Born in Lincolnshir[...] background for tw[...] **Oldham** has lived in Ilkley, West Yorkshire, for the last eighteen years, during which she has settled to full-time writing. She has gained a wide reputation for her writing for young adults; among her recent works are *Enter Tom* and *Grow Up, Cupid*. Her first adult novel, *Flames* (Virago, 1986), was awarded the joint Yorkshire Arts Association and Virago Fiction Prize. June Oldham has worked in community arts in two long writing residencies. She has directed the Ilkley Literature Festival, has been a judge for the Constable Trophy, and sometimes does talks, readings and workshops.

In *A Little Rattle in the Air*, June Oldham once again reveals herself as a storyteller of rare gifts as she explores the fierce and haunting burdens of memory and its devastating consequences.

A Little Rattle in the Air

JUNE OLDHAM

VIRAGO

Published by VIRAGO PRESS Limited 1990
20–23 Mandela Street, Camden Town, London NW1 0HQ

*A CIP Catalogue record for this book
is available from the British Library*

Printed in Great Britain by
Cox & Wyman, Reading, Berkshire

For Geoff

Chapter One

She stood by the window not caring if she were seen. It was, after all said and done, her window and it was up to her whether or not she looked out; she'd cleaned it plenty of times. She wondered if the young gentleman would find her; there was a thick fog in the street though it must be getting near spring. Nowadays you couldn't tell one season from another, different to when she was a girl. Irritably she polished the heel of her fist on a pane and flinched as the street leaped out of the mist, assailing her vision through circular streaks. 'It doesn't alter. Same mucky sight,' she reported to the cat. Then there was a woman standing on the top step.

'I've stopped the meals on wheels,' she told her when she had pulled the door open. 'The cat couldn't stomach them.'

The woman laughed, looking nice the way her mouth stretched at the corners. 'I appreciate that's no recommendation, but I'm not delivering meals.'

'No, I can see you haven't the tins.'

'I haven't the wheels either.'

She would have laughed but managed to stop in time. It could be a trick but she knew enough not to let any Tom, Dick or Harry past the door. 'You'll have to excuse me,' she said, beginning to close it; 'I have to put the kettle on. I'm expecting a Mr Green.'

'He's sent me instead,' the other told her quickly, trying to get the words in while there was still a chink. 'I'm helping him out. He's given me this letter which explains.'

'I'll fetch my glasses,' and by a miracle found them on top of the stove and read what he had to say while still keeping her waiting on the step. 'In that case, you'd better come in,' she said at last, but gracelessly. She'd been looking forward to the young man, even wondered about finding a new pinny but she hadn't, which was a good thing considering that it wasn't him who had come. It was a long time since she'd had a young man in the house so it was understandable, her being disappointed.

'Come into the kitchen,' she said; 'it's warmer,' and she could keep her eyes on the woman easier there; she wasn't having any poking

1

about. Standing by the cooker, she thought for a minute of putting the kettle on but decided she wouldn't. That was promised Mr Green.

'I hope I haven't come at an inconvenient moment,' the woman said, her nose wrinkling up at the smell.

'It's the cat food,' she interpreted, impatient because anyone with half an eye would have seen.

'Yes,' the other agreed quickly. She took a pencil and notebook out of her bag. 'It's very good of you to offer your help.'

'I didn't offer. All I did was put a tick at the bottom of the paper and leave it under the mat like he said. It's him wants to know about Neatham, not me. I've lived hereabouts for getting on eighty-three year so I don't think anyone could tell me anything new.'

'That's why Peter Green wrote to you. He was given your address by the social services department at the Town Hall.'

That was said to put a rest to any suspicions. This young woman was clever; she needed to be watched. 'I can't see how anything I have to tell would be much use in a play.'

'It may not be.' You had to give this one credit, she came right out with it, no beating about the bush. 'For example, it may not provide material that Peter could put directly into a scene, but it will help with detail and the kind of atmosphere, the feelings of people at certain times.'

It seemed to her that this play was just an excuse for stirring things up. If that's what this Mr Green had in mind, she didn't like him so much. She would have to be careful. She wished she hadn't put a tick on that paper now; it wasn't like her; generally she had more sense and she had enough to do keeping body and soul together without giving the nod to interruptions.

'I'm not so sure I can be of assistance,' she answered primly. 'It's not that my memory's cracked, it's as good as ever it was, but it's not overheated, like some's.' She could imagine what Bert Long would make of all this but she had a half recollection that he'd passed away; it was a shame how some people no sooner got the pension than they jacked it in; the government must be making a packet.

'In my opinion, information that is not exaggerated is much more valuable.'

Valuable was a strange word for anything that might come out of Neatham, and her face must have been a picture because the woman corrected: 'More reliable; it's likely to be nearer the truth.'

Now that let the cat out of the bag. She hadn't been wrong about this one being clever; there were lots she knew who, given the chance,

2

would spin a good yarn. That is, if they hadn't passed on. It was years since she'd given any of them a thought; she'd have to look out the photographs, except the box they were kept in was under his bed.

'Obviously Peter will have to be careful what he selects; if he puts in something doubtful or that could cause anyone to stand up and say, "That's wrong; I know because I was there", he loses credibility and nobody will wish to be associated with the play. Of course, I'm not suggesting that anybody would mislead us deliberately.'

The woman turned her head and pretended to look out of the window but that did not hide the crinkling round the corners of her lips; and Isabel thought: She'd be wise to mischief and it wouldn't come unexpected; she's older than she seems; they keep their looks longer nowadays. She couldn't decide whether the reason was the doctoring they got or easier times. But she couldn't let herself join in the woman's amusement. She had to concentrate.

'Who put him up to it?' she asked.

'The Council are making a grant.'

'That's fresh. They weren't always as free with money. Took them a twelve-year to stick a bus shelter at the end of this street, and now they're putting their hands in their pockets for a play!'

'They must think there will be an interest in it.'

'I'd not wonder. There's enough nosey parkers round here to fill a hall.'

That brought her face round again. 'Please don't worry,' she said. 'No bones will rattle without consent. Peter is determined about that.'

Isabel didn't like the way this woman gave her meaning back to her. She preferred it to be let lie; you never knew what might be made of it if it was taken up; but this woman had been to High School clearly and they taught them there never to let anything rest.

'You've left yourself out,' she said, to show that when it suited she was as good as the next one at picking up meanings.

'I'm only a private; he's sergeant major. I do what he says. As it happens, I think that he's right.'

'You sound as if you know something.'

'No. But I can guess.'

'You must have a good imagination inside you, then.' Which was a way of putting her down because it told her that she couldn't have come across it in any other fashion; but the woman didn't take it as an insult, nor yet flattery as some people would, which was to her credit. No, she just made a face, passing off what might be true but of no particular significance.

3

'We expect to get a lot of material from the older residents,' she told Isabel. 'You mustn't feel obliged.'

'I don't feel that. I know I can't be forced.' But she wasn't putting up with the woman's suggestion that what she could remember wasn't good enough. 'What do you want to know?' she demanded.

History of Neatham

Though today rather more extensive than the 'three streets and an entry' that one present-day resident claims was the limit of the town during the last century, Neatham still retains some of the character of the village from which it developed. Vestiges of this remain: stocks, once on the site of a now vanished green, have been moved on to a piece of waste ground opposite the new Comprehensive School; a short flight of stone mounting steps outside the Bell Inn suggests rural connections, as do names such as Pond Street, Tithe Barn Lane and Witches' Cop. There is also, under the south wall of the parish church, a horse trough and tap 'Erected in the year of our Lord 1739 by Geo. Fanhope, gentleman, for the refreshment of wayfarers'.

It is not known whether John Wesley refreshed his horse at Geo. Fanhope's trough but he is said to have preached from a great table tomb outside this church, one of the two then standing in the town. In the early nineteenth century the first two chapels were consecrated, thereby doubling the places of worship available to a population which at the first census was given as 1,278. The success of his preaching might have surprised Wesley. In his journals he refers to the inhabitants of Neatham as 'a people stubborn to move in their hearts'. Clearly, however, once convinced, they became not only enthusiastic disciples but punctilious theologians, building two chapels, a Wesleyan and a Primitive Methodist, and the strict division remains to this day. In the last hundred years there has been a continuing increase in religious denominations who have established their own places of worship, and the Victorians added two more Anglican churches.

The nineteenth-century population explosion in the towns was less dramatic in Neatham, and since its industry supplied implements for farming, the town remained closely associated with the surrounding land. Montagu Tyrewhit, a peer, owner of this part of the county, having built a canal through his private grounds as a folly, extended it into the town as a useful route for his

4

products when he turned his aptitude as an engineer to manufacturing. His son, no less gifted, inherited Lord Montagu's enthusiasm for experiment and novelty, but while demonstrating to local squires a method of ploughing which used a stationary engine to power a plough by means of windlasses and cables, was struck by one of the latter and 'his generous and aspiring spirit was summarily claimed by his Maker before the eyes of the astonished and grieving multitude'. Undeterred, however, his heir continued his father's experiments and was among the first in the last decades of the nineteenth century to manufacture the steam plough. Later Tyrewhits found this pursuit was not to their tastes and Charles, correctly prophesying the inevitable ascendancy of the internal combustion engine, sold the plant to Jeremiah Ryecroft two years before the Great War.

During that period the works turned out gun carriages, but subsequently returned to the manufacture of large-scale agricultural machinery. Though many of the working population over the last six decades have found employment in nearby towns – in breweries, a potato crisp factory, etc. – the majority have sought work nearer home and thus a large proportion of the male workers have been dependent upon the fortunes of Ryecroft's. Since in recent years these have plummeted, which has led to closures of many sections including that producing the Ryecro Combine Harvester and has left only those turning out cultivators, dryers and mowers, unemployment has risen, though never to the degree of that on Merseyside or in the North East. In the last ten years efforts have been made to create employment by building an industrial estate on the west common but that has developed into service units, offices for various firms' design, sales or computer departments, and jobs are held by commuters or professional staff who have moved in.

Work available for women has remained steady, much of it supplied by Blygh's. Opened in 1911 as a workshop making underwear, an early example of mass production in clothing, it moved into service uniforms during both wars, but for the rest of its life it has concentrated on garments for the home catalogue market . . .

'It would be better if this could be kept to one sheet of A4, Nora. I should have made that clear; I'm sorry,' apologising for the discouragement, a cardinal sin in community arts. Then, because her

5

intelligence and years made her less vulnerable to criticism and his intervention had not acknowledged that, he said sorry for that omission.

'Don't worry, Peter. I was indulging myself. This can easily be reduced.'

He considered explaining what he had hoped to convey by the repeated apology but decided against it. He found her rather daunting.

'What else should be included?' she asked.

'Modern amenities such as health centre and new schools; railway line and distance from the motorway; recreational facilities. All Glyn Mayhew needs is a quick summary of the place for his committee to read when they consider his budget. I'll fish out his letter for you. He's keen for regional arts to be involved. Don't bother about a covering note; I'll do that. Reduce the labour.' The correct reason was, of course, that the project was his responsibility, that he was acquainted with Regional Arts Association policy, and that he should deal with all official correspondence – which last, it could be argued, his particular talent equipped him better than she to compose. He did not, however, say this.

'If that is what this fellow Glyn needs, I'll concentrate on the present and cut most of the background. It's no problem.' The Shell guide covered the town in three column inches.

Her equanimity surprised him. Usually people employed the blue pencil as if painfully amputating a limb. ('I don't know whether slicing down to the viscera means this qualifies as gut writing,' a student had once commented, 'but now mine looks more like offal.') On the other hand, schoolchildren forced to attend writing workshops complied with his advice as readily as she. Generally through indifference. Yet she had volunteered her help.

'I like the traction engine bit and the Wesley quote,' he told her, contrite.

'There's a good local history section in the county library. I spent last Saturday in it.'

After a fifty-mile journey here each day that week! She could not be equated with the conscripted schoolchild. 'You ought to be leaving. By the time you've got back home to Robert, you'll be needing supper.'

'I'm considering an alternative.'

About to attempt a joke concerning diet, he was stopped by the fancy that her 'alternative' might refer not to food but to the man. Slightly breathless, he added, 'Look, if you can't shorten that, it doesn't matter; we can photostat the second page on the reverse side. Perhaps we owe it to Neatham.'

6

'Don't worry, Peter!' she repeated. 'One page does the town proud.'

When he had gone to catch a couple of septuagenarians mellowed by a lunch time's bingo, she went to the window and looked down at the playground, empty now, the chequers for hopscotch showing ghostly through the crumbling tarmac, and punk dandelions sunning round the drain's grid. Under corrugated asbestos wenned by moss and streaked tawny by rusting bolts, rubble and an iron fire grate concealed the stalls for bicycles but two netball posts, astonishing survivors, lay with rings locked and fringed raggedly by net under a wall. Such neglect offended her. Even so, she made the telephone call.

'I shan't be back tonight, Robert,' abrupt because she could have warned him the previous week.

His failure to complain reduced the importance of her decision, so she said, 'I may stay until Friday.'

Assent now bore the hint of a burden courageously endured.

Repenting, she added, 'I shall be paying out of my own account.' Unnecessary, ill managed, the assurance was answered with hurt. 'I didn't mean it like that,' she told him.

Minutes later, in the book by the telephone, she found the section which Peter had headed NORA, PRIVATE CALLS ('Though in the circumstances no one's going to suggest I charge you,' he had said) and she recorded: Monday March 18th, six minutes, standard rate.

Down in the street a woman's voice lifted without resonance to the desk at which Nora sat: 'What's to do then, chuck?' Quickly calculating the cost to date, Nora wrote the amount in the column then drew a thick line across the page.

'Do you wish to give Mr Trafford a call to tell him you've arrived here safely?' Doris Bentley asked. 'Put his mind at rest.'

'I already have done, thank you. Telephoned, I mean.'

'He must have been prepared for it, seeing that you'd packed a bag on spec. Clifford was a bit impatient that I hadn't said definitely last Thursday without waiting to check with him again, but although he only uses the room at the weekend, I do regard it as his.'

'You are sure that it's convenient for me to have it?'

'Yes. It won't put him out at all. My office is on flexitime and I always leave early enough on a Friday to get him a nice tea for when he comes in and it won't take a minute to change the bed. Now then, this is the lounge as you see, and here's the kitchenette where you can make yourself a coffee or a sandwich if you're peckish, just whenever you like.'

Responding to the cue for admiring noises, she made them.

'And there's more than meets the eye,' Doris Bentley assured her triumphantly, and went round opening cupboard doors to reveal carousels swinging cups, troughs for storing vegetables, magnetic grids for marshalling cutlery and other fixtures of wondrous workmanship. 'Clifford put them in. He likes to keep busy.'

'A hedge would have given more green,' she conceded as they stared at the six-feet-high fence, 'but there's privacy to consider and Clifford isn't one for gardening. Whereas I can get quite lost in it; so I do the borders at the front and he put the flags and gravel at the back. It's a question of give and take, isn't it?'

'A garden can absorb a lot of one's time.'

'You can get a better view from the top of the stairs,' Doris said and led her up them. Inviting Nora to crane through the narrow casement, she remarked, wistful, 'Some people manage a real show of flowers. The estate's nice for walking through, especially in a few weeks. I'm a spring person myself.'

'Does that mean you're an optimist?'

The other inexplicably tittered. 'You have to try, don't you? Else there's no telling where you might end up. It's no help being morbid.' Opening the bathroom door, she explained, 'When Clifford and me were talking about having you, I asked him, because I have the habit of looking ahead, "What do you think she needs to be told?" and he said, "Well, there's the toilet; it's often on the blink despite my efforts." And he's right, he has tried, but to no avail, so you have to keep on jabbing the handle till it flushes. Don't worry about disturbing the neighbours; theirs is just the same.' The size of the room allowing only single occupation, they stood in the doorway and contemplated the cistern. 'You can have a bath whenever you like, only you'll have to mention it about half an hour beforehand so that the immersion can heat up. That's what's in the cupboard behind the door,' crooking a finger.

'Now let me show you the bedroom,' and they both squeezed in. 'I had intended, at the start, to bring my machine up here, better than on the kitchenette table, everywhere messed up with bits of fabric and thread, and this room would have been cosy, but then Clifford came along. I have said to him, "Look, you ought to have the one at the front, a man's not so tidy as a woman and he can always do with more space," but he won't have that, being as he's only here for the two nights. If this isn't suitable and you'd like to try somewhere else, I'll understand.'

She took a photograph from the windowsill and blew an insubstantial mote off the glass. Nora thought: Now that she sees me here, feet plonked on the mat by the side of his bed, she's changed her mind; and felt a gush of relief.

'Perhaps I shouldn't take his room. It is rather impertinent.'

'You mustn't think that. Only, it is small, hardly more than a cubby, and you'll be used to a lot bigger.'

'Not much. In places we're quite tight.' Touring her home, she decided that the downstairs cloakroom would fit that description.

'In that case, you should be all right.' So Nora was left with a decision she could not retract.

'There is just the one disappointment,' Doris admitted, brisk now. 'There isn't a lot of room for your clothes. I had meant to make some arrangement but when I put the advertisement in for last Thursday I never expected to receive a telephone call the same day, so I haven't had time to put up any hooks. But you can always hang your top coat under the stairs and anything else could be placed in the airing cupboard; there's no one to see during the week.'

'I travel light.' Swinging her holdall on to the bed, Nora abandoned the suitcase in the boot of her car.

'I thought you might do. That's the advantage of having somebody in just for the four nights; they're not likely to clutter the place up. That's only guesswork, of course. I've never taken in a paying guest before. I'd not be surprised if people along the avenue think that's what Clifford is,' giggling, 'and I choose not to put them right, saves explanations. He was of the opinion, though, that I ought to have someone sleeping in during the week; you hear so much about burglaries nowadays. I'll leave you to unpack while I make a pot of tea.'

Since there was nowhere to deposit clothes, unpacking them was futile, but some ritual to establish occupation seemed necessary. Nora put her bag on the floor, unzipped it, trailed a pair of tights through the handle, hung a scarf on the door knob and dropped books on the bed. No such stratagems were demanded of Clifford whose tenancy, hallowed, could afford to be more discreet. Except for a single cuff link in a dish on the windowsill, he had left no traces unless these were concealed in a wardrobe which, sole addition to the bed, overfurnished the room. First closing the door against unsignalled discovery, and excusing her action with the argument: that's what I've

9

come for – research, Nora went through Clifford's rail. Clearly his weekend programme was a mix of household beautification and respectable leisure pursuits: a boiler suit freshly laundered but grazed with paint hung beside worsted slacks of nondescript beige, check sports jacket and a more dashing but outmoded blazer. To complement these, on the shelf above were maroon sweaters, one cable-stitched and the other rollnecked, and a number of shirts orthodox in cut and pallid in stripe. There was no denim, no rag-trade ephemera, nothing flamboyant, impudent, youthful or cheap. Depressed, homesick at the contrast, Nora closed away the Clifford relics and, looking down at the concrete garden, reflected upon why she had sought this cramped space.

The man had been leaning against the wall as she had driven through the gates and his expression, startled and slightly defensive, told her that he had been unprepared for anyone to turn in; then reflected in her interior mirror were the recovery and quick strides, the adjustment from aimless loitering to the pretended purpose of a man out of work.

'You've struck unlucky. Pete Green isn't in yet. You can give me a message if you like.'

'Thanks, but I've got a key. I work here.'

'Nora? Pete's told me about you.'

'That makes me apprehensive.'

'Why's that?'

'At what he might have said.'

'As far as I recollect, he didn't say anything you'd be sorry to hear.'

'There's time yet. He's known me only three weeks.' She had never been any good at meaningless banter; the apprehension she referred to was concerned with prejudgements, the easy categories favoured by the uninformed. But that was a subject for talk with Robert.

This man said as she opened the car boot, 'The bodywork's keeping well. I had one of these, but just the 1600. Provided you can keep ahead of the rust, they'll never die on you; you have to have them put down. I got rid of mine nearly two years back but I still see it about.'

He watched her remove a shopping bag that contained papers and books, then dropped the boot lid for her gently, avoiding unnecessary jolt, and she was pleased that she had so little to carry; she did not wish to have him following her, bearing her truck. Having unlocked the door, she made much of closing it after them in order that he should precede her up the stairs. When they reached the office she took off her coat and sat on the table in preference to taking the chair behind the desk, which would make him the applicant. But, thus doing, she obliged conversation.

'I can't work this out,' referring to the room. 'Why did the Council put this floor in?'

'They didn't. Marston's rented it for a few years during the sixties, manufacturing wigs when they were all the rage. Turned out thousands a week. The works manager, as he called himself, decided he wanted somewhere a bit private.'

'And before that it was a school? It's amazing that they built classrooms so high that they could be converted to two storeys. I feel as if I'm in a belfry.' Above them were the vaulting beams; at waist height, the pointed arch of windows whose lower half continued below the false floor.

'It'ud be the devil to heat. Mind you, they didn't bother. What the stove didn't warm up was left like a Bird's Eye freezer. The teachers would let the kids wear their top coats and the crafty ones would bind sacks and bits of straw round their boots, till they were found out.'

'Did you do that?'

'Come on! You'll be asking me next if I ever rode on a tram! My mother had me on the national health. Must have been in the first batch. She pushed me to the clinic every Friday to collect my rose hip syrup. Used it on me like tomato fertiliser.'

Nora laughed. 'We added our children's orange juice to our gin. We called it gin and welfare.'

'I wouldn't put it past my mam taking the rose hip syrup bottle down to the Admiral Nelson and spiking my dad's pint.' His smile had been brief. 'I'm holding you up.'

That was true. However, 'When was it that the children put straw round their boots?'

'Before my time, or my dad's. It was one of my grandma's stories. Listening to her, you'd have thought that, come winter, there wasn't a stalk of straw in the place, every draughthorse in town must have been stabled on bare bricks.'

'I must remember that. Peter thinks he may include a scene or two in the schools using present-day Juniors.'

He regarded her, a flickering along his top lip. 'I think the old girl was romancing,' he said.

She felt foolish, the new apprentice, object of hoaxing initiation. 'The laugh's on me.'

'That wasn't meant. I shouldn't go pulling folks' legs, not when they're new here.'

'You're obviously not.'

'Lived in Neatham all my life. I wouldn't change, either. Though there's not many that have the inclination to see anything in it,' wry, amused at the suggestion of belonging to an elite.

'People aren't sufficiently discerning?'

He nodded, grinning with her.

It certainly wasn't to many people's tastes, she thought. Once they had got away. But she had come back, not to the same place but to one similar.

'Why *there*?' Robert had asked. 'Wouldn't it be simpler to tour the old haunts?'

'They may be obliterated. In any case, I prefer to leave them in the mind intact. I think I'd like to be involved in this play thing at Neatham.'

'Nora, you aren't trying a brain drain in reverse, are you, offering some obscure parish the benefit of your skills?'

'Hardly! In *theatre*?'

'In general. But I suppose that theatre, especially that kind, is as good as anything for curing nostalgia.'

She had laughed. 'You shouldn't prejudge the fellow's efforts. What's he called? Peter Green.' Then, soberly, 'And I don't think that nostalgia is quite the word for it.'

Now, looking at this man, she knew what the word was: separation.

'Anyway, Pete says you don't mind travelling a good way to help, so you must have a nose for class,' he said.

She could not answer: I have something more acute. I have a sense of loss. Instead: 'I don't know your name.'

'Dick.'

'Do you mind if I make a few phone calls?'

'You don't have to ask. I've taken up enough of your time.'

She remembered Peter's caution: You'll find in community arts that it's the first word that has priority. So she told him, 'You don't have to go because I'm using the telephone. It's not private business.'

He shook his head. 'No one can talk the same with somebody listening in.'

12

Careful to stand well back from the window, she watched him pass through the gates and stride without hesitation up the street. She thought: He has learned to adopt a manner calculated to deceive observers; and was sorry for the business she had trumped up to send him away. He had nothing comparable, rendered inconsequential by his unoccupied days.

'Where can I find out about lodgings?' she asked the caretaker, adding, 'Temporary, of course.'

'You want the free paper, duck. It comes out Thursdays, advertises everything. Makes a nice read.'

She had come to Neatham, and taking a room made her stay irrevocable.

Squatting on Clifford's bed, answering Doris Bentley's call to a newly mashed pot of tea, Nora was glad she had repaired the clumsiness over the bank account, so that Robert had been able to say, 'What sort of time would you put in, Nora, if you were being paid? I wish my staff were as conscientious. Of course I mind your staying, but there'll be one advantage; I'll be able to snore with impunity. She doesn't complain as much as you. Sorry. I look forward to Friday evening, darling. Tell you what, I'll book a table at Henry's. Meanwhile I hope the digs are comfortable.'

'I'm made very welcome.'

'There will be a telephone call from Clifford,' her landlady told her through the door. 'So help yourself to a cup of tea if I'm otherwise engaged when you come down. I've taken the plants off the dinner trolley so you can use that, if you mean to work like you said.'

Chapter Two

What was Neatham like in the olden days, you're asking? [Nora read.] *A sight better than it is now, for a start. There was none of these shops with tills lined up behind the door and tins stacked on shelves in rows so's you go up and down, up and down, wear out shoe leather all morning and then not find what you want. I blame the government, they should never have let them be put in. It's a monopoly, that's what it is. They say, ah but you can buy things cheaper, only they won't stay cheap, will they, without competition. And who pays through the nose in the end, I ask you? Me. And you of course; that's if you come into Neatham to shop. I'd not advise it. Not nowadays. If you say to one of the little lasses at the till, will you take groceries to number eleven Corn Street, that's where I live, she'll look at you like you'd asked her how many buns in a baker's dozen. They're nice enough, but they can't do sums without pressing buttons.*

No, it wasn't me kept Raby's Grocery at the corner of Station Street and Druggist Lane. That was my cousin Benjamin, but I retain a family interest. I was a painter and decorator like my father. The night before my fourteenth birthday, schoolteacher comes round. 'Mr Raby,' says he, 'your Joseph will be fourteen tomorrow so I drew a line through his space on the register tonight.' 'That being so, Sir, he can start work.' And I did. On my fourteenth birthday! Father said to his boss, 'My Joe would like a place with the old firm, Mr Theaker, if you'll be kind enough to have him,' and Mr Theaker replied, 'There's room now Percy's passed on, so he can enter as apprentice and I'm trusting you to see he comes up to scratch.' He needn't have said that, but hearing it, it seems Father thought he was given the order to make my life a misery, and he did, no mistake. 'Joseph fetch this, Joseph fetch that, mix this, strip that,' from morning to night. Then it was, 'That paper's not hung straight, what you use for a plumb line, a dog's hind leg? You take it all off and put another piece up and your wage packet'll feel the price of that at the week ending.' He was an unremitting task master and no mistake. It was a matter of pride, you see. He couldn't have his son doing the job no better than the next. They were hard years and I think it's not a good thing for a man to be in that position with his son, there's too much at stake. But thinking about it, like you do – he's been gone twenty-five years now come October and I've had time to reflect – I think I

understand why he did it. He was just a working man, you see, and he had
nothing to pass on but his skill.

At this point Peter had scribbled a reference number in the margin. Trying to avoid Doris Bentley's gaze, Nora shuffled through the transcripts on the drinks trolley until she found the list of notes. '"He had nothing to pass on but his skill." Pick up this for a song? Could use it as a theme for a sequence showing tradesmen in the town.'

There was something Father didn't know, though it cost me a sore head. It happened like this. In those days before the Second World War, and fifteen, twenty year after as far as I reckon, the paper didn't come ready trimmed on the roll. There was a margin, see, both sides, and you had to take the scissors to it and cut it off. It fell to the apprentice to see to that. Now, Father had a little machine which you could run the pieces through and it sliced the waste off neat and clean as a whistle, only I wasn't allowed that. I had to master the old way first, and I can tell you that was much less reliable than putting the pieces through the trimmer, but according to my father you couldn't call yourself a tradesman if you couldn't turn your hand to all ways of doing. It was a job for a woman, by rights, fiddly, and with no satisfaction to it, but when I started under Father, every time paper-hanging was dawning, 'There's something to keep you out of mischief tonight, so get stuck into it,' he'd say and give me the lot to lug home. Then he would be out to his allotment or visiting his mate. He wasn't a drinking man. When he'd gone, Mother would set about it for me, though she always said she had to pray hard that night to the Lord to forgive her for the deception. She'd sit in the chair rolling the paper up from the floor on to her knee and cutting along fast and straight you'd have thought the blades grew out of her hands and coming away was this thin ribbon of paper in a continuous coil. They used to string them as trimmings across the classroom at Christmas. Anyway, this night Mrs Walmesley from down the street comes round and sees Mother cutting away and says, 'I'll give you a hand with that, Grace. Many hands make light work,' and she runs home for her scissors and sets to. Only what I should tell you is how Mrs Walmesley was the one who papered the street. The woman of the house would make the size up over the stove in the evening and Mrs Walmesley would be in first thing after breakfast and slap the paper on, top of what was there, of course, no stripping, they'd be five or six layers at times, and she'd be out for when Ryecroft's buzzer went so's the missis could get the old man's grub on the table for when he got in, and Mrs Walmesley would have had a nice gossip and a plate of cold meat for dinner and a quarter of tea to take home. Now

15

being what you can only call in the circumstances a bit on the slapdash side,
Mrs Walmesley didn't butt the paper like a tradesman but overlapped, by
which means she reduced the trimming by half, if you understand me, just
cutting off the margin on the left and pasting that over the untrimmed edge.
Well, our mother forgot to remind her that night how a tradesman on a
wage butted, so the rolls Mrs Walmesley had seen to hadn't had one margin
stripped off. It wouldn't be Mother who had left it, I can tell you that for
certain.

Upshot of it was, next morning Mr Theaker comes in saying how the
customer wants the room finished quick – they was always doing that to
save on the wages, only that time he said it was on account of it being chapel
anniversary on the Sunday. So our father puts down his breakfast and
prepares to paste there and then in full view of the boss. 'What's this, then?'
he says, unfurling a roll and seeing the margin. 'What you think you're
playing at?' he asks me very quiet but there was no mistaking his ire. He
wasn't a swearing man. Then he walks straight to me, swings his arm out
and before I know what, he's landed me a real whack on the head. I'll never
forget it. He wasn't a man for laying a finger on any of us. It was because
the matter had to do with his work, that's what it was. It was because I'd
shown him up in front of Mr Theaker. And another thing, that margin left
on made it look as if I was expecting to do a shoddy job like some labourer or
riffraff, which let him down. After I'd picked myself up, pretending I hadn't
blacked out, I didn't tell him it was Mother's fault for not reminding Mrs
Walmesley, and the reason wasn't that my head was still going round too
fast for my tongue to catch hold of the words. 'No,' I said to myself, 'Joseph,
he ordered you to trim that paper and you didn't, so you've got your
punishment.' Ever after that I did the job myself, even when I had this ache
in my head, and our mother didn't have to pray the Lord for forgiveness. I
don't know why I'm telling you this. It's not a story generally known. I
didn't blab, and Mr Theaker didn't let it out; he'd forget it the minute he
was gone from the room; he wasn't interested in what went on between a
tradesman and his apprentice, especially father and son. I wouldn't be
saying all this if Father were still here.

'Won't you have another cup of tea?' Doris Bentley clinked beside
her. 'You must forgive me for not being able to offer you a desk.
Clifford is all for me having one, you know what men are like, never
happy unless they've somewhere to store papers, but I say I've had my
fill of desks by the time I leave the office and I don't want one at
home. A drawer in the kitchenette is sufficient for my requirements.
That space behind the door would take a desk, if I moved the TV

forward. Would you mind lifting the cup up? This is a good pourer but the one time it dribbles it'll be on items not belonging to me. That's life, isn't it? That looks more like a story than a play.'

'The play hasn't been written yet. We're still collecting material. These are recollections of people we've visited.' Short of placing both hands upon the pages, she could think of no way to prevent the eyes' scurry among the words. 'We explain that we will not attribute anything to individual contributors without gaining their permission.'

Her face bland, giving no clue whether she was unaware of the hint or dismissing it, Doris Bentley returned the teapot to its tray. 'Well, you can't complain about that pile there. Some appear to have a lot to say for themselves, which isn't so surprising. It must be the first time they've had a chance of the limelight.' She rose and closed the curtains against the darkness outside. 'Of course, most will shut their eyes to anything further off than Neatham,' clearly inhibited by no sentimental loyalty to the origins which her accent betrayed.

'That should work in our favour. What Peter is trying to catch is the sense of community identity.' Nora decided it was wiser not to paraphrase the rest.

'That's not difficult to get. You can find it standing by any public house at closing time on a Saturday night.'

Nora did not comment but, silently: I've brought this upon myself.

'I'm speaking of the Bottom End, of course. On this side, the Dog and Partridge attracts a much better class of clientele.' Doris straightened the tea cosy's tilt. 'They do a very nice chicken-in-a-basket or a chilli con carne at lunch time and occasionally Clifford will say, "I'm not letting you spend all day in that kitchenette. I'm quite happy once in a while with a chicken-in-a-basket at the Dog and Partridge." So we smarten ourselves up, nothing particularly dressy because the moment Clifford has finished work on Friday he's out of his suit and nothing will get him back into it till Monday, and we're off.'

'Sounds nice,' Nora heard herself answer inanely.

'Yes, it is. Who wants to be a slave to routine? I can recommend the Dog and Partridge except that, being the opposite side to all the works, it's not the sort of place the play writer is likely to find of interest.'

'That would depend on whether anything there lent itself to dramatic presentation.'

'In that case, it won't be put in. People go there for a quiet night out. It's just been redecorated with the theme of huntin', shootin' and fishin'. There's no misbehaving and I've never once seen a man wearing a donkey jacket or a pair of jeans.'

17

Irritated, Nora told herself that she had not travelled fifty miles to discover the sartorial convention in some suburban pub. 'Why do you assume that Peter will be more interested in the people who live near the works?'

'I'm going by a report in the free paper, though it didn't say that direct. And it seems to me that what Mr Green has in mind isn't a real play as such.'

'There are many forms of plays. Especially at the moment. Surely community drama is legitimate?' Thinking that she simply could not engage in lit. crit. with Doris.

'I don't regard what's in hand as a proper play. It's not entertainment, for one thing, acting the story of what's happened in Neatham over the years; I know all about that. It seems that the Council is keen, but what I want to know is: what's the point?'

'I said I'd let you see this letter.' Peter had proffered it across the desk. 'From our very own Regional Arts Association drama officer.'

Dear Peter,
I know that by now you will have been in situ several weeks, but the run up to Theatre Work-Out (sorry you couldn't attend) and the still continuing dialogues post-The Glory of the Garden have given me no chance to write to congratulate you on the appointment and wish you every success.

It was in October last year that one of the more enlightened District Councillors contacted me with their decision to initiate some sort of local documentary drama. I attended a number of meetings. They certainly needed guidance. Their idea was to put the project in the hands of the WI – I jest not – but I was able to convince them that the scale of what they envisaged required an experienced hand. In the best traditions of Regional Arts Associations (and with an ear metaphorically cocked against the entrance of our Community Arts Officer – nowadays Constance Skrimshaw, no less) I ventured to opine that, though the WI dearies were doubtless extraordinarily capable of writing and producing a two-hour *divertissement*, perhaps first time round they would welcome a helping hand. Then one had to come down heavy and tell them that meant a playwright, bought in. Their horror confirmed my suspicions that their championship of the WI ladies was not entirely ingenuous – I didn't stoop to the tactless question: had they been asked? – because, a professional writer . . . that might cost an extra .005p on the rates! I was tempted to let them stew but conscience doth make cowards of us all so, to save the possibility of theatre in the Styx and to assist a writer – hopefully your distinguished self – to scramble above the bread line for a few months, I said that the Association might be able to help with funding in the new financial year. I also insisted that the four-month contract which, adapting to the shock of serious funding, they had at first envisaged, was out of the question. After I'd treated them to a graphic but not inaccurate account of the amount of research needed, the time spent on writing, and then rehearsals which demanded at least a four-month period, coarse amateur actors being what they are – I called them 'inexperienced', of course – they were all quite limp. But not limp enough to consider anything longer than a nine-month gestation, the best I could do, but by tapping some mysterious reserve they were able to start you in February, and we agreed that I should try to assist.

At the time my drama allocation had gone the way of all flesh but I've contrived the one for the new year – with what sweat and tears! – and it goes before the committee in three weeks. I need copy from you for briefing, the usual scenario plus a potted guide to the town, one definitely not in their itineraries. You have a good chance of something and we may try an experimental cross-fertilisation with Community Arts, which in view of the Skrimshaw termagant gives you the measure of my interest. In her favour, however, it must be acknowledged that, when she heard on the grapevine that you had applied for the job, she rang up the Leisure Services chairman and practically insisted they put you on the short list though frankly I would have thought that the kiss of death. You'll gather we don't get on. We do happen to agree in our thinking on this project, however. It deserves every encouragement.

Maybe you have already begun to appreciate the character of Neatham and therefore the extent of the task you have undertaken. I don't want to prejudice your response to it or in any way influence your judgement of the people you meet but I have to tell you that, to date, any venture supported by this RAA has met with singular lack of success. We've tried all the usual routes: local organisations, library service, schools, county council, and the populace has taken about as much notice as a leviathan to a fish's fart. They aren't hostile; merely indifferent. The only event to fetch them in has been the appearance of some character on 'Coronation Street', whose name blessedly I forget and whose connection with anything remotely resembling art is sufficiently tenuous to excuse their indulging him. I'm talking, of course, of the 'Bottom End', as they call it, with peculiar appropriateness. The smart enders, more prosperous and fewer of them indigenous, go out of Neatham for their entertainment and services. Some of them might attend a visiting show but generally they patronise theatres elsewhere. It's the general Neatham inhabitant we've tried to cater for – or rather, encouraged the catering for – and just about every time we've got egg on our face.

So you'll understand why we – I'm including the Skrimshaw scold – were so delighted by the Council's initiative and quite frankly I admit that I should have had that idea for Neatham myself. Now that the suggestion has been made and you are installed I'm beginning to feel as if I've just invented penicillin. If your play doesn't get bottoms on seats or propped against walls (is it to be in promenade?) then nothing will. Though what workable material you'll find in Neatham, I can't imagine. From my experience of the place, thankfully brief and infrequent, I'd say that looking for drama there would be an occupation bordering on necrophilia. However, clearly the punters on the Leisure Services Committee thought there was enough mileage in the idea or, philistines to a man at the last count, they have recently suffered a mass conversion. Perhaps one of them aspires to top billing! You might, after all, find the time at Neatham to be more lively than one would anticipate! I do so hope that you do. I'll keep in touch. All the best.

Then the signature, baroque: Glyn.

'He has a reputation for writing at length,' Peter had said. 'When you meet him, you'll realise that's typical Glyn.'

She nodded, turning back to reread a sentence, and he regretted having shown her the letter, worried that she might interpret the permission as vanity, letting her know how he had been backed for the job.

'As you can see, Glyn finds a town such as Neatham a strain,' he interpreted unnecessarily. 'He's conscientious and has lots of good ideas; he's also receptive to originality and he likes – can get quite zealous about – fringe stuff. However, he does find it hard to touch anything he can't reconcile with his definition of art.'

'But he seems keen on this.'

He tried not to be piqued by her quick assumption about the work he was engaged on, for he had encouraged it. 'Because a play here will silence criticism. He can't then be accused of neglect or of failing to stimulate interest. He'll wangle money somehow in this next budget, since he knows that this time he won't get egg on his face. A fact, not a boast,' he said quickly. 'The last time Glyn brought a theatre group into Neatham, loss guaranteed, they played to six. One was the caretaker and two were earnest sixth-formers in at half price. It's impossible not to do better than that.'

They laughed. 'House full every night? All the family turned out to admire their Peggy on the boards?'

'There'll be some of that, but it won't be the main attraction. They'll come because it'll be their play; they'll have provided the material; people they have known will be the characters; other people, neighbours, family, friends, will be acting in it, or being themselves; they will have made the costumes they see, the set, have hunted through trunks, sheds, for the authentic props; and they won't only be watching, sometimes they'll be invited to join the action and take part. Which they do, always in my experience they do, because what they're watching isn't a series of moving pictures for their gaze, it's what happened to them and it's plastic, can stretch out and haul them in. And it's more than just a record of events in their town. It's a celebration of their lives; it gives them a value; it insists that they are not inconsiderable though, never in the seat of power, they do not figure in the books.'

He stopped, feeling foolish. In that room, austere, scruffy, squashed under the beams, the words sounded pretentious though he meant every one; and he was annoyed at having exposed himself to amused patronising interest. He had vowed never again to invite that, after a college lecturer, having heard him out, had solemnly quoted the stanza describing the rude forefathers of the hamlet each in his narrow cell forever laid, and the obituary to 'some mute inglorious Milton'. They had both been extremely embarrassed. Now he was once more, though between that occasion and this, conviction and talent had produced an admired yield. And he thought: I must give the impression of being some juvenile fanatic, naive even; she makes me feel gauche; which brought him to calculate that she might be no more than ten years older than he was, a gap that once would have seemed almost indecent, placing her within the taboo category of his mother. Whereas now, he thought.

But said, 'Ignore all that. Routine spiel. I pull it out of stock for drumming up enthusiasm.'

21

He had not really expected her to believe the lie and she shrugged it away. 'I didn't know you felt so strongly about it. At the moment I'm not sure that I'm wholly convinced but it's good to know what principles we work from.'

Relieved, he nodded and busied himself with the day's post. He could accept her reservation. It was enough that she had said: we.

'For the life of me, I can't see the point of it,' Doris Bentley repeated. 'We, those that have made the effort, have turned our backs on all that. You ask anyone round here.'

'Turned your backs on what?' Blunt, the question discarded politeness that was seemly in a paying guest.

'Washing forever flapping about in the back yard, picking up the soot, and toilets down the path covered in frost,' Doris recalled, shuddering. 'There's no need to put up with that any more and I can't understand why so much should be made of them that do.'

Her grievance was at last out, though this had demanded acknowledgement she would have preferred not to make; nevertheless, settled in her beliefs, Doris did not flinch. She crouched in her Wendy house of contiboard walls, doors veneered with a membrane of afrormosia, the chimneyless unit fissured where the quik-dri plaster had shrunk from the electric fire whose formica base mimicked a hearth; and Nora, her impulse to contention fading, looked at her with awe.

'From my wanderings round the town these last weeks, I have the impression that there aren't many streets of that kind left.' She felt like an explorer reporting to the folks back home. 'And I don't know what you mean when you say that people putting up with such conditions are given excessive attention.'

Doris pursed her lips and adjusted the plastic tray cloth. 'You look at the television and it's there all the time. Only certain ones are given the right to a say,' she grumbled.

'The whole point about this play is that everyone has that. It's inclusive. It's different from official history. It's based on the accounts of people on the spot.'

'I can't see so much difference. That can be anything, can't it? It's just a matter of whose version you choose.'

Nora could not entirely dismiss this argument but the route to it had been so vertiginous that, exhausted: 'You may be right,' was all she could answer. She could not imagine what dispute could arise from Joseph Raby's recollections.

There was a lot of building going on in the 1930s and my father and me were hardly ever out of work. That's how it was, hunger marches in some parts, and us doing all right. I'm not saying we were in clover, mind, there was no tradesman could be that on account of the competition which meant wages was tight, but we never went without what was needful, we all had a sound pair of shoes, not cast-offs, and new suits for the Chapel fête. That was important to Mother. And she fed us well, dumplings as big as your fist and light as balloons. 'Hold that dumpling down with your fork,' Father would say, 'else it'll fly off.' He never had a bad word to say about her cooking; he was a very fair man. You mustn't be thinking he was anything else because he dropped me one that time; I shouldn't have mentioned it. It was a question of discipline, you see, and there was the stick at school. I often wonder whether, if that was still the order of the day, old persons like me would be able to walk the streets without fear.

What followed seemed to be an account of Joseph's training as an apprentice. Although she had stated her intention to work on the project during the evenings, Nora was discomforted by the other's stare which prompted an irrational apology for reading. With the feeling that every eye movement was monitored, she quickly ran her finger down the following section before turning to the next page.

Did I like the work? you ask me. Well, I liked doing the fancy stuff. Graining was all the rage before the last war and there was summat to doing it; I used a steel comb and it'ud take four hours to grain a door. Journeymen had different styles and you could walk up a street and know who'd done the houses by the graining. But I wasn't let on that until I'd finished my apprenticeship, and I was a good few years out of that when the War came, Hitler's, that is. Yes, I was in it. Joined up, I did, before being called, and I was put in the Signals, don't ask me why, and I was with them till the end. I know I shouldn't be saying this. In the circumstances, seeing all that happened, it doesn't sound right, but I enjoyed that time in the Army more than any other in my life. The wife'll understand that. She knows I'm not casting doubts upon her. We got married, you see, during one of my leaves in 1941, July time, it'ud be. Why, you ask me, have I got so much to say for those years of the Second World War? It'ud be the experience, I expect. You'll understand that? I think it must be the way it showed you something out of the usual, a bit more than Neatham or Mablethorpe where we used to go for the chapel treat.

Again Nora felt a silent reproach for her unsocial occupation, glanced at Doris and ostentatiously skimmed the next lines. Then, impatient with herself for such weakness, she started the final paragraph and read with determination to the end.

You expect that the war brought changes? Well, you're right in that. Manners were freer. After what they'd been through, men coming back didn't set quite the same store on what was laid down in the rules. And them that had been left, their lines had been given some play, they'd enjoyed a longer rein in spite of the rationing and all that. That went for the women as well. They had to do for themselves while the men were away and from what I've been told there were some not slow to take advantage. Maybe it's all rumours, the Yanks I met were respectable enough young men, considering. Yes, you wouldn't be far wrong saying the war brought some changes. But how long did they last, I ask you? The ones that mattered, that is. I've never been much of a voting man myself, but in 1945 I made sure I had my say because then we thought – you'll probably not believe this but I don't tell a lie, maister – we thought we was mekking a new world!

'It's all a matter of what you make for yourself,' Doris Bentley told her. 'Mother and me could have had a council flat but we wanted something better. Other people could have done what we did only they didn't choose, but they still think they have the right to comment. Now who would you listen to when it came to something like that?'

'I'm not making the selection. That's Peter's job.' It was puzzling how, so disapproving of the project, Doris had allowed anyone associated with it to darken her doors. 'I've simply offered to help collect the material.'

'That's what it said in the paper.' Doris's inflection suggested that, by good fortune, Nora's claim was confirmed by the authority of print. 'And what struck me and Clifford reading it, was the distance you are travelling to lend a hand with something in Neatham. "Since it's attracting a volunteer from fifty miles off," Clifford remarked, "there must be more to this play than there seems at first sight. Or there might, of course, be something else."'

Nora looked at her. A jabot of lace concealed the buttons on her blouse, the cloth across the stomach owed its smoothness to the pinch of elastic beneath; the light falling upon the spectacles glossed over the inquisitiveness in the eyes. But there was no mistaking its presence. Nora was not inclined to satisfy it, though that might have amused her. Already annoyed by her inexplicable sympathies, Doris would have been outraged to learn that her guest had an emotional attachment to streets of the kind she herself had thankfully fled.

Before the pause became uncomfortable, the telephone rang. Doris Bentley raised a finger and counted. 'Four,' she pronounced as the ringing finished. 'It's Clifford telling me that he'll be calling back. This way, there can be no mistake. I know it's not some nuisance hanging on.' She rose and stood by the instrument. 'He always gives me time to get down, if in case I'm in the bathroom,' she explained another precaution and lifted the handset as the sound recommenced.

Pleased at this opportunity to leave the house without having to make excuses, Nora carried the papers up to her room, collected her handbag, smilingly waved away the other's gestures that her conversation held nothing private, and made for the back door. Closing it, she heard Doris say, 'Well, it hasn't come out yet. She only got here at ten minutes past six.'

Chapter Three

Outside, night ringed the houses, their curtains firmly drawn, but within the radius of street lamps could be seen borders round cosseted lawns, paths bare of moss and weeds, and saplings protected in tubes of steel mesh flanking the gates. Yet it was only two Crescents, an Avenue and three Views before the single course of decorative brick or the miniature conifers marking the boundaries were replaced by wire between concrete pillars, and the glass cube round front doors had given way to a shallow canopy of timber above the step. At this change, Nora reduced her pace and sauntered, ran her fingers through the dust on cars parked by the side of the road, did not trouble to lift up a tricycle abandoned on the pavement, gave the time at a passing child's demand, and stood for some minutes under a scarred laburnum while she watched, a small garden's width away, a figure on a television screen mouthing to an audience concealed from her view. But there was no one to invite her to enter, so she wandered about this unvarying grid of roads, past houses as relentlessly uniform as those she had just left except that they lacked the superficial details favoured by private contractors to create a spurious distinction; until, depressed by the tedium and the knowledge that she was gaining nothing from this walk, she asked for a direction and came to the road which bordered the estate.

In the chip shop, while the fryer riddled out scraps, she read the notice: From now on a fish cake has to be called a fried fish filled potato sandwich!!

'Why's that?' she asked.

'It's the new name.'

'But a fish cake isn't assembled like a sandwich,' smiling at the verb.

He shrugged. 'What's it matter? I'll sell anybody one whatever it has to be called. Are you taking this out?' he demanded, hand poised with the bottle of vinegar.

Standing in a bus shelter, biting into the fish, Nora was reminded of a supper conversation. He had put down his knife and fork, sniffed his wine meditatively, then leant across to her, brows anxiously puckered. 'I hope', he had said, 'that I have enabled my children to be just as much at ease eating in some sleazy fish and chip restaurant as in a posh hotel.'

Robert had greatly appreciated her report of it. 'Poor chap!' he had hooted. 'Oh, the agonies of the well-heeled!'

'Tell you what, I'll book a table at Henry's for Friday,' he had said. 'Meanwhile, I hope the digs are comfortable.'

'I've just fixed lodgings for myself on an avenue called Belle View. Do you know it?' she had asked that morning.

He had not knocked on the door at the bottom of the stairs but had come straight up, holding a bill, half allowed visitor, half occasional helper. 'Yes. It's in a new development the other side of the Fosse council estate. I expect the buyers would have liked it a lot further away.' He put the invoice on the desk, pinning it down with a forefinger though there was no draught. The shape and condition of his hand offered no clue to his former occupation. 'This is for the typing paper Pete asked me to get. Would you mind mentioning to him that an early settlement would be appreciated? Mrs Broughton was doing me a favour letting it go on tick.'

'Of course.' She had expected more interest in her news.

'I fetched the paper in last night. Stan, he's caretaker, let me up. He was impressed by the amount.'

'I think we shall need it. Can you type?'

'Not in the regular way, but I can knock out a letter.'

'In that case, you're on. We've got dozens of tapes that have to be transcribed. It doesn't have to be perfect.'

'It wouldn't be that. You don't have to find me jobs, you know. I can invent them myself.'

She had thought: Please God don't let me blush. 'This is no invention,' laughing. 'It's all too real, and somebody has to do it. I assumed because you'd brought the paper that Peter had recruited your help and so you had agreed to give up some of your spare time.' It was too much. The rush of words admitted a compassionate motive.

'Don't worry,' he assured her, easy, more accustomed to the situation than she. 'I do lend a hand now and again. Stan's a neighbour.'

'Are there any ear phones?' he asked, arranging the table. Then: 'This job must really have got you if it's made you set up in Belle View.'

She laughed, pleased. 'You mean the reason must be exceptional for anyone to take a room there?'

'Now, I didn't say that,' but grinned. 'What about home? Won't you be missed?'

Yes. Once, during an absence of hers far less selfish, he had prowled through the night unable to rest beside the empty space. 'The arrangement will reduce the time I spend on the road; it will be less tiring and far more economical. At present I'm using over three gallons a day.' Again she had said too much, and the offered explanations where none was expected inevitably had an untruthful ring.

'Fair enough.' He was examining the labels on the tapes. 'I don't know that I'm the one for this. It's confidential.'

'Everyone has accepted the possible use of their recollections.'

'But Pete won't be putting in what he knows individuals don't want made public, will he? Not that any will be telling him stories that can't, if I know them.'

'So what's the problem?'

'They were talking to Pete, or you. Not to me.'

'But you've just said that few would mention anything that couldn't be made public.'

'They will talk differently to you two, like to the doctor. They will say things they don't want heard by people they know.'

The argument had become repetitive, had slipped and lost shape.

'You may be right, but we need the material typed out and there's an awful lot of it. Won't you have a go? If you come to a passage that seems to predict an exceptional level of intimacy, stop and leave the rest to one of us. The first half or so is often general, before they warm up.'

'I'll do that,' he agreed. Selecting a cassette, he read, '"Roland Garbutt." He must be one of the Burton Garbutts. I'd like a fiver for everything I could tell you about that lot.'

'I thought you were in favour of confidentiality.'

'What people say about others isn't confidential; it's what they say about themselves.'

'I was being facetious.' That was a social convention she must unlearn during the coming weeks. 'You know a lot of people.'

'You could say that. From the Bottom End mostly.'

She wanted to tell him: I wish to belong again. I suffer a kind of divorce. I have to find my way back to the Neathams, like the one I left. This looking on, this observing and recording, is not enough. It

28

assures me of its presence but does not restore the former pulse. I need a guide. I need to be launched upon the currents, to be borne by their spate and whirl in their pools. Is that so impossible, so ridiculous a hope?

All she could say was: 'A useful man to know.'

And wondered whether he had sensed something of her appeal and dismissed it when he answered, 'If you want showing around, Stan's the chap. He knows these parts like the back of his hand, which gives him the idea he's got something to show off.'

'I'll bear that in mind,' thinking: Anything else is all folly.

Watching him plug in the machines, she suggested he listen to a passage for the overall impression before making a start. 'Then I hear a sentence or two, switch it off, type, hear some more. Transcribing these cassettes has become a major job; you're going to find it frustrating and impossible to achieve a smooth flow.'

'I'm ready for that. I've seen Pete at it.'

Who had left a note: 'Looking at the material so far, I see it is overbalanced with accounts from men. This must be chance but has to be redressed. Could you please go back to see if you can get anything more from Isabel Driffield?'

She had already found Isabel's file and put it in her bag, but across the room Dick was hooking his anorak over his chair, the cheap nylon T-shirt exposing the bare arms and giving the illusion of sleeves rolled up in businesslike preparation. As he switched on the recorder and bent forward to hear another man's words, the light, sharpening contours of the face and squaring its planes, discovered the model for all those embroidered on tasselled banners, the copy of profiles in albums she had thumbed as a child; and she thought: One tape alone will take him hours; if both listened, we could prompt each other while I typed; I can do that faster than he.

Nora screwed up the chip paper and looked round for a litter bin. Its only remains were two rusting bolts attached to a post. For a moment she considered carrying the paper in her handbag until she returned to the house; instead, she threw it on to the stinking heap in a corner of the shelter and noticed how with what little qualm acquired habits could be given up.

'But whatever happens tomorrow, I'll certainly visit Mrs Driffield,' she promised guiltily.

* * *

29

She was not standing at the window waiting for her this time, seeing that she'd come without due word, but from her face as she stood on the step you might have thought folks should spend their time at the ready for her, looking out.

'I'm in the back, washing,' she said, though why she should give reason for the delay she couldn't for the life of her tell.

'It's a good morning for that. Plenty of wind.'

'That's right.' This one wasn't to know that she never pegged anything out.

'I wonder if you could spare me a few minutes.'

'So long as that's all it is. The cleaning'll soon be coming up and I've told you what I've got to say. We'd better go in the front,' remembering the pots stacked on the washer. She was clever, this one; she wouldn't miss that. 'It takes a bit of time to warm up,' she said, noticing the shivers. 'There's not much sun this side, on the street, but it's nice when the fire's in,' poking the ash.

'Mr Green finds that he has more accounts from men than women and wants to restore the balance,' coming straight to the point. 'I think he has an ambition to rewrite history.'

She would have laughed but didn't, not wanting to let on that she had twigged the joke. 'Men allus have plenty to say for theirsens. It's women that take the back seat. I should know. I had six brothers and they took some looking after. That was left to Mother and me, me being the first. And it didn't make any difference, you know, when I'd stopped school and was out earning; I still had to see to them when I came in. Catch the lasses doing that nowadays.'

'I certainly can't imagine my daughters doing it.'

Isabel noticed the woman didn't mention her own way of doing. 'Don't the girls help, then?'

'I don't ask them to. In any case, they are both away now.'

That gave her the chance to come round interrupting, but she would be wanting to get her hubby's dinner. So Isabel reminded her, nodding towards the clock.

It really took her breath when she heard, and she as near as nothing gave the woman a piece of her mind, but it wasn't anything to do with her how strangers carried on, so she kept her mouth shut, except to say that her husband Norman wouldn't have stood for it. She could have said a lot more but she didn't wish to give unnecessary offence; there were women knocking about nowadays that would leave their husbands as soon as spit if it took their fancy. But Isabel didn't bring up what she was telling herself, so it couldn't have been her but the other's guilty conscience that made her look stiff as she answered, 'I think Robert will manage.'

'I've no doubt,' she agreed. That way, she might the sooner get rid. She could see the woman's eyes going round, though she pretended she was following the cat. 'I've been turning out upstairs all week; his room had got into such a mess,' she explained, cross to hear herself making excuses. It was for her to decide how she did and she'd been getting on all right before this one set foot in the door. That had been a slip; it had been the young man she'd said yes to.

'You don't have to apologise,' she said.

Which was right enough but it wasn't up to this one to give permission; it meant that Isabel had admitted the state of the place. 'I've scrubbed my share of floors in my time,' and added as one in particular came back to her: 'Maisie would've told you that.'

'Maisie?' That was the first question she'd asked, which was a funny thing considering that was what she was here for.

'She was one of my cousins. She didn't pay much attention to scrubbing. She went to High School.' She had never felt like showing off Maisie before, but she did today for the benefit of this one.

'So she was clever.'

That put her in a fix because she wouldn't run Maisie down in front of a stranger but it took her all her time to nod. She didn't want to give the impression that going to High School meant that Maisie was the only clever one. 'That's wasn't always such an advantage,' she argued, which was true but the remark had a meanness, so she added, 'taking into account what she came in for.'

'You imply that people disapproved?'

She was a quick one, this woman was, getting the hang of it without needing to be told. It was her stating the words. Isabel nearly asked why she bothered coming round when she knew so much. Only, maybe out of politeness she hadn't put it as strong as she should. They'd gone further than disapproving.

And Isabel had been as bad herself at the start.

She could remember it as if it was last week. The preacher had spoken of Maisie in his prayers, or so she had claimed. Isabel hadn't been there because Norman was coming to tell her dad they wanted to get the matter settled so she had had to scrub out, and Maisie had said, 'Fancy you getting married! I hope Norman treats you all right.' And she had answered, deliberately misunderstanding, 'There won't be

31

much over for him to treat me, that's why I'm carrying on at Blygh's,' but they didn't split their sides; it weren't much of a joke. Maisie had said, 'There's some handsome young lads across at the boys' school; I see them when I come out,' but when she had answered, tart, 'Maybe you'll catch one,' her cousin had blushed and shook her head. It was years before she knew why Maisie had done that: as much as her companions at school, the boys at King Henry's looked down on a scholarship girl who wrapped the scrimped-for books in newspaper and, despite an ample train service, walked her five miles. At the time, though, she had assumed that Maisie had mentioned the young men because now she was at High School she could expect to do better than a storeman, so that's why Isabel had been sharp; and it seemed to put it in a nutshell, Maisie coming in and saying the preacher had offered prayers for her future and given thanks while she was on her knees scrubbing out; nobody ever gave her thanks for that. Maisie was her favourite cousin but she could've strangled her that day. She had not known what the girl had gone through, not till she brought it up years later. 'I was six years younger than you, still am for that matter,' Maisie had said, 'and if I'd described to you what it was like and really let myself admit it, I don't think I could have gone back.' But that wasn't known then. At the time she hadn't the knowledge which would have stopped her being jealous.

So a few months after, when they had put up the banns and she was standing in the kitchen waiting to find out whether it would be her father walking up the aisle with her or whether it would be Zac Johnson at the ready by the gate who would be taking her in, it all came back what had been permitted to Maisie and what had been denied her, when she demanded, there in the kitchen, clutching her bunch of lilies, 'Now, Dad, it's time I was off, so it's now or never. Are you going to give me away?' And he said, near tears though she had no hope they were for love, 'Why should I give away what I want to keep for myself?' She had answered him steady as she could manage; she was close on nineteen and he had to face up to it once and for all. So she chose to tell him: 'Yesterday was the last wage packet of mine you'll have, Father, and I'll thank you to see that the lads give Mother a hand.' She had been amazed at the daring but it was possible this time because she held the cards though playing them gave her no more than a skinny sort of triumph, for there was no glitter to them, nothing exciting. Even then, standing holding her posy there in the kitchen, she thought what a sour joke it was that Norman Driffield should be her ace. But still, on that day she held the cards.

Whereas six years before she had nothing, not so much as a single trump; she could only beg. 'You're in top standard,' he had stated on that occasion. 'There's nowt more you can be learnt; you're old enough to bring in a wage. That's what you should be thinking about, not imagining yourself tarted up for that County High.' She had tried to reason with: 'I could still help Mother in the evenings,' to which he had answered, 'It's my belief you'd soon be too stuck up for that.' Seeing her tears, he'd been taken aback and mumbled that it wasn't him but circumstances that weren't in favour, trying to get her to pity him, of all things! But she hadn't; though she was only a young thing that hadn't even started her bleeding, she wasn't taken in. She knew he was pleased to have an excuse to stop her.

And she wasn't sorry for him six years after when she stood in the kitchen with the lilies beginning to wither, and watched his tears start to gush, because he'd had more than his share of work out of her. So she said, pleased that she'd got Zac posted, 'I've made other arrangements for if you won't give me away. Or would it satisfy you if you could sell me?' Then a hand had darted out despite the snivelling, for the first and last time in her life he had struck her, and she had walked up the aisle with his mark on her face.

Chapter Four

'I always liked school, you see,' she told the visitor. Who looked startled. Did she think that Isabel had dropped off? 'The teacher, a Miss Freiston, said I was clever enough to go to the County High.' She didn't mention that she had passed the scholarship; she wasn't one to swank. 'That Miss Freiston was good at her job, she had a way of making you interested.' She could hear her voice losing its crack at the mention of her; it was a funny thing to sound like a moonstruck worshipper after all these years, but in spite of that she continued: 'She kept us at it all right, but we didn't mind that, we were keen, you see, and couldn't get enough of it, the way she told it. I can't remember what, now, it must be near seventy years, but I know that after history and geography, which were always in the afternoon, she'd have us reading. Round the class, mostly. We had Wordsworth and *Nicholas Nickleby* and *The Merchant of Venice*. I still remember the bits she learned us by heart – Shylock exclaiming on Antonio asking him for money when he'd called him a dog. She was a bit of a freethinker, you see. And it didn't only show up when she came to books. We used to have sewing on the Friday afternoon one week and cooking the next and instead of putting the lads to raffia work like Mr Littlehampton in standard five, she had them learning to hem and making an apron so they could cook alongside us. It caused a bit of an outcry at the time and the school managers said she had to put a stop to it so she switched them to knitting socks for the soldiers, it being about the middle of the Great War, and that shut them up.

'She was a crafty article and you have to laugh, looking back. She had us eating out of her hand, lads included. We were scared, though, not on account of the cane, she never used that, but because having her for a teacher was a bit like being perched on the top of a volcano; you were getting the chance to view a good distance but you knew it was dangerous because you might any moment be blowed up. She was very outspoken and made no allowances; she hadn't been born and bred in Neatham, like us, and she could see no reason why she shouldn't stand up and declare that women should have the vote. She was keen on me going to High School but it fell to Maisie to be the one in the family to have that.'

34

'Yet people disapproved?'

'They left her alone. It made her different.' She was growing tired and, eyes sliding, she saw under a chair one of those tinfoil trays moulded into compartments. It had been well licked and she wondered whether the dinner she'd bought last week would be thawed out. 'But it got her a job better than making up bloomers at Blygh's.'

'You haven't told me about that.'

Which was what she'd come for, Isabel remembered. 'There's not much to tell. One pair of bloomers is much the same as another, except for the size. When you've seen one, you've seen them all, you might say; and what goes into them,' cackling.

'And neither have you told me what made them leave Maisie alone, in what way she was different.'

She didn't need an answer; she'd got it in the sound of her own voice, not so much the accent because she didn't talk all that posh, but in the fashion the words hung together, and Isabel could have told her that, but she knew the visitor wasn't asking for information either about her way of talking or about Maisie.

She was asking to be taken in.

Isabel didn't know why she should be put upon like this. The woman was all right; she had her health and seemed to suffer no lack; she possessed that tranquillity which said that her husband, whether she did for him or not, brought in a wage regular. Yet she had an expression on her that reminded Isabel of her son, of the way he used to sidle up and stare, his face begging. Waiting for some word. Now again one was expected. She was flustered by the demand, exasperated that at her time of life she should not be relieved of it. So she evaded, still thinking of her son: 'I'll show you the washing machine my George bought me,' then remembering that she was supposed to be in the middle of using it: 'It's no matter. It'll wait. You can see it another time.'

She found it upsetting to be reminded of him, strangely bald now but still with that look which she couldn't change; she couldn't bring herself to try; it wasn't in her nature. But regarding this visitor, Isabel felt sorry that she'd never taken George to her, opened up to him as he had wanted and as this one did at the minute. And gently, with a sense of relenting, she offered this visitor a consolation as the request for a washing machine had been to him: 'Perhaps we shouldn't be blaming Maisie but taking it out on those that wouldn't budge, too obstinate to see owt any other way,' and felt miserable, she didn't know why, as she watched the woman walk down the path, never looking back to give even a wave, just like her son, though as Norman would point out, nobody's going to offer a wave to a shut door.

'Her husband died about four years ago. I gather that she nursed him at home,' Peter told her.

'As far back as four years?' From Isabel's remark: 'I've been turning out upstairs all week; his room had got into such a mess,' Nora had assumed his death was quite recent.

'If you think she's still grieving, then we should mention that to the social services: they've asked me to let them know if we come across anyone that might need their attention.'

'She would object strongly and it's not necessary. The more squeamish might comment upon the rudimentary hygiene, but that seems her choice. Anyway, I've discovered she worked at Blygh's.'

'Didn't they all?'

'Making bloomers.'

'Did she have much to say about the place?'

'No. Isabel isn't the world's greatest talker, though I'm sure her silences are eloquent, if one could plug in. However, she appears to expect me again, so I'll go. The only subject she gave any attention to was her teacher. A Miss Freiston. I didn't try a tape; I just made a few notes.'

'I like the sound of her,' he told Nora, reading. 'She's a marvellous antithesis to much that we have; we must find out more. Perhaps Dick could ask round. However, the priority at the moment is the pre-school play group because it meets down below this afternoon. When they've dumped their kids in the old school room, quite a number of the mothers hang about for a chat. I'd like to know whether, eventually, any would be willing to assist with props and if any of them would like to act. I've no idea yet what the play will cover but I envisage a lot of crowd scenes; some might be prepared to bring their babies into those. "My first appearance on stage was at ten months in an interesting character part." Sorry to impose this on you, but I've got a couple across the way psyched up to reminisce.'

'No hassle. It'll be like old times.'

Because she had done this before, had lolled about in a scruffy kitchen, her skin scorched by a polythene beaker distorted to a scoop in her hand, and had watched the charred paper of a spill break off and float away as the flame fired the cigarettes. But today it was different, for the talkative one was called Tracy and she had no solarium tan, hers stopped at her bra; and the pregnant one was not dressed in a Mothercare smock but an anorak constantly twitched down to conceal her skirt's open zip; and the one feeding her baby did not drop the shoulder strap of a lace camisole but shook a bottle and worked the teat between the child's gums; and none of them found Nora surprising because she didn't talk husbands' prospects, but because she was there at all.

'You must need a brain scan. Catch me working for nowt! Granted we all do that, but at least we get our keep.'

'You're behind the times,' Tracy reproved, ironical. 'She's as likely as not occupying herself with this because she can't find anything else. It's the fashion. I wouldn't mind being up in that office instead of watching his boiler suits scraping round in the launderette.'

'I wouldn't mind being up in that office, either. That Mr Green! He's lovely. Got such soulful eyes.'

However, these features left Mandy cold who, flicking her ash into the sink, declared that what she went for was Peter's little bum.

So in one respect at least the conversation did not differ from what she had listened to sixteen years earlier.

'It's our Dick up there who lends Mr Green a hand,' Mandy told Nora as she left.

And a week later, breathless because of the unfamiliar rather than the run up the stairs: 'I wouldn't mind having a go in that play. I asked Ross about it and he said it would be all right since Dick will be there.'

'What does Ross imagine may happen to you?'

She laughed, gay with the concession. 'More than you might think, or what could, I expect. I always say, with a mind like his, he's wasted down at the pumps; he ought to write a book.'

'Send him along,' Peter said. 'We could do with blokes like him.'

Next day, when he and Nora were alone in the office, Dick reported: 'There's more than my sister-in-law showing an interest. I wouldn't be surprised if a few of those play-group mothers turned up, and that Tracy Dawkins was on the cosmetic counter at Boots before she started a family, so she says she'll do the make-up provided that Pete gives her a part where she can show off her legs. I'm not kidding, before he knows where he is, they'll be passing him round like a plate of cakes.'

'Just good fun. They are very decorous.'

'There's no decorum when a bunch of women get together.'

She had not used the precise epithet. She had really wanted to say

. . . what? Narrow? Suburban? Respectable, conventional? Or simply unaware, inexperienced, green? Before Dick, any of these would have been too pejorative, and none could conceal her involuntary and surprised guilt at what had prompted it: the uncomfortable silence and the pregnant one's blush, when she had mentioned Robert at home, she living away.

So she said, 'How's the transcribing?'

'Coming on.'

'You've done masses! Who's this? Ernest Wagstaff. Peter interviewed him. Do you mind if I have a read?'

'If that's your idea of tactful checking, I can tell you for a start it's OK. I can spell.'

'Teacher's pet! I'm interested in Ernest Wagstaff, not your aptitudes. Sorry to disappoint,' and was glad that the answer was truthful.

I was the second boy in our family, there being two girls between Edward and me. Then there was Alfred, Arthur and Leopold, my parents being big supporters of Her Majesty, so we were baptised in the order the names came up. What were the girls' names? Well, one was Victoria, of course, she'd be the eldest, then there were Alice and Beatrice. Where did Beatty come in the line? After Arthur, or maybe after Alfred. My father was Albert, his parents gave him the same name as the old queen's consort who had died by then; he hadn't been king, you see, because he only rose to that position by marrying her. I don't hold with social climbing myself but my great-grandfather used to say that Queen Victoria had been very pushing so perhaps Prince Albert had no choice. My great-grandfather was born the year the Duke of Wellington won the Battle of Trafalgar, which would make him eighty-seven when I came along, but I can't remember getting that bit of news about Her Majesty from him. It were common knowledge. She was only a young slip of a girl at the time of her courtship and manners were freer then among the ruling classes, so it wasn't for us to judge. She straightened herself out later on. We was always strong Chapel.

Yes, that's right; you're not at fault in your calculating because I was born in 1902 on the day of the Derby, which is the main event in the flat racing calendar. I remember that because every year after my mother used to take sixpence to the bookie on Derby Day and ask him to put it on the best horse; I believe she thought that she would have good luck since I'd been born on that day but she never had. Or it might have been that the bookie was a scoundrel and kept the sixpence or he never gave her the winnings, I can't say what it was. She did it every year till she died when I was forty-seven so that bookie made twenty-three and sixpence out of my mother, but it was her only extravagance. She was a very careful woman.

There wasn't much money but we were better off than most, my father being a bootmaker and we lived over the shop. People came, the gentry that is, for miles around because he had a name, you see, for making boots. And when he did the mending, his boots or not, you could guarantee they'd look like new. I'm not telling a story; they did. There was a man who was something big at Ryecroft's and he would bring his boots and always said when he fetched them back that he wished Father could do as much in the renewing line for his missis. He'd say it every time, with trimmings, but you don't want to be hearing vulgar comments like that. The man's been dead this fifty year and it's to be hoped he made his peace before he went.

> Jesus, the sinner's Friend, to Thee,
> Lost and undone, for aid I flee,
> Weary of earth, myself and sin;
> Open Thine arms, and take me in!

You'll know those words. They were written by the brother of John Wesley, Charles Wesley, who was a great one for penning hymns. A bit further down the street from our house my father's brother, who was my Uncle William after King William who died the year after my grandfather was born, and he kept the smithy. There's an old poem that begins 'Under the spreading chestnut tree the village smithy stands' and I always think of it when I think of Uncle William, though Neatham wasn't a village. I learnt that poem when I was a lad for the chapel anniversary one year, and I can still say it. The verses I like best are:

> Toiling, rejoicing, sorrowing,
> Onward through life he goes;
> Each morning sees some task begin,
> Each evening sees it close;
> Something attempted, something done,
> Has earned a night's repose.
>
> Thanks, thanks to thee, my worthy friend,
> For the lesson thou hast taught.
> Thus at the flaming forge of life
> Our fortunes must be wrought.

Thus on its sounding anvil shaped
Each burning deed and thought.

'What do you think of the poetry?' Nora asked.

'I reckon whoever wrote it expected us to take note,' and smiled at some personal joke.

You're asking me about Uncle? He used to see to the carts, fixing the rings to the fellies, and he was a bit of an artist, too, because he'd make the fire-irons and dogs for grates and nice pieces of trellis for gardens. He made that communion rail in the old Wesleyan chapel though there was a lot of talk after about it being more suited to church, but most of his work was shoeing and there was a saying in the town that if you stirred out, one way or another you'd end up paying a Wagstaff because if it wasn't your own shoes worn through, it'd be your hosses'. But you might say that shoeing horses was his downfall because when the Great War began in 1914 he joined up in Kitchener's Army and became a farrier with his regiment, and when he was at Loos a horse that was very nervous after going through shells up to the line kicked him and a rib punctured his left lung. Which made two of our family lost in that war. Edward went to France in 1916 and never came back.

That made me the eldest son and I had to join my father in the shop. I didn't mind, I liked working with the leather, but I couldn't do like Father. Somehow I hadn't command of the knack. It was the lasting that gave the quality, you see, and I never could draft out all the wrinkles and pipes the same as Father could. And of course he never put a machine to a shoe of his, all hand-stitched except for the brads in the heel. He always took the jobs with a bit of class to them and I was left with the rough. I didn't object, it was his right to divide the work to his liking, and when business was slack he didn't say no to me playing about with a few fancy ideas. 'Will you make me a binocular case?' one asked me. So I did. After that, I took all manner of orders, one thing or another, and some people said I should have branched out on my own and set myself to doing nothing else only these wares, but I had to stay with Father. He'd kept five lads, and then there were the girls and Mother, which added up to nine mouths to feed beside his own, then Edward being gone I had to take his place and do my share. I was thirteen when I started under Father. You see, I was needed. What was it like, living over the shop? A sight better than this place, I can tell you, which they call a sheltered unit because there's a bell over there you can pull on if you have a turn and the warden's supposed to come when it rings but she'll not hurry if it's mine because she says it's not to be used if it's only that I'm

40

missing my glasses and I tell her I can only find them myself if I've got them
on and one day she'll be sorry she wasn't more quick if I give her a shock
and die on her before she arrives. Where did I live before? In one of those
council houses up Burton Park; they gave them a posh name in the hope we
wouldn't look too close. I moved in the day I got married to Hester
Hopkinson who became my wife on the fourth of September 1930 which
was the same day my father first drew his pension.

I kept the cobbling going, so I had to walk two miles there, two miles back
every day whatever the weather but I was ready to set up house for myself
and it would have been too big a squash over the shop. Yes, you're right. A
two-bedroomed cottage didn't offer much in the way of space for a family of
eight, boys and lasses being mixed, but it was no smaller than average and
people learnt to manage. As they got bigger, the girls' bed was brought into
my father and mother's room.

'Two bedrooms for ten people!'

He made a face. 'I suppose you could say they had one solution.'

'It exceeds the 1930s official definition of overcrowding, an average
of two over ten years old to each room, including the scullery.'

'I don't suppose the Wagstaffs lost a lot of sleep because some
high-ups said they'd overstepped the mark.' He was mocking the
academic knowledge, assuming she had nothing else.

'No, that would hardly be their first worry. Any more than it would
be your grandparents', or mine.'

She saw his expression change, though to wariness not to one of
welcome, but for the moment more important was the crush of
Ernest's family within the dense script. 'They had no privacy at all.'

Less tart, he suggested, 'That would be about the last thing they'd
expect.'

'Absence of expectation is no excuse for lack of provision.'

'I wasn't saying it was.'

'I was thinking of how they slept.'

'There's nothing wrong with sharing a bed. I've never had one to
myself in my life. Before I got married I always slept with our kid, and
when Dad was on nights we used to climb in with Mam, one on each
side. She said that way she felt safe.' He chose to explain, to vindicate
their custom to someone ignorant through the refinement of class.

Yet she could not correct him.

'When Dad was at the Front,' her father had told her, 'me and Billy
used to go in with Mam. She'd lie against the wall and us lads would
argue who was to go next till she said we had to take turns. It was the

best place, the middle, cosy, and it was funny how the night you were there you never had bad dreams. Mother'd roll over to face the wall and you'd snuggle into her back with one arm hugged round her and you were off in a trice.'

Nora could not say: I know. Because she could not have hidden her repugnance for her father's lachrymose memory which had caused her to think: He has never grown up; he is still floating in the womb. She could not risk that disloyalty in the presence of this man, not yet known.

'Don't you think that these reminiscences we're collecting are as interesting for what they don't mention as for what they do? Here's Ernest brought up with seven other children and parents in a two-bedroomed cottage and his only remark is that they learnt to manage! There's no description of how, or what it was like, or an indication of his feelings about it or its effect on him.'

'Maybe he didn't have any feelings about it; or if he did, he's not likely to put them into that machine.'

'Ernest knew that if there were anything he didn't wish to be used, Peter would rub it out. I can't judge from this whether he was employing an internal censor or whether he had no positive response to the matter.'

'What would you expect?'

At the very least, distaste; the press of bodies whose sweat gave no promise of congress or if so, was taboo. Misery; at the need for solitude denied. Frustration; the crammed rooms preventing the stretch of personal freedom. However: 'Perhaps anger,' she answered him.

'Ernest doesn't sound much of a revolutionary. It's King, Country and Chapel for him.'

'I imagine the girls would have more to say about it, three of them sleeping in the same room as the parents.'

'They wouldn't say anything about it. They don't go in for tattle round here.' She was the outsider rebuked. 'They know what's private.'

'Private!' and by a switch of vision she was no longer the girl in the crib, the great-aunt who had said to her, 'My bed was in with Mam and Dad till I was eighteen; it shouldn't have been allowed, Nora, what I heard.' Instead, she was the young wife splayed across the sheet, toes dabbling in the duvet's cumulus upon the floor, her tongue curling with his to spin the spittle to a fine thread which, as his head lifted, stretched then frayed along her chin whilst she luxuriated in words that preceded the pulse of his knob; but what had been seen through the lids of eyes squeezed into a patched shawl over a cot was the grease of sweat, the clenched buttocks between forked thighs, and what had passed into the ears through the fingers' cork was the sty's grunt and squeal.

Out of which, she said, the fragrance turned to stench by this scrutiny, 'Think of the parents.'

This man's face sharpened. 'I can't see that's doing any good.' He wished to dismiss the situation she had implied.

But she could not and disregarding his hesitancy, insisted, 'Imagine! So public!'

'It wasn't their choice.' He was not accustomed to talking on such a topic with a woman.

'I've not suggested that it was.'

As before, the talk had slipped, had gone awry, and she knew that an opportunity had passed. There had been no disagreement between them, yet discussion had separated rather than joined. She had been distanced, held away. Looking at him, she had seen no brightness of recognition in his face, drawing her in.

I have mismanaged it, she blamed herself. He resented being confronted with a subject he'd prefer to evade; he considered attempts to comprehend not as sympathy but as a kind of prying. Prying! Perhaps he would have been less accusing if I'd told him what I know, but my knowledge of my father's sentimentality, his aunt's shame is, even after all these years, still too raw for me to entrust.

She heard him murmur: 'I expect they found ways.'

Which translated the pillows of swansdown to flock and under the concealing sheet a hand slid quietly to ripple the calico nightgown, signalling acceptance, promising renewal of a neglected pulse. Within the unlit tunnel formed between shoulder and raised knee a generous though confined world was created, in which there was no disapproval, which honoured customs and conquered reserve. And though a lavish abandon was not permitted her there was no hasty fumbling; when words were suppressed it was not in deference to a listening dark. Instead, the passion was in the constraint, in the control of a motion that was precise, neat, husbanded to a compressed force and without sound.

When it was over she moved her head, feeling the stark light, and found the man's eyes were upon her. He was frowning. Stricken by the illusion corrected, then alarmed yet excited by the route it pointed,

43

she looked down at the script in front of her and wondered, as she smoothed the pages, at her trembling hands.

Dick said, 'If you're set on reading the rest of Ernest Wagstaff's story, there's a bit Pete's showing an interest in, but I'm wondering if he's on the wrong tack.'

Obedient, she read:

As they got bigger, the girls' bed was brought into my father and mother's room. They would have been no better off staying in Wesley Street where brother Edward and they were born, which was before my grandfather and grandmother died in the same week. Them being gone left the workshop, scullery and two rooms over, and they had put Father's name in the rent book so him and Mother pushed all their belongings on a hand cart to the shop. There's a story attached to that. You'll understand that they were put to the trouble of several journeys and my mother didn't like the whole street familiar with what she had, except for the good stuff, so she covered everything else with a tablecloth out of her bottom drawer that she was keeping for when Edward was twenty-one, only as it turned out it was never used, and she and my father went back and forth, back and forth, with the tablecloth lying on top. Now that brought them to the attention of Florence Moorby, who was a woman well known for her sharp tongue; she told them they looked more as if they were filling up the cemetery than flitting and it reminded her of whited sepulchres and she thought it a fine joke that despite all former appearances to the contrary, when it came to the Day of Judgement, the Wagstaffs had so much to hide. My mother never forgave that and if any of us children was found playing with a member of the Moorby family, we were denied our dinner.

After a double space, the next line read: Now it's Pete talking.

This would make a good scene, Florence Moorby cast as the street shrew. Would have lots of movement, dancing, household props, comic business with one or two of them, such as a heavy mangle, mangling the tablecloth as part of the dance, etc. Chorus song: 'The day the Wagstaffs were flitting' gradually incorporating a clothes prop revealing ribbons, moving into a maypole dance. Is there anyone around who could construct a base so that the pole would stand firmly erect?

'What is it you're doubtful about?' she asked him. 'Don't you like the idea of that scene?'

'Pete should pay attention to the next bit.'

'This?' She read out:

It was all past history by the time I was born and I didn't know the ins and outs of it so it wasn't for me to judge. Mother was the one that kept the story going, my father would grow very irritable and say we'd heard all that before. Alice once remarked to me in confidence that she was of the opinion that Florence Moorby was venting her spleen in this way because she considered the house should have gone to her or one of the Moorbys, not us, though why she should think that, I don't know. I've never got to the bottom of the matter.

'Got to the bottom of what matter?' Peter demanded, coming up the stairs.

'We've just been reading Ernest Wagstaff's recollections.'

'I remember. I thought there might be a street scene in there, didn't I?'

'Yes. Dick has reservations.'

He glared at her, leant across the desk and picked up the transcript. Tapping the sheets together, he said, 'Pete's got enough on his plate without me giving him problems. It's not my place to interfere.'

'Oh, for Christ's sake! You're in this as much as I am; you've spent almost as many hours on the job as I have this last fortnight if that's relevant.'

Dick smiled at him. 'Keep your hair on. You'll need it come a cold snap. All I have to say is, I was wondering what people belonging to the Moorbys might think of it.'

'Come on, Dick! It's over eighty years ago.'

'They have long memories in Neatham.'

'For which I am thankful. I think you're being unduly protective.'

'As I said, it's for you to decide what you do, but if you look at it, I reckon there's more here than just a brawl in a street between a couple of women.'

'Yes. Something about a house.'

'Looks more than that to me.'

'You've been doing some close analysis on this one, Dick. I didn't know that was another of your talents,' he said without condescension.

'You'd know it backwards if you'd spent best part of a day typing it out.'

'I'm sorry.'

'You should be pleased. And if you write that scene, just don't forget that if Florence Moorby happened to be my great-grandma, you'd have me to answer to. I'd take the line that I'd got the reputation of the family to consider.'

'It would already be in rags, with you around.'

The mood was now of backs being slapped, of punches feigned.

'But I tell you what, Pete; I can give you a way of overcoming the problem. All you have to do is change the name.'

'You're joking!' but he was not certain. 'This is a kind of documentary drama. A first principle is its absolute truth.'

Dick's cheeks twitched. 'Then if I were you, Pete, I'd forget it. Half of the stories they tell will be made up and the other half's missed out.'

'I've never imagined that they are telling me everything. Seventy or eighty years held in a few thousand words! I know that's not the point you're making, Dick, but think – fifty years working at Ryecroft's eight or nine hours a day, and every day in the week, in the year, no different from the next except for a joke going round, a private vendetta, an accident, an occasional strike. Thousands of hours in a life meriting no more than a couple of pages. So, if out of this barrenness some colour buds and they sprinkle a little pollen to gild their grey stories, I don't care a damn.'

They did not remind him that only one minute earlier he had declared for a play based on absolute truth; nor did Dick point out that having worked at Ryecroft's, he was better equipped than Peter to comment on the experience. They did not speak, and Nora thought: In this silence is Neatham reflected, a well drilled too deep for the fugitive sounds to rise from its base.

'Now for the comic interlude,' Peter said at last. 'I've just heard from someone desperate to put money into us.'

'You've been on the bottle.'

'No; but from his manner, I think this bloke must have been. He was incredibly insistent.'

'And so he should be.'

'Who was he?' Nora asked.

'A Mr Hipple. He seemed to be in charge of a timber merchant's the other side of Haxby: Clayton's.'

'Been there for years. Did you try begging some wood? By the sound of it, you're going to need plenty.'

'My first thought, Dick, but he wasn't interested in giving that. Only money.'

46

'That'll do. How much had he in mind?'

'There speaks the hard-headed businessman, Nora.'

'When you're out of work there's nothing else you can be. It's only artists that are supposed to live on air.'

'It's a pity I don't pay him, Nora, otherwise I'd be giving him his cards.'

'How much?'

'At first he asked what money we were getting from the Council and the number of staff. Laughed like a drain when I confessed there was only me. Paid, that is.'

'How much?'

'He offered to equal Glyn's grant. And that's not even through yet. If we get it.'

'So this would give us another five hundred,' Nora said. 'It would be a marvellous bit of pump-priming. We could bring in a firm to do the lights and employ some professional help with publicity – a designer, at least.'

'And as soon as we opened it up to the experts, the local initiative would disappear and the inexperienced would take a back seat.'

'Balls, Peter!' and saw Dick's wince. 'That's inconsistent. You're a professional. You're writing the script.'

'More putting it together. The fundamental principle is to use people in the community, not replace them.'

'But you can accept money without compromising that. You're prepared to take sponsorship in kind; you've already done so from Blygh's, and you asked this fellow for timber.'

'I admit that. I'm being irrational, I know. Any other time, I'd have grabbed. There's no queue of people out there clamouring to put money in the arts. But there was something about him that made me suspicious. I even created a management committee to whom I must refer before accepting an offer! It was weird. He was so pressing. Obviously there should be hidden benefits for him, but Clayton's is such a small firm and five hundred pounds seems a lot for them just to receive an acknowledgement on the programme. I've never met anyone so anxious to get rid of money.'

Dick laughed. 'I shouldn't worry, Pete. Maybe you haven't refused much. People who talk big often have second thoughts when it comes to putting their money where their mouth is.'

* * *

'Peter didn't agree with you,' she commented later.

'No matter. I was only telling him who he can rely on.'

Which was, clearly, himself rather than she. 'You were as astonished as I was that he could be reluctant to accept.'

'All the same, I don't think it's for us to object. If he's got a feeling the chap's shady, then he has to trust that.'

'It could have been an excuse, his way of avoiding the true reason for not wishing to accept.' Infuriated by the other's uncritical loyalty, she argued extravagantly what she did not believe of Peter, could not defend: 'Some people can be very possessive about something they are deeply committed to and interpret offers of help as a threat.'

'We all get fixed on our own notions and don't like to give them up.' He judged her, not Peter. 'But I'll go with what he says; I can't see what there is to gain from so much digging into it.' He paused, bored with the argument. 'All I would like sorted out is the where-abouts of this local initiative. I'd not want it to disappear before I'd given it a look over.'

'I wouldn't agree with him that there's initiative exactly, but there is beginning to be some interest: your Mandy, the other play-group women, and the head of English at the Comprehensive – I'm visiting him next week.' It occurred to her that she might have misjudged his remark; she had not been prepared for a slide into humour. Nevertheless she continued: 'The woman who teaches tap on a Monday has offered to help with the dancing and someone phoned yesterday inviting us to borrow a pre-war perambulator.'

He looked away from her, a nail plucking at the transcript they had been considering, and she was certain that his sobriety was contrived, that he was amusing himself at her expense.

'Then there's you.'

'I'm here because the garden looks like the pictures on seed packets and I've run out of other jobs.'

'But you wouldn't be doing this if it didn't attract you.' She saw how clean his hands were. On the other side of the desk her own were grubby in comparison.

'I met Pete one afternoon when I was giving Stan a lift with getting the big room ready for the disco; and I agreed to come along.'

The stab of jealousy was as involuntary as the movement that had just hidden her hands in her lap. 'So you're willing to give your time gratis while Peter agonises over whether he can accept money!'

'I'm happy to go along with that. Pete gabs out of the back of his head at times, but he's genuine. He's in this job for what it is and no other reason.'

Her association with the project was too equivocal for her to challenge whether by this he insinuated that her own reason was less pure. Goaded, she asked, 'But he gabs out of the back of his head?'

Dick shrugged. 'Well, he will, won't he? He's new to this place.'

He was fidgeted by the talk now; it had not the urgency of the voice on the cassette waiting to be spelt on to the typescript under his hand. His impatience reduced her to an irritation that was barely endured and she felt herself refused, a thing cast off. Before his unspeaking dismissal, her breasts flattened and sex was spayed.

And, tears pricking, her mind sought Robert. She heard his whisper, the kindling words, the articulation of feeling which ran down his fingers and on to her ready skin. So, revived, again plumped, she leaned towards the other and said, arch, 'Was it because Peter is new to the place that you thought you could pull that one on him – the need to change Florence Moorby's name to avoid offence to relatives? Really! Eighty years later!'

'There's no sense in putting their backs up. You never know what it might lead to. That is, if the family hasn't died out.' His eyes had changed. Their corners creased, they appreciated that she had detected some concealed knowledge, and for a moment she was received into his thoughts.

Therefore she did not ask him to explain. She would not invite a repulse. Under the beams which had stretched over the heads of orderly schoolchildren she was acquiescent; she was grateful for his welcome, however brief. For a moment satisfied, she knew that their fragile meeting had been bestowed by Robert but experienced no sense of him betrayed.

Chapter Five

'Another week nearly over,' Doris Bentley observed. 'Friday tomorrow. You'll be pleased to be going home.'

'It's certainly been a busy week.'

'Mr Trafford will be glad to see you again, I'm sure.'

'He's away quite a lot himself.'

'Is he, now? That makes it easier, I suppose.'

Irritated by this gossipy prying, Nora said, 'I'd be doing this whether or not it were domestically convenient.'

'That's what Clifford said only last weekend: when an author's got an idea in his, or her, head, nothing'll stop him getting it down.'

'That may be true, but Peter Green's the writer in this outfit, not me.'

'You're just saying that!'

'If I'm anything at all, I suppose that at present I'm the researcher.'

'Well, that's important. They couldn't manage without you doing that, looking up information and going round interviewing. Only, you're being too shy. In my view, whatever you say you are an author. On the counter in the library there's your history of Neatham.'

'That's a publicity leaflet to encourage interest in the play.' For it she had adjusted the brief summary submitted to Glyn's financial committee and had been rather smug about this provident use of labour.

'It doesn't matter what name you give it, you wrote that. I told the librarian when she was stamping my books. She left school the same year as me and I have to point out that, despite being a librarian, she's never had an author as paying guest. Then there are all those articles you write for the free paper.'

'One.'

'It was very nice. I showed Mrs Kilshaw in the office and I kept the paper back so that Clifford could read it. Generally I throw the papers out as soon as I've looked through; I don't like them messing up the home, but I wanted Clifford to see that one. He was very impressed,' she informed Nora, impressed.

Tired after a day spent in the Comprehensive School, Nora had not the energy to insist that Doris find a more deserving target for admiration.

'He cut out your story to show his managing director because he happened to know that Mr Wilkes was showing an interest.'

'I wouldn't have thought we would pull in an audience from so far afield.'

'I expect Mr Wilkes likes to follow what's going on because Scully and Fanhope have had several contracts round here; they put up the new school. Also, as Mr Wilkes said when Clifford showed him the article, "It's not often I get the chance to read something written by a guest of a friend of one of my staff. Next time, Clifford, is it to be one of your stories, or your lady friend's?" He was joking, of course. Clifford doesn't do anything like that; it might get in the way of his work. You have to keep your feet on the ground when you're drawing up building contracts. But he likes a good read, generally with a scientific bent, whereas I prefer books with a human interest but not sloppy, naturally. We make a fine pair, we do; never go up to bed without something in our hands, and heaven knows what time Clifford stops reading. I haven't once heard him switch off his light before I close my book. Sometimes I think he does it to show he can stay awake longest, lying there with his ear glued to the wall so he doesn't miss the click of my bedside lamp. I've considered leaving it on and trying to sleep with the sheet over my face, if that's his little game, but that wouldn't be fair.'

'Since you ask me, Becky, yes, I do think that you may be up to some little game which wasn't part of the agreement when I gave you permission to stay here, and I certainly cannot recollect extending the invitation to the rogues' gallery as well.'

'Oh, Sir! I was helping her with her assignment. She was away last week. You wouldn't want her to get behind, would you, Sir?'

'I wouldn't want a lot of things for her. Becky can go across to English One. You – outside!'

'I'll just finish looking over this page, Sir.'

'You'll go straight outside. I don't know what sort of impression you think you're giving to our visitor, arguing like this.'

'But you're forever telling us we ought to learn to argue more, Sir, and I don't know what sort of impression you think you're giving, keeping her to yourself in this pukey little stockroom when there's thousands of other places where we could all have a see.'

'Don't push your luck any further, Wayne. Out!'

'Sorry about that,' Don Clamp said. 'One of our more colourful pupils, and I shouldn't complain; we haven't many. Now when Becky here has collected her goods and arranged her cardigan to her satisfaction, you can sit down. Thank you, Becky; and next time I agree to your staying indoors during the lunch hour, just remember that the permission isn't for the purpose of courting.'

'There was no team practice, you see, Sir.'

'I can appreciate that would leave our Wayne at a loose end. Pleasant young woman,' he commented as Becky shuffled out. 'Pity she hasn't the brains to match her face, but I trust that will prove enough. I'm sorry, but I'm a practical man. Unless she behaves like a little fool, which naturally she is at the moment, she'll have more choice than many of her peers. She might even break into the white-collar league if she plays her cards right.'

He paused. 'You may be surprised to hear me say that. I don't advocate upward mobility *per se*, but by definition it's moving out of the rut, which means slightly different horizons, if nothing else. Of course, we do try to provide those.' His eyes left her and followed the titles along the shelves, contemporary fiction in the teenage lists, some abridged Victorians, school editions of proven favourites, a few cautious anthologies, one or two plays, their spines cracked and covers idly doodled upon or sometimes incongruously jacketed in paper matching that on a pupil's home walls, and stacked in class sets. 'It's a start,' he said to her, slightly defensive, 'and it occurred only three years ago when I took up the post. There was no literature in stock, merely textbooks. My predecessor concentrated on O level language. Several reasons have been given to me; the one that can be repeated without risking defamation of character is that the children had to learn to master the language before going on to the frills. From the absence of the latter I deduce that nobody qualified.'

'That's incredible.'

'I thought so at the time, but my capacity for incredulity has been blunted. However. You're wanting to know if we can make some contribution to this play?'

'Yes. Peter wonders whether you would allow your children to try their hand at verses to be set to music. He'd let you know the situation and send you photostats of the scenes. He'll be starting to write soon, mid May.'

'That would be a very satisfactory way for us to participate. I've some third-formers who've been with me since they came in, so they're used to a mild challenge. Rome wasn't built in a day. If you agree, I'll have a word with Phil, in charge of music and not hostile to novelty. We could work together.'

'That would be lovely.'

'Then I'll look into it. I must tell you I'm fascinated by what Peter Green is doing. Interesting to see how it turns out. It might prove a stimulus. Sometimes wonders have occurred; though probably not here. I keep promising myself that I'll try a school production; the boss has contrived to introduce drama on to the timetable.' He laughed suddenly. 'I mean the theatrical kind. The fact that, unlike the practice in many schools, it's the only sort, should be a relief. This community play might help. It might create an atmosphere for persuasion.'

Unable to ask who must be persuaded, Nora said, 'There'll be a lot of parts for children, particularly in crowd scenes.'

'Good. We have some who'd enjoy that, once they'd been given a costume to hide inside. I'll let you have a list of names. And as soon as Peter Green sends me details of the other, I'll have a go. He mustn't be too optimistic about the results, though. When asked to produce something about this town which happened, let's say before the last ten or twenty years, there might not be a lot of interest. My generation of teachers has made a rod for its own back. It's called relevance.' He sighed, mocking himself. 'As a concept, without resort to the carrot of examinations, that's awkward to debate with the immature mind unexercised in philosophical dialectics. Even the request that speech should bear some trace of grammatical correctness cannot be wholly justified, since it is proved every hour that you can get along with just a few interjections and grunts.'

She laughed, but: 'All the same, you should read the accounts of the old people we've interviewed.'

'I should like to. Their grandchildren also, when fired, can command quite an eloquence.'

Whose value was not to be judged by standard syntax, and she wanted to ask him what compromise he reached between that and the regional idiom because he did not seem a man who would dismiss the latter's worth. However, knowing him so little, she could not question. The difference was often regarded as more than a matter of geography, but she could not describe to him how she had first been made aware of that.

* * *

'I have no wish to discourage an individual style, Nora, provided that it is appropriate to the passage,' the French mistress had pronounced, 'but lines do have to be drawn. This is a formal piece of prose about, as you have rightly understood, two rather elegant aristocratic young people, and to describe their meeting in language at times verging upon the patois of working men's clubs is rather ludicrous. I don't imagine that you adopted it deliberately for comic effect. Or social comment, perhaps? I assure you that neither is pertinent or satisfactory. For example, instead of: "With face half averted, he admired her beauty *out of the corner of his eye*," we really cannot allow: "With his head half turned he wondered at her figure *out of his eye corner*".'

Miss Ridley waited for titters from those who had learnt to temper the dialect which she ignorantly equated with lack of intelligence among the Neanderthal hordes of the manual class. It was only in the traditional grammar schools that standards like hers could be maintained; these comprehensive schools being introduced could never do for the bright children what schools like theirs had achieved.

'I suppose we must be grateful that there is no mention of mouth or ear. Otherwise we might have had the crudities of gob or lug scattered over this translation.' She smiled at the startled faces. It was by such deft sleights that she conveyed, contrary to pupils' assumptions, that she had a broad knowledge of society, gained by choice, and that she could not be fooled.

'Then a little further down we have the young lady not "rising to sit by him" but "getting up to sit against him". Really! Why so aggressive, Nora? I do hope that the rest of you are not in the habit of approaching young men in such a fashion! I can assure you, and I don't have to say why,' allowing a fleeting, coy grimace, 'that such a manner does not find favour with the other sex. I very much doubt whether this young man would have led you, Nora, out into the garden and invited you to listen to the nightingales with him. But I am absolutely sure that he would have said: "*Listen to*", not: "*Listen at*".'

Nora had then scrambled out of her desk to receive the marked homework; and though she knew that the laughter which followed her was craven, a pretence that this defilement was not shared, she could not resist the shame.

'Perhaps if Peter came in and talked about what he's doing, they might be more ready to contribute. That's if you wouldn't mind.' She remembered how protective teachers could be over their charges.

'That's a splendid idea,' Don Clamp agreed. 'Someone appealing for their help who isn't Teach might more easily cajole an interest; they haven't met a writer in the flesh before. But you should warn him that these children are very private; they are hard to get to know. They aren't difficult or uncooperative and quite friendly, but they don't come up to you as some children will and take you into their confidence.

'You see, they are ill at ease when confronted with anything that touches on or describes feelings. They're much happier with science or craft subjects. Perhaps that's why my predecessor concentrated on exercises. Any emotion they regard with distrust and when asked to express their own, even a response apparently unthreatening such as sympathy with some character in a book, they experience the most acute discomfort. It's almost withdrawal. Part of their lack of confidence, I think, and not the same as the usual adolescent behaviour: gawky, brazen or simpering. So whatever we try, the results are unlikely to have much fervour; they won't come from the heart.'

'That won't be essential. Peter's not going to have his characters emoting all over the place and naturally he'll write the key songs himself.' Her answer was more brisk than she wished him to hear, but she was now anxious to leave him. His talk depressed her. She wasn't surprised that the children's stuff had little fervour. He'd got that, and it was infectious: the fervour of defeat. Also, she was dejected by his analysis. If these children distrusted emotions, what of Dick?

Because he had become for her synonymous with Neatham, and with that other Neatham she had long ago left. His speech described its idiom; his frame had its solidity; his gaze was level as its unslanting streets; in his opinions and humour was its independence stated and in his silence were its secrets preserved. In him she saw imaged all that she had forsaken and all that had since been closed to her, and she could not deny that consciously now she wished him to usher her back. But not merely as an intermediary. Since their talk above the crammed family of Ernest Wagstaff, his physical presence had oppressed her; and she was distressed that her need required such a resolution yet was tantalised with hope.

'Neither do I expect my children to emote all over the place,' the schoolmaster defended. 'I've been talking about their capacity to handle feelings; I don't ask for grisly public exhibitions of them.'

'What I meant was', she lied, 'that since this is documentary drama, there will be less lyrical material than narrative or descriptive.'

'I hadn't thought of it in quite those terms,' he answered, disappointed. 'But the documentary style will be very suitable in Neatham

– at the Bottom End, anyway. Anything controversial or challenging or unorthodox would have no pull.' His prediction echoed Glyn Mayhew's reports, she noted, impatient. 'The children are happier tackling narrative and descriptive forms, especially narrative, or more exactly, reportage. It's how they see life, through the television screen mostly. But that's a big subject. Evidence persuades me that its influenced cannot be ignored. However . . .'

'They do too much watching of television,' Doris agreed with him. 'The last thing they think about is having a good read, so when they see Clifford's light long after ordinary bedtime, heaven knows what they think is going on!'

In the circumstances, Nora thought, imaginations would be intolerably stretched.

'He always says that his best ideas come to him in bed. I tease him about that, but he's not intimating anything indecent; he's not the type. He refers to the way he can concentrate on problems and sort them out in his books, like studying whether it would be cheaper in the end to sell his Metro and go for a new registration. He likes a television programme occasionally, though; we all need to wind down. But we stick to BBC most of the time. That comes of the way I was brought up. When ITV started, my father used to sit by the television switching off the advertisements and unfortunately he didn't always time it right switching it back on so we'd lose bits of what had happened. It didn't make for satisfactory viewing, so I formed the habit of watching BBC.'

'Why did your father do that?'

'He'd got it into his head that the adverts wouldn't be decent for a young girl to watch, but there was nothing suggestive in them, not like there is today, as well as in the programmes. He was a man in advance of his time.'

Not sure of the other's attitude, Nora suppressed a snigger.

'Father would have had a look at the Open University programmes, though. He liked to learn something a bit out of the way. Like Clifford. They are very similar in that. If the Open University has a lesson going out first thing in the morning, Clifford'll be down here with the telly on soaking it all in. Sometimes I tell him he only does it so's the noise fetches me out of bed to get him an early breakfast but he knows I don't mean that. I don't mind; I'd rather be up and doing when he's here instead of enjoying a lay-in. And not having him under my feet lets me do a big fry-up; a man likes to be coddled now and again. While I'm at the cooker I can hear what he's watching. It can be very educational – I don't need to tell you that, I'm sure. Keeping an ear cocked while making the breakfast, it's surprising what you can pick up. Is that something else you've written?'

'No. These are notes I made after visiting the Comprehensive.'

'Rather you than me. They thought they could give it a jump-up with a new name and building but a leopard doesn't change its spots and in my eyes it's still Flood Street Secondary Modern. But you must have found plenty to take your attention, staying there all day.'

'Yes.'

'I won't keep you any longer,' she told Don Clamp. 'Thank you for giving me so much time. Good of you to talk to me,' and wondered if Miss Ridley would have commented: Not *talking to*, surely, Nora? Why suddenly so mild? I would have predicted that you of all people would have written, *talking at*. Scrutinise how you can alter the nuance with a preposition.

But disinclined to associate herself with the woman even in a thought joke, Nora forgave Don. 'I'll come again as soon as Peter has anything concrete to offer,' she promised him. 'One thing, though: what is Becky's surname?'

'Dobson.'

'I thought it might be. The headmaster suggested her when I asked if you had anyone very pretty who might consent to being Miss Blygh 1961.'

'She'd love that; her level. Just pop her in a bikini and she'll pull in the crowds.'

'I think the dress will be rather more modest,' careful to ignore the criticism. 'Peter considers all ideas as they are put to him and this one came directly from Blygh's.'

'No doubt he will include this beauty competition,' she told Doris, who was uncommonly interested in it. 'Apparently it caused a stir at the time. So Blygh's claim. For that reason they're willing to help financially; they're offering to provide a catwalk and mikes. The winner put in for Miss England and the manager at Blygh's says she wasn't knocked out till the penultimate round.'

'Is this Becky Dobson pretty?'

'Very. A conventional English rose, rather old-fashioned in a way.'

'So she'll fit what you want.'

'I think so. I shall assist with that scene under duress, however.'

Doris would have expected that comment. If anyone had challenged her to lay a pound on it, she'd have had no hesitation in making the bet. She didn't agree with Nora's condemnation but she did envy the group identity from which it sprang; only once had she been associated with the loyalties of her sex. 'Do you think some women will be against it?' she asked, knowing that she should admit she would not be one of them but unwilling to risk her guest's disapproval. It was odd that she had never felt so cautious during the first weeks Nora had stayed with her.

'They will all be against it,' Nora told her decisively. 'Fancy competing with other women! Parading wares for the satisfaction of male concupiscence.'

Though not sure of the word's meaning, Doris caught the sentiment. 'There's for and against in everything,' she appealed, tentative, and watched the other finger the papers on her knee. 'It could make a nice scene. It's not necessarily indecent, Nora, not if you look at it in the right way, and it's something the mums and dads might be proud of. Becky Dobson's might be just as happy to have her congratulated as those belonging to the prizewinner were.'

'I've no doubt. A pity we haven't made more progress in twenty-five years.'

'You'll be able to count it that we have if Becky's parents don't give their consent.' Sorry that she had permitted the sharpness, she tried to mollify with: 'I'm thinking that could put Mr Green in a fix.'

'I'm pretty certain they'll agree to it.'

'I've something that might help you, then. My first job was at Blygh's. I only stayed there six months; I wanted somewhere a bit smarter to work than their despatch office, but I was there when they held the competition. It was the first one and they didn't have any more after that, but I kept a photo. It'll be useful to you; you won't have to look up the hairdos and fashion of holiday shorts.'

Then she was running up the stairs and pulling open the door of the fitted wardrobe and pushing aside the clothes which concealed the cardboard box. Lifting it out slowed her down, though, and telling herself that all this hurry looked suspicious, she removed her shoes and eased her skirt above her knees for comfort before she knelt by the box and raised the lid. It wasn't a search she was doing; she knew what was there; she wasn't likely to forget; and the reason she'd put the photograph at the bottom was to keep it as far from sight as was possible. Anybody liable to exaggeration might have said she was trying to bury it but she wouldn't put it like that; she just wanted to make sure that she didn't come across it by chance, before she was stiffened up.

But she didn't need to prepare herself this evening; she didn't even flinch when, as she lifted the nightgown folded between tissues of paper, a crocheted edging showed unbleached, straight from the needle, and a ribbon fluttered uncreased by use. She did not lay it aside and swear she'd wear it only as a shroud, then bite her lip before scolding herself that such an idea was going too far and she would never have thought of it if she hadn't seen that Miss Havisham once at the pictures. Instead, she sat back on her heels and rested the soft package upon her lap. She didn't need to prepare herself for what came next, just as tonight she did not brush away but found almost pleasurable the light stroke of the tissue paper across her thighs.

Because tonight down there was Nora who had written so nicely about giving everyone a chance to have their say, not just those at the Bottom End (though she didn't put it like that) and by a fluke she'd hit on the bit that was for Doris to tell. Normally she would have done anything to prevent the information getting across, but Nora worked so hard it didn't seem reasonable not to co-operate. She would never have brought the matter up if Nora hadn't received word from Blygh's, not from him who'd retired but from the new factory manager and so not in command of the full facts; but ignorance hadn't muzzled him. Romancing about preliminary heats for Miss England! They hadn't come into it but you had to admit you couldn't stop yourself being flattered when somebody claimed that, even if he'd got it wrong. So tonight she could pick up the envelope without repugnance; she could empty out the print taken by the local photographer, and her stomach did not slide out of control and give its customary twist.

Because she was going to have a little corner in this play all to herself, the play that Nora was helping to write, and for a time she could be proud again and confident, could separate this triumph from the following gall. Enjoying it once more after so many years of keeping it locked up, she felt young again, stood and examined her shape in the mirror, adjusted her tights over ankles still slender, wondered whether you could buy stockings nowadays tailored at the calves, and was happy she had the photograph to show the woman downstairs.

Because she wanted her to see; she wanted Nora to appreciate how nice they had all looked; and when she heard about it she'd agree there was nothing wrong in doing it. Not in itself. It was a giggle. It wasn't to be blamed for what came out of it. Only she wouldn't go into that.

Chapter Six

Looking back, it was amazing how chancy it was, her entering for Miss Blygh 1961. It just happened that at dinner there wasn't room at the table for all the office staff, there being a salesman in pushing a new duplicator, and Doris had to go on to one with girls from the shop floor. She kept her distance, getting on with her meal, not talking, only she couldn't help overhearing what was being said and it was all about a notice that'd gone up the other end of the canteen, explaining how there was to be a fiftieth anniversary celebration.

'I don't know why anyone should want to celebrate fifty years slaving in this place,' one said.

'It's since they opened the factory, you daft!' another tutted. 'And if they're paying for a dance and supper, I shan't be one to say no.'

'There are going to be lots of spot prizes and we're all to have a bottle of toilet water.'

'Walt on the truck could do with some of that.'

'Not for the *men*.'

'The place'll stink of the stuff! The minute you get on the bus they'll know where you work by the smell. You won't be able to pretend you're with the Prudential, Marlene. She does, you know, if blokes ask. Don't know who she thinks she's kidding.'

'Leave off, Beryl; you're forever picking spots.'

'There's plenty to pick. I ought to be on piecework. So how come you know all this, then?'

'When I was clocking in this morning, Mr Fallis came across and engaged in a few minutes' conversation.' Answering the giggles, Joan defended, 'Those were his words.'

'If that's all he wanted to engage in you can count yourself lucky.'

'You have got a mucky mind, Beryl,' the other accused, and blushed.

'It comes of reading what Mr Fallis has got inside his head. I suppose that beauty competition was his notion, the old goat.'

'As a matter of fact, it was. That's what he wanted to talk to me about. He's anxious it isn't a flop. I said I couldn't speak for everybody but I'd think about it.'

'That's all right, then. By the time you've done that, he'll have forgot he ever gave it a moment's consideration.'

'No, he won't, Clara. It's official. It's on the notices. Mr Blygh's given his signature.'

'Nobody's forced to enter just because the factory manager shoves it up on a notice.'

'That's right, Beryl. He should ask us first before he starts plastering the wall with promises. It's not for him to dictate. This anniversary isn't in work time.'

'Oh, Clara, wrap up, will you? If you'd heard Mr Fallis, you wouldn't have said he was dictating. He told me it's like this: he's on the anniversary celebration committee and each one has to look after a particular part and he's in charge of the Miss Blygh competition. Stop looking like that, Beryl. And he'll cop it, won't he, if nobody enters? They're paying for a band, and giving us this supper and scent, and I reckon it's up to us to do a bit in return.'

'If you're so bothered about getting something for free, why don't you invite them to stop it out of your pay packet?' Clara demanded.

'I couldn't care less whether there are celebrations or not,' Beryl stated. 'What I can't stomach is the certainty that old Fallis is only interested in this so's he's given the chance to witness a bit more flesh than usually comes his way. Seventy-five machinists in party dresses aren't enough to satisfy him: he has to have a few take them off.'

'To hear you talk anybody'd think we was expected to do it undressed. We can choose bathing costumes if we like, but Mr Fallis says Mr Blygh has expressed a preference for sun tops and shorts. He says it hasn't to descend to a London strip club.'

'In here? Some hope of that!' but the scorn was not wholehearted. Mr Blygh's taste agreed with their own and listening, Doris detected that there was a greater readiness to be receptive to Joan's persuasion.

'It might not be so bad,' Marlene conceded. 'My mam wouldn't half create if I said it was anything less than shorts,' her modesty requiring an excuse.

'What's the difference what you wear?' Beryl insisted. 'You'll still be parading in front of old Fallis, alongside the cutters who'll be dribbling down their chops, and Walt and Ernie in maintenance,' she counted up the male workforce. 'Who wants to be glegged at by that lot?'

'They'll not be the only ones. It turns out that Smethurst's, you know, where we got that floral print for the last batch of overalls, well, they belong to Blygh's, too, and everyone there's been given a comprehensive invite, according to Mr Fallis, which means they're providing charas. They've more men than we've got. Loom overlookers, for a start. And sales representatives!'

There was a pause while this news was assimilated.

'Just for supper and a band!' Marlene exclaimed eventually.

Joan said, 'Cynth has said she'll join in. She's been on plastic pants for eight weeks and'll do anything for a change from turning out bags for wet bums. She thinks she can talk a good few into it. Like I told her, a competition will make it more of a do.'

'If she's after a cracking time, she wants to tell Mr Fallis to hire an artiste or vocalist; like Elvis or Tommy Steele.'

'In Neatham?' Marlene scorned.

'There's always Kenneth the Kunjurer,' Joan derided out of assurance that she now commanded half the votes.

'I doubt if he wagged his wand you'd end up with more sense, but at least he doesn't have a chorus of girls doing high kicks. You're a mystery, Joan, you really are. It's only last week you wouldn't walk past the cutters because Teddy whistled. The poor little sod had as like as not got a hole in his top plate, and you said he was being insulting. And now you're talking about prancing in front of lorry loads of squint-eyed commercial travellers.'

'You're a real prude, Beryl. It's not prancing; it'll be just a sedate walk, and I wouldn't think of it if Mr Fallis hadn't asked.'

'You're not at school now, you know.'

'Oh, put a sock in it, Clara. You can't tell me you're against it.'

'It's all right for you, Marlene, but I haven't a nice enough figure.'

'I can see what you're after. You want me and Joan to go down on our knees and beg. Well, we're not. You want to go to Billy Butlin's and see what wobbles out there.'

'It might be all right, mightn't it?' Clara at last joined them.

The other two didn't answer. Their decision separating them from Beryl, they felt uncomfortable.

'Since you're so set on persuading half the payroll to show a leg, why don't you ask her?' she demanded, and Doris found herself the focus of a questioning silence.

The dignified response would have been to assume deafness, but their faces were turned, their expressions waiting, and she could not pretend that she had not shamelessly listened to their talk. Therefore she answered, 'I don't know anything about it. I hadn't heard of the competition until just now,' and disliked her voice, thin with tension.

'Mr Fallis hasn't been round the office, then? He must think that queueing up to be glegged at is all right for them on the machines but if you're a typist it isn't polite.'

She could have pushed away her plate and left them but their sniggers challenged. There was, too, an excitement that she could not suppress. This was novel. Why can't I just for the once? she argued, and heard herself claiming, 'I might enter,' and was gratified by their shock.

Speechless, they regarded her until Beryl asked, 'You mean it?'

The question snagged the air in her throat; she heard it rasp, a betraying sound in the midst of their quiet. Looking round their faces, she saw them curious, puzzled, absorbed, and she was hypnotised by their stillness. They were four girls strung on a single breath. Reckless, she answered, 'Of course I mean it! The more I think, the more I reckon I'll go in for it.'

Reckless, because by doing this she would step across, on to forbidden places, relinquishing a superiority, replacing it with something unknown and without guarantee. 'I'll do it if you do,' she said.

'We're doing it all right,' Joan assured her and the other two nodded, keeping their eyes from Beryl.

Who capitulated with: 'You needn't think I've got cold feet. If she can, so can I.'

'Now look what you've done!' Marlene mimicked a rebuke. 'Got her to change her mind.'

'It's my clothes she's got me to change, that's all. I haven't altered my opinion about old Fallis.'

'You'll get used to Beryl.' The words offered more than the promise expressed.

'If that was all she has to get used to, she'd be lucky. The idea that she's got to get used to is lining up and walking across that floor for everybody to judge.'

'I suppose it does need a lot of cheek?'

'Don't look so anxious. You'll waltz through it,' Marlene encouraged, inept with metaphor. 'Nothing helps so much as knowing you look nice.'

'Carnival queen before she left school,' Joan explained.

'That's nothing to swank about. I'm only saying she doesn't need to be worried, looking like she does.'

'Nobody would quarrel with that. Is your hair natural?'

'Of course it is, Clara,' Joan answered for her.

'You've a beautiful figure, too. No, I didn't say it for you to blush;

64

it's right. Knock us all into a cocked hat. I wouldn't mind betting any money named that you'll get the prize.'

'I hope not,' Doris had answered. 'It'll take all I've got to parade in front of them. I wouldn't want to go up and receive a prize or anything. I'd rather not draw attention to myself.'

'Not draw attention to yourself!' Beryl had stuttered. 'What are you planning to wear, then, when you line up? Your nan's nightie?'

Then they were shrieking, hands flailing, bodies swaying upon tilted chairs, cutlery skidding over the bucking table, their noise and abandon turning admonitory heads. And in that gusting laughter Doris was accepted, all wariness, suspicions, traces of resentment or envy were blasted away and their fellowship was an unforced munificence that she had never enjoyed before. When Beryl said finally, wiping her eyes and renewing her mascara, 'You can come again!' she was not offering an invitation to her to sit with them at dinner but endorsing her inclusion. When Clara said, 'There's only a few weeks. We'll have to get cracking. You don't have to perm your hair, though,' she was not stating a separation but indicating a busyness to be shared.

They were fifteen, giggling, flirtatious, chaste, romantic, impecunious, coarse, their hair teased and backcombed into bobbing nests, their skirts straining over pert buttocks wagged for the pinch which would cause them distress, their diaries bearing few entries except the inescapable appointments of the days circled every four weeks. Together during the lunch hours, bunched round a table in the canteen, they planned and consulted, examined surreptitiously the contents of carrier bags and exclaimed at unattainable coiffures in borrowed magazines; or, squashed between verdigris basins in the dank works lavatory, they tried out pooled make-up, shaved legs and armpits, stood quietly while other nails removed unreachable blackheads and watched in the pitted glass the hands which, with implausible confidence, experimented with new topiary splendours upon the pleached hair.

There was no sense of competition. As Marlene had remarked, once Doris entered, all that remained was the possibility of second or third place. But this did not concern them. They were doing it for fun; it gave them a golden day on the calendar more lustrous than Saturday evening at the Palais with its tentative pairings, the assumed boldness, the longing that some glitter might be panned from the dross.

Even that unsatisfactory pleasure had been denied Doris and she became the fascinated audience for tales of intrigue, plots and preparation whose climax would be to inveigle some unwitting young man into a dance. Disarmed by these confidences which testified to their friendship, she described her years at Miss Wynne's Academy and, discovering unexpectedly that the satire she had employed for expediency was apt, she was freed from restraints. Candidly she informed them that, compared with Flood Street Secondary Modern, Miss Wynne's could be held superior only in title, uniform and assumption of refinement, and even those had no worth. After these lunch-time huddles round the table or the eager rehearsals in the lavatory, Doris would return to the women in the office and flushed with comradeship, tipsy with confessions, she would outstare their frowns. These weeks were balmy, canopied with rainbows; they shimmered and were silken to the touch, the stuff of romance.

Sitting on her heels, examining the photograph, Doris told herself that time was unique. Nothing else in her life could match it. Guiltily she glanced at a tinted portrait of Clifford taken specially for her and placed in the centre of her dressing-table, then she became absorbed in the young faces smiling at her out of the print. For a moment she wondered how these girls looked now, twenty-four years later, but the thought did not detain her; she was interested only in what they were then, pulled close, arms girdling waists; in the middle herself. And, contemplating her expression, shy but happy to be admired, she recalled something that had grown dulled and forgotten in the subsequent years: during those weeks before she had entered the competition it had been irrelevant whose daughter she was. She was elevated by this memory; it seemed a good omen for her return to the woman downstairs.

She found her reading another of those endless transcripts. However, she put it aside to receive the envelope, but not before Doris had been standing for minutes with it dangling from her hand.

'It's just how the newspaper sent it,' she explained; why the other was so interested in the outside, she couldn't work out.

Nora puzzled over the address, printed in childlike uncials as if the photographer had never reached learning how to join them up. 'You used to live in Station Street?' trying to place another reference.

'That's right, till we moved. Soon after I left Blygh's.' She didn't want to go into that. She wanted Nora to open the envelope. It was her surprise.

'There's something familiar about Station Street.'

Doris could think of no way of telling the other that a secret rested on her lap. As Nora remembered:

'Do you know,' Isabel had begun to speak again, 'to fit Maisie up with a gym tunic, her mother had to take her Sunday togs to pawn, and she didn't fetch them out on Friday pay night but had to leave them in, till that usurer Edith Bentley in Station Street refused to wait longer than the year and said they were forfeits. That didn't increase her reputation bottom end of Neatham, I can tell you, and it's my belief that she did it for spite, her own not being far short of drivelling idiots, that is till she fell for a girl during the change who had more about her. And I bet that one didn't wear the same tunic six year let down till it looked like a ploughed field round the hem and below the yoke bulging out of its pleats as she developed. Maisie told me that she was so ashamed she used to walk round with a book clapped to her chest.'

For a moment Nora wondered whether Doris had witnessed this embarrassment then, calculating, realised that she was a generation out. Edith Bentley had been Isabel's contemporary, already running a business by the time the younger cousin Maisie went to the High School, and Doris was the child of Edith's middle age.

'Did you go to the County High?' she asked Doris.

'By the time I should've gone there it was all eleven plus, and exams put me into such a panic that my mother kept me at Miss Wynne's Academy, where I'd been from the start.'

She could understand the other's astonishment. In the Station Streets of this world you don't find many children putting on a tailored uniform and marching to the other end of town for a bus to take them to a school like Miss Wynne's, and she was certain that Nora didn't approve. She wanted to describe it, wanted to tell her how every day as she walked down the street, they ran behind her calling, how on the bus she heard the cliquey sneers, how she was regarded with disdain by a headmistress who nevertheless suffered no qualms in accepting the fee. All this she wished to tell Nora, but not until she had opened the envelope. Instead, with: 'I suppose it was worth it,' she postponed the subject.

* * *

'So my Aunt Gert, Maisie's mother, lost her Sunday togs and Maisie had the same gym tunic for six years,' Isabel murmured. 'I hope what she got out of it was worth the sniggers.'

'Maisie must have thought so,' Nora had suggested.

'Doubtless. It got her a job better than making up bloomers at Blygh's.'

'You haven't told me about that,' she had reminded Isabel. 'And neither have you really told me how Maisie was different.'

She had waited but the old woman, forehead trenched with memories and lips working, offered no sounds.

Isabel would have been glad to be different herself at the time. The day after her father had said, 'You're old enough to bring in a wage; that's what you should be thinking about, not imagining yourself tarted up for that County High,' she had gone back to him and begged, 'Dad, let me have a few more years. Let me have the chance to learn a bit more.' 'What good would that do you? If I know anything, you'll soon be thinking of marrying. It's not as if you was one of the lads.' 'But none of them are interested in school, or as clever.' 'Now watch your mouth, young lady. There's no room for pride in this house. Do you wonder at me not liking the idea of you at High School when you can talk like that?' 'It's the truth, Dad. You wouldn't want me to tell lies. I've won a place at High School; it's not been given, it's won, and I'm asking you to let me have it, Dad. I want to see a bit of life outside Neatham.' 'Well, High School's not the place to find that. You can see as much of life as is good for you at a machine at Blygh's any day of the week, and you ought to be grateful to be doing your bit. I shall be pleased to tell that to the boys in the trenches when this blighty wound's healed and I'm back.'

So he had made her feel that if she didn't leave school to help against the Hun, she would be letting him down; and though she knew this was just another excuse to stop her, only one that nobody would blame him for, she couldn't make an objection. She couldn't because he had heard the rumours that her teacher Miss Freiston didn't hold with the war. If she'd said anything then, had said it wasn't sensible giving up the chance of High School to machine up for soldiers, if she'd said that, she would have been siding with Miss Freiston against him. This had confused her. She had these two loyalties and it didn't matter how hard she tried to put them together she couldn't make them bed down. Because she was proud of him; he'd joined up of himself, not waiting to be called, and he had told her that he counted on her to help their mam; and now, looking at him, his shirt neck without the stud, his sleeves rolled up businesslike as he prepared to polish his boots and his face tilted up strong and handsome as any in pictures while he waited for her to answer, she knew it was him she had to throw herself in with and she said, 'You'd better tell them I'll be sewing their breeches, then.' And she was, for the last two years of the war. While Maisie, about the time they were given the vote, started work in an office, and though she sometimes comforted herself that Miss Freiston would have turned in her grave knowing that Maisie had got herself chained to a typewriter, Isabel could not deny that was a cut above Blygh's.

'How did it make Maisie different, going to High School?' From the way that sounded, it seemed she had asked the question before but Isabel wasn't letting herself be pushed.

'Well, it meant she wasn't the same as us, didn't it?' She could see that the visitor wanted more than that for an answer, and it wasn't because it might do for the play. She had closed her notebook and was sitting as still as a statue, like a youngster holding its breath believing that you'd not notice and come out with a piece it wasn't intended to hear. This might be something like that, when she'd given it a thought.

Because, however much she'd tried to hide it in front of her, she couldn't help resenting what Maisie had been allowed; and she hadn't got away with it, of course, in spite of being six years older, the girl being as bright as a button, worth that scholarship, who had stood facing her one night and given her a shock with: 'You're as bad as the rest of them, Bella, and I don't understand why you should take it out on me. Nobody compelled you to marry Norman.' She didn't know what reply she'd given to that but she did know what she hadn't managed to say, because she hadn't got it straight with herself at the time, which was: she had meant it to be herself that would show them, show them that it was possible to get out of the rut and that the person who did it could be a girl, in honour of Miss Freiston. But that had not been permitted, she could not force him to let her go, and in any case the strength went out of her, seeing the bandage still on his wound and the hair curling over like a babby's on the nape of his neck. So it was Maisie who had been contrary, and she herself had stuck. Being stuck, she had seen it all from the angle of them that are, and though she never admitted it at the time, it can be a relief as much as anything else not to go contrary to what you've been brought up to.

69

'The rest of us were content not to step out of line,' she told the visitor.

'I learnt typing at evening class while I was still at school, so as soon as I left I could start at Blygh's. That's how I've got that photograph,' Doris prompted. She couldn't understand why the other was still twiddling the envelope; it was as if she expected something nasty to pop out. Doris smiled to herself. It was funny, sometimes, the way ideas came to you, because what was in that envelope wasn't nasty at all. Otherwise she wouldn't have wished Nora to see. Whose fingers were at last parting the mouth of the envelope, their tips going inside and curling round the edge of the print but slowly. Doris groaned to herself; it was as if she was teasing, taking all night, then they slipped out, first Marlene and next to her Clara, then on the right of Doris, Beryl and Joan. They looked lovely. And glad. Smiling away because they'd done it, and they'd had a good time. But what made their smiles really special was: they were smiling for her, full of joy because, like they had expected, she'd been awarded the prize, and it was their doing, they claimed; if it hadn't been for them she wouldn't have tried. Which was right. It was the only time in her life she'd done anything like that, by which she didn't only mean something daring. She meant it was the only time in her life that she'd joined in, and the pleasure hadn't been only from what had come of it. That hadn't given her half so much gladness as the other thing, which was being with them. Neither Beryl nor Marlene nor Joan nor Clara had paid any attention to the business her mother ran; so she had felt neither defensive nor proud. For just that time, she had been so happy, one of them.

'It wasn't parading for wolf whistles, not really, though those came into it,' she told Nora, made apprehensive by the other's concentration on the print. 'It wasn't to satisfy men.'

The other nodded. Her eyes were moving down the line; they had contemplated Joan and were on Beryl now.

'It wasn't to encourage any male . . . what did you call it?'

'Concupiscence.'

'That's right.' The other's hair was thick, strong; the stylist had left it full on the crown then cut it sleek and close to the neck, leaving a little wisp that curled at the nape. Doris wondered whether you could make it even more shiny by brushing. 'We did it for ourselves,' she explained.

70

That 'we' let the cat out of the bag and there was a pause while the other one weighed it up. 'I hadn't realised this was you,' she said.

Doris laughed. 'I didn't wear spectacles then, only for reading.'

'The hair's different as well.'

'Yes. You can do a lot with long hair. Marlene used to fiddle with it for hours, but it got out of condition afterwards and I had to have it bobbed.'

'Which is Marlene?'

She pointed, then named the rest. 'They were my friends.' That sounded like a young kid at junior school, but she wasn't to be put off by that.

'So you were Miss Blygh?'

'Now then! Don't pretend! I know you're surprised,' and nudged the other's arm, sharing the mischief. 'You'd never have expected me to go in for anything like that, would you?'

'I suppose not.'

'Well, that just proves it,' Doris chuckled, thinking: This must be what it's like when you're drunk. And she didn't care. 'You tell me what it proves, though; I don't know. Except that you didn't imagine when you were asking about a pretty girl at the Comprehensive that you'd got Miss Blygh 1961 right here, did you?'

'No, I didn't. How would you feel were the competition included? Would you be upset to see a young girl representing you?'

'I'd regard it as a compliment. So long as you don't suggest I do it myself! That'll be Clifford calling,' she said and tensed, counting the rings. They stopped after four. Glancing at the clock, she explained, 'He's early for Thursday. That's his night for the supermarket. He must have had less shopping to pick up. I've never told him about this,' leaning forward and tapping the print.

'Why not?'

Doris blushed. 'I don't think he'd understand.'

Again the telephone rang. Having sent out his warning, the man anticipated no delay. But the repeated notes were an intrusion.

'If this did go into the play, wouldn't you have difficulty in concealing it from him?'

'We'll cross that bridge when we come to it. If you'd asked me last week I'd have said I'd kept quiet about it because, knowing Clifford, he'd believe I'd been the forward type. But I'd not say that to you now.'

The telephone was still ringing; the racket jarred in her head; that must be why her tongue was sticking to her palate and she didn't seem

71

to have the breath to get the words out. 'But not now,' she repeated. 'Not this week. I didn't tell him because that night belonged with them, not him. You see, it was ours.'

She should have reached the phone by this time but she was still standing by Nora, a knee pushed against the arm of her chair.

'Aren't you going to answer him?'

'Who? Clifford?' She pondered the question. 'No. Let him ring. He'll soon grow tired, hanging on to the other end. What's he think he has to check up on, anyway?' and laughed.

Startled, the other joined her.

Then: 'I tell you what, I'll make us omelettes and chips. And I've got some sherry left over from Christmas. Would you like a glass?'

Chapter Seven

'Top of the mornin' to yer, me hearties.' Peter ran up the stairs, bared his teeth to signal a warning, was met with puzzlement, to prevent enquiry said quickly, 'Forget it,' and announced: 'Miss Constance Skrimshaw.'

'My friends call me Pug,' she told them, gaining the top step. 'You're Nora?' She delivered an assessing stare, then turned to Dick. 'And I know who you are.'

'I wouldn't be so sure about that.'

She smiled, keeping her eyes on his face. 'So you're the enigmatic one?'

'That's right.'

Peter cleared his throat.

'I'm Community Arts,' Ms Skrimshaw prevented his explanation.

'Have a seat,' Peter offered, removing a pair of khaki puttees, a Mickey Mouse gas mask, a guitar and a box of balloons. 'My God! I'm sorry. It's filthy in here. What this place lacks is the little woman's hand.'

'In that case you'll have to substitute the little man's.'

Peter winced, reminding himself that she'd had a comedectomy performed at birth. Noting as she plonked down the rich patina of her denims, he acknowledged the irrelevance of his apology.

'I was explaining to Pete that we should be opening up a dialogue on objectives,' Ms Skrimshaw began, her look oscillating between Nora and Dick to emphasise that in this team voluntary workers held equal status. 'I'm very interested in this project; we've been debating for some time how to get a toehold in Neatham, and when they had this idea for a play, Community Arts was the obvious department to deal with it. However, I don't spend as much time in the office on my backside as our Glyn, so as soon as wind of it came down the wire, he was available to pick it up. Some people are quite shameless about career politics.'

'Would you care for a cup of coffee?' Peter asked. 'We've got a kettle.'

Ms Skrimshaw shook her head. 'That's how Drama became

73

involved, though Glyn's not in the position to develop the potential, or even what you're having to initiate, Peter. And Nora and Dick.'

'I don't initiate anything. I simply do what the boss says, don't I, Pete?'

'Of course you initiate things, Dick, don't be so bloody modest. The moment you entered this room, you did that.' Sensing that her declaration had not been wholly understood and, indeed, that it might not survive impartial analysis, Ms Skrimshaw dismissed the perplexity with a gesture, enunciated clearly, 'I refer to the concept of partici-pation,' and carried on. 'In other words, it isn't within Glyn's parameter to be responsible for wet-nursing activities which have a community base.'

'I'd be happy to receive a grant from the RAA, Constance, but I'm not bothered which department it comes from. This is a community venture and I always express it as a community arts project since that's how it's run – as far as can be managed within these limits.'

'Exactly, Peter. At the moment you're out on a salient with no back-up support. I mean from the Association,' acknowledging with a flicked eyebrow the toil of Nora and Dick. 'There must be a number of resources you'd like to call upon and that's the way I can help. I can't grant the spondulicks for the drama as such, but I can make other provisions – buy in workers for a few days here and there to assist with special areas. Merely because Glyn hopes to put money into this, you mustn't think you can't call upon me.'

'No; I won't forget. At present, though, I'd say we're all right. In the best traditions of community arts, Constance, we're calling upon local talent.'

'What sort are you digging up?'

Peter considered. Unpractised in deception, he did not claim a stage teeming with hitherto undiscovered stars since as yet he'd done little recruitment; nor could he produce artists, for posters and programmes must wait for the finished script; so far, no joiner had been conscripted for the building of sets; and, about to mention Mrs Broadbent, a hairdresser, who was intimidating her clients to make costumes, he paused, remembering his failed joke about the services of the little woman. At last he managed an evasion.

'During the set-up I'll as usual be calling upon people with special skills, but there's one I mean to demonstrate on stage. We have an old chap, a retired painter and decorator, who started immediately he left school and went through his apprenticeship under his dad. A young fellow from the Comprehensive will act Joseph and learn the trade.

The pages are here somewhere,' scratching through the mess on his desk. 'Do you remember his reminiscences, Nora? They were among the first we collected. About Mrs Walmesley's helping the mother to trim the paper.'

'Yes. I remember.'

What's this, then? the father had said, unfurling a roll and seeing the margin that hadn't been trimmed. What you think you're playing at? he had asked very quiet because he wasn't a swearing man. Then he had walked straight to his son and an arm had swung out. Afterwards the young man had said to himself: Now, Joseph, he ordered you to trim that paper and you didn't, so you've got your punishment. He didn't know why he was telling this, only from time to time the ache in his head came back. It wasn't a story generally known and he wouldn't be saying it if the father was still here.

'There'll be a lot of material you can't use,' she observed to Peter, hoping that only he heard the appeal in her voice.

'I'd judge about ninety per cent. Any more, and the play would go on for weeks.' He smiled, holding her eyes, and together they honoured Joseph Raby's trust and did not denounce his dead.

'I don't know whether you'll remember,' Peter addressed the others, then added quickly, because even Constance might be subject to the orthodox vanities, 'No, of course you won't. About twenty-five years ago wallpaper was retailed with margins; it wasn't trimmed. Buried under all this lot,' still raking through papers, 'are notes for a sequence of scenes presenting Joseph. They will begin with him sitting in the kitchen trimming rolls with a pair of scissors, grumbling that he's not allowed to use the machine for the job. His mother comes in, is told that the customer is in a hurry to have the room decorated in time for the Chapel anniversary, she fetches a neighbour, and they cut at a great pace, the paper rolling along the stage in two intersecting paths. A group of children gathers round each woman waiting for the spirals of paper ribbon. These will be used as streamers in the fête. Children take part in the following scenes but keep returning to check on the progress of the trimming, which is quite a lengthy business; perhaps there'll be some mischief – grabbing before they are permitted, and rebuked by the women.

'When they have started to trim, Joseph returns stage centre to be taught by his father, and there'll be a good deal of bustle of customers, farcical bits and so on, and gradually other men will enter and do their own work. At this point there will be a strong, rollicking Song of the Tradesmen. All these characters will move into the scene of the fête

75

eventually, but before they do, they will continue quietly occupied as the focus returns to Joseph. Oh, here we are at last,' hauling up the sheets. 'I'm thinking of having Joseph's last scene straight from his reminiscences without dramatisation, spoken directly to the audience by the lad who by this time has grown older, plainly a full journeyman – moustaches and so forth. I'll just read you the previous paragraph.

Did I like the work? Well, for a start it were clean once you'd mastered it, a lot better than some in that respect, and dry; you can't do outsides when it's raining. I didn't mind that when I was a lad because apprentices didn't lose their pay if they were laid off, weather being bad, but journeyman painters lost their money. Union put stop to that after the war. I didn't mind the job once I was through my time but while I was labouring for my father, it was a real old headache, I can tell you. You never had a single minute's rest and the men were allus trying to take a rise out of you when you were still green, and no mistake.

'That last sentence provides material for an episode when he's younger, but for his last scene, I imagine him returning to his tins of paint, picking up a roll of paper and shaking it into a billowing train across the stage so that it meets if possible the lengths which still wave away from the women trimmers. Here are his words and the directions I've roughed out.

Did I like the work? Well, for a start it were clean, once you'd mastered it. (He grins as he wipes traces of garish lead primer from his face.) And it had more to it when I began. Because you mixed your own paints. You'd start with the white lead, break it up, then you'd add the stainer, keeping a nice paste; then there'd be the turps – 'Genuine American Turps' it was called, none of your cheap substitute – and linseed oil, one of that to four of the turps. You'd need a dash of paint dryer and you'd keep adjusting the colour, stirring till the paint was like cream. (During this and the following lines he mixes as he describes, testing colours by dropping splashes into the tin lid. Several other tins of paint are already prepared.) I was a good few years out of my apprenticeship when the war came, Hitler's, that is. Yes, I was in it. Joined up, I did, before being called. I know I shouldn't be saying this – seeing all that happened, it doesn't sound right – but I enjoyed that time in the Army. I think it must have been the way it showed you something out of the usual. (He takes a huge palette from under his bench and spoons round its circumference great blobs of different-coloured paint out of the tins.) Sometimes I think I might have found a roving life was just up my street, but that's only fancy and you can't pay attention to it, not when you're a respectable married man. It was a bit like thinking I'd paint pictures. (He produces several large fat-tufted artist's brushes and dabs at the dollops of colour on the palette.) On account of the colours. Brunswick green, Venetian red. Prussian blue, and yellow ochre. Burnt Turkey Umber. (He begins to walk along the stretch of paper, dappling it with brilliant circles, ellipses, stars and spots.) Burnt Turkey Umber! What about that for a name? But I liked yeller best. Got the sun in it, has yeller. (He adds stalks and leaves of green to the shapes on the paper.) Mixing them sometimes, it was as if I had all the flowers of the meadows there on the tip of my brush, the cowslips and anemones, clover and corn cockle, poppies and lady's smock, the foxglove. (As he names the flowers, he continues to walk along the paper, dashing it with bright paint; and at the same time the lights dim, then a lamp comes up lighting the stage in circling colours. The effect is of a deep, bottomless spectrum which dances, rustles, flows.) And harebells, the rosebay willowherb, ragwort and shepherd's purse. I could see them as clear as day and all it needed was just a few strokes. (Pause while the colour shimmers and breathes.) But I had to get such ideas out of my head.'

Peter stopped reading and for a few moments there was silence. Then Dick said, 'I'll make that man a beaker of coffee,' and rising, fiddled with jars.

'I'm pleased you picked that up, Peter,' Nora told him, remembering how, as she looked over the transcript in Doris Bentley's reproachful presence, she had chosen not to read those lines.

'Have you written any more? Let's hear it,' Constance urged.

'I don't really write. I just slice and stick, arranging people's accounts. I hardly change a word.' He was flustered by their appreciation and, shuffling papers, attempted to arrange them tidily on a corner of the desk. 'So,' he affected a concluding tone, regretting as always that he couldn't resolve the paradox of need to share his craft ·and the diffidence it caused.

'When can we hear some more, please?' Constance repeated.

'You must speak to his agent,' Dick told her. 'He's not supposed to be letting on about any of this yet. You have to guard against copycats, particularly here in Neatham. Would you like powdered milk in this?'

'That's fine. What do you think about it, Dick?'

'I'd rather have fresh, but you soon acquire a taste.'

'Come on!'

'I'm not the one to judge. I've never been inside a theatre in my life.'

'I wasn't asking you to judge. Leave that to the literary ponces.'

'A certain amount of judgement comes in every time you state an opinion, doesn't it? And that's worth more if you're stronger on the facts. I don't know how much you study football but I reckon people would listen to me first if they wanted an opinion on who's going to win the Cup. I can't tell whether that sort of scene is new, or being knocked out every five minutes, is pure gold or a load of rubbish. All I can say is that we shall never have seen anything like that in Neatham and, speaking personally, I reckon it's all right.'

'Which is your gut reaction.'

'You could call it that.'

She smiled at him. 'There you are, Peter. No need to worry about the pundits; you've been passed by the man on the spot.'

'He's got too much sense to worry about pundits; all he has to concern himself with is getting the words on the page like it seems right to him.'

Startled, her eyes widening, Ms Skrimshaw chased after an answer, while Dick added, 'And I'd advise you not to count me as the man on the spot. That is, not if you're set on hearing the noises you want.'

Peter swallowed the coffee in his mouth, flexed his tact to explain that her matiness was not necessarily condescension, gave up the attempt, and said, 'Nobody would ever make that mistake, Dick, and if I remember rightly, you've made enough noise already. He's taken on the job of stage management, you see,' he addressed Constance, 'and ever since I first warned him what to expect, he's been grumbling.'

Recovered, she answered, 'Certainly the lighting in that scene will be complex. You'll need a moving projector; I may be able to help you there. But is there anything you'd like brought in? Puppet craft? Murals? Banner-works?'

'I don't think I can move into any of those at the moment, Constance. Workshops need to be set up, supported, and the customers have to be hauled in. I have one, and one only, brief: to write and produce a play.'

Constance nodded, but: 'It seems you're well on schedule.'

'That doesn't mean I have any slack.' He felt a sudden gush of fatigue.

'Pete's fee is for the one job,' Dick reminded her. 'There's nothing in his contract about anything else.'

'I'm afraid we have to adopt a more flexible approach in Community Arts.'

'Maybe so, but he's Drama.'

'You should have warned me you'd got a resident shop steward, Peter,' she answered thin-lipped.

'I'm sorry, Constance. I really haven't the time. I cannot possibly get involved with, or follow up, any other activity.'

'Naturally I wouldn't ask you to front any work that wasn't in your field.'

He guessed her purpose and saw her eyes move to Nora, her face assuming a preparatory sweetness which, not ungenerous enough to dub gruesome, he nevertheless found alarming. 'Look, Constance, I shall be at home the rest of this month and all June, incommunicado whilst I write. I'm going at the end of next week and when I come back I shall be fully occupied rehearsing and staging the play. Nora and Dick have plenty to do. They will each have a list of jobs as long as your arm and I shall be sending more as I make decisions about props and set. I'm also having to leave them to tie up recruitment for all the backstage jobs. Added to which, Constance,' he appealed weakly, 'they're both volunteers.'

'I might be able to manage a small wage.'

'What for?' Dick asked.

'Another paid worker,' Nora interpreted.

He blew out air, vibrating his lips.

'I'm serious,' Ms Skrimshaw assured Peter unnecessarily. 'As far as I'm concerned, your coming in to do this play is the best thing that's happened round here for yonks. We can't afford not to build on the initiative. It must be used to spearhead other ventures. There's no need to pussyfoot around any more, skimming a toe across the water to try the temperature,' she pictured the comfortable days before her advent. 'In any case you've already done that. By the time the play is in performance the areas that can be developed will have been identified. That's what community arts is about, finding ways of giving people the confidence to discover gifts that have been repressed. It's not in society's interest to nurture individual talents among the telly-viewing and assembly-line fodder.' Her face glazed with proselytising zeal, she turned to Dick and Nora. 'I take it that you agree.'

'Constance isn't accustomed to speaking to the converted,' Peter apologised.

Dick drew breath to comment, reconsidered and said, 'What are you thinking of doing about it?'

'I wondered when you'd ask,' she crooned, oblivious to atmosphere. 'Eventually I'd like to build on this with a team of workers, but that's impossible in the present financial year. What I should like to do is pick up something for which the main work has already been done and develop it.'

Peter sighed. As he had guessed, Ms Skrimshaw was about to propose a publication of the reminiscences and since that was 'in his field', he would have no trouble attending to it.

'I can't do it, Constance,' he repeated. 'If I had more elbow room I'd have started on it already. As it is, I shall be writing with a stopwatch clenched between my teeth.'

'I can believe you. You could supervise it, though, I'm sure,' she smiled, and looked at the others.

The undertaking would be effortless as Constance described it. Once they had decided on length of copy, haggled over estimates and chosen a printer, there was hardly anything left to be done. No editing in the sense of fiddling with the text would be required because the principle was to publish, warts and all, exactly as the words had been said. So it was a walkover, really. The printer would advise on typeface and point size – that sort of thing – and proofreading could be farmed out. Such a publication presented so few difficulties it was surprising that Constance devoted any time to dismissing them, and conscious that the observation might have occurred to her audience, she conceded, 'But one thing that might be a problem is the cover, unless any of us is into illustration and design,' careful to say: 'any of us' rather than 'either of you'.

'Perhaps the school could help you,' Nora suggested, demonstrating a greater freedom from proprietorship in the matter of pronouns.

'Do you intend to approach the school?'

'I've already visited it. Your mention of a cover reminds me of the head of Art. He's anxious to be involved, as are a number of staff.'

Constance sniffed happily. 'I'll bet. That way they can give the impression of doing something energetic without expending the sweat, riding on the back of other people's labour. They take their cue from the Education Authority. Time and again we put things in that in my opinion should be funded from City Hall. It pisses me off. I try to keep most of the community arts work within the general community and let the schools look after themselves. We make provision for the adults they messed up as kids.'

'Are there many like her about?' Dick asked later.

'Unfortunately, no.'

'Bloody hell, Pete! She'd lop it off!'

The other nodded and gently zipped up his flies. 'I mean as an agitator. She has plenty of ideas and gets things done.'

'I wouldn't dispute that for a moment, not if what I witnessed this morning is her usual form. The minute I saw her, I knew we had to be careful, yet we've let that woman go away thinking you're in agreement about supervising – what did she call it? – "a preliminary selection of material for an oral history of Neatham".'

'I didn't agree, did I?'

'No, but what's that to do with it when she's around? You'll have to put up a fight. She's a persistent woman.'

'It's not her persistence that people find so difficult to overcome but an insidious loyalty to her, and to her principles. She seems to inspire that.'

'You're not being sentimental about Ms Constance Skrimshaw my friends call me Pug?'

'Only when she's gone.'

'I'm pleased to hear that. You know,' Dick continued as they left the lavatory and climbed the stairs into the office, 'when she was reading that piece about Freddie Bell, it wasn't him I was imagining; it was her.'

'That really would outrage her in view of her attitude to the police.'

'Yes. I'll have to mention it to her some time. But I could just see her standing there with a truncheon clouting the Micks as they jumped out of the van. It's a shame you've decided against using that story. You could have dressed her up as Freddie and she'd have been – what's the word for it?'

'Typecast?'

'That'll do.'

'What have the women to say for themselves?' Constance had asked.

'Not a lot.'

'That's an exaggeration, Nora. What about Freddie Bell's widow?'

'She's called Clarice.'

He took the pertinence of her reminder. 'Yes. Sorry.'

'Just about everything she says refers back to him or his work.'

'True, and though I found her recollections fascinating, I doubt if I shall use them much. A shame. Her character would demand more sensitive treatment than I could draw from inexperienced actors.'

'I'd like to hear her account,' Constance said.

'I'm not sure that I can find it,' annoyed that his enthusiasm had seduced him into inviting this request. He did not wish to expose Mrs Bell to Ms Skrimshaw's scrutiny.

'Is this it?' She reached up to a shelf and took down a folder.

'I haven't asked permission to publicise any of that material, so in a sense it's confidential.'

'Good heavens, Peter, you don't have to be so scrupulous. It'll remain between these four walls.'

He could devise no other excuse.

They won't have it, naturally, but the youngsters entering the Force nowadays have a much better time than ever came our way. People used to say to me, 'You don't know when you're lucky. Your Freddie's uniform's given and he's got the boots.' Boots! That was all that impressed them! I used to tell them, the miles he tramped, it wasn't a boot allowance he needed, but a spare pair of feet. I'd tell them what I thought of their notions, I'm not afraid to say, but I stopped when he was made sergeant. It didn't do to get too close.

Then there was the house. Not paying rent, we were the object of envy, but how many of them would put up with moving like you had to when you were with the police? Not many, I'll guarantee. And they don't today, either. There's constables will stick in one place for years so I'm told and even be permitted to buy their own. That's what I always wanted, a neat little bungalow, nothing fancy, but it wasn't to be; the wages weren't what they are today. You want to know about the moving? What is it you want to know? It was moving, uprooting yourself; it seemed like every month. I packed and unpacked every pot and stick six times in the first ten years we were married and once I'd been downstairs after Gavin only three days. But that was no argument with the Force. You see, Frederick was at country stations a long time before he entered the one at Neatham and he was anxious to get on. I daresay some of the stations we were moved to, it was hoped would lead to promotion, but he didn't tell me. A born policeman was Frederick, he could keep his counsel and was a stickler for getting things right. And his memory! I used to say that with Frederick around they didn't need a filing cabinet down at the station because he'd got everything he'd ever seen and heard filed in his head. I don't tell a lie; it was true. He'd take note of everything that was going on, things you'd never even realised had happened, then sure as eggs, he'd put his finger straight on it if required. 'Never think a single detail, however small, is beneath your notice, Mother,' he'd say to me. That's why he was a great reader of Agatha

Christie, practically an addict, though he would tell me that he could've put her straight on a thing or two relating to the Force.

Yes, he had a marvellous memory, and it came in handy when he got the station bottom end of Neatham. Being born and bred within the sound of the station cells, as he used to describe it, there wasn't much he didn't know about the residents of Neatham when he came back. Nowadays they talk about putting in officers they call community policemen. I say they wouldn't have to go to the trouble if they had more like Frederick in the Force.

At the start, we were in the police house at Broughton and Frederick had Haxby as well. I suppose you'd call them hamlets. All the children had to walk to the Elementary at Longthorpe but there were chapels. There wasn't a lot of crime, really, except poaching and regular stealing, mostly by gipsies. What went on inside some of the houses wasn't Frederick's concern. Midday he was in for his dinner; I used to like that. I didn't mind the country. In the afternoon, when I'd finished in the house, I'd push Gavin in his pram down the lanes for miles and if I got thirsty I could stop at one of the farms and the wife would sell me a glass of milk. It wasn't so lonely as you might think, and often they'd give Gavin a brown egg for his tea, but I couldn't stay for long; I had to think about Frederick's position. We had a dog and she was quite friendly but a bit big to handle and I didn't take her on the walks.

'I can see why you're not using that.' Constance tapped the desk, impatient. 'Not very exciting.'

'You've come to the wrong place if it's excitement you're after,' Dick told her.

'I think it's sad,' Nora said.

'Yes. She's so completely unaware of what she's revealing.'

'That's bloody tender-minded of you, Pete! She wouldn't care if she knew. Snobbery's second nature to her and not to be ashamed of,' Constance interpreted. 'She didn't have a bad life, either. Other women more intelligent than she were putting in eight hours a day.'

He was constrained to defend. 'As a matter of fact, she was practically Freddie's assistant. When he was on the beat she had to deal with enquiries, complaints, people coming to the station. She acted as the left arm of the Law. Yet she was lonely, never taken into his confidence; but still a mouthpiece for him.'

Ms Skrimshaw dismissed this with a shrug. Any woman foolish enough to marry into the Force automatically disqualified herself for sympathy.

'And often frightened,' Nora supported, provoked as Peter had been to protect the woman against Ms Skrimshaw's scorn. 'There's that description of the cells; I think I can find it.'

As, stretching forward, Nora picked up the sheets, he said, 'All right, but we ought to get back to work. Just the one page.'

'We have to support our argument!' and, finding the place, began to read.

I expected changes when we were posted to Neatham Druggist Lane station, and one thing I did rely upon being different and that was the house. It was, too, in one respect, and that is: it had a toilet with a chain instead of an earth closet at the end of the path. But it was still outside and until they built the new station it was next door to the cells. Sometimes I felt as if I was taking my life into my hands, running across the yard at night with a felon there lurking. Frederick would always check and double-check the locks before he went on duty but I couldn't rid myself of the worry that one night the prisoner would find a way to get out. I didn't tell Frederick, of course; he didn't want to have his thoughts taken up with worries of mine, but there were nights I'd sit wanting to go and not daring till Frederick came home, and it was worse when Gavin was a baby, I was anxious for him. Now I think about it I wonder why I got myself so nervous. They were mostly only drunks waiting to be taken before the magistrates next morning but you can be inclined to silliness when you're young. That was before the last war.

'I shan't lose any sleep over that, but hang on.' Constance intercepted the return of the sheets. 'There may be something more interesting coming up. Don't be so possessive, Pete!' she rebuked his objection. 'Don't tell me it's a juicy bit!'

Keeping the pages well out of reach, she began rapidly:

I wish I could tell you all that happened in the Force. Frederick had a great store of tales. 'Never a dull moment when you were down at the station, if your account is anything to go by, Freddie,' his friends used to say. 'You ought to write a book.'

'Imagine that!'

You mustn't think that Frederick could not be trusted with confidential information. He could shut down like a clam if need be but once he'd retired it was all past history and he could open up. And some of it came as a surprise to me, I can tell you. Because when they took over the new offices, Frederick didn't do his book work in the one attached to the police house any more and I hardly saw him, he was that busy, what with the war and all the extra that caused. I was kept out of it. Then, too, Gavin was getting a big lad and didn't want me fussing around. So I had to make do. That's how it goes, isn't it? There was one benefit, though. You have to look on the bright side. Having the new station meant I didn't go in fear of drunks. And there were plenty. It was disgusting, in the summer months, the riffraff that used to come in. Irish, they were, mainly, and of course, gipsies, doing seasonal work out on the big farms. They'd help with the hay, then pick fruit or see in the harvest and maybe go on to potatoes, out in the fields as long as there was light and sleeping in the barns I expect; I didn't ask. But by tea time on Saturday they were in a lorry and coming full pelt to Neatham. They'd drink anything, Frederick said, until it sent them insensible, that was their aim. It was the policeman's job to see to them when they came out of the public houses; the landlords didn't think of that when they let them in. Some would go quietly, just trudge into the cells and be snoring in seconds; they looked really sheepish when they were cautioned next morning. Others were not so amiable. They would get nasty, you see, with the drink, and although Frederick and Constable Alsop were big men and didn't stand any nonsense, sometimes it would be the devil's own job to round them up. That all changed after one night. I could tell the minute Frederick came off duty that Saturday – it was gone midnight but I always sat up in bed to wait – I knew by the smile on his face that trouble had passed without a hitch. I say, smile on his face, but really it wasn't that, I know you want me to be as correct as I can about Frederick. No, the smile was more inside, if you understand me; it was something you sensed rather than saw, that's if he was amused. It came of being in the Force. He had formed the habit of not letting on what he was thinking; he said when you were dealing with miscreants that was what was needed. This night he was pleased. I didn't ask him; and of course I couldn't put my finger on it exactly, not being a witness to the event. I heard about it eventually, years later when, as I say, he'd retired and could be more free, telling friends that came round. He and Constable Alsop had taken the van and gone about the public houses at closing time and collected. When they reached the station some of them were so rowdy and ready to put their fists up that Frederick said, 'Now, Constable, it's about time we gave these Paddies a taste of their own medicine. You back that van up to within three feet of the cell doors and we'll give them a swipe as they come out.' And it seems they did. As soon as each one of the drunks dropped out of the van and made for the cells, Frederick and Constable Alsop gave them a clout and, as you can imagine, it quickly became their desire to get into the cells without catching it. Frederick had never in his life seen such a scramble to get locked up but he and

Constable Alsop didn't let any of them get off without feeling their truncheons. And they knew what it was all about, despite being drunk; they knew having too much wasn't right, especially barely an hour before the Sabbath. And they were pleased to have it pointed out because no sooner had they picked themselves up than every single one of those men touched his forehead and said, 'Thank you, Officer,' and as Frederick used to declare, you couldn't learn your lesson better than that.

'And you couldn't be treated to any better material than that, could you, Pete?' Ms Skrimshaw exalted, slapping the typescript on the desk. 'It's perfect. Like a fairy story; about another period but absolutely relevant today and people will make the connection with more independence than they would if they were more closely involved.'

'They can make connections well enough without fairy stories,' Dick remarked.

'All right,' ready to concede where there was no loss. 'It'll make a most powerful scene.'

Peter opened a box file, laid the papers to rest and released the spring. It pinned them down with an echoing snap. 'It won't make any kind of scene.'

'You can't omit an account as dramatic as that!'

'That's why I can.' He could be firm, unhesitant about this; it was an artistic decision, not an issue to be argued in open court.

'Pete doesn't go in for Irish jokes,' Dick told her. Then, seeing the woman's bewilderment, explained ponderously: 'It was a van full of Micks and they queued up for the stick, and as they got it, they . . .'

She snapped, 'I'm not a racist either, and I find nothing at all comic in the episode. I don't know how anyone could. That incident just can't be left out! It's a gift! It doesn't even need dialogue. It's a concise, visual, totally explicable representation of violence.'

'So is any punch-up.'

'But this is the behaviour of authority.' She turned back to Peter. 'Why not use it?'

Despite his resolution, he was obliged to answer. 'I'd like to include a local bobby and no doubt will bring in Freddie Bell in some way, but not in this one. Such a scene, in the context of this play, would be intrusive.'

'So you're playing it safe, are you? Kindergarten stuff? We mustn't have anything controversial? I thought you were being paid to write a play about what goes on in this community.'

He flushed. 'Yes, Constance, I'm being paid to write a play about

Neatham and I see it as a kind of documentary pageant. And, as I've said, such a scene would be out of key. Taking up that account in the way you'd like would be, simply, wrong. It wouldn't be in the style.'

'Bollocks! If you're claiming to present Neatham, then it all has to be there. You shouldn't be leaving things out on the grounds that they might be uncomfortable. Obviously, with all that stack of material you can't put everything in; but without certain incidents – and I'd say that roughing up Irish drunks is one – you won't give a true portrait.'

'Ah, now that's a different matter.' Peter suddenly glinted. 'You're chasing a will o' the wisp. It's all in the eye of the beholder, Constance, particularly the one looking into the glass. If I, or any other writer, were capable of a true portrait of Neatham, nobody would recognise it.'

'Especially since it would be based on what the folks have to say for themselves,' Dick laughed.

'In that case you might come nearer to it by putting that scene in.'

Wishing to hide his annoyance, Peter collected the polythene beakers and dropped them into the metal wastepaper basket. They keeled over and oozed dregs of coffee across the other litter. This was neither the time nor the company for debating any concept of truth. 'By including that account I would come nearer to your requirement, Constance, that's all, and if I were writing any other kind of play I'd probably use it. But this play is restricted in its aim and is designed for amateurs to perform. Even so, it's still art of a kind, so there's selection and that episode would stick out like a sore thumb. I don't for that reason consider I'm employing what you would call censorship. You're only arguing for it because *you* want it said. I'm not in the business of scoring points.'

'For Christ's sake! That beating up at the police station happened.'

'It was roughing up a few minutes ago, but yes, it happened. And so did a lot more, but much nastier. Only unlike this recounted by Clarice Bell, it isn't so overtly stated.'

'Such as?'

'In the two or three years running up to the last war, several refugee families rented houses by the common. German Jews. Later there was a US Army station up at Haxby, that's about three miles out. Some of the GIs were black. The refugees were gone in a couple of years and the black soldiers, along with their regiments, went into Europe, but they're still remembered. They're still here amongst those people who knew them. Traces of them are to be found in pauses, in sudden abstractions, in the fractured syntax of unexpiated guilts. I shall not

87

bring those ghosts back to confront them, just as I shall not reveal Frederick Bell's sadism. I am not the appointed conscience of the people of Neatham.'

She stared at him, scratched in a pocket for her car keys, which seemed to be her total luggage, and walked to the stairs. 'Thanks for the coffee. I'll be in touch about the publication and I do hope that when you flee this eyrie and get your head down, the writing will go well. It was good of you to give me a preview. It's going to be great.' But she could not leave on such a line; her honesty was too relentless. Drumming her palm upon the banisters, she qualified with: 'Provided it's not a cop-out.'

'Well, it's like this, Miss Skrimshaw,' Dick answered for him. 'I don't know how people go on in other places, but there's not a single person in Neatham – and I mean that – not a single one that'll sit in front of a play that runs them down. They can find that without going to the trouble of paying for it. But Pete's all right. He's lucky because he can always check with me. I can tell him what Bells are left apart from Clarrie. An uncle of mine married Freddie's niece.'

'I don't believe it!' Peter exclaimed, his voice suppled by thanks and relief which became laughter, cathartic; while Constance, without risk of compromise though with humourless incomprehension, could observe and grin. As Peter hooted, 'First you suggest I change the name of a street shrew because you're concerned about the family reputation, eighty years on, as if Florence Moorby were your great-grandmother. Now you're related to Freddie Bell! Every time I turn over a page I bump into your kith and kin, adoptive or real. Do you consider yourself guardian for all the families in the neighbourhood, Dick?'

He chewed a thumb, pretending to calculate, his face expressionless. 'I wouldn't say *all*, Pete. There's a fair number can look after theirselves; but for the rest, and others that might need my services, I'm their man.'

It was impossible to determine whether he joked.

Chapter Eight

'You'll be late home tonight,' he commented.

'That doesn't matter. I couldn't miss this evening.' Nora threw her jacket across a desk and returned to the stairs. 'Better check that everything's ready.'

'It's done. Me and Stan have put the seats out in the big room. You needn't have come so early.'

We shall have to organise ourselves better than this during the next six weeks, just us doing the job together, Nora thought and tried to suppress the spurt of excitement with: 'I didn't know you were setting up.'

'I should've mentioned it.'

'No matter. I wasn't sorry to get away.'

He nodded, incurious, and the pulse was quietened. Disappointed, she could not avoid the comparison, could not deny that Robert would have asked her what had occasioned her last remark and she wanted to force the knowledge upon him; accustomed to empathy, she required it, however contrived, to justify her present choice. She would also have liked to confide. Doris Bentley's attentions had grown persistent; they were difficult to shake off, and they were not to be explained as symptoms of benevolence or admiration; there could be no delusion about that. Nora wanted to ask him: What do you do when someone develops a passion for you? but the question was too pertinent, her situation painfully ironic, and she feared his response. So she said, looking at her watch, 'Leaves us with half an hour to kill.'

He did not answer but sat on the floor by a triangle of window and slantingly looked out. In half profile, again the face showed cubistic, modelling tradesmen, and under the flesh polished by shaver the bone's structure was durable, giving the sense of weight.

'I want a word with Pete before he goes in,' he told her. 'There may not be time, after.'

'He said it might take about an hour and a half.'

'That's good. He'll be able to start back in the light. The night doesn't begin to draw in till about nine.'

About Peter's journey he was solicitous; hers prompted no concern.

'This meeting isn't necessary anyway,' he repeated an objection

89

already made. 'Those who are interested will turn up without having to be lectured.'

She wanted to shout: Christ, Dick, fuck all this shop! Why so bloody uptight? We've been working together in this outfit for nearly three months. But she was silenced by his manner and the physical removal to the window; perhaps he, too, was thinking of the weeks ahead and this was his warning of the terms she should expect.

'What Peter intends is hardly a lecture. I know there's been quite a lot in the press, but to give people a résumé of what will be covered, as far as he can at this stage, seems not a bad public relations exercise and it should help with recruitment.'

He shrugged. 'I told him I could do that with less effort over a pint,' and turned back to the segment of glass. They were strangers filling in time before Peter's arrival.

'If you have to go immediately after the meeting I can pass on a message to him; I don't have to rush off.'

'Like that, is it?' She could not determine whether the lips were screwed with disapproval or envy. Yet he had been one of the few who had shown no puzzle at her arrangement. 'I'd rather tell him myself; it seems indecent just passing it on.' He paused, considering. 'I suppose you'll find out in due course. It's no secret really. Do you remember Pete asked me a bit back to enquire about that school-teacher, Miss Freiston? It's taken some time because it's been the devil's own job to get the old ones I know to open up. She died, you see, second half of the Great War. Piecing it together, I reckon it would be the winter of 1917. One old chap thought it was soon after the Passchendaele offensive and I went into the library and checked the date: back end of July 1917 it started. Another one said there was ice on the canal by the lock.' He stopped, looking down into the former playground. 'That's where she went in.'

It was an accident, a stranger's death, but Isabel's admiration prompted a vague sadness. 'And she had so much to give.'

'Maybe there weren't any to take.'

'That's not true. At least, Isabel Driffield wouldn't agree.'

'I was only following on what you said. I didn't mean anything.'

'You must have.' She was not sure why she was being so persistent. 'Speech can't occur in a vacuum without reference to thought.'

'Mine can. Where did you learn that theory?'

She ignored the sneer. 'To quote Isabel: "She had us eating out of her hands, lads included." That doesn't sound as if there weren't any to take.'

He fidgeted. 'It was only an expression.'

'But you used it as if offering an explanation.'

'All this diagnosing, worse than the doctor,' he tried to mock but was compelled by her stare. 'She left her hat and a book, it was the Prayer Book, by the side of the sluice wheel, up on the bank.'

'Why?' She tried to make the sound neutral.

'Who knows?' Then, struggling: 'She was against the war.'

'From what Isabel says of her, that doesn't surprise me.'

'That must be the answer, then.'

She knew it was not; she had not found the right question. 'You're suggesting that Miss Freiston committed suicide because she could no longer bear the knowledge of that war?'

'She'd be at the end of her tether.'

The banality was repellent; it plucked at her face.

'Well, what else?' he demanded, aggressive, but scrambled up as if squatting on the floor were an unsuitable posture, disrespectful; then he didn't know where to stand.

Startled, she caught the hint of apology and sensed that it was she now who determined the conversation.

'She must have been a remarkable woman. Surely when people are driven to suicide it is by more private nightmares?'

'Driven,' he repeated as if about to object, then sagged. 'Nora, have you looked at the names on the memorial in the park? Hardly a family in Neatham went through that war without sending a man, particularly at the Bottom End. You've met some of the relatives. Isabel Driffield's father was in it, wounded but survived; Ernest Wagstaff lost an uncle and brother, and some came off a lot worse.' His eyes touched her face but could not rest there. 'I'm not excusing, but what I am saying is that it's easy for us to judge. It's seventy year since, and we weren't there. All past history now.'

Gradually she interpreted. She could not move; speech had congealed.

'No,' he denied quickly. 'It wasn't that. There was never any doubt what it was, though Frederick Bell always maintained that she hadn't intended to do it but slipped on the ice as she walked across the lock gates. That's no more than a theory and useless. Because it ignores the Prayer Book and hat.'

'Frederick Bell?' was all she could manage.

'Yes. Not a policeman then. He was in her class at the time. Perhaps that was why he preferred it to be an accident.' His voice drained away.

'It was right what I thought,' she told him slowly.

'No!' He fisted the beam at his shoulder; he was defending the streets that had reared him. 'They never placed a finger on her.'

'That wasn't necessary.'

'She could have left. She didn't have to stay here forever lecturing the folk that war was a sin.'

'Is that what she did?'

'She wouldn't let it rest.'

'You said, "Maybe there weren't any to take." You should have said, "There were too many who chose to reject."'

'What else could they do? You remember Joseph Raby? One of his uncles, Samuel, went to prison for her. Joseph didn't mention that in his story. But there were things he said struck me as funny coming from a quiet chap like Joe. Pointing out that he'd volunteered for the Army and going on about how much he'd enjoyed it. Then I remembered Sam and came to the conclusion that Joe had got used to saying what was wanted, righting the score.' As Nora turned away her head: 'I'm not arguing they acted right, but she spoke out too loud. Feelings ran high. People kept their kids from school. She might have got away with it in a bigger place.'

'You mean, she might have saved her life?' As she had hoped to save some from the trenches.

'She was stepping out of line and wanted them to. It got so she started on them before they left here.' She looked back at him questioning, not wanting it to be true. 'Yes,' he assured her quietly, 'this is the place.'

Watching her, he said, 'I'll make you a coffee.'

As he fussed with kettle and powder he squinted down into the yard and reported, falsely jocular, 'The crowds are beginning to roll up. If we're not careful, there'll be a record gate. Pete's just arrived, though perhaps we shouldn't count him, and a big lad with a real smasher holding his hand – could be your Becky Dobson – and the woman who plays the organ at the Wesleyan in John Street, and the wimp from the *Gazette*, and that teacher with no hair and a beard.'

'Don Clamp.'

'That's him. This water'll be warm enough now,' and filled a beaker. 'There you go. Just get outside that.' He hesitated at her side ready to mother, to supervise her while she drank.

'Dick, what was her name?'

'Miss Freiston. You know that.'

'Her first name.'

'I can't be sure,' he evaded.

'Someone must have mentioned it.'

'She's just spoken of as the teacher, Miss Freiston.' His discomfort told her that the address did not indicate a respectful formality; rather, it distanced them from the fact. Less intimate, it permitted a relegation of guilt.

'You know.' The admission was necessary for the woman who was dead.

'I think it was Tryphena,' he said at last.

Her look softening, thanked him, and his breath whispered as if in some measure their practice of concealment had been absolved.

'It's a nice name,' he murmured, 'though it wouldn't be heard here,' and he led her eyes up to the main beam and along the pitched ceiling that had once taken the chants of children, unstopped by the false floor.

'For her pupils she'd definitely remain Miss Freiston,' Nora agreed. 'But I wonder who was bold enough to call her Tryphena. Or perhaps someone used that as his intimate right.'

So she received her just attention; the treatment of her was not extenuated by impersonal address. She was given flesh, a woman who could embrace a lover as Nora suggested and, imagining this, the two were quiet, momentarily joined.

A rush of sound on the stairs pushed him a pace from the desk but Mandy had seen it and, fingers clenched over the dusty newel, she halted her greeting.

'Thought it'ud be you,' Dick said. 'All that noise. Ross said you might get.'

'So long as Barbara'll look in and listen for the kids if he wants to nip down to the pub. She's my sister,' speaking to Nora; then, nodding towards Dick, 'his wife.'

'Yes; you've told me.'

Mandy appeared to consider an answer then rejected it; censure had been hinted and family loyalties honoured. Therefore, relenting slightly, she made do with separation. 'Are you coming then?' she asked Dick.

'Save it for Ross, will you, Mandy? Then we'll not fall out.' Deliberately, stating independence, he took Nora's beaker and tossed it into the bin. 'About time we went down,' he told her.

'I'll join you in a minute.'

Tryphena, a woman persecuted unto death. Nora shivered.

She had walked by the side of the canal several weeks earlier.

Unused, its water stagnant, its wharves empty, it was a trench between warehouses fissured, pocked by winds, their gutters clogged by scorched grass. Occasionally evidence of a tenant was presented by whole, glazed windows through which could be seen fork-lift trucks manoeuvred by men in T-shirts and denims, less appropriate to the decaying floors than the starlings that nested inside the adjacent roofs. These ended as the canal reached from the town centre and the horizon dropped to corrugated zinc balanced upon newer walls, to serrations – shallow slope, abrupt pitch – above machine shops and sheds; whose windows faced car parks and meshed fences beyond which were the pinched streets and somewhere the town's principal road. These factories, squat, shoddy, the ironic justification of temporary architecture, had never shared in the life of the canal.

But beyond them, at the town's edge, the allotments were eternal. Defined by short paths, they were furrowed by rows of potatoes, webbed by blossom colours, screened by stick crutches ready for sweet peas and beans. Forming a settlement on either side of the water, they were quiet, compliant to the pace of the seasons, and their sheds, cunningly improvised, were shanty habitations which had grown with the crops, had creaked with them under the rain and opened with them to the sun. They were private, unassertive, a refuge from the year's push. That morning as she had strolled down the path Nora had enjoyed the gardens' solitude.

Now, sitting at her desk, she saw them clenched in frost, the clinker alleys sharp as flint, the doors padlocked; inert and abandoned, the place menaced. And she thought: Had Tryphena Freiston looked at that on her last day? Had she, acquainted with the landscape of that path, relied on its emptiness? Or had she been obliged to acknowledge a greeting from one of the plots, to stop and sympathise with a tenant ice-banned from occupation?

But that was unlikely. When she approached, people turned away or shouted abuse. Did a jeer clang across the iron ground and jolt the canal's stiff reeds on that frozen day?

These were ghoulish reflections, but excusable because somehow required, and rising from the desk Nora stood in the space which had once absorbed the voice of that other woman and repeated the lines of the Jew which she had made her class learn:

> Shall I bend low and, in a bondman's key,
> With bated breath and whispering humbleness,
> Say this:

'Fair Sir, you spit on me on Wednesday last,
You spurned me such a day; another time
You called me dog;'

Did they remember that when others of Shylock's tribe looked for
sanctuary in Neatham? Did they weep at the Pathé News six years
later and, questioning their own humanity, wonder at the futility of
remorse? Isabel Driffield had made no such confidence; but she had
learnt the speech. Miss Freiston had kept them at it, but . . . 'the way
she telled it, we couldn't get enough.'

One of whom had been Frederick Bell. Contrary to circumstantial
evidence, his devotion forced him to argue that an accident had caused
her death. Then, appalled, Nora discovered another interpretation:
inclined to bullying, the boy had brought the adult hatred into the
classroom then, when a man, had proposed this theory to deny his
part in their guilt.

Isabel had explained: Having her for a teacher was a bit like being
perched on the top of a volcano, you were getting the chance to view
a good distance but you knew it was dangerous because you might at
any moment be blowed up.

'It's not a case of "Ah, but a man's reach should exceed his grasp/Or
what's a heaven for?" It's more a question of there being no reach in
the first place,' Don Clamp had told her. 'This is not to suggest these
children don't work; they'll put in a fair amount of graft, but that's as
far as they'll go. They have little initiative and almost totally lack a
sense of adventure. You could argue that the latter's atrophy is no bad
thing, given their economic and environmental constrictions. However. We manage to handle that, they and I, and the diffidence, the
absence of self-confidence. More worrying is the cause. I think it is
the symptom of something else, deep-seated, unrivable, immovable as
bedded rock. These children seem to believe – even invite, comply
with, as if it had been written in the tablets – the immutable edict that
the best things in life, its stars sparkling the dark firmament, talents,
passions, personal freedoms, are not for them.

'Don't ask me why. When I first came here I could find plenty of
answers at hand and there were others waiting to be plucked from the
files of previous experience as well as the theories that low expectation
is programmed by birth. But I came to the conclusion that these were
inadequate. Too slick. None explained the consistency of the attitude.

So now I cannot give you an answer. If I could, I wouldn't still be here. I remain because of the search. Or until I've come to terms with their acquiescence, with their instinct for the flat which keeps their eyes turned from the hills, with their conviction that there are no veins of gold running through their clay. You should not mistake this for humility; in the more sensitive it is expressed as a kind of embarrassment or a shamefaced retreat; in others who are influenced by parents' claiming it with pride, it shows as complacency. To adopt this attitude is safer; it doesn't risk the cold winds that come when you attempt distinction from the rest; it's comfortable. Snuggled together in the firelight, you can stop your ears to the knocking on the door.'

'The rest of us was content to work at Blygh's and not step out of line,' Isabel agreed.

'And they could be right,' Don Clamp had said. 'Such an ethic permits a lower reach; it moderates ambition. You'll never become unstuck through aiming above your ability. Nobody in my Fifth will develop ulcers through stress. I call myself a practical man. They should receive my applause. Because, if I gave them anything else, if I were to succeed in lifting their eyes away from the cosy firelight and point out the vast horizon above the peaks where they could conjure the sun, would I not be imposing my values? Couldn't it be arrogance that makes me assume that mine are more valid than theirs? Does not history instance the dangers of missionary zeal? Is it my job to replace one system with another? Or should I be acting within the framework that is already there? Philosophies change. I'm in the propaganda business but no one has yet decided the text, or who should make the decision.'

'She was keen on me going to the High School, but she made no allowances,' Isabel went on. 'She hadn't been born and bred in Neatham, like us, and she could see no reason why she shouldn't stand up and declare that women should have the vote.'

Tryphena Freiston. An outsider, a dangerous woman, challenging them to stretch, to leave the firelight and reach for the blistering sun. An uncomfortable woman, dismissing the vacuous content that comes through never stepping out of line. Until, finally, their resentment was given an admissible vent: she spoke out too loud. The excuse for that floating corpse was still passed down the decades; Nora had heard it repeated that evening. Confronted by her pacifism, they had repelled it. And her. They were committed to a more terrible recruitment.

Condemned, she had taken the path which led to the lock gates. There Nora had paused on a spring morning when light sheened a grid of roofs beyond the canal, but the animation suggested was spurious: the sheds were empty, awaiting demolition, and intervening walls concealed the débris of neglect. When Tryphena Freiston had stood by those sluices, Ryecroft's had been throbbing, a piston of war. It sanctioned the hatred she had come to escape.

It was a silent place. The wharves with their traffic, the untenanted allotments, were long past. The only sounds were a plover's reproach above the rigid fields and under her boots the snap of cat ice lidding the puddles along the path. There had been no one to witness. No one had observed how long she had stood, her hands on the narrow rail surmounting the gates. There had been no exchange of comforts, no final words of comradeship or love. The moment came without another's ceremony; that, she had performed herself: the final, private and neat act.

Nora leant against one of the beams browned by the heat that had risen from the classroom fires. They had been kindled for many children but only Samuel Raby had gone from them to enter prison, despite the town's contempt. She wondered how he had received the woman's death; certainly his grieving would be untainted, free of guilt.

Nora walked down the stairs and entered the kitchen. Through the partition which separated this from the main hall she could hear Peter's voice. He was describing the content of the play and telling the meeting about one of the characters. She heard him say, 'Therefore, since he wasn't fighting in the war, he saw what happened in Neatham. I'm going to read you a passage from his recollections that I shall use. I haven't yet decided on the best method of dramatising it, but however we do it, this scene will be very solemn. There will have to be an atmosphere of respect; it's our memorial.'

The tuberculosis made a patch on my lung, so I wasn't passed as fit. I did everything I could besides. I passed the Air Raid Precautions test by correspondence with the Bennett College and they sent me the certificate. I've still got it somewhere. So when the war broke out I was first in the line for badges and orders and a bit after that I got the tin hat. Most of the war it was a question of checking houses for lights and night duties. We were not required to combat many air raids, though we had plenty of warnings as they came close, making for Notts. I'm not making out it were a holiday, we got a fair number of bombs, but most were what you would call random: a bomber would be intercepted and he'd drop what he had left. That would

lighten his load, you see, and so give him a bit more speed to evade being
shot down. I said most were like that, didn't I? But not all. And the worst
was a daylight raid. Have you heard about that? It was near the start of the
war, first summer, maybe, and a Jerry bomber, one of them sneak raiders,
got hold of the canal and followed it straight up to us. You can't credit
that for impertinence, can you? A Jerry nosing his way into the middle of
this town, large as life! We would have been flabbergasted, except that we
didn't have the time. Because he found Ryecroft's, found it there, slap by
the canal.

Slap by the canal, a short distance from the lock; but on that afternoon
the Ryecroft sheds did not beat out a judgement. They were themselves vulnerable, a prey. Nora shuddered. It was another war.

Right slap bang in his path, Ryecroft's was, and he thought, 'What manner
of place is this? It behoves me to find out.' So up he went, round about
Boston Hill yonder then came back over Little Ringby, circling, you see, to
get a better look, and of course no matter how much they camouflaged it,
there was no hiding it was a factory. And do you know, he chose his position
as if he was running up for a jump and he came back low, sweeping down
like one of them great birds – albatross, isn't it? – crossing over Bramble
Lane as it was then, that's buried now under that new road, motorway, and
he dropped all he'd got on the works. Ten minutes past four, it was; another
hour and twenty minutes and the buzzer would have been going for home
time. He must have been laughing fit to do a mistake in his trousers, if
you'll excuse the expression. Till he was caught. One of ours got him over the
North Sea, we was told. I've often wondered what he thought, that German
pilot, on his last afternoon. I didn't worry about it at the time; I was born
an Englishman and that's always been good enough for me, but sometimes
nowadays I look back and think: How did he feel up there with no fighter
protection? Scared out of his wits, no doubt. Then he finds Ryecroft's and he
says to himself: I'll let them have it, at least then if I cop it, it won't all be
in vain; then pleased with hissen, singing as he banked and made for the
coast, shouting to his crew he'd be standing them a drink, till there was the
puncture of bullets across him, wing to wing.

Then the collision of air crushing out that in the lungs and the drop
out of time reeling out the past in a parabola of fear. Until water
sagged, lifted, sluiced back and, drawing the lonely body into its
currents, sheeted it with insensible coldness. While for a short time

buckled and sliced wreckage tossed, marking the place; or on the frozen edge lay a hat and a book of prayer.

She had been followed and harried; she had been reviled. She had prodded their complacency and opposed their beliefs. Unlike Isabel and the rest, she had stepped out of line.

Nora was tweaked by a memory. There had been another also who had been punished. She did not know why she should recall this, standing in the Centre kitchen waiting as Peter searched for the next page, but she knew that the memory came from one of Isabel's grudging confidences: 'Dot was one of my nieces, my brother Jack's girl. I had a fair bit to do with her back end of the war, so I know what she came in for.' Reflecting on this, puzzling why the sentences should return prompted by thoughts of Tryphena Freiston, Nora heard Peter read again from the script.

I often think about that German bomber now. You see, we were never told how my brother Edward went. Just 'killed in action' was what was put on the list they pinned up. It was April the 9th 1917 and the lieutenant who might have written went the same day. Of course, you'll understand I wasn't thinking of this when the bombing occurred. I was on nights that week. Like I said, as soon as war started I gave up shoe mending in favour of the factory and it gave me a shock to be woken by the noise of the siren. Before it had finished there were thumps and rattling and the town shaking as if there was dynamiting under the ground. I got up sharp but my bicycle had been lent so by the time I was on the spot the fire brigade and ambulances were there and they were beginning to carry them out. There was a fire in one of the sheds but most of the load had fallen in the yards which you might think was a saving, but it wasn't, you see, because of the blast. You'll never believe how it can shift things: walls, fire escapes, machines that weigh a mighty bit I can tell you, and there were four hundred workers in the middle of that. There was sheet metal standing in one of the shops and it acted like so many bacon slicers. It was something I'll never forget.

Peter stopped reading. Quiet, they listened to his finger tap into place the leaves of Ernest Wagstaff's memory.

'That will come at the end of the first half,' he told them. 'Perhaps we should have five minutes' break.'

Chapter Nine

They were not as Nora had hoped, those six weeks of Peter's absence, and as they progressed she rebuked herself for fantasies, attempting a protective cynicism, and failed. Because, she argued – and a great many hours were spent in silent involuted debate – there had been moments that Friday evening when something had flickered, when something, little more than a breath but enough to sustain her, had escaped from him in harmony with her thoughts. Though defensive, his acknowledgement of Neatham's conduct towards the schoolmistress was a kind of confiding; paradoxically, in talking about a woman they had made an outcast, he had drawn Nora in; he had admitted her, no alien. And he had yielded the other's name. But that was not all. His behaviour in the last minutes before Mandy's entrance had persuaded her that their feelings had coupled and she cradled that belief to her, unable to surrender it, telling herself that, listening to her charm up a lover for Tryphena Freiston, he had heard and answered her desire.

Yet there it had ended; the next time they met he had been neutral – neutered, she sneered, but to be vicious was no comfort; it offered merely fleeting relief. After their talk about Tryphena, his return to a polite working day depressed her. She had run into the office on Monday morning expecting more, and he had greeted her without excitement; almost, it seemed, with dislike.

'You're early,' he accused, looking at his watch. 'Stan's only just opened up.'

The contrast between anticipation and reality cramping her stomach, she heard herself apologise, 'There wasn't much on the road.'

But, she thought, goading the reluctant brain: He has had time to reflect; on Friday he was receptive to my emotion though it was obliquely expressed, but the conventions in which he labours have since recovered and what I disclosed, since it was stated through a dead woman and her lover, seems to him obscene; he is perceptive and intelligent but there are concepts and intellectual liberties too distant for his catch.

They had never been too distant for Robert whatever the length of the journey, and the thought shamed her. It was on such freedoms that her present conduct was fed.

He had said, 'I've been looking at the lists Pete left and I've marked the jobs I can start on. One's seeing about timber so I'll take a walk to the Do It Yourself, have a word about off-cuts. Kev might be able to put me in the way of stuff going cheap,' and left her, his haste vindicated by Peter's request.

Occupation outside the office was his frequent choice during the early weeks and inclined to discover a reason less painful to herself, Nora decided that this manoeuvring was caused by Peter's absence; the man's relationship with her was not freed by it but constrained. In another's presence he could relax, could be natural; feel no threat. That last possibility, once named, disturbed her; it belonged not to social assurance but to sexual cowardice and she was not convinced.

But there could be another more obvious reason for this man's behaviour – or lack of it, she corrected unsmiling: perhaps Mandy had spoken to Barbara her sister his wife. Having suspected a relationship they had not yet enjoyed, she had split on them, Nora repeated, temporarily eased by an expression belonging to childhood and the dismantled home. A clat-tale, a blab-mouth, who could confess to lusting after Peter's little bum without risk to her knickers – the coarse spite she considered appropriate – and who elected herself moral custodian of her brother-in-law. And though Dick had taken pains to flout Mandy's insinuations, if he were also faced with his wife, his continuing to come into the office was surprising, it could be argued; which Nora did, adding always the explanation that his persistence, defying suspicions, was on account of an interest in her. If so, she reminded herself tartly, he had a strange way of showing it.

Because he was courteous, but little else. And though not exactly unfriendly, his manner was studied; he made her a suffered guest. Reference to people, to incidents, to businesses, streets and buildings unknown to her grew more numerous; his conversation, when it occurred, was an encyclopaedia of local allusions, at times so convenient and pat that she wondered if he were making them up. He did not quote them to inform or give pleasure but to emphasise that she was a stranger, and when she attempted to contribute an observation showing that her experience, though not derived in Neatham, was not entirely alien, he sulked. It was as if he comprehended her reason for coming, her wish to tap the overgrown springs, and he was determined to hold her off. She could not understand this. It was more than a statement of distinctions; it was exclusion, and the insularities she had

101

met elsewhere, and conquered, had not trained her for one in this sort of club.

So one morning when he introduced a private dilemma her gratitude was disproportionate and she was not inclined to examine how incomplete the confidence was.

'I've been offered a job,' he told her abruptly.

'That's splendid.' But the floor tilted as she anticipated separation.

'I've got till Monday week to make up my mind.'

'Surely there's no question?'

'It's temporary, over by Christmas, and the way it works out I'll be no better off. It doesn't help with the gas bills or rent.'

'But it's something to put down, to say you've done.'

'I'm not so sure about that. Seeing what it is, it might be more sensible to keep it dark.'

'In that case, when you quoted it later, you'd simply have to adjust description.'

'Try a bit of romancing to bring it in line with what a boss wanted to hear?'

For a moment they were grinning. 'That's right.'

'However much I dressed this up, it wouldn't carry weight for any other job I'd be after.'

She was disappointed rather than surprised that he did not describe the nature of this offer. He had not told her what his work at Ryecroft's had been. She had asked the caretaker and, having learnt Dick's former employment, had remembered his smile, unexplained, at Ernest Wagstaff's quotation about the village smith: 'Thus at the flaming forge of life/Our fortunes must be wrought.' Then she had been obliged to ask Stan for a description of constructing harrows: flicking the glowing rod out of the furnace, flinging it on to the bench, forging it with deft, swift, unhesitant strokes into a curlicue link and lacing it to the last before the steel was grained with grey. She had explained Dick's silence about his work on his assumption that she knew what it was or that the information was irrelevant. Now that this reserve was repeated, she saw it as deliberate secrecy.

This was a painful conclusion. It reduced her tolerance, so that she heard as self-pitying excuse what was stoical armour against future knocks as he said, 'Though I don't know why I worry; I was rubbished three years back and nobody's been interested since.'

Therefore she answered, tight, 'If so, you've got nothing to lose.'

He stared at her. His throat clicked but the retort was suppressed; and she saw herself through his lens, a person less vulnerable than he, cushioned against hardships. 'Yes,' he said at last. 'That about sums it up.'

She could not deny that her tone had been modulated by her adopted class and, guilty, she also felt helpless. She wanted to banish the pessimism, urge him to seek work, but his accusation prevented her.

'What I was trying to say was: I don't agree with your attitude,' she struggled.

'I did notice. Best keep that one buttoned up. It wouldn't be polite.'

'Not out of politeness. Obviously we aren't inhibited by that.'

'If you want an argument I'm afraid I can't oblige at the moment. I've to go along to John Street, to see if the chapel kept back any of their old forms.'

It was a characteristic evasion and enraged her but, the unnamed job waiting, she regretted that their acrimony should sour the few days that might be left.

Gradually, however, she became reconciled to the possibility of his abandoning this project; and her. For she believed that soon she would no longer rely upon it; soon, she believed, they would spend time together, their meetings independent of the play's convenient excuse.

Because he was in good humour, and catching its reflection, her own mood lifted. For the first time he seemed to welcome her company and wished her to participate in what he did. The offer of work had given him value; recognising this, she reviewed her examination of their relationship and, ashamed, decided that it had been unimaginative and self-absorbed. Focusing upon her own dissatisfactions, she had ignored the dispiriting effect of being unemployed. Thus she argued that his behaviour over recent weeks had been a defence or that she had wrongly explained it. Certainly there is a difference, she observed to herself, watching, noting, interpreting every intonation and gesture, every flick of the man.

'I've been having a word with Ted White,' he announced. 'He's done a bit of acting. Used to belong with the Swinethorpe Players till he got tired of travelling eight miles after work, but he kept it up. Puts on a nice show at Christmas down at the Jubilee, bit of everything, singing, a comic, a magician for kids. Him and a few mates generally do a turn.

'He'd be useful to have. Pete'll have seen better actors, but not here. Ted says he might be interested always provided it doesn't cost too much time because he's got to plan for the Jubilee. Any road up, he's willing to hear a bit more and I reckon you're the one for that. You've got more of an idea than me what Pete's got in mind and what might be in it for Ted. I've put down his address,' handing her a strip of paper. 'Most nights after half-past six he says he's free.'

It was a longer paragraph than any he had proffered during the previous three weeks and she almost simpered, a young girl selected by the heart-throb of the class. 'I'll go this evening,' she promised.

Promptly next morning she reported, 'I think we can count on Ted White. Luckily he appreciates the number of rehearsals amateurs need, and he should be able to manage two or three a week here in July and August. After that, probably Sunday as well.'

'I told him you were the one to consult when it comes to dates.'

'I was merely following Peter's timetable. I said that if there were any props or costumes in our play that he'd like to use at the Jubilee Hall, he was welcome to borrow them; or hire, I suppose. I wasn't sure of the form.'

'Form's not something to bother Ted overmuch. So he jumped to a bit of bribery, did he?'

She laughed. 'That wasn't necessary. Having discovered the town's potential, I was meeting its needs by offering our resources,' mimicking Constance Skrimshaw. 'That came after I'd persuaded Ted.'

'He was always one for the ladies.'

And, ridiculously, she was flattered.

'Look, Nora,' he said a few minutes later, 'I've got to size some hardboard. Kev's stuck it down in the little ones' room,' using the designation it retained from its shelter of standard one infants. 'Have you got a minute?'

'Of course. This letter's not urgent,' beginning to rise.

'Well, it's those days Pete sent for rehearsals. As far as I can see, nothing clashes, but the booking has to go through the Council so Stan needs the dates. Do you mind making a list for me? Then I can see it's definite with him before he knocks off.'

She agreed, though dashed at being denied the hardboard and standing companionably sloshing, side by side. But she was warmed by his asking a favour; it was a sign that he was less unbending, not shutting her out.

'Did Pete say something about a VE Day party?' he asked the following day.

'Yes. In a street.'

'That's right, with house fronts with windows for people to lean out of. I'm going to have to fetch in a few mates for them; my joinery isn't that clever. I told Pete he doesn't want a carpenter but a blinking construction firm. And it's real food he has to have, too, isn't it?'

'He's determined not to lower standards. It generally is real.'

'I wouldn't know about that, but since that's what he wants, I had a word with Millie behind the bar at the Admiral Nelson and she said she's willing.'

'To prepare the food?'

'See what's needed. She likes cooking for numbers, in charge of that side of things for all weddings and dos.'

'That's very good of her. Does she understand that this is ration book catering?'

'I mentioned there were drawbacks but she didn't mind. Her mam worked on the counter at Raby's grocery during the war and Millie said she'd give a few tips. I told her that she wasn't expected to foot the bill and we'd be giving her a float for when she wanted to be buying, but as soon as she started on questions about amounts, I told her you were the one for that. I was making initial enquiries. When it comes down to deciding what goes on plates and how many pounds of flour and marg are needed, I said that was your business.'

'I was beginning to worry whether I'd ever find someone to take charge of the food. Thanks very much, Dick. I'll do the same for you some time.'

'You don't have to wait. You can do something now, if you like. I've to go along to the Fire Station in a minute, have a word with the Station Officer about fire precautions and what's required in the way of flameproof paint for scenery. There's going to be a lot of timber in those flats, as Pete calls them, if we manage what he wants. You're not so new to that typewriter as I am, and I can put the time to better use, so I wouldn't say no to you doing those letters. It won't take you long; they're all on the short side, enquiries about donations of paint and asking whether me and Vic, he's an electrician, could spend a few hours over at Stage Illuminations to get our hands in with the lights.'

It was some time before Nora allowed herself to define Dick's behaviour; but until given irrefutable evidence, such honesty she chose to postpone; even the rational will retire from facts when they are in conflict with self-deceit. During a conversation with Peter she did not ask him to explain some curious allusions, sensing they endangered her calm. Like a betrayed wife, she resisted hints she did not wish to hear.

'I'm taking the morning off,' Peter greeted. 'How's everything your end?'

'Under control. So far, Sir, there have been no crises to report and no exciting incidents, not even an outbreak of hysteria.'

'That'll come. They peak late round there. Mug up your first aid; you'll need it for the last month of rehearsal.'

'I can't wait. Do you want to speak to Dick?'

'If you're too busy.'

She could ignore the surprise in his voice; her question had become automatic and no one else thought it strange. Peter didn't know how she and Dick allocated the jobs in the office, working as a team. 'I asked because, if you do wish to speak to him, he's not here.'

'A good thing I didn't say yes, then,' and laughed a lot. 'Sorry. Working long hours and late nights gets me like this. It lowers the reactive threshold: I laugh like a drain at the feeblest of jokes and weep buckets at the slushiest of songs. Where were we? Dick. Who isn't in the office at the moment. So you're holding the fort.'

'Carrying out the current assignment.' It was an obvious economy on labour for the quicker typist to dash off the letters.

'Well, I must say that the pair of you have got it gripped. I also have the strong impression that Dick is exceeding expectations, which must reduce your workload, Nora. I'm relieved that he's giving you so much support.'

'Yes.' It was less onerous if he made the approaches and the decisions he reached were the same as hers would have been.

'Our very own Constance Skrimshaw is greatly impressed.'

'She phoned a few days ago and left a message with me for Dick to ring her back.' Which, presumably, he had done when alone in the office.

'He has become her blue-eyed boy.'

'A pity they happen to be brown.'

'Now, now, Nora! No bitching. Constance may be a pain in the arse but she has her strengths, among which I'd place her aptitude for catching hints of things that might serve her purpose, then homing in and encouraging them to grow. And if they ever need a boost, she'll pump in her own conviction and drive. But, from what I hear, that's not likely to be necessary with Dick.'

'I imagine he could rise to the threat.'

He laughed again. 'I think it advisable we don't tell him that Constance claims his latent abilities are about to flower.'

'How awful!' She did not ask why Constance should predict this. 'Does she think she's Galatea to his Pygmalion?'

Peter said, 'She's simply being lyrical at the scent of success. I must

106

get off this line. Though it's recuperative to be idle, it sets a bad example to the staff. Have you fixed the printer yet?'

'I think Dick may have done. The estimate is very much lower than offers I've received. He put in a word.' That appeared to be his favourite pastime. 'He and the printer played football together when they were in their teens.'

'The old school tie isn't the only network. Good that Dick can get the job done more cheaply, though. I must remember not to mention that to Ms Skrimshaw; she's already smug enough at the vindication of her argument for involving a local man.'

As Nora finished the typing and attacked the letters ready for Dick to sign, she did not reflect upon Constance Skrimshaw's admiration of Dick's talents or question how she had discovered them. Instead she concentrated on debating whether the other woman would have approved of this traditional division of labour. Theoretically she would not; but, eyes fixed on the higher reaches of accessible art, the Community Arts officer would doubtless ignore the skirmishes at the foothills of endeavour. If they came to her notice she would despise the failure; like Clarice Bell, submissive women merited domination. Or desired it. But I'm not that kind of woman! Nora protested. I'd no more take directions from Robert than fly!

But he had never issued any. And this was another place, a different man. For a moment, her guard raised, Nora was appalled.

The printing firm stood at the junction of two streets, a good position to intimidate slackers in the congregation at the time when it was a chapel. The flight of four shallow steps had been chipped by trundled machinery and across the brick arch had been hung a plywood door faking security with two enormous padlocks, both open. Inside, three men defended their redoubt against the monstrous regiment by closer attention to their work until, after a decent pause, one raised his head and shouted, 'Walt!' Interpreting signals from a watchtower above him, he permitted one economical flip of a finger and reported, 'He's up there.'

Board stairs, uncovered, led to a gallery. Then there was office clutter squeezed upon or straddling a bank of steps. 'Cleared the pews out but never did level the floor except at the bottom,' Walter Price told her, placing a chair. 'I keep promising myself I'll do it.'

'That would make it run of the mill. This is very unconventional.'

'That's a handy argument. I'll remember that next time my married daughter starts grumbling. She comes in twice a week to do the paperwork. Now before we get too far into this order, I have to tell

107

you we're a bit tight on dates. I'll need to have it out of the way second week in September.'

'That's fine.'

'Good. I'm not trying to sound difficult, but I have a lot of work coming in that time of year, Christmas catalogues and such.'

'I'm pleased you're in that position.'

'Oh, it's nowt new. That's why I can see Dick right. As he said, if anybody's going to have the benefit of discount, it ought to be them at Bottom End, not those smarmy lot with briefcases on West Common.'

'We appreciate your offer.'

'Mind you, you mustn't go away thinking there's no reasoning behind it all. I stay in business because I stay here, which I wouldn't call the most suitable premises, but we manage.' Perched in the balcony, they looked down the room to the dais separated by the communion rail, a frill of ironwork lace. Nora wondered whether it was the one that William Wagstaff had forged. Where the pulpit had once stood a young man bent over a drawing board pasting up. 'I could've taken a unit on the West Common Estate but if I'd done that, the rates are so high they'd have doubled my prices. So I stayed here and all them on West Common send me work, brochures and whatnot for their products, because nobody there gets their hands dirty, it's all admin. Funny, isn't it? I mean, here am I turning the stuff out and I do it in a converted chapel while they have smart modern offices just for sitting by the phone! But they provide the work, and it keeps me and the wife and three men and theirs, so I'm not objecting. Here, young Graham,' he shouted without a pause, 'put the kettle on and fetch this lady a cup of tea.'

He was a likeable man, quick and effective with constructive suggestions that he did not impose. 'Surely,' he agreed. 'If Martin Chapman can get some in his top class to have a shot at a poster it'ud mean we didn't have to put out the job to a designer – I've no one here can do that – and there'd be some interest shown by the lads and lasses, which wouldn't do any harm. Only, some pictures come out better than others, so I'd appreciate a view of one or two you'd got in mind before settling on the one.'

'I'd be happier with that.'

'That's how I like my customers. The programme side's straightforward.'

'I should like to rough out a working design myself.'

'You do that. You don't need to have been to art school. Half of what we do here is measuring and the other half's tending machines.

But while you're doing it, you could bear something in mind. I know it's not my place to butt in, but I've been thinking it might be nice to settle on the same style for the lot, make it all hang together so folks recognise they're all connected.'

'I rather expected that, and I shall carry it into the artwork for the advertisements. The publicity needs to have a uniform look.'

'That's the right idea,' he agreed comfortably. 'I wasn't thinking about just what's coming off for the play, either. I had the book in mind as well. Perhaps when you're choosing the poster you might consider whether you could take anything out of it for the book cover and we could use the same typefaces and colour as in the programme, then people will recognise it and know they're already acquainted.'

The explanation was interminable. She watched his lips, willing them to stop, because if they did not soon, she would choke on the question she had tensed herself to ask.

'It's good psychology, that is. You look round you and you'll find it's easier to sell summat people already know about; it's the new they run a mile from.'

'The book?'

'The People's Neatham, or words to that effect. But that's Dick's sideline, isn't it? No matter; you're working on the same bench and you're not in shifts.' He laughed. 'So when it comes to you making up your mind on how you want your orders to look – and that'll have to be mid August – it might be an idea if you and Dick put your heads together and think up something on the lines I suggest. You can drop in any time to check if it's feasible.'

'Thank you, Mr Price.' She got up. The steps angled down the gallery, precipitous. She thought it would be safer to crawl. 'I appreciate your suggestions; I imagine we shall take them up. So far, though, because the play is the priority at the moment, we haven't discussed the book much. I can't even remember the date we're supposed to be bringing it out.'

'Fortnight before Christmas,' he obliged. 'Dick's going to be pushed. Or will you be giving him a hand? He'll have no more than two or three weeks after the play's over to get the copy ready for the typesetter. Then there's the proofs and he's got to get the books into the shops. He wants one hanging on every Christmas tree in Neatham. A good job that contract that's been fiddled for him goes to the year end.'

'Yes.' At last she had reached the door of the gallery. All that separated her now from the elusive air were the stairs to the ground floor. 'It's been good of you to give up so much of your time, Mr Price. I've learnt a lot.'

Chapter Ten

After that, the days were stagnant and dreary, without tweak of hope.

'Two huge parcels of photostats of the interviews have come from Peter this morning,' she told him. 'They were addressed to us both.'

'He wants them filing.'

The lie was prompt and implausible but she did not challenge it. She made no reference to his appointment; she could not have done so without an accompanying rebuke. Nor could she have been forbearing towards the deviousness or his pretended surprise that she had not known the nature of the offered work. She did not wish to give him the gratification of observing her hurt.

Neither could she admit it to Peter.

'Is our SM there?' he asked the following Monday.

'He's out. Shall I ask him to ring back?'

'There's no need, if you'll pass on that I'm pleased. He's sent me a copy of his letter to Constance accepting the job with a covering one in which he went into the reservations he has about publishing such a book but, fortunately, he's decided they aren't prohibitive. The letter has given me pause. I feel that I've never really made the effort to get to know him.'

Suppressing sarcastic advice to choose material more tractable, she soothed with: 'You've had a lot on.'

'Yes; but that doesn't excuse.'

It occurred to her that Peter gave to personal relationships an attention they more often received from women, scored too by the typical self-castigation for failure; and her impulse was to respond with the information that Dick had kept her ignorant of this job. But she could not confide. The man's conduct had humiliated her and she remained silent. Realising as she did so that this lack of openness was uncharacteristic of her, she was shocked that involuntarily she had adopted his way.

'I was astonished that he wrote a letter about it. All very formal. A quick word on the blower would have sufficed.'

'He said he'd been given till today.'

'Left to Ms Skrimshaw, it would have been a demand for a reply within the hour. Not one to allow second thoughts, our Constance.'

Would the woman have had second thoughts herself, Nora wondered, had she known that she was giving licence to a small-town dictator, one who had established so smoothly the customary delegation of tasks?

'I'm afraid there was only enough in her kitty to finance one assistant, Nora.'

'I think you've done well to get that.'

'Perhaps, but the motive is not entirely altruistic. There's a certain amount of competition between departments.'

'So I gathered.'

'Of course. When she visited. I'd forgotten that. I manage to flush away inessentials when I've got my head down.'

'How's it going?'

'You'll probably laugh at this, but I'm superstitious about answering that sort of question. Shall we say pages are being covered?'

She giggled.

'There you are: just as I said,' joining her.

For a moment she puzzled over the irrationality of attraction which could draw her to another before this man whose temperament and language had more consonance with her own; but that quality was Robert's also and it was not for that she searched. 'It's a good thing I'm doing publicity. I'll make sure that claims about the play are not weakened by the author's modesty.'

'We'll have to see about that.' He paused, then hesitant and awkward: 'Look, Nora, I want you to know that your not being at the receiving end when we were handing out tin doesn't indicate that I don't appreciate what you've done.'

'There's no need to say that.'

'I want to. But for you, I wouldn't be at this stage now. You've helped me to meet the deadline. Apart from anything else, by your interviews you've doubled the material I have to work on.'

'Some of it isn't so marvellous,' trying to deflect him. 'I haven't got very far with Isabel.'

'No matter. In fact, I can't deny having a sneaking respect for those determined not to Reveal All. Anyway, Nora, I'm truly sorry that there's no wage for you.'

'Don't worry about it. I didn't come to Neatham with that expectation. In any case, payment would jeopardise my amateur status.'

'When I was uneasy about the Clayton offer to equal Glyn's grant – that's definitely through – I wasn't objecting to payment for workers.'

'It was a joke, Peter.'

111

'Sorry. But you may like to regard it as a compensation, of sorts, that your area is the one selected to benefit from a little windfall. I've accepted the sponsorship from Clayton's and they want the money to be spent entirely on publicity.'

'You've accepted? I'm pleased you were able to change your mind.'

'Yes. I decided that my original hesitation was stupid. If one refuses sponsorship there should be a more tangible reason than the sense of being manipulated, quite without evidence. So you can have car stickers, banners, what you will; up to you to cost it out.

'But I hadn't finished, Nora,' he persisted. 'When we chose Dick, there were two factors we had to consider. One was political: it was necessary to stress the involvement of someone who belonged to the town because that would strengthen argument for future ventures, Ms Skrimshaw was very keen on that. And the other was that he's unemployed. His need seemed to be greater than yours.'

'And you were right. Stop anguishing over it, Peter, and get back to the play. Remember I've got a sugar daddy.'

'Wish I had,' he answered, relieved. 'Or a rich leman. Trouble is, nowadays they interpret independence so relentlessly, as soon as I qualify for a small allowance, they shoot off. I'll return to the workbench. You should soon be receiving copies of the early scenes so you'll be able to organise a more precise building schedule and continue with props. Thousands, I'm afraid. Look after yourself, and give my regards to Dick. Eventually I'll have to rearrange our programme to accommodate his work on the book. Constance didn't try to force me to supervise it; she decided to do that herself. No hard feelings over that. Releasing Dick for part of the week shouldn't present an insuperable problem; you're in advance of target already and he seems to be tackling jobs with great gusto, showing lots of initiative as well, which is good.'

Which she had acquiesced to. Attending only to her delusion that he was accepting her and inviting her into his life, she had assented to his requests, had permitted herself to be used. More than permitted, Nora relentless now corrected. Offered. And by this behaviour was he deliberately showing what he could do or, provoked by her tactless encouragement to accept the offered work, was he punishing her for that? But she dismissed these theories. After obsessively playing back those scenes between them, she knew they could mean only one thing. Jaunty, competent, resourceful, occasionally even charming, he had been nothing more complex than the man taking over, electing himself boss.

And the reason: a wage. Leaving her in the amateur and inferior position, taking orders. Of course it was both politic and practical for Constance and Peter to favour someone living in Neatham and she must not pretend that because a man less able than she had cut her out of a job, she felt this chagrin. That was caused by the man's deliberate exclusion. And she was angry with Peter, not because he had implied that they were justified in not paying her since she was supported by Robert – an indefensible argument – but because Peter had touched upon an area of personal morality she had attempted to evade.

She was using their income for something very private: for this, a kind of homecoming. There was no place in it for Robert and it brought her to another in preference to him. But the infidelity that might occasion, should hopes be realised, was commonplace and superficial; within the language of Nora's ethics it had little weight. She felt no guilt about carnal licence; for her, infidelity was not to be expressed in terms of sex. With Robert there existed a greater refinement. So there were more important breaches of communion, and one she had already committed. There was not only infidelity of her body but of her mind.

Thus having betrayed their spirit and compromised her intellect, Nora thought sardonically that it was a pity there had been no compensation of physical joys. Nor were there any other. Dick's withholding all description of the job she interpreted as indifference towards her feelings, practically contempt, and this conclusion was endorsed by his behaviour over the book. He kept it to himself, a miserly hoarding. He could not deny her the material, for she already knew that; what he could refuse was her association with the work. It became the symbol of the fence he had erected between them and just as, in the early days of Peter's absence, this man had made her alien by flaunting his possession of the town, he now used this anthology to hold her from him and the contact she sought.

So jealously he would not permit her to contribute or even be a witness to a task that he made entirely his own. That would have been a degree of fellowship, however meagre; instead, only his presence was suffered her, a constant reminder of what could have been. Finding this intolerable, during the last fortnight before Peter's return she shortened the time spent with Dick in the office by arriving very early, staggering their lunch breaks and leaving before him.

In the hours thus released, she took to wandering and sought the strange confluence of country and industry at the edge of the town.

113

It was the canal that most drew her. Starting at the bridge not far from Walter Price's deconsecrated chapel, she would walk under the dank arch, pass the high warehouses, the squat factories, the field gardens whose free and lovely first name had been debased to allotment, until she came to the lock. Since she had walked there once in the spring, the landscape had rounded; the green which had hazed the bushes was now a deep pelt. Pink bindweed spiralled through hedgerows frothed with hawthorn, and vetch blued the tall grass. Sitting by the lock gates, she caught the scent of honeysuckle as the breeze lifted its blossoms and she was reminded of the flowers that Joseph Raby had wanted to paint. Perhaps he had walked here, too, crossed the lock and sauntered through the meadows preferring the curiosity of romping heifers to the grumbles of fishermen required to move their tackle from the tow path as he approached. Or it may be that the sport was already discouraged by a depleted stock so that Joseph's walks were solitary, as Nora's were now. Though his meadows were today chequered by desirable residences, few owners ventured to the canal where pet dogs would have scrambled filthy out of the suspension of mud and whiskery rust of weeds. No one had been exercising a dog on the day Tryphena Freiston had come here. Her body, glazed with a membrane of wrinkled ice under the bank, had been found the next morning by a man from the village of Haxby who, walking the four miles each day, strode across the lock as a short cut to the works. Ignorant of Neatham's persecution, he had been shocked by the way his news had been received.

'They didn't want to be told,' Isabel had attempted after a long silence, consoling herself that it was this woman, not she, who had brought it up. 'They wouldn't go and lift her out; they left that to the constable; they didn't want to know.'

'Why?'

'She spoke out too loud. She called it evil when the preachers called it good. It doesn't do to be churning it up after all these years.'

'We're not doing that. Peter thought he might put her in the play, but of course he won't now he knows this.'

'I wouldn't expect it; Mr Green's too much of a gentleman for that.'

'Had you started work when it happened?'

'I'd been at Blygh's a year or more. I was let in to skivvy but they had learnt me the machine a good few months past when I picked up the whispers. Folk never raised their voices, putting it round how she had passed on. I would've liked to go to the funeral but things being as they were, I was too frit to say, besides they would have stopped my money and Mam needed that. I'm telling you this, young woman, I don't know why; I've never mentioned it to nobody else, least of all Norman, though I've noticed him being a bit more understanding in recent months. Maybe it's you getting me talking and bringing him in.' She referred to her husband frequently nowadays as if he were alive. 'I'm telling you, lady, that I've been sorry ever since not standing up to them and going to the church. She weren't chapel. I don't know how she would have fared there but she couldn't have been worse off because the vicar seeing to the matter wouldn't give her a regular service, her taking her own life, and him and the sexton, that was all there was, they laid her at the end of the cemetery that hadn't been blessed, by the ash heap and where they chuck the dead flowers off the graves. I went to look for hers once, fifty years after. It took me that long! But I had reason; we'd just buried our Dot, my brother Jack's girl, and in a way they was birds of a feather. But I couldn't find where they had laid Miss Freiston. There was nothing to see but great mounds of rotting wreaths.'

'You did your best,' Nora had comforted.

And the woman had looked up, eyes dry and sharp. 'Not what that one would have said. She wouldn't have considered that when you are old, soft words are the order of the day. I don't want my head patting.'

Only the vicar and sexton had attended to her committal; no consecrated place had been suffered her in a parsimony of rites. It was the vicar's conscientious decision, but nothing could justify the ostracism of the rest. That was the more cruel. And restless, comprehending something of the woman's defeat through the lesser misery of her rejection by one man, Nora would leave the lock, note how the afternoon sun flushed her arms, and reflect wryly on the fallacy of summer optimism.

It was on her third walk by the canal that, with the lock behind her and going further than she had done before, Nora found a stile in the hedge. Nettles grew through the planks and a bramble's barbs wired the crosspiece, but she forced a way over, crossed verdigris land bordering the corporation tip, and came to a narrow lane. Once metalled, its surface had crumbled to grit but dandelions and grass tufted the centre. Undisturbed, it seemed more abandoned than the canal though there was evidence that it had been important: the verges were wide, suggesting room for pedestrians; there were passing bays for vehicles and a sign restricting speed. Stimulated by this slight exercise in detection, Nora continued down the lane, its gradual bend roofed with beeches taking her back in the direction of the canal. Then there were high mesh gates and an expanse of concrete and empty sheds. For a moment this fractured, deserted place was the works as Ernest Wagstaff had described them, twisted and disfigured by a solitary bomber who had followed the beckoning glint of the canal; but Ryecroft's had recovered then; the dereliction she looked at was not through explosives but neglect. Under the board painted with its name was a notice, blebbed by storms, announcing closure and referring enquiries half a mile on, to the remaining section of the plant. It was from here that Dick had been made redundant.

Behind these gates everything had halted; three years before, Dick had switched off his furnace, put down his tongs and hammer and strode out with the final shift. After which, the brief noise of the auction, the lorries collecting machinery, then silence shivered by the tinkle of glass and the grate of wrenched downpipes, and at last silence protected by a fence patched against trespassers and topped with barbed wire. The loading bays, the pussy willow and elder sprouting out of the arid grids, the cracked skeleton of a harvester, the sodden and decomposing mattress never absent from deserted wastes, reminded Nora of aerodromes whose use had ceased at the end of the war: runways invaded by plantains, sour latrines and damp-furred huts too cold and still to tempt the homeless to lodge with their ghosts. But that was a disquiet Nora did not share. Though saddened at the decay of Ryecroft's works, she was excited at the thought of whom they had once held and she rested her face against the links of the fence and peered, imagined him emerging from one of the doors, hair gummed to his forehead with sweat, his bared forearms lifted to the wind and his boiler suit unbuttoned to entice a draught round his chest.

Creating him thus in a situation that she could control, she overcame the barrier he had erected and made him a bridge to the place she had left: to the dungarees soaking in a bucket, to the homework pushed to one side of the laid table at the sound of the buzzer, to the compliment at the first relished cup of unstewed tea, to the farcical humour, the uproarious hooting as a guest selected the squeaky cake, to the fortnight-long packing of two cases for the holiday of one precious week. Intellect told her that this was mawkish nostalgia. It forced her to recall the constrictions, the defensive scorn

116

of the unfamiliar, the hearty simplistic pronouncements from which she had escaped. Reason and the critical faculties could argue and condemn but, her face squashed against the fence until her flesh was impressed with the pattern of its mesh, Nora listened to the notes of Dick's flattering whistle, watched him nudge the other apprentices handing out fags, and waved boldly: she would accept next time he asked her out; and felt a movement at her youth's core.

'You're looking more cheerful,' Doris Bentley remarked, watching Nora eat her supper.

'Really? I didn't know I'd looked anything else.'

'Moping, is the word Clifford supplied when I described it. He pointed out that you would be missing your husband.'

'I see him at weekends.'

'That's exactly the answer I gave Clifford. I don't see him all week but I don't mope, I could have told him, but I didn't, of course; men can be so prickly about what touches them. Things are different now I've got company.'

'I'm pleased,' flinching at such a word for her unyielding hours.

'And don't forget I've told Nora she must feel free to give Mr Trafford a ring any time, I reminded him . . .'

'Yes.'

'. . . So she'd do that, wouldn't she, if being away from him is the cause? I said. And I know for a fact that Nora's not miserable – quite the opposite – living here with me.'

'I'm more than satisfied.'

'So I've decided it must be that office,' Doris concluded, triumphant. 'It's the work getting you down.'

'I suppose it does sometimes. There's a lot to think about.'

'Too much, I'd say, with only you there at the present.'

'And Dick.'

'Oh, him. I can't see what use he'll be in an office when all he's ever done is labouring at Ryecroft's.'

'He was a smith!'

'Oh, I'm sorry; I didn't mean to demote him. But whatever he did on the shop floor at Ryecroft's, it won't have given him any practice in office procedure.'

'Which leaves him in about the same position as me.'

'You'll know more about it, bound to. That's where education comes in.'

'Perhaps.' Nora was tired of these flashes of jealousy, not least because they obliged her to defend a man who caused her distress.

'It seems you can trust him with a few bits and bobs anyway,' the other diplomatically pretended a concession. 'The minute you came in I could tell that some of the load's been removed.'

'Yes. I was able to go for a walk.'

'Now that's what I call sensible, especially in this lovely weather, giving yourself a rest for a while. You certainly deserve one, and you'll feel all the better for it when you go in tomorrow.'

She nodded but did not agree. The restoration she had enjoyed in Ryecroft's lane would not survive the reality of the next morning.

'I went out in the lunch hour and bought a punnet of strawberries,' Doris told her. 'It's nice to spoil yourself now and again, and I don't suppose you've had time to notice they're in season. Would you like cream?'

'Please.' Then, providing the awaited appreciation: 'This is a treat.'

'The pleasure's mine. And I can tell you, I shan't be buying any for Clifford. One bite of these, and he'd be out in a rash so it's a fruit I have to forgo, but today I thought: Why not? Nora will help me eat them and I can cover the punnet up in the bin.'

'Whatever for?'

'It'll be for the best. What the eye doesn't see, the heart doesn't grieve over.'

'Do you mean that Clifford would object?'

'I wouldn't put it as strongly as that but it might cause some upset, me buying strawberries for us when I know they don't agree with him.'

'I see,' but Nora wondered whether the offence was imagined in order to give their sharing an illicit zest.

'I've been delving in some old boxes of Mother's,' Doris said. 'There's things I haven't set eyes on for years, not since she packed to move here. The spoons come up nice with a polish, don't they? But of course they aren't the plated variety which can look so garish, not like real silver.'

'They're lovely,' Nora compensated for not having noticed.

'Mother couldn't abide anything common on her table, for high days and holidays, that is. I found something else you might like to see. In fact that's why I started rooting in the boxes; I had an idea Mother might have hidden it away. I mean, stored it somewhere safe,' she corrected quickly. Fetching a limp package, she placed it on a chair and folded back the tissue paper. 'There you are,' holding up the sash. 'It was given to me when I won the competition.'

'It's magnificent.'

'Yes. That's what we thought.' She lifted it to a shoulder and stroked the glossy cloth over a breast. 'I've put on a bit of weight since then, not overmuch, but it's times like these you notice the difference. I don't expect it'd look anything now.'

'Well, not over a twin-set.'

'After they'd announced the result and I'd been given the sash and bouquet, we went into the office – it had been made into a cloakroom just for the night – and Marlene and Clara and Beryl and Joan, they all tried it on.' She hung the broad ribbon across her wrists and handed it over the table to Nora, and as she received it Doris held her breath for a moment, then let the hope go.

'It's beautifully made. Presumably a product of Blygh's.'

'Yes, and it got a mention in the paper on account of the time it took to attach all the sequins, all hand done, you see.'

'May I borrow this so that Mrs Broadbent and her sewers can have a look at it?'

'I'll lend it to you. No, really, I don't mind. It's doing no good shut away. Might as well give it an airing.' Although Nora had not looped the sash round her neck like a garland as Beryl had done and gone round the room doing a hula dance, she had forfeited nothing; Doris could trust her. So she attempted: 'Sometimes I wonder whether it's best to keep the past bottled up.'

The other laughed. 'You're hardly doing that! Here you are, going through boxes!'

Forced to an answering smile, Doris could not bring herself to explain that she had not referred to the sash and she was immediately despondent. To confide had never appeared so possible; this evening they had been getting on so well.

'I really do appreciate the loan, Doris, and we'll take good care of it. What else have you found to show me?'

'They're nothing, just the shorts and top I wore for the competition.' She wished she had not disinterred them.

'Yes, I remember from the photograph. It's difficult to believe, isn't it, that not so many years after this, the mini was in? Do you mind if I take these to show Becky? I don't expect they'd fit?'

'If she's got a waist more than twenty-two inches, they won't.'

'No; this is minute. I suspect that she is intent on exposing as much flesh as she can negotiate for, so these will be a great disappointment.'

Watching Nora refold the properties of a long-ago evening, Doris, miserable, commented to herself: It doesn't make any difference whether you show more or less.

'I can't march on to a catwalk wearing those! You're not calling them shorts!' was Becky's anticipated outrage. 'The zip's down the side! And the only place they fitted was round the waist. She must have had corsets to squeeze herself in.'

Becky's concept of fit was demonstrated by a denim skirt which would have shamed any corset except in the matter of stiffeners, and her sartorial judgement was evidenced by adjustments to the school uniform calculated to enhance the attractions of her sex: the top button of her shirt was unfastened above the pendant of tie casually knotted; the cuffs had been turned back and pushed to bracelet the arms; and the cardigan slung from a shoulder suggested an elegant cape.

'You'll have to wear what was in fashion at the time, Becky.'

'But these are so naff.'

'The girls at Blygh's managed what they could afford.'

'That doesn't mean I have to look like a right old hag.'

'In the end, the decision will be Peter's,' Nora evaded. Soothing prima donnas was not a chore she had envisaged.

'Will he say I have to have my hair like the way you showed me in that magazine? Beehives or something, my auntie says. They're disgusting! Enough to give you the runs.'

'You'll be going to Pam's Place to have your hair styled.'

'Her!' Becky shrieked. 'Do you know, that Mrs Broadbent has been there since the year dot. She can remember hunting in evacuees' heads for fleas.'

'She could be exaggerating, but if she's been a hairdresser for so long, then she's right for the job.'

'Not for my hair, she's not. Do you know she hasn't heard of setting gel? Me and Wayne have to trail right across town to Shearer Magic. Why can't we have them?'

'Probably because they haven't offered.'

'It seems to me I'm going to look a real mess.'

'We'll see that you don't, if only to convince the audience that you deserve to win the contest. What you should be more concerned about is whether you look and behave the right way for the part.' Nora began to appreciate Peter's forthcoming difficulties in producing a group of amateurs. 'You're a character in a play, not Becky Dobson.'

'How many people will think that?'

Since sophisticated audiences frequently failed to make the distinction, this was not an argument to be discounted but, impatient now, Nora told her: 'If you are truly unhappy about Miss Blygh, then you mustn't take it on.'

'I shouldn't want Mr Green to have gone to all the trouble of writing that bit for nothing.'

Trying not to smile at what could be construed as a plucky attempt at blackmail, Nora assured her that Peter would not cut the scene; the only debate was whether Becky played in it.

The girl nodded. 'I suppose he could find someone else. There's plenty wouldn't mind, and Debbie Slingsby'd grab your hand off if you asked her; she doesn't care a toss what she looks like. She's got no pride. If I had legs like hers, I'd either cover them up or buy a razor.'

'Well, you must think about it.'

Becky picked up her bag and dawdled over arranging its straps under the cardigan-cape. 'I wouldn't mind for myself, Nora,' she said hesitantly. 'It's Wayne. He says he'd like to be a GI. Mr Green mentioned them at the meeting and it got Wayne interested. He wouldn't have bothered, but it's the uniform.'

'A uniform has seduced stronger men than Wayne. And women. Good. I'll put him down.'

'I thought you would. That means he'll be there. If it had just been a case of him coming to the performance, I could have thought up something to put him off, but if he's in it, he's there, isn't he? So he'll see.'

Now she heard Becky's true objection to her appearance. More sympathetic, Nora said, 'But Becky, you'll look fine.'

'I thought it'd be a bikini or something nice, but I'll look a cow with my hair backcombed and in shorts like that.'

'These shorts aren't so different from many that are in the shops today, Becky.'

The girl snorted. 'Wayne's very faddy. It'd be as bad if these were cut-offs. He wouldn't be seen dead in *them* now. I know what you're thinking, but you don't need to bother any more.' Then seeing Nora wince: 'I mean, I'm not married to Wayne yet.'

'That's what you want?'

'Of course. I've been going with him since I was fourteen.'

'How old are you now?'

'Sixteen in December.'

'Don't you think that's rather early to make a decision?' tentative because she had no sanction for comment.

'My mam got married when she was eighteen. She says keeping house is better any day than working at Blygh's. Do you know, all she did for three years was sew zips into trousers? She goes back now and again, temporary, when they're short and she needs a bit extra, but never again would she work there full-time. I had to go in to give her a message once and she was sitting in a line, one behind the other, and she was doing the top stitching on pockets. I watched. She was that quick, it was a miracle, and she hadn't time to stop to listen to me, just cocked her head, but before she had hooked the jacket on the rail and pushed it down to the next machinist, there was another one waiting. You get out of there as fast as I did, she tells me. Only there's no need. She always says that stuck to one of those machines you're no better than one yourself. In your own house, you're the boss.'

'I understand that, Becky, but surely there are other alternatives to working there.' She had almost said: Better things you can do. 'You're taking O levels.'

'I'm doing an English O level and four CSEs. That's not much bottle when it comes to getting a job.'

'It might be worth looking round. You don't know what you are capable of till you've tried.'

'I couldn't do that. I mean, what would be the point? I've never been in the top stream. I reckon you're best sticking to what you can do.'

The girl depressed her. She remembered Don Clamp's account and felt his dilemma. Yet she could not entirely deplore Becky's resignation; what could be scorned as cowardice could equally well be complimented as realistic good sense. And the uncomfortable fact was that they both stood in clothes produced by this system. To release the regiments at work in Blygh's, they would have to turn back the clock a century.

'I shan't mind Blygh's all that much. It won't be for long. You can put up with most things when you know that, like school. Wayne's hoping to go as an apprentice electrician; he's cleverer than me. He works out that in three years, maybe four, we can save enough if we're careful.'

Nora wanted to shout: No! Planning is for later; you are too young to shrink your life to the measure of one man, to a post office savings book, too young not to take risks, Becky, my daughter. But her own rendered her helpless; they had provided her with no practice in this kind of talk.

'I shouldn't have kept you so long. You'll think I'm a real gasser and I'm not generally. Only I can't get past that hair and those shorts. I just couldn't stand Wayne laughing. You can't afford to neglect yourself, can you? Men like their girlfriends to look nice. I don't have to tell you that. If you don't mind me saying, Nora, I wish I'd got a blouse and skirt like that.'

The compliment was innocent of guile, but, shocked, Nora admitted the care she had taken with her appearance during the last month: the selection of clothes, the attention to her hair, the daily manicure, and the calculated casualness of becoming postures opposite him at the desk. Humiliated, she knew she could never confess this to her daughters; their brash independence would condemn such stratagems. But Becky was no stranger to them; for her, they were unquestioned necessity, and Nora regarded the girl, seeing herself.

'Look, Becky, perhaps we can modify the hairstyle and I don't suppose anyone would challenge us if we altered the design of the shorts.'

'Oh, if you would! But I don't want to get you into trouble.'

'That's not likely. If I need to, I'll find some way of squaring the change with Mr Green.'

'You look exhausted,' her husband remonstrated. 'I don't like to interfere, but don't you think you're taking this project too much to heart? If it makes you so miserable, why don't you give it up?'

'I've had more on my mind while Peter's been away. The load will lighten when he gets back.'

Chapter Eleven

'Any gum, chum?'

'That'll do for tonight. Rehearsal's over,' Peter told them.

'Naw, be a mate, chum, and gi'us some gum.'

'Any gum, chum?'

'Look, if you aren't home soon, you'll get me into trouble,' locking the playground gates. As the boys began to circle other members of the cast walking ahead towards the public house, he groaned, 'My God! They learn fast.'

'Three words! And two of them rhyme.'

'I meant the begging.'

'Better than asking for cigarettes, and they aren't getting either. You're not tempting the youth of Neatham into bad habits.'

Patient, she humoured him. First, as always after rehearsals, there was some ridiculous worry which postponed expression of his true anxiety.

At last: 'How did it go?'

Nora could have answered quite genuinely, 'Fine; it's coming on marvellously,' but at such a moment compliment made him suspicious. So she had learnt to hedge. 'I can see what you're after in the scene when Neatham gets its first sighting of American servicemen: the flurry and wonder and the girls almost instantly blossoming with sex.'

'God! Did I say that?'

'No; and you didn't mention orgasm either.'

'That's a relief,' unsmiling. 'You don't think I've gone over the top? I know the situation is a bit of a cliché, but it happened. It's there, hinted at, in the reminiscences. You remember Joseph Raby's? He said that the women had "to do for themselves" while the men were away and "there were some not slow to take advantage. Maybe it's all rumours, the Yanks I met were respectable enough young men, considering."'

'Yes. The usual oblique style. It's OK, Peter, really.'

'Well, I thought it was rather messy tonight. I want those two groups on the pavement to be absolutely absorbed in gossip, then a switch to stunned silence when the GIs walk down the street, but I just can't stop them from anticipating what they are going to do.'

'If you'd like to explain the moves to me, I'll go over them with that lot in the small room while you're rehearsing other scenes.'

'I'd be grateful for that. Co-producer, eh?'

'Assistant. I notice you've restricted the Americans' girlfriends to spinsters, despite Joseph's hint.'

Isabel had said: Don't talk to me about Yanks. Not after our Dot.

'I'll say.' He was more cheerful now. 'It's only just over forty years ago, so any skeletons in closets are still jangling, I imagine.'

They had reached the public house. Through the window she could see a game of darts in progress, Dick checking his position on the mat before his throw.

Isabel had insisted: Taking advantage of our Jack's Dot when the one who should have been with her by rights was away. I'm past judging now, but I can't pretend I was sorry the day they went.

As they entered the Admiral Nelson, Peter said, 'My turn to buy the drinks,' and struggled towards the bar.

'You may have my seat,' Don Clamp offered as she reached him through the crush. 'I've twenty-eight essays to mark before dawn. Would you mind conveying my thanks to Peter? Good of him to invite me into a rehearsal.'

'A sort of thank you for your children's poetry; but the rehearsals aren't in camera. Peter likes folk dropping in. That helps to accustom the cast to an audience and it's good public relations.'

'No problem with the latter. The play's attracting a lot of attention now. That, I'd say, can be attributed to your very capable promotion.'

'Thank you; I can always take praise,' forgetting Peter's generosity. It was the other's parsimony she remembered.

'After all the work you've put into this play, I hope that you're getting something out of it yourself.'

'Is that relevant?'

'I think so. Giving so much time to this project, surely you can be excused a little self-interest, some expectation of personal benefits?'

'I'm learning a lot.'

'No doubt. But I meant satisfactions.'

'They are more elusive.'

'Perhaps you will capture some.'

He was not prying as Doris had pried; he was offering support, the reason for which indicated an observing eye. This alarmed her, but she was relieved that he had chosen to speak through abstractions. They were undemanding and protected them both.

'I've almost accepted that such satisfactions are a chimera,' she confided silently as he left.

Then Dick was at her shoulder, carrying a dripping glass. 'With Pete's regards. He's just taken over my darts.'

As if bearing the drink obliged him to act as Peter's surrogate, he did not discourage the busy rearrangement of customers on the settle and sat down.

It was unusual to be with him outside the office and the situation irked her. The crowd offered no shelter; she felt like an inexperienced girl at a first meeting anxious to disguise nervousness made worse by a public place.

'I don't know how anyone can talk against this noise,' she excused.

'They aren't here for talk.'

The rattle of a collecting box saved her. 'You'll give, Mr Coulbeck, won't you?'

'On the scrounge again, Peggy?' His hand was already in a pocket. 'I'll have to have a word with the Social, see if I can qualify for any extra, the amount I dish out to you.'

'God will reward, Mr Coulbeck.'

'Maybe, but he takes his time about it.'

'It is easier for a camel to go through the eye of a needle than for a rich man to enter into the kingdom of God.'

'You say that every time, Peggy, and if you're trying to give me a helpful shove by relieving me of cash, then I have to remind you that I don't suffer from the disadvantage of a rich man.'

'In that case, blessed are the meek, for they shall inherit the earth,' she laughed. 'And the lady?'

'That's for her,' Dick answered, dropping in another coin. 'Though why I should bother, I don't know. You're growing slack. We haven't even had a tune tonight.'

'The landlord wasn't in favour this evening, but I'll leave you a hymn sheet,' laying it on the table.

'Right. That's just the job. We've got very noisy neighbours, you see, Peggy, and I can stride round the house now, singing hymns at the top of my voice. That'll pay them back.'

'You're a caution, you are. May the good Lord give strength to those that have to put up with you,' glancing at Nora. Then for a second a veined hand covered his.

Astonished by this exchange, Nora would have found difficulty in suppressing comment had Peggy not been replaced immediately by another.

'It's last orders,' Mandy announced. 'So I thought if you were drinking up, you could see me home.'

'I don't plan to leave any in the glass, but I might take longer than you were banking on, Mandy.'

'I can wait,' she told him, unperturbed.

'You'd not be advised to do that, else you might find yourself staying out all night.' The affability had vanished; the shoulders were tense; the face, impacted anger. The change was swift and complete.

Mandy was not to be thus intimidated. 'Why's that, then? Weren't you thinking to go home?'

'What I might be thinking of doing is none of your business. Since when have I had to lay out to you what's in my mind? But I know what muck's in yours.'

'It's your mind needs cleaning up because if you think that, then you must have a guilty conscience. All I asked was for you to see me home.'

'You don't need me to see you home! It's still light out there, Mandy. Or was you imagining somebody might accost you on the way? I don't think there'ud be much hope of that, when they got close.'

'You rotten bastard,' against the quavering. 'I told Ross you'd see me home. What'll he say?'

'I can tell you what he'll say: nowt, because you never told him. You haven't been in the habit of waiting on me this past month, after rehearsals. It's only tonight you've come across. And don't think I don't know why. You're not talking about me seeing you home, Mandy, but the other way round. And I don't need no chaperon. I can look after myself.'

'If you feel like that, I'll be going, then. I'll tell Barbara you're still here.' She turned with a flounce but was jerked back.

'You'll tell her nothing, do you understand that?' His voice grated with threat. 'I'm not standing for you, Mandy, or no one else, putting anything between me and her, and just you remember that, you bloody busybody. Anything, anything, any single thing that crops up with me and Babs is between us. Between us, you understand. And there's no place for interfering buggers egging us on.'

His eyes checking on her departure, he acknowledged his audience with: 'That woman would make a saint use language,' and drank slowly, rinsing it out of his mouth. 'It's always been a wonder to me how her and Barbara could come out of the same stable. It's about time Ross straightened her out.'

Nora was repelled by this brawling; she would have criticised his abuse but, its cause an interference she also resented, she said nothing.

But he had refused to be intimidated by Mandy's convention, as he had refused to be weeks before in the office on that evening in May. When for a short time, as they had talked about Tryphena Freiston, she was certain that their thoughts had come together, when there had been an intimation of shared desire. Remembering, she could not dismiss her belief in that evening's unity. Nor, as it crept upon her, this night's hope.

For which reason, when he interpreted her silence with: 'Forget that woman; she's not worth it; I'll walk you home,' she rose with him; though her mind insisted that she did so only because the people along the settle were squeezing to let her pass and because their appetite for sensation had already been handsomely supplied in the previous scene.

However, on the pavement she managed a salve to her pride, saying, 'I don't have to have an escort but thanks for the offer.'

'You're not telling me you're bothered by that Mandy?'

'Why should I be? I'm not interested in her opinion. I don't wish you to walk home with me because I don't want to be used.'

'Used?'

'I'm not prepared to be crutch for your ego.'

'You have a funny way of putting things at times, Nora. I don't know what you mean.' But he did and was not disconcerted because her words were a token, a sop to her intellect; she could not make them sting, and that he had heard. So he was encouraged and answered, 'I could do with the walk, that's all. It's a lovely evening. Twilight, best part of the day.'

'Some people would say that was dawn.'

'I wouldn't know about that. I'm never up that time nowadays, and when I was, I was still too asleep to notice. Just look at them swallows!' raising his face to the racing and swoops above them.

She could not resist the correction. 'They're swifts.'

'How do you know that?'

'By the shape of the wings, and if they came in close you'd see they have neither the pale belly of swallows nor the white saddle of house martins.'

'Would I now? I didn't suspect you knew about that sort of thing! In which case, come on. I'll show you a bit of Neatham you'll like.'

Later she tried to persuade herself that it was only curiosity that caused her to follow him.

'It's not so far when you take the short cuts.' Quickly leaving the streets, he guided her down passages, along cinder ways between the backs of houses, through dock and nettles camouflaging rubble on stretches of waste ground.

'Mind where you put your feet,' he cautioned. 'This used to be a regular path through to the works but there hasn't been much call for it recently.'

'Did you use it?'

'Every day.'

With that he became expansive. 'I'd drop in first for a packet of fags from Maudie Thompson at the beer-off down there, open all hours, and even when she did manage to lock up shop and try to take the weight off her legs, she'd never refuse anyone knocking at the back. Done that myself dozens of times when I was a youngster, mostly for a quarter of tea; Mother never anticipated running out. Seemed to regard the caddy as a widow's cruse despite years of evidence to the contrary. Maudie was dearer than the supermarket, of course, but I still went. It was a ritual, a kind of pacing myself. If I could be at her counter by twenty-three minutes past seven, I knew I'd be inside the gate by clocking-in time.'

In five months he had not told her so much about himself and he rewarded her further, describing friends living in streets they crossed, inviting her to enjoy, showing himself a charming companion.

'Nearly there now. The other side of this lane, a meadow away, is the canal. I'll have to break back the hedge; it's grown through the fence,' careful lest she were scratched, helping her through. 'We're making for some old sand pits the other side, but we'll take a little humpbacked bridge further along.'

They could have crossed by the footbridge over the lock, and she took his choice to indicate that he remembered her response to his description of what had happened there, and was affected by his tact.

'Why the old sand pits?'

'Because they have plenty of birds, water hens and mallards and some coots. I played round them as a kid, swam in them, too, only we never let on; they're dangerous. Don't worry, I'll see you don't fall in,' sensing a hesitation.

Understanding, she answered, 'It's not that. It's that I know this lane, I think.'

'Up there it leads to the old works. You've been along it?' surprised.

'Yes.'

A memory opened. Isabel had said: Ryecroft's Lane was a popular place.

Sitting down, Nora pretended to search for a pebble in one of her sandals and to hunt between her toes. The grass was deep there at the verges; already seeded, it tickled her skin; the scent from crushed stems was liquid and sweet.

'I didn't know you'd been wandering around.'

'One way of getting out of a stuffy office.' She did not add: And away from you.

'I could've told you what to look for.' Undoubtedly, she thought, but without bitterness. 'Not exactly beauty spots, but nice.'

'I enjoy exploring without help.'

She delayed further, placing the second sandal in the grass and massaging her tanned flesh while he crouched beside her waiting. Afraid lest any moment he would suggest they continue as he had planned, she tried to prevent him with inconsequential talk. 'You left this,' going to a pocket and offering the hymn sheet. 'Peggy would be disappointed.'

He screwed it up, chuckling. 'Not her. She knows where I stand.'

An hour earlier she could not have said it, but: 'You seem to contribute regularly.'

'That's right.' The tone was easy; he was relaxed, half reclining in the grass.

So: 'I was puzzled.'

'I'm not surprised. It's not that I've ever fancied myself banging a tambourine.' He laughed. 'Only, they did something once I respect them for. I suppose there's no harm in telling. They christened a babby one time that nobody else would.'

'I don't understand.'

'Well, no; it does take some crediting. Her mam went round to every church and chapel in Neatham and none of them would do the christening, till she arrived at the Sally Army.'

'But that's dreadful! I haven't come across anything like that before.'

'You hadn't come across Neatham before this February end.'

He had remembered the month. Pleased, she asked, 'You knew the mother well?'

'God Almighty, no! It happened before the First World War, only my grandad knew the circumstances and he always had a shilling ready for their box. I picked up the habit from him, along with the feeling. I suppose it wasn't so unusual in those days, with the number of illegitimate kids there were about, but it just happens I know about that one, and that particular piece of charity. It mattered more then, getting baptised.'

'It mattered more having a bastard, too.'

'You're right there. They were outcasts both of them, mother and babby, and that started before they arrived at the font. It was never forgotten. They would carry the stigma for the rest of their lives. At least they did round here. Still do, except folks are a bit more careful the way they talk about it.'

He was more critical of Neatham than he had been on former occasions. In referring to the rejected woman his voice was compassionate; he did not attempt to excuse the malice she had received. This, Nora thought, indicated a trust between them.

'You get short shrift round here unless you toe the line,' he added.

'What happened to that uncle of Joseph Raby's that went to prison for being a conscientious objector?'

Plucking grasses, he answered, 'Samuel? I don't know. Maybe, by the time he was let out, people wanted to forget.'

Beyond the lane and one field lay the canal; along the towpath was the lock.

Isabel had explained: She could see no reason why she shouldn't stand up and declare. Fifty year after I went to find where they had laid her, at the end of the cemetery that hadn't been blessed. There was nothing to see but a great heap of rotting wreaths.

Nora shuddered.

'We'd best be getting on. It's turning chilly,' he said, considerate.

'I'm not cold.'

'Someone walked over your grave?'

'I'd rather not put it like that.'

'Look, Nora, like Sam Raby, people don't always take it lying down, accept what's doled out to them. Some folks stand up against the spit. Or their families do.' He paused. 'That woman I told you about. She was one of the Moorbys. You'll have forgot. It was Florence Moorby that started that row in the street when the Wagstaffs were flitting.'

'She had the baby?'

'Oh, no. Its mam wouldn't have dared start bawling for her rights. Florence was its auntie, and she reckoned Jessie, her sister, should've been let have the house, seeing how old man Wagstaff was the father.'

'Ernest's father?'

'Yes. Got her in the family way while he was courting Ernest's mam. It happened, even if you were chapel. And from Ernest's account, Florence was a clever devil right enough, saying the wheel-barrow covered with the tablecloth looked like a whited sepulchre and it was a fine joke that when it came to the Day of Judgement, the Wagstaffs had so much to hide. It was no wonder the wife wouldn't let Ernest's old man forget it; that's why she kept on about it and why he'd go off the deep end and try to shut her up.'

He had known this when the episode was discussed, yet he had not told Peter. Neither had he admitted it to her when she had challenged him later, though his eyes had told her that he appreciated her suspicion. It was not unreasonable that he should choose not to reveal it to her; but to hide it from Peter, whose work depended on such assistance, was indefensible. This was a secrecy different from his keeping her ignorant of his job; this was practically dishonest.

'And you didn't tell Peter.'

'I wasn't forced to,' with a flash of the old petulance. 'Because he was writing a play about Neatham didn't oblige me to give him just what he wanted. I can't see what the bother's all about. Peter hasn't even put Florence Moorby in!'

Alarmed, she saw him tightening a shoe lace, heard him propose they move, heard him say that it was too late now to look at the sand pits: by the time they reached them you wouldn't see a hand in front of your face.

'Well, it's been a healthy walk,' unable to say: The pits will still be there some other time.

However, lingering because she must rescue the evening from sulks, that was not how she wished it to end, she said, 'I remember your comment that there was more in the story than simply an argument over a house. Poor Peter! There he was, admiring you for a talent in textual analysis when really you were hinting at what you knew! I reckon that amounts to having the playwright in your pocket.'

He laughed, flattered as she had intended. 'And why not? That bit's my story more than Ernest Wagstaff's because, as he said, he never got to the bottom of it, so deciding what came out was my privilege.'

She did not argue. She could not suggest that by undertaking to work on the project he had accepted certain principles. She could not say that by just so much as he evaded those, his loyalty to Peter was lessened. His was another code.

'First thing, knowing the circumstances, I'd got my mind fixed on the Moorbys and was against what happened there being stirred up. It didn't seem fair to me that Florence should be put in a bad light when all she was doing was trying to grab something for her own that

132

needed it. It struck me you might have an opinion,' reminding her that he had pointed out that section. She smiled, grateful for that brief impulse to confide. 'Then, second thing, I decided I'd got it arse end up. Because, you see, if that bit went into the play, the people who knew the story wouldn't be laughing at Florence Moorby; they'd be remembering the Wagstaffs – very big at the Wesleyan – and they might say that Joseph's favourite hymn had the right idea: "Jesus, the sinner's Friend, to Thee,/Lost and undone, for aid I flee." In the end I reckoned that people'd say that scene showed the Wagstaffs' reputation getting it in the neck, and they'd be clapping to see that bunch of hypocrites being taken to court.'

'Often there can be many different interpretations of the same scene.' Had she interpreted him incorrectly? He had considered inviting her opinion. 'Those are not only influenced by the producer,' she added, her voice breathy, 'but by what each individual person brings to it.'

'You know more about that than me,' but not sneering. 'Only, how I saw it was that Jessie Moorby who'd taken their medicine, though sixty years dead might have got her own back a bit. But it still wouldn't have mattered whether folks realised that or not. It would've made a little rattle in the air, and I'd have been satisfied. That would've been enough.'

'Yes.'

A private reparation. His emotion was unexpected, apt for the masking shadows, and she thought: He would protect a woman whom others threw out; he can embrace the outsider.

Though Isabel warned: There was no peace for our Dot, my brother Jack's girl.

Preparing to join him, shaking the confetti of seeds from her dress, Nora felt the stems against her calves, saw above her head branches pricked by the sky's opalescence, peered at the trees' boles thickening with night. And she heard Isabel repeat: I suppose it must've happened down that Ryecroft's Lane.

'I'm glad that Peter doesn't have the American servicemen strolling down here,' she said.

'He's got more sense! How could he do that?'

'Anything's possible in the theatre.'

'So I'm beginning to learn. Why are you glad?'

'Sentiment, I suppose. Like some stories, places too can be sacred.'

'You wouldn't count this as one if you'd worked back there.'

'That's likely, but I didn't. It's how I feel about it after talking recently with Isabel Driffield.'

'But Pete's finished the play! He doesn't need any more histories.'

Such material might have been useful in the publication that was his special task, but he did not mention it. Later she acknowledged to herself that, still retaining this jealous ownership, he kept her shut out; then, the moment was too delicate to admit fracturing thought.

'I've got into the habit of visiting her. I'm not sure whether she wants me to; it's hard to tell. I go because she worries me. She seems so lonely.'

'That must be her choice. I expect they'd let her into a home if she wanted.'

'I'm sure there would be no difficulty about that, and she has a son. He visits occasionally Not that he's made very welcome, or so I suspect. Luckily she has a cat; that seems to provide some kind of companionship. But when I go, she doesn't have a lot to say.'

Out of the long silences and Isabel's few words, Nora remembered: I haven't been near the place, not since our Dot. I reckon it was there it happened.

He had forgotten why she had mentioned Isabel. In the tunnel of trees he was a shadow, but solid, almost too swift for her feet.

I'll not say more about her. It's over and done with. There's the living to think of. And the old woman's cackle had been disquieting.

'Here, let's be having your hand,' Dick said as she stumbled against him. 'You don't know this lane like me.' His face leant over her, its features ambiguous, its colour taken from the passing dusk; and as he guided her over the ruts his hand was warm over hers, making her secure, no longer displaced. In the looping darkness, distinctions vanished.

You can put two and two together as well as me, the voice came, impatient.

She had thought the old woman asleep.

You must make what you can of it. Mebbe you can get to the bottom of it. All I have to say is, what a story there'd be if our Dot could speak from the grave.

My God, he was beautiful, but it was his shyness that got me at first and that look, like a young kid begging but expecting you to say no. And all he was asking was for me to walk across the floor and invite him for a dance. It was the ladies' excuse me. The floor was a mile wide and his eyes were on me for every inch but they slid away as soon as I reached him checking first one side then the other for the soldier I could be addressing though I was looking straight at him. The first thing I noticed was his hands, a sort of faded maroon in the palms and between the fingers but with the brown filling up the lines. I mentioned that once, after, and he made a joke, saying it was because, being in the cookhouse, he was always scrubbing up. A cut above me, I told him, because I couldn't even keep my nails a nice length greasing ball bearings. My answer astonished him, though it was one of those things you say, casual; it wasn't meant to make a point. I suppose it could have been the first time anyone had said he was a cut above them.

It didn't happen the first night, nor yet the second. The amazing thing was, he'd never done it before, while there was I not twenty and with a young one near eighteen months. And I know at first he was trying to hold off, rubbing my ring round and round between his finger and thumb as if it was a charm that would stop us doing the wrong thing, but it didn't work because I loved him and that mattered more than anything else. I'd stopped worrying about what Mam and Dad might be thinking, me not coming home straight after the dance. I said to myself, the babby's safe in his cot and I'm a married woman now. I can do what I like.

I had to help him when we did it first time, with him showing me because I didn't know how, Eddie had always been that quick, but I knew the reason without being told. It was because where he came from it wasn't allowed, not illegal but still not customary. So he was going against strictures and he was going against the Bible, too, me being married. It was the thought of Eddie that bothered him most, no matter what I said to him, because it was wrong what we were doing and besides that he had a sort of fellow feeling for Eddie out there in Burma which he said was nothing but jungle and flies. So when it worked, him showing me, there's no wonder he said it was a greater victory than any that General Eisenhower would ever dream up.

After that it was easier and what I did was not in order to help him but because he liked it; I didn't tell that I did as well, but I think he guessed. He was that sort of man, whereas Eddie never had any idea what I was thinking. There was something he couldn't understand, though, and that was how I could go with him when I already had someone, because he never heard me say a word against Eddie. I don't think he really believed that I loved him as well, especially since

I'd known him only a few weeks. He wanted me to love him because that took away some of the guilt but he didn't really believe me when I told him I did. And I didn't want to talk about it, not as much as him; I'd rather listen to stories about his folks as he called them. Because it wasn't kindness that made me do it, like he once suggested, or hating Eddie, or a daredevil shrugging at the risks. After all the rowing about me going to the dance – Dad even said that being a matron I ought to act like one, and if they'd guessed what he was, besides being an American, I'd have been thrashed – after all the rowing, by the time they'd finished you wouldn't have thought there was any difference between dancing with a soldier and sleeping with him, and to tell you the honest truth, not doing it after all that seemed such a waste. Anyway, I think that's how I felt the first night, but if I did, no longer than that. I'd say that waste was still the way I looked at it, only not for that reason. I was thinking it was a waste having feelings and bottling them up; and I couldn't see how I was doing Eddie any harm. I didn't love him any less.

Soon we didn't depend on the dances. We'd meet whenever he had a pass and our favourite place was the lane down to Ryecroft's, the only snag being we had to wait till the night shift had gone in. It was August time and the grass was high; there were places under the trees where you couldn't be seen. At least, I thought so, but I was daft because we could have gone to Timbuktoo and done it and somebody would've found out.

Afterwards it would be like pitch. I could never see a thing, but he was more sure-footed than me and sometimes, with my hand in his as he guided me round the potholes, I thought that was the best bit, in the dark. I could pretend I was black, like him.

Chapter Twelve

'You're not planning to go back to the Centre, are you, Nora?' She shouldn't have put it like that. The other gave her one of her looks.

'Yes. There's a rehearsal.'

'That play ought to be good by the time you've finished with it. They've been practising for weeks.'

'Five or six, I suppose it must be by now.'

'And it's not being shown till October! I never knew it took so long.'

'It doesn't with a professional company; these recruits have to be drilled move by move, and however enthusiastic they are in theory, they don't all appreciate the necessity to turn up regularly. So often there isn't the full cast.'

'It would be a shock if there was. They soon tire of anything costing them an effort.' She could sense the other tutting to herself. It was a constant puzzle to her why Nora should always take their part. 'Though I must admit, when it comes to this play, a good few seem to be putting their backs into it.' She added the concession quickly. She wished to rescue the talk from disapproval. That was not how she wished the evening to proceed.

'I'd say there are a dozen, probably two, who seem to do little else.'

One of them being, of course, that man. 'In that case, I'd have thought you could give yourself a rest, Nora. You've been at it all day.' She lifted the coffee machine out of its hiding place in the top cupboard and placed it carefully on the fitted unit by the electric point. 'What you need is a nice relaxed evening.'

'You may be right, but that's a pipe dream at the moment. I want to see how the play's progressing. It's over a week since I went to a rehearsal. Every evening last week I spent at the Institute with a gaggle of women making paper flowers.'

So that was the reason she'd got back earlier. Watch him turning his hand to paper flowers! That other night it must have been after rehearsal, but perhaps if Doris could manage a little cunning, that wouldn't happen again. Best start was to delay her; she was pleased she'd folded the filter paper ready and placed it in the top. Now it was just a question of measuring the grains and pouring in the water up to the mark. She'd been practising all weekend. Clifford had told her that he couldn't understand why she'd gone to such expense; if she'd asked, he would have looked round for something more reasonably priced – the direct sales warehouse near him did special offers; even the gadget in Mr Wilkes's office was nothing like such an extravagant little job, and he hoped that she wasn't going to be forever playing with it; she knew he wasn't fond, the way it could upset his stomach; much more of the stuff and it would be chafing his system all week; he feared he might be taken badly at work.

'You'll have time for a cup of coffee,' she stated, flicking the switch. 'It won't be long before it starts perking.'

'Have I seen that before?' the other asked, noticing at last.

'No, you won't have.' But the question had been only a polite gesture and, disappointed, Doris said, 'It's been up there years, but you get into lazy habits, by yourself.'

'I can't believe that. And if you ever did, I imagine that Clifford would help you out of them.'

She wasn't quite sure how to take that, particularly as Nora was rinsing her plate and cutlery under the tap instead of filling the sink with bubbling suds, but she said, trying for gaiety, 'That's why I'd have to make sure he didn't know about them.' She didn't like hearing herself saying that; it sounded disloyal, but you can't satisfy everybody, and she had an excuse. She turned and noisily inhaled the scent of the coffee to hide the sniffs.

'It's very tempting,' Nora agreed, 'but I don't think I have time.'

'It's not fifteen minutes past yet.' She must not sound aggrieved; that would be a mistake. She must appear unaffected, light-hearted, persuading her to stay with amusing talk. 'Just listen at that noise!' she tried. 'It's a real show-off, this. Some just pop away daintily, acting respectable like old ladies hiccuping into their handkerchiefs, but not this one. It's really belching, you need ear plugs. The way that water seethes and the noise it makes, you'd think it was suffering from indigestion.'

Nora seemed to appreciate that. 'With flatulence,' she said.

'What an idea! If that's what it puts you in mind of, I'll carry the tray into the lounge and we won't be disturbed by such thoughts.' She had exhausted any silly notions about the spouting water.

'Please don't bother, Doris. Since you've started the coffee, I'll have a cup but I must be quick.'

'It hasn't finished yet.'

'You'll have to slide the jug out and pour before any more coffee splashes through.'

Obediently Doris followed the instructions. Attempts to delay her had been futile; they had been temporary stratagems which foolishly she had thought would be enough. She had imagined Nora saying, 'Heavens, is that the time? If so, I don't think I'll bother to go along. After all, I've already put in a good day's graft. You make me too comfortable, Doris,' or, 'You're leading us into bad ways,' as Beryl used to tease. She had not imagined beyond that. Elated by her purchase, by its promise of success, she had not prepared any other persuasion, and she had not developed the evening. It had rested in her mind furnished with cushions dropped without attention to tidiness, lit by the electric fire which would gild her mother's best silver tray and hold back the lurking dusk.

'It's hot,' she rebuked the other's haste. 'I wouldn't want you to scald your mouth.'

Nora shook her head, impatient, blowing into the cup.

The machine had finished its work; the last drops of water were sinking through the sodden grains; the level of coffee in the jug was lower than it should have been by the volume of one cup. Over the quiet thing, Doris whispered, 'I bought it specially.'

Thinking that she referred to the coffee, the other answered, 'It's a decent blend. One of the more reliable of the vacuum packed.'

She should have bought beans, only then she would have had to buy a grinder as well. Not that one would have made any difference, she thought, her eyes on Nora. Helpless, she knew that only a few seconds remained for her before the final gulp.

And the woman could not pretend to linger, take her time, appreciate the offering. With the hand not round the cup she was buttoning her jacket, arranging files and papers ready to tuck under an arm.

Miserable, Doris asked, 'You'll not be late in?'

'I don't know, but I've checked that I have my key.'

She was not paying attention. She had not understood what Doris was trying to say. She had set down the cup and picked up her bag. Having suffered Doris, she was at last free to do as she had planned, her expression eager, her faith in the evening to come making her hands deft.

'Well, I don't mind sitting up once in a while.' It was something Doris could do, denied the first place. She had heard it said that the one confided in sometimes grew more important than the other.

She had not expected that to stop her. Nora was already at the back door, but she turned. Encouraged, Doris felt the tingle of a small hope.

'Sit up? Whatever for?'

'I don't feel easy till you've got back, and generally there are things I can find to do, pottering about, so it's no inconvenience; but the week before last, on the Wednesday, I'd got through everything I could think of doing and I'd prepared the kitchen for the morning, so I thought: I'll give it till midnight before I take steps. Then I heard you at the door and rushed upstairs. I look such a fright in rollers.'

'I can't believe it! I'm a grown woman, Doris. I've knocked about. I haven't had anyone wait up for me since I left home.'

'Probably not. But Neatham's a new town to you and while you're my paying guest I have to know that you're safe.' At least she'd been able to admit as far as that, even though she supposed it sounded ridiculous.

'That's ridiculous. Please don't stay up again; I'd find the possibility very inhibiting.'

Which was an argument for going past bedtime if ever there was one! Cheered, Doris told her: 'I don't know that I can promise that.'

'Then be it on your head.' But she did not reach for the door. Her eyes were on the fitted unit, considering; it seemed as if, for the first time that evening, her mind had pulled from him.

'You haven't drunk any of the coffee, after going to all that trouble,' she reprimanded.

'I'll have some when I've tidied up.'

'There isn't a thing out of place, Doris.'

'That depends on how you look at it. At the moment everything's out of the new place I'm about to find for it.' When you were feeling a bit happier, you could sometimes find your way to a joke. Beryl always said that those weeks before the competition having Doris around was better than living with Frankie Howerd. 'And there are other things that might be better for a change round,' she continued, because the other's smile had been an inspiration. 'I'm thinking of requesting Clifford to move his things out of your room.'

'Why's that?' the other asked wonderingly. She now leant against the door, a position not for leaving but for keeping out intruders.

'You're in it for longer each week than he is, aren't you? When you consider, it's not sensible, you having so little room to hang your clothes and him taking a whole fitted wardrobe for what he parks here just to see him through a couple of days.' She had never realised before how exciting it was to make things up, what Nora called

140

improvisation. 'Really, he can get by with a change of slacks and a sweater, and he can keep those in the airing cupboard. Anything else he thinks he might need he can always bring on the day.'

'But there's no necessity to prohibit half the man's gear, Doris! I've managed satisfactorily up to now.'

'No, I've been remiss. If you're not careful, you can get so as you take the first idea that comes and that was: it was Clifford's room because there were his clothes staking a claim,' she smiled, 'and he comes regularly. But so do you, and you stay longer.'

'The comparison isn't valid; and I would say that length of stay is less important than another factor, permanence.'

'I wouldn't call it that but I suppose you could say that he's formed the habit and it'd be no bad thing to have a bit of a shake-up.'

'Look, Doris, it isn't worth making an issue about providing a little more room for my clothes.'

She laughed at the way Nora had missed her point. Sometimes these clever ones could be so slow on the uptake whereas her feelings were racing at such a pace. 'I wouldn't go to the trouble over just that,' she assured her. 'It's not only his things forever littering the house like a lodger's on full bed and board; it's the way the weekends slip by with him under my feet so I can never get myself properly turned round. I've been thinking I'd suggest an alteration. That would give me time for plenty of baking and bottoming the house. Ready for Monday.'

Nora offered no answer to that, looking so taken aback that Doris giggled, and as she went on she could hear that her voice had almost a trill in it because there was no hurrying to go to rehearsal now.

'I've begun to suspect that I'm not cut out for all this coming and going, and showing an interest on Friday evening when I'd rather give my mind up to something else. That can be as good as company any day, and I've got all of that I can want for during the week.'

She was surprised to notice that Nora looked embarrassed; perhaps she would feel awkward herself listening to talk like that, but she had nothing to go on. And she would have liked to tell her something else but didn't because she wanted to save it, they had hours ahead of them and you shouldn't spend all your sparklers in one go. She wanted to tell Nora something she had just learnt, something she hadn't known five minutes before, and that was: it was a waste having feelings and bottling them up.

But at the moment it seemed she had to be careful not to overdo it. Perhaps she'd gone too fast; perhaps you had to lead up to it more gently. She didn't know; she'd never had any practice. She didn't wish to be thought crude. Nora would go all cold and critical if she thought that, which was a manner she couldn't bear. It could be that, just now, she'd been too direct; maybe the right way, the polite way, was to start with hints.

'If you consider, it could be of benefit to Clifford to have a rest from coming here every Friday. He's always complaining of jobs crying out for attention in his flat. He might even take the chance to look round him and I wouldn't voice an objection; the arrangement here can't be entirely satisfactory though to do him justice he's never intimated a requirement for any other, but there are times when I get the impression he'd be happy to settle down. I've never let it come to the fore because I was content to let the matter rest as it was; and it worked out perfectly well till you started sharing his room.' She paused; that sounded clumsy and wrong. 'You're not to blame. It's entirely my decision who stays in my house; all you've done is shown we were in need of a change. I was, I can see that now; I'd got too set in my ways, and it'll be nice, a real tonic, to regard the weeks in a different light. Saturday and Sunday I'll be able to do at my leisure; I'll enjoy that. There are some pillow slips that came from my mother's bottom drawer and never been on a bed, the most beautiful linen, and for years I've been saying I'd embroider them for that spare room but up to now I've lacked enough motive; I look forward to starting on them. And I'll out that old mirror; you could do with a pretty cheval glass, a woman likes to see her full reflection, not like a man. I'll have time to pay attention to more than the everyday comforts, things that wouldn't have been appreciated but that I'll be glad to occupy myself with now, knowing they'll be seen the same way. I have quite an artistic bent. You may not have noticed, but I have. Only it hasn't been much in demand.'

She laughed, unable to disguise the happiness, because Nora was dumbstruck listening to all these plans. She couldn't even answer when Doris offered her a second cup of coffee; she merely shook her head.

'I'll think I'll have one,' Doris decided, though a glass of water would have been more thirst-quenching after all that talk. Beryl used to say there was no muzzling her once she'd started. 'I'd better climb down from my soap box and iron his shirts. That's what some women go on about, isn't it? I always considered they were making mountains out of molehills, but I'm beginning to wonder.'

She saw Nora glance at the clock. That second hand was a real

142

nuisance the way it clicked round. No wonder people were startled and were suddenly distracted from what was being said; she'd noticed that before. She'd have to replace that timepiece with one less busy. 'It's quite exhilarating to think I'll be taking a holiday from that,' gesturing to the shirts folded and smoothed ready for the iron.

'I'm sure it's not too early,' Nora agreed. She looked a little recovered. 'But what will Clifford think?'

'If he's not here he wouldn't expect to get his washing done by post!' she giggled again. She had not felt so careless of opinion since that evening the five of them had lined up, arms circling waists, and had done high kicks to make the photographer blush. It was a shame, the way Nora seemed to be taking it all so seriously. 'You mustn't worry about him,' Doris assured her. 'I don't reckon he's given a thought to the way you've been putting up with the inconvenience.'

'I can see no reason why he should have considered me, Doris. Neither can I understand why you imagine it's necessary to go to such lengths. You enjoy his company at the weekends; you love coddling him.'

'As I've said, I'll have plenty to occupy me,' laughing.

'Please don't be set on going to any more trouble on my account, or to any expense. The looking glass in the bedroom is adequate, and I don't need any more space. Other decisions, obviously, must be left to you but I do hope that you think carefully before ejecting Clifford.'

She was such a sensitive kind of person, Doris rejoiced, that she was upset about hurting Clifford, but that was an obstacle soon removed. 'I've been giving the matter some thought quite a bit recently and it'll come as no surprise to him. We had a long chinwag about it only last Saturday.' It was amazing how, when your heart was in something, you hadn't to think of the words. They said themselves; and if they were lies you didn't feel guilty at all because the only harm you were doing was to your own conscience and at the moment she could live with that. 'Though he didn't like to admit it outright, I could see he would welcome the excuse not to get into his car and drive here every Friday after work.'

'You think so? Well, you know the man; I don't. I hadn't picked up that you'd discussed the idea with him.'

It was a pity she hadn't had notice of the way the conversation would go so she could've worked the story out from the start and everything would have fitted without fuss. 'A different arrangement has been in the air for some time now. He'll be only too ready to follow my plans.'

'I hope you know what you're doing, and that you haven't misinter-preted Clifford's assent. In spite of the talk you've had with him, he might claim that you'd sprung the idea upon him without warning.'

'I'd never do that,' she answered, very firm. Then: 'I don't know why we're standing here in the kitchen when there are easy chairs in the lounge.'

'I don't know why I'm standing here when there's a rehearsal in the Centre on the point of starting.'

'No, you mustn't let them down, not without prior notice,' showing that she could be reasonable, that she accepted there had to be some give and take, that she wasn't the demanding sort. Some people had to have a bit of leeway, especially a woman like Nora.

For she was confident now. Her blood was dancing; she felt good all over, absolutely A1; and it wasn't the kitchen she was seeing with the units meticulously installed by Clifford, the oscillating shelf for pans, the paper towels printed with floral border, the rack of plates each illustrating a historic moment in the lives of the Royal Family and shining a little purple and gilt upon the formica under the tubular lamp. The visions in front of her eyes were softer, amorphous, their planes fuzzed with down; their colour, pastel; their habitation, shade unlanced by stark light; their warmth, modest embers; their breezes, words' gentle drift.

But she must save those, treasure them up for a time more appropriate. Tonight she must try to be a little more matter-of-fact, which would not be easy. 'Yes, you'd better be going. When you've got an appointment we shouldn't stand here gassing; that'll not spoil,' she said to Nora, who was pulling at the Yale lock. 'You have to give that a good yank; it's taken to sticking, something to do with the weather, no doubt. I intended to mention the fault to Clifford but, since I forgot, we'll have to tackle it ourselves, now.' The thought made her dizzy; again the imagination throbbed. 'Look, I think we ought to do something after that rehearsal, give ourselves a treat. I'll leave the ironing, have a bath and a change, and I'll give the manager at the Dog and Partridge a ring.'

Nora had the door open. She turned, her face one big puzzle.

'I shouldn't have mentioned it! My mother always said I never thought before I spoke; she could rely on me to let the cat out of the bag if there was a surprise in the offing. Don't think any more about it, Nora, only come straight back. I know the caretaker likes the Albert Street Centre closed by ten. That'll mean the occasion begins late and is short, but still nice.'

'I don't know what you're talking about.'

'Wizard!' she chortled. 'I won't say any more.'

'Please do.'

'Not another sentence, not a single word, not a teeny little letter.'

'I want to know,' Nora begged, her voice a whisper.

'You are a caution! You'll be telling me next that you're allergic to secrets and that you'd rather look forward to an outing than have it popped at you all of a sudden.' It was years since she had teased like this; it was times with Beryl and the girls all over again and there had been nothing nasty about it, nothing spiteful. When she remembered how all five of them had teased, she knew they couldn't have done unless they'd trusted in one another's feelings, and she knew that there had been no other teasing, either before then or since.

'I'm serious,' Nora insisted.

'All right, if you're one who likes to savour what's coming, only you've got less than two and a half hours! As soon as you've dashed off, I'm going to phone the Dog and Partridge and book a table. I told you once how they do very tasty bar lunches, chicken-in-a-basket and such, and they have a restaurant as well. It has a good reputation; it caters for weddings and big receptions and the reports in the free paper are always complimentary. Clifford and me have been promising ourselves for ages we'd go when we had a special something to celebrate but we never had. It strikes me I don't have to wait any longer.'

'I've only just finished eating, Doris.'

'You can't call a salad and a dollop of curd cheese a meal. Every time I set out a plate of thin stuff like that I can't help but shudder. I wish you'd let me prepare you meals with more body to them. I'm not sure what time they take last orders but I'll speak to the manager,' talking over her shoulder as she bustled round, wiping the breakfast counter foldaway, shaking detergent into the sink, pressing tea cloths under the foam to soak. 'He'll make a concession, if necessary, for a regular customer. The chickens-in-a-basket I've consumed in that bar lounge!'

There was nothing she couldn't do tonight. She was soaring, head right up in the clouds, gliding, curving, swooping and rising in crazy aerobatics that flushed her cheeks, kindled her flesh and combed her hair into a thick flambeau tress. Because it had not yet been bobbed and the pinny she was wearing was a spangled sash and the woman behind her was still, overcome with admiration in that suspended moment before the clapping began.

'I think that by ten o'clock I shall be too tired, Doris.'

'And you such a late bird! I shan't be, so I'm sure you won't.' Drying her hands, she turned and as she folded the towel against her breasts she regarded the motionless woman. 'You're looking a bit pale, duck, but however much I say you're working too hard, you won't take any notice; I wish you would. A good meal in a relaxed atmosphere will be just what the doctor ordered,' smiling.

'I rarely pay attention to orders.' Nora paused, teeth digging into her lip; and the smooth spiral was distorted as Doris felt the supporting air begin to sag.

Bravely she said, 'When you've finished the rehearsal you'll soon perk up and you don't have to take the car out again. I can order a taxi.' There was no glow in her voice; her body had lost its spring; laying the pad of towel across the radiator, her hands were clumsy, old, the skin over the knuckles stretched and creased. But, not quite believing, not yet able to assimilate the other's refusal and striving to see in her face merely a doubt about the expense of a taxi, she delayed with: 'I'll pay for it; don't worry about that; I'll stand the fare. For the two of us. Like I'm going to pick up the tab for the meal. It's my idea. A little fling on me.'

The other clicked her tongue. 'Doris, I'm trying to tell you that I'd rather not go.'

'Some other night then?' She had to grip the cooker because the floor was slanting up.

'I'll see.'

The back door was opening now. The draught stiffened the goose pimples already roughening her flesh; it stabbed the fading embers which yielded a trickle of smoke beyond which the evening stretched blank, without sounds. 'Look,' she said, her eyes dragging at the fingers stern on the knob, 'why don't I put a little supper together and we can have it in front of the fire as soon as you get back? Better than going to any restaurant, more comfy.'

'Please don't go to the trouble, Doris. I can't be certain when I shall be coming in.'

And finally the air opened; she was sucked through the jagged crack, was twirled towards the lurching ground upon which were scattered the clinkers of a gilded evening, their colour ash. For the circle of twilight had drained and vanished, leaving a darkness which gave her no strength, not even an echo of applause because the hands were not raised to clap but to press clammily, the nails snagged on the sequins and the fingers printed the silk with sweat. She heard her voice say, 'You'll be going with that man.'

146

Other fingers returned. They curled round the wood. One was ringed with gold, an insolent deception. 'I'm going to the rehearsal.'

'Afterwards. That's why you won't come to the Day's Bag restaurant with me.'

'I'm sorry, Doris. I really am not prepared to discuss my reasons.'

'You'd rather sit with drunks in the Admiral Nelson.'

'I don't know where you got such an extraordinary idea from. It's the usual commonplace sort of pub.'

'That's it: common. You wouldn't find me setting foot in it. But we know why you do, don't we? It's so's you have an excuse to walk out with that man.'

'Good night, Doris.'

'Oh no; don't think you can run off now, not before I've finished my say.' She felt fabric inside her fist, felt the pain of her shoulder's blow upon the glazed door, heard the lock snap and watched the shock on the face of the other, the jacket sleeve dangling deformed, a heel angled clubfooted on a dropped book.

'Ever since you came here I've known, but I tried to deceive myself. I've made you welcome, haven't I? I've made you as comfortable as I could; I've put myself out; but you look down on people like me that are respectable, doing an honest job, paying our way, not thinking it's the government's responsibility to keep us and blueing what we can scrounge on beer and cigarettes. We're not interesting enough for your kind, are we? You can get all that at home, can't you? And more. Oh yes, so much more that you can sneer at them that would like to do as well but haven't enough to pay for real style. When someone like you wants a change, leaving behind them a smart detached house with, I suppose, five bedrooms, one with a bathroom *en suite* and an Aga cooker in the kitchen and a utility room that opens on to the double garage and another room built above that as a study with a proper desk for correspondence and papers; yes, when you want a change, you drive up in a big car, look out for a box room to squeeze yourself into and take up with labourers and rough elements, or the workshy and spongers. And if you imagine that means they've got out of the rat race, as it's called, and their minds are on higher things than money, which makes you think you can be buddies since you're not bothered about a wage packet at the end of the week, then you've got another think coming. As I confessed to Clifford only last Saturday, "It's all beyond me, and there's her husband, too," I said. "Sometimes I wonder whether he ought to be told." But Clifford advised me not to get mixed up with that. "She's a grown woman," he said, "and knows what's she's doing, or not, as the case may be. While she's in Neatham she's on a longer rein and it's more customary for her category of person to be a bit loose. For all we know, the husband might be taking advantage himself. You've heard the saying, when the cat's away." But he hadn't a word of explanation to offer when I asked, "Why *him*? Why one of his sort?" '

She was finished, shaking. Her head ached; her voice was raucous in her ears. 'Why a man like him?' she repeated, the air scratching down her throat. For the lights were switched off, the others had gone their ways taking with them the laughter which was in celebration of her, and fingers were splayed across a breast, rooting under the sash whose joy had been so brief. Like another thing she had prized. Swaying towards that, where it stood by the electric point, she whispered, 'I'll not delay you any longer, but I wish I knew why you should let him when we two could have got on. He can't even claim to have been a foreman though that makes no difference. That sort are only after one thing.'

'If I got into a car like that, I'd want to be behind the wheel,' he answered.

'That can be managed.'

'Don't tempt me. I'm out of practice. Haven't driven anything more complicated than a push-bike for two year.'

'I'll leave it here, then.'

'What for?'

'There's something I want to tell you.'

'There's all tomorrow.'

'Not if it's anything like the last week.'

'Once up the street and back, then. I told Barbara I'd be home as soon as the pub closed. She's not feeling so good.'

'In that case, I'll leave it. It's a story that deserves longer than a turn up the street.'

'You look as if you need an early night yourself. I reckon there must be a bug going the rounds.'

'If that's so, I'll order a medicinal nightcap. I suppose that Trust House down the motorway will be able to supply a toothbrush?'

'You're taking a rest from 9 Belle View for the night?'

'Longer than that. You know that empty house attached to the old cloakrooms?'

'The schoolhouse.'

'Oh, of course. I hadn't thought. What condition is it in?'

'Mucky, I'd say. Stan keeps the key. You wouldn't think of moving into that?'

'I don't see why not, if I can circumvent the red tape.'

'In that instance it doesn't stretch any further than Stan, as I remember. You'd be taking something on, squatting in there, though. Primitive's a kind word for it and you'll be lucky if they haven't switched off the water. I wouldn't set much store on those rabbit hutches the other side the Fosse estate but they can't be worse than that crumbling old house.'

'In one respect it can only be an improvement,' and added silently the answer to the question he had not asked, 'because I have to escape.'

From the sight of a face begging, accusing, spiteful, punishing, prising out guilts, and finally abandoned, cheeks swilled with despairing grief; and the hands grabbing filter and heater and jug to smash them in an eruption of splinters and russet spouts upon the burnished taps.

Chapter Thirteen

'So where's the action?' Constance Skrimshaw demanded before she had gained the top stair. 'The place looked shut up, then I saw the light. Is this a one-woman sewing circle?'

'I'm mending. Would you care to join me? I can guarantee the pursuit is non-addictive.'

'Why are you doing it yourself? You need a team for wardrobe.'

'We have one. I'm carrying out running repairs.'

'I thought they only came during performance. You must be at least six weeks off those.'

'If we were any closer, Constance, I wouldn't be sitting here with needle and thread. It would be a matter of a quick snap with the stapler. As soon as they are ready, costumes are donned and props used because Peter wants the cast to be as familiar with them as they are with the text, which isn't saying much.'

'Do I detect a note of cynicism?'

'No. Candour.'

'You have to remember that for people totally inexperienced, there's an enormous amount to be absorbed and I expect that as usual no concessions are being made. It's a great challenge to them.'

'And to Peter.'

'And to you and Dick as well.'

Nora forbore to add: Without whom this list of grateful acknowledgements would not be complete, and whose unremitting labour, reticent dedication and unquestioning loyalty, this project has exploited to the full.

Instead: 'As far as work goes, I wouldn't claim to have been greatly challenged. Everything I've been responsible for has been well within my capacities.'

'I can appreciate that the satisfaction in this job is limited,' Constance sympathised, with no apparent reference to the mending. 'However much latitude you are given, the fact remains that Peter is the boss and even though he's reasonable, he's still a bloke. Hard to find work without them around, unfortunately.' She flipped open the appointments diary on Peter's desk and skimmed through half a dozen pages. 'But it's still possible to find jobs, here and there, that aren't defined so rigidly that there's no scope for freewheeling enterprise. Look, Nora,' she continued briskly, moving from generalities to practical solution of the other's problem, 'since after this you'll be on the hunt for something that demands more stretch, I might be able to help. The job I have in mind is administrator with a well-established base. The position has overall responsibility. Within the parameters of the budget there'd be one hell of an opportunity for personal choice and putting your own stamp on the product.'

'I'm not sure if that would be appropriate, whatever my stamp may be, Constance.' Cravenly she felt unable to confess that she was not looking for future work. 'Or whether that's my sort of job.'

'What else are you interested in, then, if it's not community arts?' Since an alternative to the latter was unthinkable, the question was clearly rhetorical. 'But I didn't come here to discuss your career prospects. I can do that on the phone. According to the schedule Peter sent me there should be a rehearsal tonight.'

'There is; at the school. It's no longer practical to hold them in the big ones' room here. I mean, the bigger room where the top standard children used to be taught. The education authority has been very co-operative,' recalling Ms Skrimshaw's prejudice.

'There's nothing more gratifying than charity that doesn't pinch the pocket. If there's a Keep Fit class in the gym, the caretaker will be there on duty till nine anyway,' she answered, unabashed. 'Dick will be there, won't he? Good. I've come for a word with him about the anthology. I've heard nothing for over a month; must have been about the beginning of August. I presume everything's going all right?'

'As far as I know, it is.'

'No sweat, then. I'm certain he's an OK bloke,' adding, 'and thoroughly competent.' There seemed to be a chink in her assurance she was asking Nora to plug.

'Absolutely.'

'Well, of course, that's what we're trying to encourage. We make the expertise available but once people understand what they want, my department fades out. One of the core tenets is avoidance of imposition.'

Nora was quite awed by the other's capacity to make that final statement; she was equally awed by the configuration of reasons that could bring Constance to choose work whose principles were so contrary to her temperament.

'The thing is, if the process were to reach its ultimate stage, I should be redundant. The better I do the job, the less I'm needed.'

'We've a long way to go before you're superfluous, Constance,' laughing at her sobriety. 'There are quite a number of nooks and crannies still unblessed by community arts. I think there's room for you yet.' Nora felt abruptly maternal. It was by such freakish signs that she recognised a longing for her daughters. Suddenly homesick, she looked down through a dunce's cap window and reminded herself why she had come.

'There's also room for a few questions,' the other agreed, looking happier. 'I'm funding Dick and I want to know what he's doing. I don't suppose he's dragging his feet?'

'He's spending a lot of time on it.'

'In that case there must be queries that have to be talked through. I told him several times that he was not to hesitate to consult me. Perhaps he interpreted that as an available service rather than a requirement. Though I'd have thought there could be no doubt about what I meant. A job at this level of subsidy cannot be left in inexperienced hands without supervision.'

'Perhaps he may not have reached the stage of needing any other opinion.' She was amused that she was assuming the role of peacemaker.

'I doubt that, and I'm surprised he hasn't asked yours. You've got a hell of a lot more experience with the written word and thus more discrimination.' She was too angry to remain circumspect with inadmissible probability. 'If the decision had been based on knowledge, then we'd have given you first option, Nora. It's the sort of dilemma one has to cope with. What would you have done in my place?' The question was totally serious.

'I don't think I should venture an answer to that. It might be slightly blemished by prejudice.'

'I don't see why. I'm only asking you to be objective. You can be that, can't you? I would have thought that was among your strengths. One of the reasons I reckon you'd be right for that administrator job. It won't be advertised till mid October. I'll send you the application forms.'

This seemed a clumsy attempt to compensate Nora for the other preference but, employing the objectivity which Constance admired, Nora decided that the other was unaware of any connection.

'I'll dash along to the rehearsal,' and noticing that Nora had finished her task: 'Would you like a lift?'

It had not been Nora's intention to return. To sit by herself mending was less lonely and dispiriting than, separated by others' jostling needs, to watch him the length of a room apart, rehearsing his stage crew in his newly acquired skill of cleating flats. But she felt unable to refuse the other's offer without an excuse. Irritated, thinking: Nowadays I can't even assert myself with another *woman*, she followed Constance down the stairs.

As Nora locked up the main doors Constance asked, nodding towards the corner of the building, 'Is that where you're living? It's strange how you don't realise until it's pointed out that the end bit's a house, not part of the school. Couldn't you have found other lodgings? Or isn't it as primitive as Pete makes out?'

'I can't answer that since I haven't heard his description.' She was neither flattered nor surprised that her move had been considered sufficiently interesting to merit discussion; it was their equivalent of small-town gossip. Instead, she felt wary and defensive.

'He says there's not even water.'

'There's a tap outside.'

'So what do you do for a lav?'

'Abstain,' wanting to add: which is what I do for sex. 'Don't be alarmed, Constance. I wasn't being strictly truthful. There's an earth closet in the yard at the back and when I'm in the mood for real luxury I come into the school.'

'Sounds all right,' Ms Skrimshaw conceded without conviction. 'But there's no electricity now?'

'There never was. However, there are many ways of making light.'

'I suppose, on the credit side,' Constance laboured to project into another's reasoning, 'you may gain on something . . . like privacy.'

'That was what I calculated.'

Erroneously. Because the privacy she had planned had been for concealment, not solitude. But there had been no pleasures to hide.

She had stood by the window for hours on end, keeping herself by the wall to make sure she wasn't on view. It was a long time since she had said he could come if he wanted. By the state of the tree outside it could be months, though the young hooligans were being forward if it was conkers they were after, throwing up sticks. She wouldn't generally have said yes, putting a tick on the paper, but the way he put it down he sounded a nice enough young man, and God knows, she hadn't come across many. She should know better at her age than to be waiting on anybody, let alone some pipsqueak who never got any further than dropping letters on the mat, but she could do with a change from the company of him upstairs, though he wasn't so demanding as formerly and in past weeks he'd shown a willingness to hear what she had to say, which was a novelty. She wasn't doing so badly, either, in the novelty stakes, rearranging the settle in front of the hearth and keeping the kettle on a low gas for Peter Green Esq., with every good wish for this coming year. Of course, that probably wouldn't go down very well with Norman, she sniggered, but what the eye doesn't behold, the heart doesn't grieve. Only she made the mistake – she had an idea it wasn't the first time she'd done it – opening the door too quick and smiling, when it was Mr Green's helper, not him. It was the trousers that did it; nowadays you couldn't be sure which it was, man or woman, till you'd had a good gleg at the face. And not always then, she cackled, startling this missis in the middle of asking after her health. She didn't bother to answer that one. Anybody with half an eye could see she was sound.

'You'll have a cup of tea?' she asked, inclined to forgive her because it wasn't her fault that Mr Green was too busy and had to send a replacement.

The visitor mumbled that she didn't want to put her about, which was a thought but senseless because there's nothing to spooning leaves into the bottom of a cup and taking it to the kettle, but she could see no reason to insist. Anyway, she forgot it, next minute, seeing her taking in the pillows and blankets screwed up on the settle.

'They wouldn't be there,' she explained, 'if it wasn't for him. He's grown that restless and his noise keeps me awake.' Then quickly, to cover the slip: 'I'm referring to Puss. He likes me to stay with him, so that's why I'm here. Puss isn't allowed near the beds.'

'You must be having me on,' was all she could say to the woman's remark, amazed because she'd never come across a young one like this sleeping in front of the hearth; though not for the sake of a cat, it was stated, but for reasons of choice, it being simpler to clear just the back room, and Isabel laughed because this one was as wily as she was, pretending it was only the rubble in the bedrooms which kept her out. They were a real pair, when you thought on, which she hadn't done till now.

'They're a trouble, men are,' she agreed comfortably. 'It's best to stay out of their way. I'd keep your coat on if I were you; you can catch a chill coming into a house you aren't used to. I was thinking of putting a fire in.' Like the young one said, it was cold for August. She would've given it November but there was no sense in arguing, she wasn't particular which month. Just to show her that she didn't stand

154

on ceremony and meant the invitation about the coat, she buttoned her own higher and, feeling easy because he was napping and the cat had been fed, she gave her mind to what the woman was telling her, not asking questions for once or hoping Isabel'd talk, but going on about her own doings. She could spout, there was no doubt about it, like the parson for words but with a friendlier sound, and you could see what she was telling you about as if it was here in this room. All the same, she could hardly believe what it boiled down to – her going into a musty old house without as much as the gas, and carting a fold-up bed and a primus, expecting the summer'ud keep the place warm, but it hadn't. Mind you, she didn't seem bothered; to speak the truth, Isabel suspected that this young one had enjoyed it at the start, making do. It takes all sorts. What she didn't explain was how she'd managed to move him and get him upstairs but that was a detail; this one had plenty about her and would easy find a way. She wasn't satisfied, though; they never were. She had hoped there'd be callers, but they hadn't come and she got lonely stuck there downstairs by herself.

That made Isabel think and the other kept quiet while she did. You could have heard the clock tick if it'd been wound up. Because she didn't rightly know what folks meant by lonely. It wasn't being just by theirsens and though she didn't as a general rule put what other folks said alongside herself, she did try to decide whether for what she was she'd give lonely the name. She supposed that anyone feeling like that was after other people's company rather than their own but that seemed daft unless you could exercise a bit of choice, whereas she'd never had the chance of that, people pushed theirselves at her whether she wanted or no. Except that Mr Green. So she asked, 'Was it anyone in particular you was expecting?'

This Nora – it came back to her that was what she called herself – gave a jump, coming out of her own thoughts which she'd let herself get into believing that Isabel was asleep, and she nodded but didn't say no more. Usually Isabel wouldn't have taken it further; people were best left to fend for themselves, but she'd been feeling different lately, maybe she was going soft, she chuckled not letting the other hear, or maybe it was because he wasn't so difficult, easier to manage despite his whimpering now and again, or mebbe it was this Nora, a bit different to them round about. Whichever reason, she could afford to give it some brain space.

What struck her when she began thinking was the way this Nora had looked when she nodded. It reminded her of someone she'd known. She wasn't used to puzzles but she didn't like to give up, not once she'd started, but before she could put her finger on it exactly, finding the memory of who that person had been, it came over her that the caller this Nora referred to was some man. Why she should think that she didn't know; she'd have a better idea if the memory would come back all of a piece, but she was certain she wasn't wrong. For a minute or two she was shocked, but then she had to admit that she wasn't really bothered. She'd just taken the line that people think they ought. After all, him upstairs wouldn't be doing her much good. She told her as well, only like as not she got the names muddled – as far as she knew, this one's hubby wasn't another Norman – because this young one looked a bit dismayed; her eyes went round as they used to do when she came at first, and she looked upset to see the cat meat tin on the table open and the two mucky plates. So she explained, not wanting her to be worried: 'Puss doesn't mind if I have a taste.'

Isabel didn't say any more on that subject because she'd got another one nagging and she didn't want it to go before she'd got topside of it, because it was giving her this ache.

She couldn't understand it. A woman she hadn't known before the cat arrived – that was a better way of calculating than any calendar – a woman who had the boldness to get past the door when it should have been that polite Mr Green, who hadn't sat in this room more than half a dozen times, she came back with a story about moving house and a friend who didn't visit, saying it with a look which she didn't know was stuck on her face, and Isabel caught this pain. It was as if all of a sudden there was nothing to hold you up and you knew that it could never be set right and that you'd never have peace to speak of again. If anybody'd said that dying was as hard as that she wouldn't have minded, it was no more than you'd expect, but it was the living after that was the trouble. You see, she said to herself, this wasn't the first time she'd had it.

Then she remembered one time as bad as any other, worse than when the news came that her mother had had the stroke, and she knew why she'd got it now. Because of the way Nora had looked when Isabel had mentioned the friend. She had stared into the ashy hearth with a face saying she'd travel the world for him, and her cheeks had twitched with the tears she was holding back. It was the same as what she'd read on another young one's face years ago, only that one was hardly more than a girl at the time, and the pain it had given her tonight wasn't so much for this one but for the other.

Their Dot. Hers, she told herself secretly, more than their Jack's. She'd wished for a daughter when she was carrying, but it wasn't to be. Yet if the amount you felt for them followed on from the pain they'd given you, then she had to admit that Dot had meant more to her than ever her George. She couldn't be blamed for that; she was too old to be fussed finding ways of giving herself stick, only she did wonder at times whether he sensed it and whether that was the reason he tried so hard to go up a few pegs in her esteem, like bringing that washer, and when he was a lad always wanting her to know the minute he'd done something a bit out of the way and hoping for praise. But he'd not cost her tears, never shed but boiling in the belly and choking you with their gas. It was Dot that had done that. It was her she'd been thinking of because of this one here, and she chuckled, pleased with herself for remembering but, suspicious of congratulation, pointed out that she could keep ideas in her head when they belonged to years earlier; it was the present that got shuffled about.

Therefore, contemplating Nora, she told herself that she should be annoyed with this one who had arrived out of the blue without warning and brought this pain back, but she was able to raise no more than a frown, which was really anxiety. She said to her, 'I've heard a "friend" mentioned once before and I can tell you that nothing good came of it.'

The other looked taken aback. 'All I said was that it's nice to have a place to myself so that I can invite people to drop in. I didn't mention anyone specially.'

Isabel could have sworn that she had, but that was no matter; nobody could deny that look on her face. Which was why the pain had come, the pain for Dot and now for this one as well. This one could pretend as much as she liked but she'd not deceive Isabel. With that expression on her face, you'd have been hard pressed to tell the difference between her and Dot.

It hadn't been there the first night. Isabel had never seen a lass so lit up, sitting in that very chair and bursting out the news that she'd got a soldier. 'Why you telling me?' she had asked. 'I have to get it off my chest. I can't keep it locked up and Mam would kill me if she knew.' 'How d'you know I won't?' she had asked and the monkey had giggled, 'I've known you take off your corsets, Auntie, and you're not so set.' 'I am tonight,' she had warned her but there wasn't much heart in it. The little devil could twist her round her little finger and no mistake. All the same, she would have rebuked her; she would've told her she was being a fool, that she'd regret it for the rest of her life, that she'd got to straighten herself out, if it hadn't been for one thing. She couldn't give Dot a piece of her mind because that piece might have shown her up. She was aghast, no doubt about that, and she had no second thoughts that it was wrong, but one piece of her mind that might have slipped out was that she might not have been averse to the prospect of a bit of a fling with a soldier herself, and she forty with a husband in a reserved occupation and a son a rear gunner! So how could she chastise Dot, twenty years younger, pointing out she'd already got a babby and a husband – and him out fighting – as if she'd forget. Instead, she listened, letting the girl talk on. Dot had never been as full of Eddie as she was of this other one and Isabel couldn't bring herself to do more than caution, telling her to watch that she didn't do anything silly. She couldn't possibly play the vicar or even be proxy for Dot's mam, not when she was wishing she could be in Dot's shoes herself, not when Dot's happiness made her tingle all over in a way she'd not experienced before and, knowing that was so, wanting to be sick. Dot got what she wished for, an audience and no row, by telling an aunt who, she had said, would sometimes take off her stays. Which was a bitter joke considering; Isabel would have given a month's housekeeping to have taken them off then.

So she didn't offer correction, a fact that she couldn't forget when, a few months later, the girl came round so early in the morning that the ashes hadn't been cleaned from the grate and, keeping her eyes on them, she told Isabel that the worst thing had happened.

It was then the pain grabbed and the tears broke like the waters but flowing inside. She didn't like to put too big a word to it, but that grabbing like a fist screwing her innards was despair. It seemed there was never happiness without some blemish. She'd never expected anything different for herself, but she had for Dot. And there was this other thing, which didn't make it worse because that wasn't possible, but it added to the worry: she couldn't be sure that by not speaking out, by not making the girl see sense, she hadn't helped it to happen. Whatever excuses she tried on, she couldn't get away from the fact that she was partly to blame; and she would not have accused herself of that if she hadn't sat there that night lapping it all up, imagining it was as much her as Dot. She would blush to think on, but not now; then, she'd wonder if it showed, like a stain on your frock when you've started sudden, but nowadays it seemed a waste that she couldn't enjoy feeling like that and couldn't try to put it to some advantage; but in the end you have to accept that it doesn't do to be lax. She didn't say any of this to Dot. How could she? Dot's mam was her brother's wife; they'd sat together at school and Isabel had been there for her lying-in; you can't say to a young girl the age of your own son that you

158

are sorry you didn't try to prevent her but you couldn't in all honesty since you were thinking what it would have been like if it'd been you.

That is to say, until a week or two after, when Dot told her at last what he was. She couldn't stomach that one at the start; and she knew that if Dot had told her first off she'd have put a stop to it. She'd never have imagined herself lying with a darkie! But whatever he'd been, that didn't alter the mess Dot was in, and disgust didn't take away the pain when she saw Dot growing more swollen and knowing what a disgrace she was carrying. Now, forty years after, when she remembered that time, all that was left to her was the grieving and he could've been all colours of the rainbow for what it mattered to her, so long as Dot had been happy. That could not be. It would've been bad enough Dot going with another man when Eddie was away fighting. But this was worse. And everybody knew. She had stared out the street, had given them as much as they gave Dot; it was none of their business. Dot's mam was a flimsy sort, too scared to answer back, but Isabel had done. No matter what happens, you stick to your family, and Dot had her heart. Yes, she'd given them back as good as Dot received. She frowned, trying to recall her answering abuse to that bit of censure that took their fancy in particular, and she repeated it now, out loud: It's against nature, mixing kinds.

This one tonight – she'd forgotten what name she gave herself – didn't half blush when she heard that. 'I'm keeping you from your bed,' she answered, prim as a Sunday school teacher, which was her way of showing offence, ready to walk out; and it came to Isabel with a jerk that maybe this Nora thought she was making a comment on this 'friend' she had mentioned, which wasn't what Isabel had intended. So there was no need for her to be going; Isabel didn't mind if she came visiting; she could do with a change from seeing to his sheets and you might even say she was grateful to be given the excuse not to be forever tending the cat.

Trying to make it right with her, Isabel said, 'You mustn't take that as personal, mixing kinds. It wasn't meant for you.'

That stopped her from going quicker than Isabel could have hoped; she could guess this Nora wanted to know who was the target for that spite. She had done her best not to let Dot hear it, and by the end, when the girl was close to her time, Isabel had got so she'd have walked down the street with that soldier herself, to show how she spat on their whispers.

'I've never had much time for folks,' she told Nora, 'though I've given them most of my years. They can make life a misery if you don't follow the regular path.' Hadn't this one said it was the old school-house she had moved to, where Miss Freiston had lived?

But she mustn't let herself be distracted by that idea; one was beginning in her head that she wanted to hold on to, not let it fracture into splinters before she'd looked at it close.

'When I was a young one I kidded myself it was no matter if tongues wagged.' But she hadn't searched for her grave, not till they were burying Dot. Yet the feeling was growing in her head more solid than wispy thought. 'I have to admit not a deal came my way like to set tongues off along the street.' Until that time. It was wicked, what they had said, and Dot carrying. 'It can't be ignored, what they think, but that's not to say you always have to tek notice,' she told Nora, and there was this knocking at her heart. 'There are times when you have to go your own way, listen to your own voices, not theirs. Even if, at the end, you've nothing to show for it.'

Then she heard this Nora come in quiet. 'But who's after a show? Something remains; something which nourishes. Something to treasure.'

She was right. It had taken her, practically a stranger, to tell her that, making the sensation sharper, an incandescence like a mantle glowing, waiting to be turned up. She wanted to tell this Nora but she feared that if she concentrated on words there would be nothing but the twilight again and the grey hearth. So she said, impatient, though sorry to be brusque, 'If you haven't got the electric in that house, it'll be too dark to see soon, when you get home,' and cupped her hands round her own wick to keep it safe against draughts.

This Nora got up straight away. 'Would you like me to put a fire in before I go?' she asked. 'It might be a help.'

For a minute Isabel was confused by the other's anxiety, not sure what it was that a fire might help. As far as she knew, she hadn't mentioned the pain. The suggestion of a fire, though, was a proper joke and she laughed because with this lamp she needed no heat.

'I'll be going then,' this Nora said, for all the world like a neighbour, the decent sort, who had just dropped in. 'I'm pleased we've had this talk.'

It struck Isabel that she might have said more than she imagined and she couldn't remember a word the other had spoken. She didn't want to try now, either; she had to keep her mind clear of everything to make room for this light. And it would be wisest if she made sure of that for the future, not allowing anything to interfere, risking its loss. She suspected that there hadn't been much in her life to stand comparison with this.

'I'm asking you not to come again,' she said loud as she could so there'd be no mistake. 'I've been getting behind with the jobs.'

Watching her go down the path, head bent, Isabel whispered through the glass, 'I've nothing against you; in fact I've everything to thank you for, starting thoughts again about Dot and what happened and the scandal they made of it Bottom End. But if I hadn't got rid, I'd have mebbe lost track.'

With an unexpected sadness, Isabel watched until her visitor had turned out of the street. Then she sat on the sofa, wrapped blankets round her legs and stared into the lifeless grate, certain that if she kept quiet she'd grow used to the dazzle and without a blink be able to make out what was there at the light's core.

Chapter Fourteen

Constance Skrimshaw had to employ an unpractised patience before she could speak to Dick. With his electrician friend he was bowed over a bank of dimmers checking light cues in the script.

'It's too complicated to follow from this. I'll have to make a separate copy and get it typed. Those spots with the gold gel need to be brought in gradual before the moving projector is switched off. And I reckon we'll have to do something to tone down that red. I could see Pete wincing and he's got a point. It's the flowers of the bloody field the man's talking about, not the hothouse in Harlaxton Court. We'll think on later. It's all yours now, Vic, while I have a word with that bunch of mental defectives pleased to call themselves stage hands. I've told Pete that it'ud need Brian Clough to get any joy out of that squad of costive nuns,' indicating how smoothly a parade-ground image could be married to a theatrical manner, both adopted. Nodding to Constance and Nora, he went on his next mission.

'He's just gone right through the apprenticeship scene without a single mistake and he painted the flowers lovely,' Phyllis Baker reported to Nora on the progress of her nephew cast as Joseph Raby. 'Some of them doing tradesmen aren't a patch on him. I always knew he was clever,' more impressed by Mark's public achievement than by his four GCEs. 'I'm pleased you've come back, Nora. You can see whether I've sorted out the props right for this scene. There's that many, and to guarantee that all of them acting holds on to their own gets me fussed.'

'Oh, come on, Phyllis! Everyone told me you took the biscuit for bossing about.'

'The cheeky devils! Who, I'd like to know? Mind you, I can't deny I'll stand no nonsense.' They smiled, conspiratorial. 'It's all a story, isn't it? You're only trying to get round me.'

'Why should I want to do that?'

''Cause that's what it's all about. You needn't give me a look! That Peter Green and you, and I suppose we have to include Dick since he's as bad, the lot on yer done nothing for the last – God knows how long – but coax. If it weren't for you, I could be sitting in front of our telly with my feet up. Bored stupid, of course, but peaceful. Instead,

I'm standing here collecting varicose veins fretting whether Charlie Hopkinson is going to get that awning up without tearing it. Peter Green should've been warned.'

'He chose Charlie for his appearance.'

'I hoped he had some reason; I couldn't find one. Charlie's the most uneppen person in Bottom End. He's the only chap I know has slung himself into canal throwing sticks for his dog.'

'He'll be OK when he's had more practice.'

'He doesn't need any practice in shredding paper. He mastered it first time.'

'Poor Charlie. He knows you're talking about him.'

'He's lucky that's all I'm doing,' waving cheerily across the room to the offending man. 'Now just you remember what I've told you,' she addressed others returning to their places in the centre of the hall floor. 'You have to put every one of those tools on your benches into the Tesco carrier and leave it underneath. Your clobber for the chapel fête is all there, nothing missing as yet, where I put it, same place, only in the Easy Saver bag.' They nodded, slightly glazed.

Taking up their positions behind tables borrowed as substitutes for benches, they quickly cleared away tools, masked by dappling colour as Vic switched on the lamp.

Peter called, 'Don't forget, Vic, that before you take off the projector Kev and John have to fling the sheet across stage front,' referring to a prop appliquéd with blossoms, still in the making. 'Now you're just walking the moves, so no song, but stall holders can do their cries if they like. I think they'd better; helps the rhythm.'

'One of my favourite bits,' Phyllis Baker whispered and checked the cast's progress by running her finger down the text.

When the colour has quietened, the stage is revealed decked with blossoms and the tradesmen's faces are glossed with summer sun as they convert their benches into stalls. They are setting up an anniversary fête and there is much jollity, hailing of one another and shouting. They stroll about examining and discussing the goods. Women enter, their movements interweaving with the men's, then together they raise the lengths of paper on which Joseph has painted flowers and place them across frames, showing that the undersides are decorated with wide stripes and these form the canopies for the stalls. As this is going on, the children who have played round the women trimming wallpaper at the back finally join in and, snatching the coils of paper ribbons, toss them about carnival fashion, looping them over necks, wreathing shoulders, curling them round hats.

'Here you are, Zena: six lengths of rag.' Phyllis lifted her eyes from the script and intercepted a young woman making for her place. 'You see you get them off those little devils as soon as the race is over, else they'll go waltzing home with them draped round their ankles and I'll never see them again.'

'You want me to sign for them?'

'Now why didn't you suggest that before, duck?' the other answered unperturbed.

'I can see Julie's remembered to take on the barrel for the lucky dip,' she remarked to Nora. 'There's parcels in it for them to practise on; I'll not put the prizes inside till the time comes.'

'You don't imagine that anyone would steal them?'

'I don't go in for imagination much, so I'd never think the kids round here are all saints. There's no sense in putting temptation before them. Even a busted hair slide in a parcel looks better than the one on your head.'

Nora could not have wrapped up empty parcels. The possibility of pilfering would not have occurred to her; had she discovered any, she would have made up the loss out of her own pocket, arguing that dishonesty was a failure of reciprocal trust. 'I'm thankful you've taken this on, Phyllis.' The sentiment was unqualified.

'I don't mind helping out.'

Nora did not quibble over definition of roles, but she did congratulate herself on having managed the switch of responsibility so smoothly that Phyllis had accepted it gladly rather than with reluctance, predicting the jealousy of peers. This achievement would have qualified for the approval of Constance Skrimshaw; it was a neat example of her definition of built-in redundancy, an ideology with which she appeared to be tussling at that moment. Nora could see her across the hall, her forehead rumpled with annoyance as she talked to Dick.

A greeting, low, to conform with Peter's rehearsal discipline, turned her eyes from the man's glowering face. 'I told Mr Green my mam wants me home before ten tonight, Nora, so he's letting me off practising this scene, and Wayne as well, though I said there's no need for that.'

'Peter regards himself as responsible for your safety.'

'It was Wayne insisted. He likes to look big. He could've stayed till it finished.' Becky's tone was almost a whine.

'It sounds as if the pair of you have fallen out.' That was a pallid description for the argument raging on the other side of the room. Two boys tied together by one of Phyllis Baker's fetters of rag skidded boisterously into the chairs round the edge of the hall. She saw Dick's head jab towards them; he was complaining that Constance was holding him from his duties.

'He hasn't fallen out, but I might,' Becky told her. 'It doesn't fool me, him leaving here to see me home. Kills two birds with one stone, showing everybody he considers it's his job and no one else's to see I don't get stopped – at nine o'clock on Gethsemane Terrace! – and it gives him a chance to get at me, same way as that old hag.'

'You shouldn't call your mother that, Becky, just because she wants you in earlier tonight.'

'It's not my mam!' Shock clashed the girl's whisper. 'She hasn't said about being in. That's what I told Mr Green because I had to have an excuse. I couldn't bring myself to go into it with him. I calculate if I leave early, I'll miss her; maybe she doesn't start on the prowl till nearly the time practising ends.'

'Becky, I've no idea what you're talking about.' The girl's presence was irksome. Between the bobbing shoulders of the cast she could see Dick's face turned towards her and interpreted his expression as an appeal.

'She talked about it with you. She says that, underneath, you're in agreement only you can't go against Mr Green. You know her. You used to lodge with her.'

'Doris Bentley has been discussing the Miss Blygh scene with you?'

'She doesn't reckon I should do it.'

'I don't understand. She was very enthusiastic about it. She showed me the photograph, lent us the sash.' Now there was Doris also hovering intrusive, accusing her with echoes of splinters spattering tawny gouts into the polished sink. These claims were untimely; they encroached upon the space he was making for her, his eyes beckoning.

'Well, she's not keen now. She's not right on top, Nora. She says it might give men wrong ideas. It wouldn't be so bad if it didn't encourage Wayne to keep nagging the same.'

'Look, Becky, you shouldn't be standing here talking; it's setting a bad example. Try to get into the office after school and tell me all about it.' She was impatient that she should feel guilty. It was not her duty to supervise the girl. Someone more important wanted to talk with her. 'You're being summoned. Wayne's signalling. Better not keep your fellow waiting,' and Nora tiptoed away to join her own.

'I expect there wasn't a soul that *didn't* notice we were having a slanging match,' he answered. Waving a clipboard and baton, he directed his stage team as they cleared up.

'I deduced you might welcome support but unfortunately I couldn't get across.'

He smiled. Victory made him charitable, disinclined him to cavil at the notion of such unnecessary help. 'No need for you to worry about me,' he told her, magnanimous, and remarked to another, 'We don't take orders lying down, do we, Monty?' Receiving the answer: 'I can't say, Dick; you've never tried one on me when I've been stretched out,' he feigned a punch and crooned affectionately, 'Get away!'

'Were they orders?'

'As near as makes no difference. Mind you, she didn't like it when I asked her, "Are you telling me that's what I have to do?" "It's not a matter of *telling* you; we're discussing it," she said. "That's funny," I said, "it sounded to me like you were issuing instructions." She couldn't let that go, of course, and she spends the next five minutes denying it, ending with saying, "It's only a question of us reaching agreement."'

'And did you?'

'I'll say. We agreed it was my job to get on with as I thought fit and if she wanted to put her spoke in, all well and good, I wasn't averse to lending an ear. But it isn't up to her to decide what's best for Neatham and if at the end it comes to her warning Walt that she won't pay for the printing, which would mean an idea she's fixed on goes down the drain along with a few hundred quid she's paid out in my wages, then that's how it'll have to be. Only that's all theory because it was against her principles to do anything like that. I never thought to see that woman bested; she was running round in circles so fast I expected any minute she'd disappear up her you know what.'

He laughed uproariously, showing his teeth large and flawless, and Nora thought irrelevantly: At his age Joseph Raby was wearing dentures, as was my mother; at least we're matched in the condition of our teeth. She laughed with him, amused by this whimsy and infected by his mood. Then, quietening, thought: Poor Constance.

The hall was emptying. She heard the caretaker tell a man stacking tables that he would replace them in the classrooms the next morning rather than be delayed in locking up. Nora began to feel anxious.

Here was an opportunity for talk with him opened by a reason unspoilt by hesitant excuse and it was seeping away as the people left. At the door, laden with Phyllis Baker's props, Peter shouted, 'See you.'

'You didn't object to his deciding what's best for Neatham,' she improvised, desperate to stay him.

'Pete's different. He's not a Constance Skrimshaw,' and laughed again, jubilant. 'Interfering bag.' He dropped script and clipboard into a child's satchel, plastic and scratched, and assured the waiting caretaker, 'We're on the move, Harry.'

Disheartened, she walked with him down the hall. But outside, a voice from a parked car inviting them to a lift, she decided she had nothing to lose and called loudly, 'Thanks, but I'd rather walk, Vic,' then asked as if nothing had intervened, 'Would you have resented the interference less if it had come from Peter?'

He could have fobbed her off, but her declining the lift and the firmness of her question were a challenge. To remain with her did not appear to be a capitulation; rather, to stride across to the car would smack of flight, and tonight he was the victory boy; his nostrils still throbbed, appreciative, at the scent of the other woman's defeat. So he regarded her, not speaking, calculating the expression in her face, and she considered the obscenity of this unprecedented attention excited by another woman's collapse. Yet though disgusted, she was not deterred, asked herself: Am I doing this now for Constance? But could not assent to the salvaging lie. Whose thought caused the air to swirl in her throat and she coughed raucously as Vic shouted, 'Remember me to Babs.'

'You've swallowed a frog,' Dick commiserated and slapped her between the shoulder blades, all strong man assisting the casualty, then toyed, stroking, to assert his disregard for Vic's reminder of Babs his wife. And wishing to be deceived, for a moment she accepted this as tenderness before remembering Constance, and pulled away. It's only the second time he's touched me, she thought, and I withdraw; through loyalty to Constance. To Constance! And discovered without surprise that this small private victory was irreducibly bleak.

Recovering, she said to him, 'You haven't answered my question.'
'Which one?'

She repeated it, using the exact words. This amused him. 'What a memory!' he exclaimed, but not in compliment, more in the spirit of indulging a characteristic that was paltry, one to be ignored if you had trounced an interfering bag.

167

'Pete would've used more tact. He would've talked it over, man to man. It's ones like her give men a bad name,' chuckling.

She should have defended, but in the September dusk, alone with him as she had not been for weeks, she kept silent, not wishing to impair this tenuous contact with hostile politics; and sighed, guilty at reneging on her daughters whose principles she had formed.

'Bossy women really get me,' he stated unnecessarily. 'They stick in my craw.'

By now everyone had left. Cars, their horns sounding farewells, had accelerated past; Mark Baker, upper lip still hidden by crimped instant moustaches, had checked the rev count of his bike and been propelled in a couple of deafening circuits; parents, grumbling amiably, had collected children and led them home; the caretaker had locked the door behind them and, with dog spirited from some unknown closet, was setting out for a nightcap, his customary reward for the obliged walk.

Nora said, 'Only another six weeks, and this is all over.'

He didn't answer, giving to the limp comment the disregard it deserved, but she said to herself: He could have shown some regret that I'll be gone; even insincere, such a remark would have indicated a little concern for my feelings. But there was none, no hint. Yet he did not move and she, restrained by his criticism of Constance from taking the initiative, could not suggest they walk away. So, resorting to social habits by now instinctive, she must fill in the silence with chat. All she could think of was: 'Of course, I'm not supposed to know about the anthology so I've really no idea what you and Constance were arguing about.'

She had resolved never to admit that she was aware of his exclusion but now spontaneously she had done so, plaintive.

For a second he frowned, then evaded. 'You can be a dry one at times, Nora. That's good!' and laughed, appreciating the complaint but untouched by it, still merry because of his treatment of Constance.

She thought: There is not and never has been a meeting place for us.

The humidity of the day was misting to rain. She regarded the place where they lingered and saw that the school's narrow concourse was greasy, already covered with a film of mud. Rubbing a shoe across the shallow step, she remarked, 'In wet weather the children tread this stuff over every floor, in classrooms as well as corridors. It's produced by as little as a tentative shower. In fact, damp is enough to bring the whole place out in a sweat.'

'It was built on a swamp.'

'What?'

'That's a bit of an exaggeration, but most of the winter the ground used to be standing in water; and it wasn't so good in summer, either. Apart from heat waves, it'd be slimed over, of no interest to anybody except kids and dogs. So going for a song. Just the place for a school. All it needed, so they said, was draining. And they were right. It still does.'

'Do you mean that they didn't put drains in?'

'They had a go but the builders had to economise. They were doing it on the cheap. Have you seen round the back?'

He led her along the side of the school down a path too narrow for them to walk abreast, which explained its borders of grassless churned earth.

'No wonder the inside is so filthy,' she observed.

'Why lay a double course of flags when you can get away with one and say that the kids'll keep to it when the shrubs have grown up at the edges? Only they didn't get the chance.'

They passed between a couple of huts erected within months of the school's opening and called, Dick told her, temporary classrooms in the pretence that the description could conceal an inaccurate prediction of the numbers on roll. 'That was sixteen years back.'

Behind the school were similar paths strung out to the canteen, the block of laboratories, cloakrooms. In the deepening twilight these strips of pale scarified stones floated precariously on the sodden earth. Unevenly laid, they seesawed jerkily as she followed Dick and their cracks snared her heels.

'Neatham's answer to Wembley,' he announced, leaning against posts. 'Across the other side there's the netball courts for the girls.'

'But it hasn't rained since the weekend!'

'I told you it takes a heat wave to dry it out.'

'It's all part of the shoddiness of the whole place.' She looked back at the buildings, mainly one-storey, flat-roofed, flimsy constructions of wafer panels and membranes of dusty glass.

'According to one of the lads, it was thrown up in about six weeks. The components arrived on a fleet of lorries and were slid down the tail gates straight into position. Where the sections didn't quite fit, a piece of hardboard and a couple of nails cobbled up the gaps.'

'That would be funny if it weren't almost believable.'

'Taff does let his imagination run away with him but you might say the proof's in the pudding.'

She recalled seeing along corridors the tidemark of damp, a scallop border under the lip of windows and the warped panels here and there cracked, edges of cheap compressed material frayed. In some places these splits had been plugged or sutured with tape.

Don Clamp had said, 'This stuff is so brittle, a football or less legitimate projectile can splinter it. They could stave in every wall in the school just with their boots. God knows why they don't.' 'You and the rest of the staff must be the reason.' He had surprised her with his blush. 'Realism disallows such flattery. No, lethargy comes nearer to the reason. Or it might be fear of doing the wrong thing.' 'Would you approve if they kicked in the walls?' He had smiled, rueful. 'I was expecting that question. And obviously I have to say no.' Then, after a pause: 'But it would be a protest.'

'It's a disgrace,' she exclaimed to Dick. 'Worse than that, it's a scandal.' Her words were an echo of the speech of Neatham. Robert had remarked on the occasional change. Curious and scholarly he had pointed out that this was in idiom or vocabulary, not the accent; her adopted one she retained, and he had teased her, considering it a comic mix. She sounded like Eliza Doolittle after the professor's training; and she had told him that when he could hear the accent as well, he'd know she'd truly regressed. 'It's dreadful that the education authority let it pass,' she said to this other.

He shrugged. 'They had a budget and most of the classrooms were up before any inspector was on the site. But that's no excuse. They wouldn't have dared be so stingy anywhere else. This was good enough for Neatham.'

She did not ask him why, feeling so strongly, he had not protested. Don Clamp reminded her: As it is, most of them consider it our job to wave banners. She did not wish to provoke Dick with such a question.

For in this sinking light they were companionable, united in disgust, and she thought how strange it was that they should be standing there so easy together, harmonious in their contempt of this school. And she asked silently: Why couldn't it always have been like this; why have you been so unbending, holding me at a distance; was it through some policy or dislike? And lastly: What have I done wrong? It was the timeless inquisition, the woman blaming herself for failure with a man.

The paving stone under her moved, flicking her momentarily off balance and, his hand coming out and fastening upon her arm, she thought: Soon I shall invite him back to the house. To prepare for which, she told him, 'This depresses me. The country's infested with muck like this.'

'You'd consider it was a palace if you had a look at some of the other ruins Scully and Fanhope have shoved up.'

'I seem to know that name.'

'You ought. It's on boards on just about every site for miles. They've practically got the monopoly round here. The local crooks.'

'I haven't noticed; but I know why I recognise the name. Clifford works for them.'

'Well, we shouldn't be too hard on him. We can't all have shares in the DHSS,' and his hand gripped more tightly as, laughing with him, she rocked on the unstable base. 'Who's Clifford when he's at home?'

'Good question. Whose home? He's Doris Bentley's feller, or sort of.'

'What do you mean by that? Are you telling me there's some doubt?'

His salacity was new to her and, taking it as an indication of greater intimacy, she could not suppress the excitement. 'I don't know. I've never met Clifford.'

His hand was under her elbow, ostensibly steadying. Perhaps he preferred deeper shadows, not the subtle tones she could provide with a lamp's jabbing flame. He had been her guide, dark and moth-gentle, down Ryecroft's Lane. This place was equally undisturbed. And the question about Clifford had been a hint. 'But certainly his libido isn't overcharged,' she delayed with a tease.

'How's that?'

Then she told him. She described the cautious four rings on the telephone to ensure readiness for the imminent call, the careful extravagance of a chicken-in-a-basket lunch, the handyman weekends beginning with the arrival on Friday evening and the consumption of the lovingly prepared supper, then the ascent to the chaste bed, the retreat into a long read disturbed only by Doris turning the pages of her book, the thin sound fluttering against the separating wall. 'And now, can you believe it, Doris is getting at Becky Dobson not to play Miss Blygh because men might get wrong ideas!'

There was a silence, a short concentrated hiatus in which intentions assembled. 'I see,' he said, and his breath touched her cheek.

And she was propelled along the catwalk of sinking flags, slithering on patches glossed by rain and skidding through the pricking scree. To the wall of the school where there was a recess backed with glass, two knobs and the clinking grid of a metal shoe scraper twisted, bucking under her feet. While in this corner of no light, as shutter against the sky's paler dark and the limitless drop of the indistinguishable earth, his bulk stayed; he murmured, 'This rain,' and there was a movement, a sway, a bob and fabric's crackle. Waiting, sliding along the glass until she found the frame and the angle of hinge, she listened to the sounds, traced them among his clothing and cautioned herself to be patient, not permit her hands to search, be first to caress; she must relearn, forget the liberty which to him would be unseemly; she must be modest and compliant for him. He must lead the way; that was his prerogative. It was his right, the right of the system to which he would return her; and secretly not to rustle their quiet, with joy at the approach of her wish granted, she prepared herself for him and found the slick ready for his reach. So, without speaking, in accordance with his wordless signal, she moved to his touch and parted for him, first breasts and buttocks and finally the tangled shag; then obedient to his stretch she followed where he conducted down mazy passages and into roofless chambers where she was lifted and carried along underground streams for years lost to her but now recovered, turbulent, swollen, chattering not of neat banks or poetic sedges but bawling of rocks, of hidden fierce currents and jutting weirs. And as, spinning in terror and ecstasy, she was sucked into the whirling spate, she felt on her skin the delicate filament of its spume.

Gradually her mind levelled. She saw him featureless, his body without shape against the cavernous sky, and he seemed as intangible as the air which lay between them and which had not yet wavered, scurried, split or bulged in the grapple of their beat.

'It's coming down faster,' he observed. 'Can't shelter in here all night. You'll have to borrow my cagoule,' crackling once more. 'We'll have to run for it.'

She pushed away from the door, dragged her hand down the hard glass and knew the ache of the thing unfinished, the vitality soured. The juices in her body set, were impacted, bowed her with their weight, and the distension was so great, she thought that it would show. As she stepped clumsily out of the shallow doorway, something flicked up and scratched along her leg. Startled, she gave a small cry and drew back.

'It's nothing,' he told her. 'Only a screw of paper. Some kids must have been eating fish and chips. Probably up to no good, either, round here after hours.'

His gentleness cut her like a lash, raising the bitterness of what could have been and, interpreting his remark as a deduction that youngsters had coupled in this place, she was revolted, and frantic

172

with disappointment and shame. 'They shouldn't have dropped it,' she snapped. 'Leaving behind their filth.'

'You make it sound like a sin.' He was astonished by her anger.

'They foul the environment. Haven't you noticed the litter round this school?'

'I've noticed.'

'They throw it down everywhere. There are weekly rosters for harvesting it, but that doesn't work. All the wet is bad enough but with this muck on top, it's disgusting – a layer of sodden wrappers, flattened straws, pieces of moulded polystyrene, empty crisp packets, discarded cartons and card. It makes a glutinous scum on the mud.'

'Hang on, you ought to be writing that down for a newspaper or summat, not wasting it on me.' The voice was no longer gentle.

'And it would be wasted on them, too!' She was almost shouting; her words carried across the marshy grass and knocked against the school's flimsy walls. 'They can't care about their surroundings, can they? Otherwise they wouldn't do this. They make it ugly and scruffy and drab.'

'This isn't some prettified estate.'

'You don't have to tell me that! But are you implying that would make any difference? This school was new once. There were a few strips of garden. They choke them in rubbish.'

'That's all they're worth.'

'So that's an excuse for clogging up the grounds with effluence, reducing them to a tip?'

He was trying to understand. Her fury and viciousness were out of proportion to the words. He was trying to hear their true meaning.

'It could be the reason,' he suggested carefully.

She was aware that he was meeting her with logic, that for once he was not attempting evasion, and the irony of this incensed her. He proposed lucid dialectic at a moment when she had regressed to signs. Her speech had only superficial connection with what it appeared to express. The words which came to her mouth were simply channels for her despair and fury. She was wild with the knowledge of a hope lost. And that it had been an illusion.

'I'd expect you to stand up for them,' she hissed, poking her face at him. 'I'd expect you to do that. You're only interested in seeing that nobody round here gets put down. And you'll never admit there might be anything wrong with it; you'll not stand back and take a good look, see if it's got any flaws. Which is laughable because you're such a dog in the manger, guarding what isn't all that marvellous. As if anyone else wants a share! And the funny thing is, while you're so busy admiring your own patch you don't give up a minute to turn your head in another direction, which suits you in fact, because if you did you might catch sight of what you'd missed. So don't stand there surrounded by all this muck and try to give me some smart reason. You can't tell me any I don't already know, Clever Dick!' She was practically hysterical, pushing against him, daring him to strike her. She felt his body tense, taking her weight; that was all.

'If you already knew it you wouldn't be carrying on like this,' he answered, insulting her with control. 'So I'll tell you the reason, the one that strikes me. Mebbe it's their way of showing what they think to them that can stick up such a rotten school. Why should they show pride in it? No one else has. Why should they say thank you sirs for putting us in the way of sodden football pitches and classrooms dripping damp? And shall I tell you something else?'

'Why not? Enjoy yourself. You don't often let anyone into your secrets.'

'I agree with them.'

'Surprise! Surprise!'

'Because if they kept the place tidy, what would they be doing?' His speech was relentless now, farcical but without humour.

'According to your hypothesis, of course.'

'That's right. They'd be complying with what others thought fit for them. They'd be saying it was all right for them to be given less than was just. They'd be saying that, whatever was doled out, they'd make the best of it; that no matter how their lordships carried on, they'd wipe the spit away and show their gratitude for such notice sprayed on them by keeping tidy and respectful. Only they don't. They sling their litter about, which is their way of putting their fingers to their noses and telling the high-ups where to stuff their lousy chipboard and slimy grass.'

He had been indifferent to her signals. He had not bothered to explore what was stated by her attack; he had not risen to her contempt. But she was a match for him, she told herself fiercely. If it was logical argument he wanted, then she could provide it; and what is more, it would be superior to his. After all, she had had more practice. It was her habitual mode.

'I don't think much of that idea,' she told him, her voice crisp, hysteria banished. 'Neatham doesn't produce rebels. People are far too conventional; they keep to the rules. They are excessively wary, truly circumspect. They're afraid to wander from the straight and narrow,' she mocked him. 'You've said yourself that you get short shrift round here unless you toe the line.'

She wanted to cheer, to stiffen her fists and beat out her triumph upon his chest, for the last sentence had probed to a weakness; her quoting it was almost a foul. Because the context of his comment had been his defence of Florence Moorby, when he had condemned those who had ostracised Jessie. Then there had been no questioning of customary edicts; only the sister had put her finger to her nose.

'It's their own rules they keep to. It's the line they've made for themselves that they'll not step from.' Then languorously, like one replete, 'How they manage is their business. They'll not be pushed. They'll tek no notice of how others want them to act, unless it suits.'

The reprisal was effortless. Defeated, she acknowledged his intelligence and that he was more cunning than she. Yet worse. As he removed her hands from his chest and stepped back, she understood that his speech, too, had been a matter of signals and that his last words had been directed to her. It was the nearest he had come to verbal repulse. Receiving this, she leant against the door's frame, her spirit numbed.

'Time you were getting back to that house,' he said, his voice curled with remorse. 'You can hardly see the path now but you'll be all right if you keep behind me.'

'It's too late for that,' she answered. 'You should have offered before,' and glad of the small gratuity of the night's veil over her face, she pushed past him and stumbled round the building the other way.

Chapter Fifteen

Peter replaced the handset and made a note on the back of his hand. 'Glyn would like five tickets for the Saturday night,' he reported. 'The argument was over their category, paid for or complimentary. I told him only your actual sponsor, not funding bodies, could pick up the latter.'

'But we've only the one sponsor who's given cash!'

'So we shan't be handing out many free tickets.'

'He's coming on, isn't he? He'll make the businessman of the year yet.'

'People who think that concessions are their right get up my nose.'

'I wasn't criticising,' Dick assured him.

'No. But I do wish I weren't placed in such an invidious position. The money Glyn's provided isn't from his own pocket. He has no more claim to a complimentary ticket than Joe Bloggs. Kept his head down, too, these last five months. Had you noticed?'

'You didn't want him dropping in?' Nora asked.

'I certainly didn't. Constance is enough; not all of us possess Dick's talent for seeing her off. It's just that I know what will happen. Glyn will arrive with his party, all bustle and fuss, and by the time the show's over it will have become his baby entirely, sired by him years ago in some inspirational converse with a receptive town councillor, painfully gestated in the mayoral chambers, massaged slightly by myself and finally brought forth in the school hall.'

'I hope you don't reckon me as midwife,' Dick said through their laughter, adding the afterthought, 'And I can't see Nora as nurse. You shouldn't be taking on like this at the minute, Pete. I'll tell you when it's time to panic. There's nearly three weeks yet before you need to start,' correctly interpreting the reason for the other's irritation.

Formerly Nora would have smoothed away anxieties; now her solicitude was less prompt and Dick frequently supplied a jokey care. Her relationship with Peter was undamaged. It was merely that a small feature had been rubbed out, for which she felt relief rather than regret. Her resources were required for herself and there was little space to devote to anyone else. For the hope that had given her vitality at the start had petrified, leaving her with nothing but a weight she must drag until the prescribed term was at an end, and she found herself counting it off, first the weeks, then the individual days.

'There'll be no difficulty in finding good seats for Glyn's party,' she said. 'Fewer people have booked for the final performance than I expected. Usually Saturday night is the most popular.'

'Two pubs have a darts match that Saturday, but not to worry, we'll fill the hall. They don't like to commit themselves, rather make out they'd come on spec.'

'I'm pleased to hear that, Dick, otherwise I'd begin to think these months had been a waste of time.'

'Not on your nelly. Best in your life, Pete. I can guarantee that.' Then, to the other's remark that it was really Nora that he should be cheering up, he answered, rising, 'I need notice of that. I'll think out a few stories while I'm away.'

Peter waited until Dick's steps were thudding across the deserted playground before he asked, 'Aren't you well?'

'Just tired.'

'This is a temporary low. As soon as preparations accelerate to their climax – let's hope it's not crisis – the adrenaline will start pumping again. We're falling into the usual pattern.'

She thought: There will be no renewal during the next three weeks. But she was touched by his pretence that he shared her weariness, wanted to ask him: Why is it always the nice ones that are valued less? and wanted to stroke his hair, to kiss his forehead lined with worry for her, let him soft-fingered draw the tears off her cheeks.

'Can we run through the next fortnight's schedule to make sure I've missed nothing out?'

'You haven't. I've examined it. And you've reserved far too much for yourself, Nora. I can relieve you of some of your load. I don't have to potter round during the day offering last-minute boosts to the morale of helpers and it doesn't take me three mornings to give interviews on the radio and to the local press; they'll be lucky if they get ten minutes. I like the idea of your dressing those two shop windows with memorabilia, but it'll take you ages; and you mustn't try to leaflet every house. That's impossible. Leave that job to me and I'll recruit a sizeable band. You aren't obliged, as a matter of principle, to finish this project in a state of collapse.'

It was Robert's admonishment, exact even to the intonation, and she shuddered at the resemblance of the two men. Were she inclined to be fanciful, she told herself, she might imagine that her husband had been present witnessing her shame; and as she had answered him, she lied to this other: 'Believe me, that is not my intention. I'm no more busy than everyone else. I assure you that I give myself plenty of time off.'

Whereas she filled every hour, often with unnecessary jobs. Because now she must cram her thought with distractions; she must stuff every fold and cranny with the small and insignificant to prevent the banished condemnations from squeezing back: the sound of Becky's innocent admiration; the love on the face of Doris whose trust she had not deserved.

'Anyway, from now on I'll make sure you're not overloaded,' Peter was saying. 'You've had to carry the can several times recently, but honestly I had no idea last Monday how critical the situation was.'

She flinched. 'Don't worry. Becky had already confided that she didn't wish to go into it with you. Through shyness.'

'I should have come out with you the other night and confronted Doris on the spot,' she had apologised to the girl. 'I'm afraid I didn't really understand what was happening.'

'That's all right. I could see you'd got other things on your mind.' The answer had been free of sarcasm. 'All I was wanting was to keep out of her way. She's been on at me for weeks – well, two or three. First time I didn't think anything of it, she was there at the corner of Drove Lane, and she said, "Are you the girl who's playing Miss Blygh?" Wayne told her interviews and autographs by appointment only and she didn't half give him a look. She said, "I was the real Miss Blygh." I didn't know where to put myself, I really didn't. I mean, she's such a dog, and I'm supposed to look like her! That scrawny neck! I made a vow there and then I'd never be seen looking like that. Catch me wearing a scarf stuck with a pin big as my gran has in her hat, and pearls, loop after loop, and a watch dangling like a medal on her chest. I wish she'd button her coat up or wear a bin bag or something. It's embarrassing. "I'd like a word with you," she said, so I had to stop. She stared at Wayne but he didn't budge. Then she said she reckoned I shouldn't be doing Miss Blygh in the play. "I didn't push myself; I was chosen," I told her. "Mr Clamp gave my name to Mr Green and he said there could be no one better," thinking she was making out I didn't come up to scratch, though generally it's how I do in class not the way I look that comes in for comment on that score. "I was referring to the moral position," she said, pulling her mouth tight, only she didn't know that showed her lipstick was

smudged. "Lining up like that isn't the thing for a nice girl to do."
"You did it," I told her. "That's right, and I was innocent as a
newborn babe." "You saying I'm loose?" I was put out, I really was. I
don't know who she thinks she is, poking her nose in. Some people
imagine that just because they're old, they've got every right to go
round handing out insults. I walked off that night, but she was there
again soon enough.

'"I have to correct an impression," she got out before I could push
past. "I don't wish to insinuate anything about you. It's the way others
look at it. It's people watching that are in the wrong." It had come on
to drizzle and she was frightened it would mess up her set because
she'd tied one of those plastic pack-a-hat things over her hair, you
know, squares of plastic with a ribbon at each end and they fold up
like a concertina to stick in your purse. It looked awful, the creases
sticking out and a mangy knot of white ribbon under her chin. "She's
suggesting there'll be some that get ideas," Wayne told me as if I
needed an interpreter. He wasn't half pleased; he'd been grumbling
about that for weeks so this Miss Bentley suddenly interfering and
backing him up free gratis gave him a buzz. "I can look after myself,
thanks," I said back. "And if she can't, you can rely on me," he said,
preening himself like any old peacock. She shot him another of her
looks and it didn't seem that she was impressed, more distasted. I'd
have laughed if I'd been in the mood.'

'I wish Becky had let us know earlier. It's ridiculous, a member of the
cast being subjected to criticism of a scene I wrote.'

'That bothered her less than meeting Doris.'

'Because Wayne didn't catch on, Nora. In spite of being the one that's
supposed to be clever. He thought she'd taken a shine on him, silly
sod, and he got all smarmy. I told him after and he said, if she was as
old as his mother, so what? He hoped I wasn't implying his mother
was past it; she'd have plenty to say about that if she heard. I reckon
he deliberately took it wrong way. It was spooky standing there in the
twilight and drizzle, watching Wayne making up to an old bag that I
had been practising to be, when she was a girl my age at Blygh's. I
thought: She's supposed to have been a beauty and look at her now!
Could I ever be like that when I'm that old? She'd won a competition;
she'd had her photo in the paper, and was this the best she could do
– baby snatching? And I thought: Stuff that.

'She was going on about how parading in front of an audience might give the men an excuse. "They'll accuse you of being to blame when all they've been interested in is bringing you round to their notions," and I looked at Wayne and I said to her, "You're right."

'Don't get that wrong, Nora. Wayne's in agreement that we don't have any of that till we're engaged, so he's not the sort Miss Bentley was referring to. It was him siding with her that got me. He was grinning all over his face not just because he imagined they'd clicked but because her seeing eye to eye with him about me in the beauty contest gave his nagging more weight.'

'*Against* your taking part?'

'Yes.'

'I know that you never wholeheartedly approved of my including the competition but I didn't do it lightly, Nora. It seemed just that Blygh's should be represented. They have provided work for a substantial number in the town for over seventy years, and from accounts some of the sewers gave us, the Miss Blygh contest was a jolly occasion.'

'Certainly that's how Doris described it.' But the description was incomplete without the epilogue over twenty years later, of a woman tense, lips tight against the confiding, as she sat beside the hearth in a derelict schoolhouse.

'It appears to have been so innocent. Perhaps I'm naive. You don't think that in putting Becky and the others up on that catwalk I'm doing a Rupert Murdoch?'

'You're directing that scene beautifully, Peter. It has a lovely period flavour. You're getting the youthful diffidence yet eagerness.'

'It is after all Neatham. And before the swinging sixties were invented.'

'Exactly. It's thoroughly decorous.'

'My God, I hope so. But that doesn't seem to be the general feeling.'

'Peter, this objection has come from one person only, and she hasn't yet seen the play.'

'I know; I know. The trouble is, she's the one that Becky is acting.'

Nora sighed, thinking: It is Dick's job now to give reassurance. 'That's not the only point you have to bear in mind, since this is a community play. You have to consider those young girls. And I can assure you that Becky for one is getting a lot out of it.'

The benefits that Becky had claimed were unexpected.

* * *

'You see, Nora, Wayne doesn't like me showing myself off. "I wear shorts half this size to play netball," I tell him; "anybody'd think I was going to skip in front of that audience with nothing between me and their eyeballs except a G-string and a couple of milk bottle tops." But he won't be persuaded; he says it's an open 'nvitation to every man that turns up on the day. That's why he was like a dog with two tails when that Miss Bentley barged in, getting at me the same way. I wasn't having it, though. "So what?" I asked him. "If any feller starts drooling at the sight of me, it's my worry, or for that matter, my pleasure," I said, because I didn't see why I should hold back what I was thinking just because it was something he wouldn't like.

'I know what you're thinking, Nora. You're saying to yourself: Here's a turnaround, this is different to what she was mumbling on about when it came to wearing them old-fashioned shorts. Well, you're right, and I'm not too proud to admit it. But I don't want you to conclude that it means me and Wayne have fallen out. We haven't. He's lovely, and he is properly clever, not just a know-all; that is, when he's not being thick. It still seems like it would be a dream come true, me and him being married, but I've decided there's more to it than I thought – you know, the wedding and presents and that, and us in a flat with nobody butting in. I've decided that if you're not careful you can easy lose your head, and funny thing is, Nora, that's just what I mean because losing your head is losing your thoughts, how you think, letting somebody else's thoughts be inside your head instead of yours. And the thoughts Wayne has in his head are that if I show my legs off to a few seedy old men, they'll form the idea that they have a right to see when really it's only Wayne that has that, and if he can get that idea into my head then I'll be thinking like him and he'll have nothing to worry about namore. I'm sorry, Nora, if that sounds like a load of rubbish. Mr Clamp says that in the exam I have to choose the essay that wants you to describe, not argue, and though he rates my talent for the discursive (I reckon he was being sarcy) the examiners aren't quite ready for it yet.'

'You're analysing this very well, Becky.'

'Am I? Well, that's a change. Only, I feel as if this is a matter I know summat about. You see, how I work it out is this: if Wayne can get me round to his way of thinking, which is that I've no call to show my legs off to anybody else except him, or to them he says I can, then I'll be agreeing that my legs aren't so much mine to be doing what I like with as they are his. It's daft talking about legs like this, but you know what I mean, Nora?'

181

'I know. And it's not daft.'

'All right; but it does get my goat that all this comes about over *legs*. I mean, when all's said and done, what's a few inches of leg to write home about? But it's them that started it, so I've no choice. He pretends that I only took the part so's I had licence to wag them around and get the praise, legal, which was mebbe right at the start but that doesn't make me nympho, and however much he declares that every time I walk on that stage proves that I am, he'll not get that thought stuck in my mind because I know he only wants it there so's I'll not do it in order to show to him that I'm not. Do you get that?'

'Just about,' smiling.

'It's like this,' Becky repeated patiently. 'He isn't arguing whether I'm nympho or not because he knows very well I'm not; what he really wants is me feeling I've got to prove I'm not because that'll suit him. He's trying to put me in the position of doing something I don't believe in so's we don't fall out.'

'I think I've got the point now, Becky,' Nora said quickly.

'Oh, good. And another thing. It's not even as if it's a leg show, sexy in the way he says, because Mr Green won't let us do it like that, spite of us trying that on at the start. And he never rants on at Judi or Bridget or Kath or Gail, only me. So it all adds up. It's definite that he wants me to believe that I can only do what he likes. I'd never of thought I'd want to do anything else; I allus believed we liked the same when, now I look back, I was bearing myself in such a way to keep him liking me. But I'm not letting him sneak his ideas into my head and alter my way of thinking when my mind is made up, when I know I'm right and he's wrong; and he's wrong to say the competition's sexy because it isn't; and he's wrong to say I'll be egging the fellers on because I shan't; and he's wrong to put it in such a way that he wants me to believe that I have to give it up or else I'll be considered forward; and he's wrong to say I should never have got mixed up with the play in the first place when *he's* not turning his back on being that GI. He's wrong, and this play's lovely, and we've never had anything like it before in Neatham and my way of saying thank you to Mr Green is to keep on acting that part.'

'I'm pleased you say she's enthusiastic – and pleased for her as much as for myself. And you feel that Doris will stop pestering her now?'

'Yes.'

'You dealt with her, too, better than I think I could have done.'

182

'I doubt it.'

'Of course, you have lodged with her, so I suppose you know the way she thinks.'

'Yes.'

'She seemed quite cordial when I phoned, said I could visit her any time. It's a pity I didn't manage that before she went round to your house. It wasn't your problem.'

Doris knew better than he.

'I was partly prepared. Becky had warned me that Doris had declared the intention of approaching me.'

She had also said: 'So I shall carry on being Miss Blygh whatever they say, though I don't mean her – I couldn't care less about her opinion – I mean Wayne, because I'm not his to order about; I'm not married yet, and I'm not sure now that if I was, he'd have the right. Hey, do you know what? First thing I did after I'd thought that one out, I went to Shearer Magic and Marge did this. Do you like it? "I don't know why it's taken you so long," she said to me. "You've been dreaming about streaks for months. What's made up your mind for you?" And I said, "I'm a slow learner but when I get the message, I get it loud and clear." She didn't cotton on, of course, but you do, I know, Nora, and I know you'll approve – of the action, even if you're not excited about the streaks. I suppose they're what Mr Clamp would call a statement. Trouble is, I don't reckon Wayne catched on; he doesn't seem to have understood that it's more than my hair I'm changing. I banked on you being pleased about that.

'I don't want to put upon you, Nora, when I tell you this, but it was thoughts of you that helped me to see straight. I said to myself: Nora won't let anybody dictate to her, she's different; and I asked myself how you're different to my mam who'll argue but in the end she'd rather not be thought pushy if the other one's a man. I'm not blaming her; I'll never say anything against my mam. Just describing. Only, you're not like that. You'll not let any man dictate your views or alter your way of going on to fit any old requirement. That's obvious when you'll come and live the weeks in crummy old Neatham instead of staying at home looking after Mr Trafford.'

'There has never been any disagreement between Robert and me about that,' and turning, Nora had pretended to tidy the office in order to hide the mortification struck upon her face. 'He appreciates my reasons for wanting to be here.' And now her fingers, clawing through a heap of files, reached *Ryecroft's, the History*, and she watched the title crimped by the breath of a furnace out of which tongs drew the slim rods and, directed by the hands, twisted and curled the malleable steel into the determined shape.

'Well, I think that's nice,' Becky cooed, a woman of the world now, believing she spoke to an equal. 'Blimey, is that the time? My dad won't half give me it in the neck, being so late for my tea. Only I wanted to tell you about me and Wayne. I hope he doesn't throw me over; I'll cry my eyes out if he does, but it's no good believing one thing and acting another, is it? So if I'm not letting him fashion me how he wants, I have to stick to my guns. I'm not going to be like some, Nora. You know the sort,' she confided, newly smug with platitudinous wisdom; 'I'm referring to those women that'll do anything to make up to a man.'

'I know only too well,' she had answered and, unmindful of the evening's advance, had sat alone at the desk appalled by the girl's unwitting ironies and marvelling at the intersection of these two women's lives with her own. And the point where they crossed was jagged and stony and she could neither circumvent it nor scramble over its barbs. For standing in the doorway to the cloakroom of the school, she had allowed her tongue to stroke him with: Clifford's very much the well-behaved gentleman, no irrepressible passion for him. After arriving on Friday he partakes of a calm undisturbed meal and spends the evening with feet comfortably planted in pre-warmed slippers, his conversation never straying from discussion of the Saturday domestic jobs, his eyes sedulously hooked to the little screen and his hands never anywhere but on his lap. At bedtime he ascends to his monastic cell, lies in his narrow cot and does penance with a book until Doris, weary with waiting, puts out her light and he feels it's safe to sleep.

Peter fussed, 'I wish you had mentioned Becky's warning that Doris might bother you. I wouldn't have delayed visiting her if I'd known of that possibility. Offers to relieve you of work sound rather empty when twice during these last two weeks I've left you to cope. I'll have to do better in the next three, otherwise Robert will be suing me for neglect.'

'Doris would have spoken to me whether or not you had gone to talk with her.' His apology was irksome; his self-reproach excessive, of so little moment in comparison with her own. 'It was nothing.

184

Practically all I had to do was listen.' And found herself offering up the desperate, age-old, futile prayer to forget.

She'd never meant to do this. She'd vowed she'd never speak to Nora again but young Becky Dobson had said to her: 'You shouldn't be picking on me. I just do as I'm told. It's Mr Green who wrote it you should be telling off. Or see Nora; she'll put you right.' The vicious look on her face was enough to turn your stomach and Doris nearly advised her: Switch that on much oftener and it won't be beauty competitions you're chosen for. But she had been pulled up by the girl's words. 'I'll go and see Nora,' she had answered. It came out like that without thinking, not stopped by vows in the head, and she was glad because it was like a promise, so no matter what, you couldn't go back.

Though she almost did as she crossed the empty playground, its surface so deteriorated that she felt the prick of gravel through the soles of her shoes. It took all the courage she possessed to turn round the end of the building, through the broken gate held up by the ground not the hinges, and enter the walled-in yard. Because now she was ashamed of herself for all she had said to Nora that evening nearly two months back but it seemed like only last week, and she felt she ought to be standing here straddling the drain – it could do with a grid – ready to offer apologies, but that wasn't why she had come. She'd meant every word she had said at the time, however terrible they sounded; she'd said them in the heat of the moment, not bottling them up as she had been taught since that was polite, but she couldn't decide whether or not that made her glad. The result was that Nora had left. As she had walked through the estate then trekked along streets recorded on the tickets of her mother's customers, her memory sniffing the route they plotted like a hound recovering overlaid scents, she had said to herself that she was making the journey in order to mend what she had fractured. Now she admitted that was not so. Such an ambition was hopeless. She was here because she wanted to speak to Nora again. But when she paused to select a path over the cracked slabs, her resolution faltered. The yard was a tight rectangle bounded by brick, its light cavernous under thick elders, its air stagnant, crusted by the faint stench which seeped through the soil closet's vent. She thought: This is what I escaped from, one time. And turned to do so again but found one of her heels was clamped between stone edges and that Nora was standing at the door.

'Becky told me you would be coming,' she said.

So, freeing her shoe, Doris stepped over the webbed fissures and entered the house.

It was not how she had imagined the meeting while she had bathed and changed, putting her hair in heated rollers to revive a limp set. This was not how she'd seen it before she started having the doubts, and she realised now how unrealistic the idea had been, stupid, since you couldn't ignore what had gone on the last time they'd been together; it was there between them like a freak creature that you wanted to turn your eyes from but couldn't forget. She'd be willing to soothe it over and say it was all her fault, but that didn't seem appropriate and Nora looked edgy, asking her twice, as if she hadn't got the answer first time, whether she'd like a cup of tea. Balanced uneasily on a canvas camping stool, she repeated a memorised formula: 'I thought I'd drop in to see if you're all right and if there's anything ...' but becoming aware of the room, broke off and exclaimed, 'Nora, you needn't have come down to this!' And immediately rebuked herself for being spontaneous.

She saw Nora's lips straighten. 'We're sorry you've been pestering Becky,' she answered her, prim.

Having to adjust, Doris frowned, concentrating. This subject had not held priority during her preparations.

'It would have been better to discuss the matter with one of us. We're puzzled, too, why you have changed your mind.'

Wan, she told her, 'That's my privilege.'

'It's not possible now to alter the play.'

'That would be too big a concession to expect.'

'Look, Doris, had you objected at the beginning, Peter would not have included such a scene, but you were very keen on it, a lot keener than I was. Added to which, your warnings aren't valid. You'll agree when you see it. Why don't you come into a rehearsal and watch? Truly the only prurience it could possibly excite would be among the pathologically oversexed.'

'There's plenty of them around.' She had not come to argue about this. She had not had any great hopes that they would stop the competition. Her intention had been to make the girl aware. Becky was her proxy. She could not see the girl in any other light and, just as it had happened all those years ago, she thought it might happen again if she didn't get a word in first. It was possible. History, they say, has a habit of repeating itself.

'I think we can cope. And Becky,' she heard the other say.

She felt responsible. She had encouraged the scene of the beauty contest, had let it go on, a bit out of vanity but more in celebration of those former friends and in memory of their vaulting days whose happiness she wished to share with this one who had come to her, welcomed though so late. So she had allowed herself to return to that time, rub bright its faded brilliance and prevent its loveliness from going to waste, contriving in her exhilaration to keep the destroying sequel locked away.

'Surely you wouldn't wish the scene to be withdrawn because it might provoke molesters? Is there a reason that we should know for your changing your mind?' Nora persisted.

She shook her head and not wishing to meet the other's eye, Doris looked round the chill room. The wallpaper, its pattern grimed by the years, was blistered with damp; the window frames were seamed with mould; scales of ceiling plaster scurfed the floor, whose boards were splintered and, gaping, funnelled the draughts. A thin mattress rested on a flimsy tubular base; clothes zipped into a cover hung from the picture rail; a number of books and tins of food were stacked on newspaper inside the hearth. Shocked, Doris thought: She has deliberately chosen this; it's no more than what they call a squat; I doubt whether she's given it a good brush-out and mop; she's come here when she could be living in 9 Belle View! The other's preference was a snub; it was an insult dealt out not only by Nora but by that man. Because he was the reason why Nora was pigging it in this hole; he was the reason why Nora had left; it was him whom she favoured, passing over Doris who had been nothing more than a mere convenience, who had been pushed out to make room for him who couldn't be excused even on the grounds that he was a gentleman, like Clifford. Because he was common, with rough hands, which had unfastened all the memories and confronted her once more with the fear and the shame. You could say, if you liked, that speaking to Becky was her way of getting her own back. It was the nearest she could come to that, a kind of settling of a debt after twenty-five years. Without having to go into explanations.

But she answered, 'The reason's what I've said.'

The other shrugged; and Doris thought: Would I have been able to tell sitting on cushions piled on the hearth rug, shielded by twilight and turned from the dazzle of the electric fire's glow? But the chance had gone. There was no curtain across this window and no quiet flickerings came from this hearth; it was full of ash. Doris shivered.

'The oil heater is in the kitchen,' the other responded and, rising from the edge of the bed, straightened her thick jacket.

'It's all right. I don't want to put you out.'

'Well,' Nora said.

She was being dismissed; she supposed that was reasonable since she'd given nothing away, but she couldn't do that, not here, not where Nora and him met. She had told it only twice before and both times had taught her to keep silent. Which was easier, in the end, because it had taken more effort than anybody could imagine to spit out the words, even to her mam.

'I'm thinking about the girl,' she stated aloud. 'If anything should happen. It's not only that, itself, that would upset her but the way other folk look at it. They might say it was her fault.'

The other was staring.

'I don't refer to her mother. She'd understand.'

'I wish you'd put the dinner on the table for your father,' her mother had said, coming back flustered. 'It's enough having you mooning about the house without being useless into the bargain.' But Doris had known that the grumbling was to give indignation an outlet. 'Well, he says they won't take my word. He says you'll have to go into the station and make a statement, which means you have to describe exactly what happened. I told him nobody should ask that of a young girl not yet sixteen, and he could hardly keep the smile off his face, pointing out that meant you were out of rompers. And I asked him, "What do you mean by that?" and he pretended to look knowing – in front of me who can give him a few years! – and he answered without a moment's hesitation, "Nowadays girls aren't as innocent as they were in our day, Mrs Bentley; they get wind of it before marriage and that can excite them. So some'll make allegations." I was flabbergasted. "How can you insinuate that about my Doris? You'll remember her in her pram, not so long after you came to Druggist Lane Station.""Eight years after, to be exact," he answered prompt; "retirement hasn't addled my memory." No doubt he was expecting congratulations. "Well, you know there's never been anything of that nature in Doris." "Maybe winning that contest went to her head; you have to allow for that," he insisted, and it quite turned me up because he wasn't at all as I had expected, ready with sympathetic advice. I think he was enjoying himself, though he kept a straight face. I said to him, "I'd never have thought that of you, Frederick; I'm disappointed, I really am." I shouldn't have said that, Doris, because it didn't allow for the big idea he has of himself, which hasn't shrunk with the years.

"Look, Mrs Bentley," he said, "I didn't ask you to come here after my opinion. I was looking forward to a game of bowls before you interrupted, and all I can do is tell you what the Inspector will say. First of all, he'll not take the report second hand, so no matter how Doris feels about it, she'll have to go in; and he'll definitely say that she should have done that straight off. He'll take less notice after a week's delay. But without that, I doubt whether she'd get much change out of the Inspector. He'll advise her to consider what she's alleging. It's a very grave accusation and Mr Fallis is a respected man in the neighbourhood and highly thought of at Blygh's. I'm given to understand that he's standing for the Council next year."'

'You say that the girl's mother would understand. So would most people. Provided that she could bring herself to confide.'

Doris saw that the other had not fetched in the oil stove but was sitting on the bed again, watching her visitor, her hands clutched in her pockets against the draughts.

Doris thought: She knows I wasn't speaking about the Miss Blygh in the play and she was answering the real one, me.

She shook her head. 'Telling only aggravates matters.'

'Clara's been told you've handed in your cards,' Beryl had announced at the door. 'So I told the girls I'd come and fetch the story. You're a real caution, you are, Doris, sneaking off without so much as a word. Marlene will have it that some chap's popped the question and you're too shy to say. You know what she's like. There's a lot of talk in the canteen; people think it's a bit funny you no sooner being chosen as Miss Blygh than you bugger off.

'Well, the mucky sod!' she had said finally, outraged; her arm round Doris's shoulder was trembling. 'And of course you should've told me, you silly fathead; you did right, letting it come out. But it's no surprise. I'm sorry to say that, but it isn't. I allus told Joan that his only reason for introducing that contest was to give him view of a few more inches of bare flesh but I never reckoned he'd not be satisfied with that. I'm going to report him to the boss; he's not getting away with it; we'll settle him. Doris, please stop crying, do; I can't stand it, I feel so useless; you make me wish I'd got a gun. And look, duck, we shouldn't be carrying on like this; we should be laughing – I mean, it's funny, looked at one way, please have a go – because when it came to the point he couldn't do nothing, could he? Must have taken all the strength out of it getting you laid out behind the hedge. Try to see it like that some day, maybe, if you can't now. Doris, I don't understand why I shouldn't go and tell the boss. If I don't the rotten bugger'll get off scot free and he ought to be there in the *News of the World*, Doris, he qualifies for nothing less. All right then, I won't, if you're set against answering questions, but there are others to consider so I'm not promising I can keep my mouth closed.'

And she hadn't. With the best of intentions, Beryl had told her friends what had occurred and the whisper had gone round Blygh's. So that for years wherever Doris was she felt him pushing, squeezing, ripping, tearing, against the counters of shops and within bus shelters and along the church pews, forever closing upon her in the monitors of their eyes, while their heads tilted sometimes calculating, sometimes sympathetic, sometimes satisfied (had she not received her deserts for the title, Miss Blygh?), always curious and never forgetting. She had said to herself later when the experience had dulled that it was from her rather than from Mr Fallis they had exacted the price.

'So you see, I worry about this Becky. I don't want anything to happen that might do her harm.'

'It won't, Doris. We'll see to that. And you'll be pleased to learn that she appears to be benefiting from playing the part. She's already learnt an unanticipated independence.'

'Has she?' She didn't understand. 'Well, times change.'

She was certain that Nora had guessed and though she blushed she was glad. Because it was a relief – more than that: a marvellous thing – that Nora should know without Doris having to go into it, without having to reconstruct what had happened detail by detail, not having to spell it out. And this being unnecessary was a measuring rod for the amount they understood each other. It showed how well they could have got on. But they had been prevented. A man had seen to that; a man, she imagined, like Mr Fallis who had worked on the shop floor before his promotion and had been heavy with pincer hands and cannibal teeth and a still lingering smell of grease. Chilled by the room, her buttocks numbed by the uncushioned stool, Doris looked into the hearth, could discover no way to circumvent the bulk of the two men between them, and felt the tears scorch under her lids.

'I know you won't mention this to anyone,' she told Nora. Beryl had, though for a good reason, and she had not realised it would bring

Doris pain, for she wasn't in the same rank for friendship as Nora, who could sense how Doris felt. 'I know how careful you are not to let on without permission. I saw this right from the start. I remember the first night you came to my house you were reading somebody's reminiscences and when I came close you would've put your hand over the page if it hadn't looked rude. I noticed that, but I wasn't offended. It proved you were someone to trust.

'I know how easy it is for some people to let things out,' she continued, nodding wisely, thinking of Beryl. 'Not because they want to hurt but sometimes because they want to create an impression, you know what I mean? I hope I would never do that. I'd never be able to forgive myself if I did.'

Obviously Nora felt the same because her face was all twisted as she tried to declare that she, as Doris, regarded as sacred all private words of confiding and deeds and thoughts. And she was trying to agree what they could have been to each other if third parties hadn't intervened; but all she could gasp out was: 'Oh, Doris, I . . .'

'You don't have to say,' Doris answered her gently.

Because they understood each other; they knew what was going on in each other's minds. Tonight had proved that. And as the tears, washing back, refreshed her eyes with coolness, Doris told herself that this was a precious thing to possess. Circumstances had been her enemy but she had not been totally defeated. It was melancholy-sadness she felt, not barren misery, for she would leave this derelict room with her knowledge to treasure, to protect, to hold to herself, stroking its loved lineaments by which her spirit would be renewed. A flower pressed in a book.

'You don't have to say,' she repeated. 'I know what you're thinking.' For she saw that the other woman could not answer. She was too full up.

Chapter Sixteen

'Despite all the duties crying out – nay, shrieking – for my attention this crisp autumn morning,' Glyn Mayhew wrote, 'my priority must be to pen my most sincere congratulations. Naturally I was vastly disappointed at having to back out of attending the Saturday perform- ance. A lucky thing I hadn't sent the money for the ticket, which I'm sure you'll have no difficulty in selling.'

'I'd suggest we invoice him for it,' Peter offered a line commentary, following her eyes as she read.

'And lucky, too, that you had a dress rehearsal on Monday, a blank in my diary, but nevermore! The entry: P. G.'s Neatham saga, *A Bit of All Right*, deserves to be illuminated. At the end of the year I shall have the page framed. Because, Peter dear fellow, it was quite splendid. I sat entranced.'

'Glyn's appreciation is very exaggerated. At least fifty per cent is insincere and the rest is unwarranted,' Peter said, clumsily trying to conceal his pleasure. 'So I'll shog off. The banner's guy ropes at the fish shop end are coming adrift so I'm doing my act again on the roof. This time with Stan's help. I didn't know when we put it up that Dick suffers from vertigo.'

'Don't forget the *Evening News* is sending someone in at eleven. They want your photo.'

'Yours would be much nicer. Didn't they take enough last night?' Tuesday, their final dress rehearsal, before the first performance on Thursday, leaving the cast free this evening to manicure, pedicure, shampoo, curl, tweak, gargle, check moves, frantically con parts; while stage hands set up, tested equipment, baked, cleaned out baskets for the transport of pigeons, ironed costumes, washed the pre-school play group's soft toys; and she, Nora, having ensured that this activity was in progress, tinkered with a few insignificant tasks and waited for the last dimming of the lights. At approximately twenty-two fifteen on Saturday.

Only her intellect could respond to Glyn's enthusiasm.

'It was in your very best style, Peter, superbly theatrical, though that's probably not a word to be pronounced too loudly in the context of a community play! Some people – and I don't have to mention

192

names – might object that too high a degree of professionalism is contrary to the principles of this kind of production, but frankly I've never agreed that *anything* vindicates tat. You are clever, of course. (I'm not so out of touch with the boards, can still feel them occasionally springing under my feet, that I don't recognise how it's done!) Drill the cast in dense business and moves – no mean achievement, I admit – and the audience believe that if they don't project adequately it's because they're absorbed in their tasks and the dialogue is kind of spontaneous. Add some unexpected contrivances – you've got them well trained backstage – and the illusion's complete. We even begin to be persuaded that when Joe Brown comes in with the wrong line, it is inspired direction!

'And what effects, Peter! For the first minute or two I was a bit dubious about staging the bombing of Ryecroft's outside the hall. We all know about regulations imposed by philistine fire brigades, I said to myself, but this is ridiculous, the man doesn't have to simulate the real thing out there on the football pitch. Where in the name of God are his lights? But it worked marvellously, the old fellow – pro Ernest Wagstaff, wasn't it? – standing by the French doors silhouetted against all that stuff crackling behind him, describing what he'd seen. I declare that yours truly was scared out of his little cotton socks. By what wizardry, Peter, did you get those windows to rattle? I loved the painting scene dissolving into the chapel fête; pure Peter Green, that, I thought. And I liked the street party on VE Day, too; there was a good feeling of relaxation after labour. I particularly applauded the photomontage of the lads in khaki (you've found a gifted photographer there, Peter) grinning down at the revellers scoffing the baked meats. There was a sense of families reunited.'

The telephone rang. Pleased at the respite from Glyn's fulsome praise, Nora answered the request for Dick. 'I'm afraid he's out at the moment. Can I help?'

There was a brief hesitation, then: 'All I really want to know is what time it starts on Saturday.' Informed, the speaker said, 'I thought it'ud be about that.'

'We shall do our best to see that it begins on the dot,' she assured him, amused. 'Do you wish to book tickets?'

'Tickets? Dick never mentioned them. I'll leave it for the moment if you don't mind. Check it with Dick.'

Wondering whether he was running a private system of complimentaries, the probability of which was quite high, Nora returned to Glyn's letter.

'There were some lovely touches. As a rule, Peter, I don't generally go for pigeons, rather too heavy-busted for my tastes and without the wit to manage more than a couple of notes, but my heart unreservedly warmed to the one that refused to take off. There lies in the pea-sized brain intimations of independence, I joyed, though I knew that wasn't the interpretation required, so I capitulated and acknowledged the frustration and despair of its owner – a talent worth encouraging, there, Peter – whose attempts at cajolery not only failed but left him bespattered. That's one certain laugh. It was a relief that the bird concentrated its attention upon him, otherwise I'd have been unfurling the umbrella. Was the creature specially trained? Of the livestock, I predict that the chinchilla rabbit will be the show stopper; and may I say that I admire your restraint in drawing the line there? After that imitative piece put on by you-know-who at Centre Six, deservedly a flop, I don't think I could look another whippet in the face.

'I found something curiously affecting about the last scene. It was a strange way to end, rather teasingly ambiguous, I thought, a mix of the accusatory and hopeful. I wasn't sure what I should be coming away with. Yes, I know you made a statement *v.* the system through the unemployed and men made redundant by Ryecroft's, but weren't you rather softening it by having them turn their hands to assist with a play about their own town? Were you criticising a narrow perspective, presenting a kind of narcissistic retreat from the harsh world? Or was it an affirmation of the healing power of art? I'm probably straining its intellectual content. Or is it a satisfactory, home-grown solution? Thinking on, that must be your point. Certainly that's how your friend and mine will interpret it, so as far as she is concerned, it'll be a winner.'

Bored by this as she would not have been three weeks earlier, Nora flipped over the page, saw that Glyn had twirled his prose through a further two pages, and fled. Downstairs a woman was washing jars marbled with poster paint; seeing Nora's kettle, she jerked away. This recoil had become a habit begun as Mandy's retaliation for Dick's choice in the public house that summer evening. Nora's conversation, studiously unperturbed, was part of the ritual.

'Play group finished for the day?' After the surly nod, 'Has the slide been collected yet?'

'Ross said he'd bring the van at half-past.'

'It's a relief we can move the slide. It keeps the children occupied in the pre-school play-group scene much better than the original toys.' Not waiting for an answer she knew would not be offered, and deciding that on this probably last private meeting she would shame the other's incivility with generosity, she said, 'I expect to be in the office for the rest of the morning so if you don't wish to hang about with Cindy, I'll show Ross where the slide is and lend him a hand.'

'I'm staying.'

She had been tolerant long enough. She was tired of diplomacy. In three and a half days she would have left. She no longer felt obliged to maintain good relations with everyone in the interest of the project. So, turning off the water, squeezing the tap tightly in the hope that Mandy would have a struggle to reopen it, she pronounced, 'I think you're very wise to stay. If you can't trust Ross.'

The other flushed. 'I can trust him all right, only I wouldn't want him to have the embarrassment.'

'You're too protective, Mandy. He's old enough to cope with it himself. On the other hand, he might not be in the least embarrassed.'

Hearing herself, the salacious lilt, she turned from the sneer on the young woman's face and for a moment regarded the unwelcoming room, squalid and greasy as are kitchens for common use, and appropriate to her joyless game. She herself was the one whom she had shamed. Her eyes kept from the other, she left the sink, walked through the arch and towards the office stairs. She did not pause when Mandy shouted, merely twitched as the words struck her back: 'If you're thinking to invite him into that mucky house, you're wasting your time. I can tell you it's a dead cert that none of ours is busting a gut to take up with *you*. Their mates wouldn't half laugh! As I said to our Babs, "When she slunk into that hole I bet she reckoned that Neatham wouldn't notice, and she must have a tile loose if she thinks we don't know the design she's got in her head."'

'Not in my head, Mandy,' she murmured beyond insult as she re-entered the office. 'A design, but not in my head.'

Busy with enquiries, photographs, and a visit to the local radio station, Nora did not return to Glyn's letter until the end of the afternoon.

'How you manage all this, Peter, is a mystery, quite apart from training an epic-size cast. The play makes Neatham seem almost attractive – I stick at *almost*; it doesn't persuade me to move house. Your success with this play is all the more impressive because on this occasion you weren't working with material that offered you an inherent shape, nor is the society cohesive like mining or agricultural communities, and nothing spectacular has ever flourished in the Neatham air. Even so, you did find a way of giving it structure and the whole thing had a pulse which kept my attention, even interest. As you know, this isn't a genre I've ever been wild about. I really cannot be excited by clan rivalries over the Sunday feeding and watering of itinerant preachers or by the oldest inhabitant's countdown for *The Telegram*, though that was a nice running joke. Appreciating your dedication, I won't go on. I know why this audience will love all that, however – as have all your others. It must be very enjoyable to watch yourself reflected in such an affectionate mirror, and to hear your own words quoted must convince you of their enduring worth. To build up a play by this method is another technical triumph for you. And, I would have thought, to have extracted the copy in the first place! What spells and charms did you and Nora employ to persuade such frankness? Was it a matter of their surrendering all? It very much looked like it, because as I listened to characters, particularly where their dialogue was extended, I felt that you had penetrated to the inside. The trouble is, Peter, I still don't think there is anything much there!'

Coming from Glyn, the last sentence was not surprising. It was necessary for him to restate a sophisticate's scepticism after such a tribute to the play's conviction. However, he was wrong. The documentary format, the idiom and cadences of transcribed speech, encouraged the assumption that the characters were confiding their innermost feelings but it was an illusion created by Peter's skill. Which had led to Glyn's mistaken conclusion.

Nora thought of the omissions: the ecstasies preserved against intrusion; the horrors and guilts withheld. Then, the partial unburdening, by an allusion sometimes ponderously calculated, sometimes an involuntary relief. And the confessions in codes too esoteric for her to decipher, signals made laboriously and desiring neither her understanding nor answer. The shutters raised for a moment then let drop. The pacing round a mental obstruction whose nature was never clarified since it was thought visible to her. The long silent retreat into the contemplation of years whose face only could she observe.

'So Peter, once again congratulations on pulling it off! After your pioneer work, the good burghers of the place may not disapprove of the occasional theatre group's bringing a show, so your work and our money will have been worth while. It was a marvellous piece of theatre. I only wish, dear fellow, that the inhabitants of Neatham had provided you with rather more sensational grist.'

The fact that they had not done so was a triumph he had not guessed at. The lack of sensationalism was the exact measure of their success.

'I don't know why Pete is so pleased with that letter,' Dick commented as he entered the office for the first time that day.

'He needs appreciation other than ours, which can't be objective. Most of this is very flattering.'

'When it says that, in the end, Glyn Mayhew reckons there's not a lot there?'

'He's expressing what he deduces about the people, not evaluating the play, but I can understand your objection to that.'

'I'm not bothered what Glyn Mayhew has to say about Neatham; he's talking out the back of his head anyway. But if he doesn't find much of interest in the characters, then the same must go for the play, except what he calls effects and contrivances.'

'That's possible,' and hoped that never in the future would she sink to describing him as a man with an untutored intelligence.

'There's too many backhanded compliments for my liking: that one about drilling the cast to look so absorbed in what they're doing that the audience believes that's the reason they don't speak up; and though Pete kept it going, there's not a deal of scenes he can get wild about – like chapel preachers and so forth.'

'His sense of humour.'

'I'd not want any truck with him in a bad mood.'

'Well, that's not a likely danger.'

'Do all folks in his sort of job spend their time arguing the toss?'

So, she thought, his criticism of Glyn's letter was the introduction for another irritation. But she did not wish to hear it. 'I can't say; I've never worked with them. Would you mind locking up? I'm clocking off. I've been confined to this office all day, most of it answering the phone.'

'Did you tell Constance Skrimshaw where I was, then?'

'No, but I would have done, had she telephoned. Aren't details of your movements for general release?'

He did not object to her tone. It was a welcome fuel for his annoyance. 'She must have checked with the school, expecting I'd be there. Came bouncing into the hall when me and Vic had the projector stripped and in hundreds of bits, wanting to give her views on the anthology.'

'What anthology?'

'Look, Nora, don't play silly buggers. You always take that line. I don't know why you pretend you've never heard anything about it.'

'I've heard about it but not from you, so adopting your principles I have to pretend it's a great secret.'

He glared, sucking in his cheeks. At last: 'Do you want it, i's dotted and t's crossed?'

'Not now. You've missed your chance.' It was a playground squabble, its syntax repeating her youth's; but the desire to reconstruct that had passed. 'I'm going. I need something to eat.'

He waited until she had completed the words then, as if their sound had not reached him, demanded fiercely, 'Can you remember Clarrie Bell's tape?'

'Not in detail. The last time I read or heard any of it was when Constance came in. My acquaintance with the transcripts is neither as close nor as recent as yours.'

'The section I'm talking about is her description of Freddie waiting to scare off the dog.'

'You may talk about any section you like, Dick. Feel free. Only I shan't be listening unless you hold forth in the house because that's where I'm going. Now.'

To her astonishment, he flicked the switch on the answering machine, followed her down the stairs and locked the doors behind them. As she led him round the school, across the house yard and through the back door, she reflected upon the effortless manner in which she had at last achieved her aim. But too late.

In the kitchen she lit a camp stove, filled the kettle from the tap out in the yard and put it to boil while he paced the next room, raging against community arts officers, political interference and underhand manipulation.

'I thought that you and Constance had reached an agreement,' she said, fishing a packet of biscuits out of the hearth.

'Some agreements I'd rather not have. I don't want her being all lovey-dovey and making out I'm including things just because she approves of them.'

'I can imagine that doesn't suit.'

'It's bloody infuriating! She came into town today to return my choices for the book. I'll have to do a lot of cutting down yet, but I said she could have a look when I got to this stage. And she was all over me. Mainly on account of one piece. Vic had to go into the bog to stop laughing. It's these pages.' He opened a briefcase, a recent purchase, and took out a ring file. Inside, the extracts from reminiscences were carefully typed; there were pencilled instructions to Walter Price. It looked very professional. He found the place. 'Read that, to bottom of the next sheet.'

She could have quibbled that a request would have been more

acceptable than an order but his excitement had punctured her lethargy and she was curious.

It wasn't so lonely as you might think, and often they'd give Gavin a brown egg for his tea, but I couldn't stay long, I had to think about Frederick's position. We had a dog and she was quite friendly but a bit big to handle, I think she had some Alsatian in her, and I didn't like to take her on the walks. It's her that made me start on this story.

You see, when she was in season the dogs from all over would come sniffing round. It was amazing; they'd turn up from farms three and four miles away. It was a real headache; we used to keep Bess on the chain but that only stopped her running off, it didn't deter visitors. Frederick used to bawl at them and their owners when passing would whistle them away but there was one that used to hang about day and night, a little Scottish terrier that belonged to the shopkeeper the other side of the road to the police house. I suppose when it was hungry it could just pop across for its meal and run back. In the end Frederick decided he was going to put a stop to it good and proper and one day after tea as the night was drawing in he made preparations. 'I'll settle that little . . . once for all,' he told me, and he did!

He fetched out his notes for the day, to study them as he always did before making a neat copy, and walked down the yard to the earth closet and put his book on the shelf by the seat. Then he came back. 'It's raining,' he reported; 'I'll need the umbrella.' This on account of the fact that the roof had a leak, and he took that down the path and propped it alongside his notebook. 'What are you after now?' I asked, beginning to giggle when he returned a second time. 'I'm about to issue a caution,' he says and fetched his air pistol from under the stairs. By this time Bess had sensed that Frederick had some business in hand and she was leaping about at the end of her chain and whining, so Frederick had to hesitate and give her a stroke to calm her down before he carried on. Then he took up his position in the closet, but not seeing any sense in lolling on the lid when he could put the time to use, he dropped his trousers and sat on the seat, though of course he left the door open to watch out for Scottie. Now I know it was against the proprieties, but I just couldn't help taking a peep through the kitchen window and I'll never forget what I saw. There was Frederick sombre as a judge sitting on the seat with his trousers runkled round his ankles and his notebook open on his bare knees, and in one hand – it'd be his left – he was holding the umbrella over his head because the hole in the roof was immediately above where you sat on the closet, and in his other hand he had the air gun cocked. I could've died laughing. You mustn't think I was mocking him, there was nothing disrespectful, he wasn't wearing his uniform, but I'd never thought how anyone must look sitting there under the umbrella when it was raining. To tell you the truth, ever afterwards when Frederick went down that yard with that brolly I couldn't keep my face straight.

Anyway, I hadn't been long at the window and Frederick told me after that he hadn't read so much as one entry in his notes, when Bess starts the chain clanking and there's Scottie sidling in. It was ridiculous, a dog that size showing an interest, which I hadn't thought of because I hadn't felt like watching before, but I didn't watch for long. No sooner does Scottie come between Bess and the closet than Frederick lets rip. Scottie yelps and goes up like he's on a spring and starts racing for the gate while his feet are still in the air but Frederick manages to pepper him again before he disappears round the wash house. And that was the end of the nuisance. We never saw him again. 'That's taught that old dog a lesson,' Frederick said and, for years later, that's all one of us had to recite to start us laughing. Only it was the umbrella I was thinking about.

I was right when I said that was the end of the nuisance but it wasn't quite the end of the incident. Next morning Frederick was on duty when the shopkeeper came round. 'I've got an offence to report,' she said. 'Oh, have you?' I answered. 'What's that?' 'There's a soldier at large prowling about and wants seeing to. My hubby has sent me to tell the constable.' 'Well, you give me the details and I'll pass them on,' I answered, though they were a couple spent most of their time on the doorstep with complaints. But when you're in the Force you don't have to let personal feelings come into it but abide by procedure. 'He's been tampering with our Scottie,' she said and I asked, 'What makes you say that?' 'Because our Scottie came home with his coat full of pellets,' she said. I can tell you that by this time I had my hand over my mouth. 'Perhaps he got between somebody shooting pigeons,' I suggested; 'he always strikes me as a nosey sort of dog.' 'I'll thank you not to make remarks about our Scottie,' she answered; 'and please inform Constable Bell that that dog is so frit now he'll not leave our side of the road.'

'In that case, you should count your blessings,' I answered. 'When it comes to being run over he won't offer the market bus a chance.'

As soon as Nora had finished reading, Dick demanded, 'Well, what do you make of that?' His urgency would have persuaded anyone to deduce that the story was his invention.

'I've always had a soft spot for Clarrie although I can't approve of many of her principles.'

He burst out: 'It's a gut-buster, a side-splitter, that's what it is. It'll have them rolling about on the mat. That's why I'm putting it in; folks like a laugh and a sentence or two from that on the cover and it'll be a sell-out. First run of a thousand will be snatched up fast as Walt can turn them out.'

'You know your market.'

'It'll be a bestseller inside a week. In Neatham the only time a person'll buy a book is when it's stood in the 5p basket in the church bazaar. But that picture of Freddie Bell – and it's only the babbies'll not remember him – with his trousers round his ankles sitting on the lav and taking pot shots at a Scottie will have them in stitches.'

'Certainly the comedy is very broad.'

'There isn't so much that's funny in the book that I can afford to leave that story out.'

'I didn't think there was any danger of that, except that for some reason you'd prefer not to have Constance's approval.'

'It will go in for my reason, not hers, but I can't get that into her thick skull. She's crowing about it; she sees it as compensation for Pete refusing to put that other story about Freddie in the play, the one where he and his mate took their truncheons to those Micks. She says that it's a bigger indictment of their behaviour, Freddie shooting at a dog. It was an air pistol! I tell her. No matter, she answers; that episode puts into a nutshell the whole argument for not issuing guns to the police. It was an air gun, Constance, I tell her again, patient as I can be although by now it's certain she must be daft in the head. That is irrelevant, she tells me; it's the mentality that went with it that's significant.

'After that I thought I'd better try another tack so I said: Look, Constance, this book is a collection of stories about what it's been like living in Neatham over the last seventy or eighty years; that's what people want to read, that's what I shall tell them on the cover they're going to read; and I'm not out to make any points in respect of the police force or anything else. You can't help it, the silly bitch answers; everything you do is a political act.

'It was then Vic made for the bog. I should've asked her what brand of politics she reckoned he was favouring there. Instead, it was her said next words: I see the ease with which Frederick Bell took up that gun as highly relevant social comment, relevant to the community, she says. I have to inform you, I say, that you're up the creek. Folk here know how farmers and such go on, keeping a gun behind the back door to mow down the rabbits and pigeons when they line up to attack, and Freddie having had village stations it was natural for him to have a gun. Only he sat with it on the lav, Constance. It's a funny story, and nowt else. But that didn't floor her. She answers: If it's as good as you think, then like all comedy it has a serious intention and in spite of what you protest I know that when you include it you're being more subversive than you'll admit, you cagey devil. I'm delighted you've taken it on board. It redresses the balance. When Peter bobbed the other police issue I was really pissed off.

'So now when I put that story in she's going to say it's only there to make a daft point about police mentality.' Anger scored through his speech.

'Does that matter?'

'Of course it matters! Every time she issues out compliments for something I've done like she wanted, even though she's wrong, she's creating the impression she's got me under her thumb. It's a manner of manipulating after the event.'

'You're tarred with the same brush. Has Clarrie agreed to that story's being published?'

'What a question! I wouldn't print it without.'

'I think it's possible that she wouldn't have done so had she imagined that the readers' amusement might not be quite so respectful as hers.'

'All this bloody analysing! I reckon I'm the best judge of how Clarrie will look at it. But she's no different to other folks, wanting summat. Mind you, I sent her off with her tail between her legs, last time. But nobody's telling me what's best for Neatham, or how folk'll take things, or imagine them.'

Through this slight incoherence she learnt that his speech was no longer directed against Constance solely but was straddling two targets. Though the prospect of confrontation with him no longer excited her, she did not avoid it. 'You're right: nobody is telling you what's best for Neatham. If anyone tried, Constance would be the first to criticise. So, at risk of being analytical, I'd suggest that she wasn't interested in interpretations of Clarrie Bell's story. Today she was set on revenge.'

He stared at her. 'What the hell do you mean by that?'

And suddenly she was light-hearted; laughter twanged the air in her throat. 'You haven't allowed for her not liking to be dictated to any more than you do. How would you feel if she could claim she'd sent you home with your tail between your legs? There wasn't much she could do on that occasion because she's committed to the anthology – emotionally. Today, though, without risking it she found a way of giving you hassle. She's succeeded in making you quite impotently angry. Her method of paying you back.'

'As a rule, anger is impotent unless you lash out,' according to her intention stung by the word. 'That's wanker's talk. I know who she was getting at – Freddie Bell. Him and the law of the gun mentality as she calls it. The story puts it in a nutshell, remember?' he jeered. 'The whole argument for not issuing guns to the police.'

'Which means that the laugh's on you, Dick. There's no lobby for general issue of firearms and the police don't want it. You missed that. She played you like a fish on the end of a line.'

It was a harsh answer, a sneer at the naive, contempt for the duped, and she was elated. This statement of Constance's revenge was a convenient vehicle for her own. She waited as the words circled the darkening room until finally they settled and incredulity was transformed to chagrin on his face.

'And you think that's OK?'

The question was low, appalled, asking for contradiction. He was acknowledging her, reaching to her, a palm outstretched, and she thought: It is possible; it could happen; I could make it happen; now. But the realisation did not affect her; the skin remained temperate, the juices placid. She wished to savour her victory; it was overdue and too recent to be surrendered in haste. 'I can't see that it can matter to you what I think one way or another,' she dismissed him and walked into the kitchen, where the kettle of water had at last boiled and was filling the room with steam.

He followed her. 'I just wanted to know where I stood.'

She grimaced at the expression's inadequacy and, still avenging, answered it appropriately to its echo of pulp romance. 'I wasn't aware that we had an understanding.'

A hand made a gesture, crimping the mist. 'I would've expected you to take a different view when you considered her laughing behind her hand, pleased at the thought of making a fool of somebody.'

'A private satisfaction.'

'That's no excuse. It's mortifying.'

Behind the gauzy swirls there was the slant of a face, the loved profile. Her triumph receded. 'Constance may have no such intention. She may have meant every word.'

'Don't try to kid me. I'm not to be taken for a ride twice.'

'What I said was a suggestion, Dick, an interpretation. I've no proof.' She could not maintain her detachment. Though desire had ceased, she could not dismiss entirely this man who for so long had inhabited her thoughts.

Her tone betrayed her. She knew this as she saw his head lift, his eyes through vaporous wisps regard her. 'It's not so much better if she did mean what she said about the guns, on the level. She'd still have been trying to twirl me round her little finger. It's bloody insulting.'

'Now who's analysing?'

'You've got me as bad as you.' He pushed a finger along the edge of hair on his forehead, drawing off the damp. 'Stirring it up.'

She did not answer.

'All I want is to get this anthology together, but I'm not let.'

She poured water into the teapot, shook it round, then stood cradling it against her breast.

'Ever since the idea for this play was taken on, folk couldn't let us be. They had to have a finger in the pie.'

'Help was necessary.' She could have said to him: Omit the preamble; cut the cackle; you must have more important grumbles than this; I'm sure this isn't what you wish to say. Instead she waited, warming her hands against the pot.

'I'll not dispute that, but there's some kind of help that's suspicious. I'm not just referring to Constance Skrimshaw, or Glyn Mayhew for that matter, snatching the chance to make them look better at their jobs.'

'No?' She threw away the water and from a packet of tea on the sill dispensed two measures while over her shoulder his voice pursued her.

'No. There's others about who consider they've got you in their pocket if they dish out money. But we'll get even with them.'

She turned, questioning, and saw the grin creasing his face; it hinted a mischief but she did not ask him to explain, saddened that, after so many months of working together, she should find the expression novel.

'One way or another,' he stated, his face again sombre, 'people have been out for what they could get.'

Returning to the gas burner, she tilted the kettle, watched the spate of water rush through haze on to the leaves, and wondered whether the moisture she felt on her cheeks came from this steam, from her eyes, or from fear.

'They had their own private reasons,' he insisted.

'I understood you.' She dragged the carton from under the sink and took out the second cup and saucer. This was the first time they had been used.

'They thought there were benefits in it for themselves.'

'Not many were gained, Dick.'

His eyes glinted. 'Maybe they were expecting too much.'

'It was less a question of expectation than of hope. A pipe dream, really. An attempt at rediscovery.'

'I got hints that was the case. But it can't be done. There can't be any going back. What happened years ago is finished with.'

'You say that, and you come from Neatham! Where past and present are indivisible.'

'It's only the play that gives that impression.'

'It merely makes the fact more evident. The whole referral of people here is to an ethos established for decades.'

'Mebbe,' he conceded. 'They've allus kept close, Bottom End.'

'Therefore is it so outlandish for anyone to come here hoping to make contact with things similar to what had once been experienced?' She heard the plea in her voice.

He did not acknowledge this. It was not how he had intended the conversation to progress. He had wanted punishment. Resentful, he looked round the kitchen then behind him into the main room. 'They can be wide of the mark, though. As far back as can be remembered there's been gas piped in Neatham as well as water, and I'd be surprised if any hadn't got as much as a table or chair. And if it's considered that brings the person nearer to the way Neatham is, was, and shall for ever be, there's been some mistake. Nobody here lives in a squat and we've got used to a bit of comfort; we've the electric Bottom End and there's even baths and lavs that flush. I know some people get a kick out of slumming, in fact some think they're doing it just by setting foot in the town, but they don't go in for it round here, not even on a temporary basis.'

She had begun to pour out the tea but, her hand shaking, she put down the pot. 'I suppose it's not surprising that anyone's choosing to live in a derelict house should provoke hostility.'

'I wasn't saying folks would be hostile,' trying to correct the personal fervour. 'More suspicious.'

'Why's that, do you think?'

He frowned. He was not there to answer questions; that way, you lost control. 'It's out of the ordinary.'

'Yes; it doesn't fit the accepted pattern, living in a derelict house, and no doubt the only explanation would be some rather disreputable motive.' It had failed, but there was a small compensation in his blush. 'I don't want to overstate the comparison, Dick, but I think little has changed here since the days of Jessie Moorby.'

'I'll not agree. In any case, though she got out of line, there were them that backed her up.'

'And Tryphena Freiston?'

He winced. 'That was different. She didn't know Neatham like those had lived their lives in the town.'

'She must have done. She taught their children. What you're really saying is: she was outlawed because she wasn't one of them.'

'Anybody would've been, going on as she did.' But his answer convinced neither of them. 'This is getting morbid. You knew this was her house?'

'Yes,' she said. 'But she is a forgiving ghost.'

She found that her hand had stopped trembling and, taking up the teapot, filled two cups. 'The milk's powdered, I'm afraid, Dick. I know you'd rather have fresh but you soon acquire a taste,' quoting his answer to Constance so many weeks earlier, before his rejection had hardened, and the words had an elegiac sound. She held the cup to him. Above them, a few rags of steam still clung to the ceiling and collected into swatches in corners. They no longer masked but burnished his face. 'Please take it,' she appealed. 'For this farewell it is suitably decorous.'

He accepted the cup and, responding to her mood, said to her, 'It wasn't just because she didn't belong here, Nora. It was because she was trying to get folks to act different to what they wanted, trying to make them into different people from what they knew theirsens were.'

'I know.'

'And it's a bit the same as those that have other ideas fixed in their heads, like thinking they can get back to the way it once was, because they'd like people to be different, too, the way they would like. But a person can't fit in with requirements that easy, Nora.'

'There were never any requirements.'

'I have to disagree with you there, duck. The requirement was to be a test sample for the one who'd arrived.'

'No!' she whispered, appalled.

'Well, we're all entitled to our own opinion and that's mine. And the trouble is, a person turns obstinate when he suspects that somebody's got him lined up to be put to some use.'

'I once did think of you as a way of contact,' she admitted, 'but, Dick, that became less important than other thoughts.'

'I'd hope so!' He grinned, affectionate, and the shape of the face altered, became an arrangement of curves. 'And I'll tell you something, Nora, something to buck you up on the days when you look out of the winder and it's teeming with rain: there's many a time I cursed myself for being an obstinate bugger. Since I shared the other thoughts that you had.'

She was able to smile back, not only in pleasure at his admission but because at last his speech had broken free of its impersonal shelter; he had stopped pretending. At last he had said: you.

She watched him step across the yard and squeeze round the tilting gate, then she closed the back door. The steam in the kitchen had dispersed now and had bequeathed no residual warmth. She considered removing her clutter from the hearth and lighting a fire but excused herself from the task, arguing that the sticks in the wash house would be damp and that there would be few nuggets of coal in the tiny cairn of cinders and slack. So she put on her jacket, zipped it to the neck and went to pour herself a second cup of tea; and could not remember which cup had been hers. For a moment she debated but, her mind sliding back to him, she reflected on how little had come of her hopes and remembered the first occasion she had seen him, standing by the gate into the deserted playground, trying to look as if he were employed. And she had loved him.

Without rinsing the cup she had selected, she filled it with tea and raised it to her mouth. He may have drunk from this, she thought, and mourned the uncertainty; even this symbolic communion was a possible fiction. But it was all she had.

'I can remember it like it was yesterday,' Isabel had said. 'Our Dot came round so early in the morning the ashes hadn't been cleaned from the grate and she said the worst had happened.'

'I've heard a "friend" mentioned before,' the old woman had rebuked her, 'and I can tell you that nothing good came out of it.'

'I stared out the street, gave back as much as they put on Dot. It wasn't meant for you when it was said it was against nature, mixing kinds.'

It was hard because she was breech and I had to hold the screams in for the sake of not bothering the neighbours. They were all morning setting up the tea in the street. I didn't want to draw their attention. Auntie had been good enough having me and Will for a three-month without putting her out any more. 'You'd do better if you let the shouts come,' the midwife said. 'Don't you tek no notice of what's going on out there. Nobody down there's trying to drop a babby. You're lucky it's only the VE celebrations. There's no lads turning up demobbed today to ask the meaning of any racket you're making.' She'd never have dared to say that if Auntie had been there.

She was downstairs keeping Will out of mischief but she tied dusters round the knobs so they wouldn't spang in the draughts while Mrs Garbutt went in and out. She made some jam buns for the boy which meant that she must have gone under the counter for the eggs, and she brought one up each for me and Mrs Garbutt when it was all over, but she would give no more than a glance at the girl. 'It's sickly,' Mrs Garbutt told her; 'and couldn't come without help. It was a breech, and the cord was twisted round the neck. I did what I could, and there's breathing but if it were mine I'd take it to the doctor. Any other babby, I'd say it ought to be taken, but maybe this sort always look this way. It's a shame she hasn't owt better to show for her trouble.' 'Dot'll decide what's to do for the best,' Auntie told her; and she slept downstairs that night on the sofa leaving me and the babby to the bed by ourselves.

When they had finished with the singing in the street and had fetched away the trestles, I got up, pulled the blackout across the window out of habit, switched on the light and sat on the edge of the bed. I stared at her. She didn't look like a newborn babby; she was wizened, veins standing out on her temples and the patch of hair over the soft spot pumping frantically up and down, up and down. She didn't look like a newborn babby; her skin was wrinkled, shrunk, folded like a pickled walnut and the same colour, the way they say bodies go when they have laid for years under peat. She was already old, her eyelids crunched together and corners creased as she concentrated on dragging breath back and forth inside her throat; she did not look as if being born had been the beginning for her, but the start of the end; an old woman given a push towards the grave by illness. I realised then that for those nine months that I had carried her, all the hatred and malice that had been flung at me had got through to her; and all the time I'd assumed she was safe.

It might have been different if she'd been healthy. If she'd had a bonnet of springing fuzz, smooth cheeks and bright eyes, she might have shamed them to respect, but she was already crumpled and frail and her eyes squinted round lids joined together with webs. She would be the butt for their mockery, the living reminder of what her mother had done. They hadn't spared their disgust and, being like this, she proved all they had said. You have to be handsome and sure of yourself to withstand wagging tongues. I had only just managed to do so myself before I was saved by Auntie.

I dropped from the bed, switched off the light and drew back the blackout. The lamps were on in the street and coming suddenly to them made my eyes prick. They were hard, not gentle like the dusk and the stars, and they jabbed into the bedroom and showed up everything there, only not in a warm and friendly way but sharp and sneaky as frost. Their light made the linoleum sting like ice as I walked back to the bed and the cold scratched up my legs. I said to myself: Without a covering you could soon die in this cold. Which was all wrong for early May. But I was too tired to think of anything like that.

I climbed into bed and with a piece of the sheet I mopped the spittle from her chapped mouth and wiped the pus out of her eye corners. Then, pulling the blankets over us, I turned on my side and held her to me. As I went to sleep I whispered to her: This isn't how it was when I fell for you in the grass.

She seemed pleased to return to the darkness, curling back into my belly's sag.

The next morning when Auntie got me up so that Uncle could have the bed, all she said was: 'Now don't you let Will see you crying,' and she massaged my nose through a hanky while I blew. Then she said, 'She'll be seen to.'

I never asked where. It was enough that Auntie had said: she.

Chapter Seventeen

Had Nora been in a satirical mood she might have resorted to the sub-literature of theatrical cognoscenti, real and pretended, to describe the Neatham cast. Certainly they could have provided material for one of those timeworn sketches deriding amateurs; they could have inspired another blindingly original treatment of the parallel drama in progress behind the scenes; or, slightly adapted, their endeavours might have supplied stuffing for an obsolescent farce that tweaked the dust sheets off weekly rep. Observing them, however, surrounded by them, encouraging them, assisting them, she felt no such inclination. Most were first-time performers and this experience was an agony; their commitment, though as parochial as the old-style repertory casts', could call upon none of their professional expedients. And though something was occurring behind the scenes in this play, Nora knew nothing of it as she sat at the entrance to the school hall selling tickets on the final evening; nor did she recognise hints.

'I'm feeling spare,' Peter told her. 'Everything's ready down to the last brass handle. Apparently Dick's been here all afternoon, "taking delivery", Harry reports, so the cooks must have been sending the food as it came out of the ovens. I was actually shooed from the side hall when I put my head round the door. "If you're after doing something useful," Dick yelled at me, "then go and keep the party from the Town Hall happy, and stay with them." I think I shall. If there aren't any seats on their row, I'll sit on one of the sides.'

'I can squeeze you in by the sponsor. The side seats have all gone to a couple of party bookings. They weren't made till this afternoon but that means it's a full house, contrary to prediction.'

'Marvellous. So I'll watch from the front. I can always slip out if I suspect an imminent crisis. Though that's unlikely. I've suggested to Dick that he try for stage management jobs; he'd fit in fine with TIE or small-scale touring. He warned me that I might be less inclined to recommend him by the end of the show but I said that if we get through this performance as well as we did the first two, I'll be handing out references gratis for the whole pack of them. And you, Nora.'

'I'm not looking for anything else.'

'No? That's a pity. You're good at this sort of job. You can organise without being officious; you're imaginative and enterprising; you're prepared to put in plenty of graft; you can make things happen.'

'And you can compose a flattering testimonial.'

'Not flattering; and incomplete as it stands.' He twiddled with the programmes stacked on the table in front of her. 'Do you know, I found you rather alarming at first.'

'Yes.'

He was surprised by her knowledge. 'I can't imagine why, now. It might have been that you were so in control, but I soon adjusted,' grinning despite the blush. 'It's been good working with you, Nora.'

'And with you. You have been a most delicate boss.' A man like Robert. She was caught by affection, wanted to lean across the table scattering tickets and pull him on to her breast. 'A rather well-bulled car has just arrived,' she nodded towards the forecourt behind him, 'containing a personage garlanded with chains, equally well bulled.'

'Chairman of the parish council hoping to be taken for the mayor. Join me soon, won't you? Phyllis Baker's husband will carry on at your post. I was going to add, Nora, that the most important characteristic I'd quote is your capacity to form good relationships.'

'He's managed to hoist himself out of the car.'

'It's an invaluable gift in this kind of project. You've fitted in very well. People have trusted you. Been one of them.'

'Please, Peter.'

'Well, there you are. I expected you'd be embarrassed, but it had to be said. I wanted you to know that there's no excuse for being miserable on all counts.'

'He's labouring up the steps.'

Peter's last words told her that he knew of her feelings for Dick and was attempting to console her. She was also certain that his view of her was totally sincere, but her perception was otherwise and there was nothing that could relieve its ache.

Before agitation had quietened, Doris was at the table flourishing complimentary tickets. 'Clifford was of the opinion we must use them,' she informed Nora. 'You see, in the end I told him. I suspect that secretly he wants to imagine that it's really me!' Then, bending over her, Doris whispered, 'I didn't mention about the other business. That wasn't necessary.' She dropped a coin for a programme and, straightening, drew Clifford forward. 'Let me introduce you to him.'

He was no different from how she had imagined: neat, colourless, a man immediately forgotten, provident with his life's pulse. 'Pleased to meet you,' he said, and released a narrow hand.

'Clifford's voiced the suggestion of taking up residence on a more permanent basis now that you've gone,' Doris told her. 'It's not ideal but compromises generally have to be made.'

'It's not such a long journey to undertake daily; no more than nineteen and a half miles,' he explained to Nora. 'That's if I go the back way. I'm not a motorway man.'

'I'm pretty certain that you'll be the only member of the audience who has travelled so far. Peter Green will be delighted.'

'Well, Doris sprang her piece of news on me and then she received the tickets, but I was giving serious consideration to attending anyway. After all, what's good enough for our MD is good enough for me.' Seeing that she did not comprehend, he prompted, 'Mr Wilkes. Interested in new ventures, Mr Wilkes is, and not afraid of taking risks.'

That seemed an extravagant reason for attending the play, but she nodded. 'I hope he's booked a seat; the few left don't have the best view.'

Clifford appeared to be surprised. 'As I understand, Mr Wilkes will be sitting next to the civic party, as is only right in the circumstances.'

Even so, it was a few more seconds before Nora made the connection. 'The complimentary ticket for the sponsor went to Mr Hipple at Clayton's.'

'One of Scully and Fanhope's subsidiaries. I expect it was thought best that Mr Wilkes should attend, him being behind the idea from the start.'

She sensed something odd in this indirect subsidy, remembered Peter's instinctive reluctance to accept it, and was about to ask: Why has the name of the parent company been concealed?

But Doris was saying, 'If it hadn't been for Clifford, they'd never have known about it. Isn't that right, Clifford?' She was showing him off, proud. 'Remember it was Clifford brought your leaflet on Neatham to the attention of Mr Wilkes.'

Clifford agreed, complacent. 'That's quite correct. I lent Mr Wilkes the pamphlet out of general interest, you being Doris's house guest at the time, and without a doubt I scored a hit there because he came upon me in the corridor weeks later and made a point of stopping me to thank me for the trouble. It had given him an idea, you see.'

It was too late to seek an explanation, probably no more than a quite legitimate organisation of the parent company's accounts.

'We're pleased that he did get the idea. We didn't know that we had you, Clifford, to thank for five hundred pounds.'

'In a manner of speaking, you might say that.' It was impossible to guess whether it was a smile he had attempted to score with on this occasion or the attained smirk.

'Yes. I'm sure that Peter would be delighted if you'd join the party in the staff room. One way or another you both qualify for a glass of plonk.' Mr Baker had arrived, signalling her change of duty, and was negotiating tickets and cash with a large florid man in charge of one of the party bookings. 'I'm about to slip in. Won't you come? There aren't many invited: a few district councillors, parish councillors, your Mr Wilkes.'

'That would be nice!' Doris accepted, flattered.

'I'm afraid it isn't possible, Doris. It might look pushing.'

Nora acknowledged her mistake. Clifford was not the person to challenge any hierarchy. 'Very well,' rising. 'Scully and Fanhope built this school, didn't they?'

The shoddy result was around them. Once she and Dick had raged against it in the September dusk. But she did not linger now over that fleeting unity; something more urgent, an unfocused disquiet, hovered on the edge of her mind.

Clifford answered, 'That's right; and I do believe that Mr Wilkes has had a soft spot for Neatham ever since.'

'That'll please Nora.' Tonight no scratch of malice could be detected in the other's voice. 'Some time, some day in the future when she pays us a visit, she'll be amazed to see what a hive of activity Neatham's become, cleaned up, a proper town with some decent shops, and she'll know that only a firm like Scully and Fanhope could have brought that about. And who would've thought Clifford, when he took in Nora's pamphlet, started it all off?'

'That's going a bit far, Doris,' he reprimanded without conviction. 'Don't forget the matter is confidential as yet. I think we'd better find our seats.'

She hesitated. 'We may not catch you at the end; I expect you'll be busy. So I'll say goodbye now.' Formally she held out a hand. 'If you ever do think of visiting us, do bring Mr Trafford. We'd like to meet him.'

'Have a safe journey,' Clifford said.

'Yes, you be careful, Nora,' in a gush of her former solicitude. 'There's still a lot of ice on the road. What's November going to be like, I ask, when we've already had such frosts?'

213

Nora looked after them. Doris's hair had been newly styled; her two-piece suit, a fine worsted, had been freshly groomed and pressed; she walked firm and sure on high heels of mirror patent; and Nora said to herself: The cut is healing; she is almost serene; and she will never know what I did; Dick will not reveal what I said; he will honour that as a confidence. His secrecy, once used as a weapon, would become her protection.

She watched them turn into the school hall, he gesturing Doris to precede him, a hand cupped under her arm. Silently Nora pledged them: She will be safe with him; he will shelter her; his blood runs too thin and sluggish for eruptive passion; he is too fearful to invade her fenced dark. She'll know no ecstasy with him, but neither will she know anguish; that is her choice, made for her long ago and to which she assented. He is prim, vain, a deferential snob, but considerate and unthreatening, a man she is able to respect. Small wonder that she was disgusted at the thought of mine!

Who approached her ten minutes later, waving at the door of the staff room, shaking his head in refusal as she beckoned him to enter.

'I'm not coming in,' he said as she reached him. 'I can't go back to the lads stinking of drink.'

She laughed. 'Hardly! One glass!'

'It's the time. Only eight minutes before we start.'

'Don't worry.'

'They're on pins back there. They shouldn't have to wait for stuffed shirts.'

'They won't do. In three minutes I'll start the rounding up. It's you that is on pins, Dick.'

'That's right. Nerves.'

'We all suffer from those.'

'Unless there's a chance to pull in a few jars of sherry.' They smiled like children sharing a secret, companionable, and she thought: Why couldn't we always have been like this?

'Don't worry,' she repeated. 'It went without a hitch on Thursday and Friday. Or are you reacting to the full house? That'll make it better. Did you know that those seats booked over the phone this afternoon represent almost the entire clientele of the Wagoner and the Admiral Nelson? Mr Baker was incredulous. He said he couldn't point to a single member of either party who had ever been to a play or, for that matter, had set foot in school since leaving it.'

His lips twitched. He looked across the room at the group standing by the table, at Peter desperate under civic talk.

214

'I'd better go back to him,' she said.

'Hold on a sec, Nora. Will you do me a favour? Will you tell Pete that if anything happens it's not because we have anything against him and, thing is, we don't want him to interrupt?'

She was startled, apprehensive for Peter; but first on this last night she must pay heed to herself. 'I'm sorry, Dick, but I can't be your messenger boy.'

'Fair enough,' he said, seemingly without surprise and with no rancour. 'I'll have a go at catching him in the interval. If I don't, I'll just have to do a spot of speechifying. I reckon that there's a first time for everything.'

She stared at him. 'Dick,' she said quietly, 'I won't blab.' And noticing the sherry lift in her glass as her hand shook, knew that this was the test.

His answer was not immediate but at last it came, permitted, not sucked out by her will. 'I argued at the start that Pete ought to take that money, I admit that, because what I didn't know was where it came from.'

'Peter didn't either. Throughout, the correspondence has been with Mr Hipple at Clayton's. I've just heard.'

'I found out a few days ago.'

'I can't understand it. Is there really something fishy or are we paranoid? There's no logical reason why Scully and Fanhope shouldn't filter the money through Clayton's.'

'The reason is Scully and Fanhope want a local firm on the programme. Looks better, doesn't it? Especially since folk in Neatham regard them as crooks. If it had been them and not Clayton's making a handout, it would have been suspicious. Of course them on the Council know that Clayton's is under control of Scully and Fanhope, has been for ages, but it's not the first news any of the men'd see fit to pass on over a pint! You see, Scully and Fanhope are putting in a tender for a theme park half a mile beyond Ryecroft's Lane; easy to reach, only three miles off the motorway. And they reckon: Show the Town Hall they're ready to spend money in Neatham, throw out a bit of bait, and they'll land the big catch.'

She wanted to ask: Is this theme park any more than a rumour? Don't you think that five hundred pounds is too paltry a bribe for such a huge investment? But it was unkind to unsettle his conviction. So: 'However they've gone about it, shouldn't you be pleased? The project has benefited and such a development will bring work.'

'Work? You mean, when it's built? Taking tickets at gates, going round with a nail on a stick jabbing at litter, wiping lav seats? You call that work? And you reckon the play's benefited? Five hundred quid! Compensation money. Have you forgot what that stipulated? To be spent on publicity, a good percentage of that outside the town. You've been doing their job, Nora, bringing Neatham to folk outside's attention, so that it'll ring a bell when they hear that theme park's on the way. Scully and Fanhope know the value of that; worth more any day than five hundred clogging up the till. And we're their stooges, too. Peter and you and me and that fifty-odd out there have done all the graft; and they're drawing the dividends. They're using the play to promote their interests, bribing the Town Hall on the sponsorship ticket. Well, Mr Wilkes can stuff it. If he thinks we're a pack of nincompoops who'll jump to Scully and Fanhope's whistle, he'll think different after tonight. We don't want their theme park in Neatham; we're happy with it as it is. But as like as not we'll get given no say in the matter. There's summat we can have a say in, though, and that's letting them know that we're not a sideshow for folks from outside to gawp at, or be manipulated, or bits of local colour providing a background for their business ventures. No, we'll be letting them know that it's best not to tangle with us and that we've got our own thoughts and we'll do things the way we decide. We're not so lacking that we don't know how to take a hand in things ourselves.'

'It's your hand really, Dick, isn't it?'

He grinned. 'You could say that. Being in charge of what happens on that stage, I'm in the best position to intervene.'

'Yes.' She did not ask what he planned. Knowledge would have brought responsibilities she did not wish. Instead she looked at her watch, herself now, like him, anxious. 'I'll insinuate the idea that we ought to be going in,' she told him. 'One thing, Dick. Aren't you afraid that you might prove Constance Skrimshaw's maxim that everything you do is a political act?'

'That's a sly one! But if once in a while I agree with her, so be it. I'm not proud.'

He stepped back from the door and she was no longer interested in the performance, in plots and politics, or how Dick might contrive to make heard a dissenting voice. Her only thought was that her own participation was completed. 'I'm going immediately the play ends, Dick.'

He nodded. 'You be careful. There's still bad patches on the road after last night's frost.'

She was pleased that he did not consider farewells necessary. They had already been said. Watching him stride down the corridor, she was grateful that tonight they had been at ease together, that they had achieved a tranquillity. And at the last, she whispered to herself, he had confided; he had not kept her out. That was something to treasure. It was less than she had desired but perhaps one day she would think it enough.

So she watched him stride down the corridor as she had watched Doris and Clifford, and was struck by the thought that they were all going away from her rather than the reverse. It was as if they were moving on and she was the one left to wave at their departure.

'She never uttered a word about the babby after it was gone,' Isabel had said, 'and she didn't mention her soldier, either, only to tell me one time that they never wrote to each other. That was their understanding. She had Eddie to think about by then. How she explained herself to him, I'll never know, but there's one thing I'll swear to, and that is: she were never sorry. Any more I can't say.'

Watching him stride down the corridor, Nora thought: Did Dot feel as I do, that last evening?

I didn't feel guilty, I'd never done it with anyone besides Eddie and that goes for ever afterwards, too, so nobody could claim, though they did, that I made a habit of it. I can't be sure why I didn't feel guilty but I think it was something to do with Eddie being so far away. He was practically the other side of the world, and he didn't seem a real person any more, just handwriting that you read weeks after it's been put down, and it was getting on for three years since he'd gone, and no man had so much as kissed me since then. But it wasn't all to do with that, with being lonely and wanting to nestle inside the crook of a man's arm. I'd be wrong to pretend it was; I'll not have it sound like I was making excuses. I went with him because I was in love with him; that's the plain fact. I always said to myself that he was my seven weeks' wonder, which is an improvement on most. No, I'll not make excuses, and I didn't feel guilty. It wasn't guilt that made me cry that last time when I helped him button up his jacket so smartly tailored and the cloth so smooth and I thought of Eddie's rough khaki with creases poking out of the battledress top in all the wrong places because it had to be squared off; it wasn't guilt that made me cry when I remembered how he'd looked that first evening begging me to walk

217

across the floor and invite him to a dance, because it seemed it was Eddie who was the young soldier asking and expecting me to say no.

And I wanted him home.

'I'm enjoying this,' district councillor Christopher Morley said to her in the interval. 'I had really no idea what to expect. It's quite a polished job, isn't it? For amateurs, I mean. All credit due to everyone concerned. I'm sorry – I was rather late in arriving so I haven't picked up exactly what has been your role in this, Mrs . . . Mrs . . .'

'Trafford. General factotum, I suppose. Though I've had nothing to do with the set or stage management. They were Dick Coulbeck's responsibilities.'

'So I'm told. I do apologise; my question was unnecessary. You were Peter Green's right-hand man, woman.'

'We all worked together.'

'In itself an achievement. And I gather that the town disgorged dozens of willing hands.'

'Less the town than the bottom end of it, probably because that's where, physically, we were based.'

'I see. Am I right in concluding that it was in the older part of the town that you found most of the material? Some colourful characters, eh?'

'At the bottom end they have deeper roots.'

'One certainly gets the sense of that. Peter tells me that you interviewed and recorded many of the personal histories. You must have come across lots of bizarre incidents.'

'Not very often.'

'Perhaps that's rather strong,' he answered, suave. 'Does that mean that you really were not bombarded with skeletons in the cupboard, as the play would have us believe? I've sat for an hour with bated breath waiting for one to pop up but so far everyone has behaved with the utmost decorum.'

His condescension was repellent. She wanted to swing round and walk away but a necessary civility restrained her. 'This is a true representation of their character. More sensational tastes will inevitably be disappointed.'

'It is tension, not sensation, that one would hope for,' he flashed out, defensive. Then recovering composure: 'But perhaps I'm applying the wrong criterion. This is not the traditional form of play, is it? More·in the nature of a pageant and therefore really very suitable.

218

Would you say that it catches the flavour of the place?' And, after her assent: 'I thought so. I'm pleased to have your opinion. Parish councillors, however sound, rarely appreciate the degree of objectivity which has to be employed by us sitting in the council chamber at City Hall.'

'I wouldn't have thought you could have any doubts that your grant had been worth while.'

'Absolutely none. What I have to assess is how this kind of project might fit into future schemes.'

'Future schemes?'

He swung out an arm in a gesture taking in Neatham. 'General presentation of the place, raising the profile. I don't have to tell you, after what I've seen of the way you've tackled the job already.' He smiled, flattering. 'Fact, if you were interested, I'd be delighted to drop a word in the right place.'

She suppressed her incredulity. 'That's considerate but someone has already offered to back me in another post.' What would Constance say to that? she thought.

His question was automatic: 'What sort of figure?'

'Very realistic, but I never close the door,' and she saw by his look, the abrupt contraction of the muscle in a bottom lid, that he was revising his measure of her; and she thought: I've heard more conversations like this than you've had hot dinners, and heard Isabel's appreciative cackle. 'I might be happy to talk though I can't imagine why there's an interest in marketing Neatham of all places.'

'I take your point. Why indeed?' They were confederates now. 'The argument is that eventually the Council would receive incalculable returns. If we could contribute to the whole package of making the area look lively, interesting, a place to visit, we should eventually benefit from the commerce we'd helped to attract.'

So this was the hive of activity Doris had envisaged, a Neatham cleaned up, a proper town with some decent shops. Was this a complement or an alternative to a theme park? Had Dick been misinformed? However, the precise nature of the development was not important. Whatever the proposals, they were covert, had almost a furtive quality, and they had not been adequately communicated.

'And who are the other contributors to the package?'

This was too presumptuous. His face closed. 'It's still early days.'

'Of course. One indiscreet word . . .' Her laugh enticed his. 'But perhaps you can tell me why you're so interested in this play. I can't understand the attraction.'

His right eyebrow tilted. One side of the mouth was carefully creased. 'Surely! I'd say it was improving by the minute!'

My God, she thought, I'd forgotten how predictable they are, out there; and wondered how long it would be before he dared drop his eyes to her breasts. 'I think Peter would be astonished if the play were expected to be a draw beyond the boundaries of Neatham.'

'Amazing what will take at times.'

'This is the last performance tonight.'

'Of the first edition. It could be revived; might benefit from a rewrite, jazzed up a bit. What do you think? Would the locals co-operate in anything like this again?'

Locals. She felt them gathering round her, joining in her muted hiss. 'Co-operate? You mean to attract trippers and coach parties?'

His eyes snapped away. She was breaking his rules. That was the kind of brutal question jabbed across the council chamber, not one that should come from a handsome woman. 'I imagine rather a better class of client is envisaged.'

'To gawp at people here co-operating to provide a sideshow full of colourful characters?' She echoed Dick; it was his anger she felt.

'That's a very biased way of expressing it.' He was confused; her accent had changed, had become unashamedly Neatham. He should have been warned that some of them were Reds.

'Not really. It can be defended. This play is restricted to Neatham and holds little interest for anyone outside. It is quintessentially parochial. That is its strength.

'Because Peter's aim was to celebrate this place and the people who live here. He wanted to assure them of their worth and that they aren't to be dismissed. Also, when they took part not only by acting but by assisting in dozens of ways, he knew they would discover other things than a community identity, things in themselves.' She paused, thinking of Dick. And what of the others who had taken part or made their contribution? She considered Becky and Doris. She remembered Isabel's hesitant, incomplete yet unclenching confidences. Whether the play's touch were strong or glancing, few people had gone unaffected in these last months. 'They found new capacities in themselves,' she insisted. 'That may sound pretty humble to you; indeed in the context of many so-called achievements, it is; but it has its own criteria that have nothing to do with those.

'All of which has no connection with commerce,' she told Christopher Morley. 'Its material, and effort, and devotion – yes, devotion – are not appropriate to be exploited, spectacles for tourists or trippers.

They require the professional, the slick, the red nose of farce. If this play or any other activity drawing upon the same source were employed to attract that audience, it would be amputated from the spirit which gave it birth and everyone associated with it inexcusably used.'

She saw the astonishment in his face and knew it mirrored hers. Such febrile expression was light years away from learnt objective appraisal, and she was shocked to hear it. She was repeating Peter's conviction, first heard one March afternoon, and though he had dispelled her first reservations, one still remained: that the project, by validating the town's inversion, discouraged wider horizons. But she would not admit that to Christopher Morley. Confronted by this polished committee man, this outsider, she identified herself completely with Peter's faith and spoke for them all. And she thought: Nine months' hard work with little coming from it for myself, ending in a declaration of loyalty with only a stranger as witness! Wryly she added: The final service I perform. So now, she did not care if her words were too passionate, if such evangelism were not the received manner to accompany a cup of tea. She did not care that the man who stood with her was fiddling with his spoon, his eyes stumbling embarrassed about her face, discomforted and alarmed. As well he might be, she said to herself; he must think I'm mad.

However, to her surprise he contrived to utter. 'Well, I can see you are very committed and can articulate the creed – which, frankly, is new to me. I sympathise with the theory, absolutely necessary for somebody to have one, but I imagine that, in practice, the locals don't think of this as anything more than a way of getting together and having a damn good time. I'm confident that they'd be happy to agree with any suggestion. They're an orderly lot, don't generally rock the boat.'

'You mean they don't complain? Take what's handed out? I'd advise you not to be so sure. They can be independent all right on issues they consider are worth the sweat.'

He made a moue. 'Well . . . I suppose we'd better see how they shape up in the second half.'

'Yes,' she answered, and knew for the first time for many weeks a soaring vertiginous elation.

Dick had been careful not to disrupt the flow of Peter Green's production. His intervention came within one minute of the final lines, and for a moment the warning of it was so apt to the previous action

221

that the audience simply took it as the coming and inevitable climax of the play. Which, of course, it was.

Two of the men cast as unemployed tradesmen walked to the front of the acting area carrying a tight bolt of cloth.

'He said to us: So you're interested in doing summat for the show, are you? Well, that Nora's set on having a banner strung across the street with the name on. Folks'll not be able to claim, after, that it weren't brought to their attention, will they?'

'And we said: No, they won't.'

'So if you're after doing summat useful, get your brain boxes going on that, he said.'

'And we did.'

'Hold on a mo, I said, what's measurements, then? What colours are you after? What do you want us to put?'

'You can use a ruddy tape measure, can't you? he said. He's like that when he's pushed, straight out with it. And you can choose the colours; you've had plenty of practice with football team.' (Laughter) 'And the couple on yer are like what I'm aunt to, asking what should be put on. You work it out for yourselves.'

'And we did.'

'It's your show, he said.'

'And it is.'

Separating, and encouraged by a drum, they unfurled the cloth, then they climbed step ladders and raised a banner above their heads. The audience watched, eyes raised. The title of the play was expected. What they read was: Darts Tournament second round, Wagoner v. Admiral Nelson.

Immediately the stage was full of people. Cast standing at the edge ready to climb on for the final applause had to stand aside as patrons of the two pubs leapt up. First they pushed back moveable parts of the set then, hooking dust sheets from shrouded cubes behind Dick's barrier of props, they handed out beer crates and passed them between the shoulders of the astonished audience, carried them on to the stage and placed them in a generous circle within which, miraculously, grew a concentric ring of bottles, each topped by an inverted glass. And as the two parties abandoned the rows at the sides of the stage to seat themselves in two opposing crescents on the crates, a dartboard was brought forward. Mounted upon a flat made stable by an iron brace, it was placed stage centre, the totem to which both teams turned their eyes. The length of the throw was measured out. There was the clink of bottles against glass.

Then, rising from the squad representing the Admiral Nelson, one man walked to the front of the stage; he was nonchalant, relaxed, gripping darts in one hand and in the other a glass of frothing ale.

Dick said: 'We know you'll be wanting to get back to your beds, so this is no more than a taste. Or, put more exactly, a short demonstration. Show you what we can do.' From her position, Nora could see that he was looking along the row of official guests, fixing each face in turn, patient until he reached that of Mr Wilkes. 'Some of you'll know without telling that this isn't on the schedule, but for those who don't, it'll come as a bit of a shock. It's allus best not to count chickens afore they are hatched. Now, these arrers are burning a hole in my hand, it's a good while since I had time for them, only before I start, there's a bloke we'd like to drink to, and I know you'd all join us if you'd been handed a glass.' Behind him, the circle of men levered themselves to their feet. 'We're drinking your health, Pete. Being a sentimental bugger despite appearances, I want you to know that I reckon you've done right by Neatham. Only thing is, we have to take law into our own hands, when it comes to.'

There was a pause filled by the sound of beer slurped down, and Dick remained, waiting.

'Your good health!' Peter's voice came at last from the still audience.

Satisfied, the other grinned, strode back and, raising his arm, delivered a powerful shot at the board. Before his third dart had settled the Wagoner's resident vocalist had begun to croon, 'We'll do it our way'.

It was doubtful whether the audience fully understood. During the ninety seconds that had elapsed since the banner had been stretched across the stage, they had looked on, at first confused by the sight of a quarter of their number suddenly taking to the boards and next struggling to make sense of Dick's statement. But whatever was going on had received Peter's blessing so, the disquiet of the serious ones placated, the slight discomfort of the unreflective removed, and all thrilled by an occurrence they suspected to be not quite legitimate but was unlikely to be contagious, they settled down to enjoy watching the two teams. And soon they had converted the event into a vigorous spectator sport.

They were not invited to do this by the supporters on stage. Those savoured their beer and said little, disciplined by the convention of low-toned, undistracting encouragement. Or they might have been gripped by stage nerves. Neither consideration inhibited their audience. Up to that moment, though they had followed the play intently

223

and with unconcealed enjoyment, they had ventured only hesitant and feeble participation on request. But this was different; this was the real thing; the men hunched on empty crates were not representing others, they were simply themselves; the match was part of a tournament which would be reported the next week in the local rag; the supporters had deliberately left their hearths and had consented to this ritual. The audience had the feeling that they were present at an incident soon to be elevated into myth.

Rising to the challenge of a competition, they chose their allegiance and became instant fans of the elected pub. (Five minutes into play, one cheerleader in the third row rose to exhort the crowd to redistribute themselves according to loyalties. 'Admiral Nelson left terrace; Wagoner, right,' he was heard directing, but he was peremptorily ordered not to block the view and nothing more was heard from him.)

Every score marked up received cheers and derision; every dart let fly battled against the current of a hundred noisily indrawn breaths; a dart hitting the wire and plummeting crestfallen earned both laughter and sympathetic groans; when a young man untried in tournaments and brought on as a substitute bedded three trebles for the first and only time in his life, he was given a standing ovation and an embrace by a nubile opportunist on the front row.

But very soon this level of response became unsatisfactory. The energy was superficial; it had a passive quality; what was needed was more true engagement. That took the form of advice.

'Eighteen and double twenty to finish, William,' would be one shout, corrected subversively to: 'Make it twenty and double nineteen,' from the other side.

Or, from the less interested in mathematics than aesthetics:

'Pull your belly in, Ted.'

'You've forgot the little finger, Matt.'

Or, 'You'll rupture yourself throwing that way, Colin.'

'He'll do hissen a mischief.'

'And his missis wouldn't like that!'

Accustomed to some assistance and banter, though from the regular devotees less loud, the teams were not affected at first. Their demeanour was impeccable; they played with solemnity and an admirable phlegm, but gradually their concentration was invaded by this irreverent and holiday spirit and they began to talk back.

Some – generally those wearing tie, sleeveless pullover and braces – asked for suggestions on what to aim for, scorned the folly of the ignorant, approved the subtleties of the informed, and discussed tactics with the experts.

One, a septuagenarian playing for the Wagoner, took the opportunity of testing contemporary aptitude in mental arithmetic. Acknowledging the applause after a cunning finish, he retrieved his darts, fixed his audience with a contemptuous stare, and shouted: 'Right, then. All you young lads on first three rows, take away double thirteen, threbble eighteen and seven from one hundred and nine. Now!'

Others attempted a less cerebral alliance. Their dedication to the game a little blighted by an element of personal showbiz – evidenced by hard-man kits of singlet and chest hair or waistcoat in denim plus woad-bright tattoos – they simply came forward and declared they knew they could rely on the ladies.

It was at this point of boisterous anarchy, when Dick, tipsy with success, had just challenged aspiring champions to equal his score, that Nora was called to the phone.

Chapter Eighteen

'Pleased I've caught you,' Don Clamp said. 'I wanted to have a word before you freed yourself of the Neatham mists and drove off, though I hope not for ever. How's it gone tonight? I would have come a third time but the family was looking neglected.'

'It's a pity you didn't.' She told him. The description allowed her to assimilate what had occurred and increased her pleasure.

Which he shared. 'I can't believe it! One cannot claim that putting on a darts match is breaking new ground but it's certainly a pragmatic use of the play. Should we be laughing? What about Peter?'

'I kept checking on how he was taking it and he looked almost as smug as if he'd devised the episode himself. He doesn't know the reason for it yet. I'll have to tell him the whole story before I go since Dick will be incapable of coherence.'

'I'm sure. What about the guests?'

'Most looked bemused, but one councillor, Christopher Morley, was far more alert; as was Wilkes. He looked very angry. Even if he couldn't penetrate Dick's ambiguities, I'm sure he picked up that the intervention was some sort of challenge to him. But was it justified? We don't know for certain what the schemes are for Neatham – park or shops or both. The Scully and Fanhope tender may be only a rumour.'

'Yes, but something is going on. Your talk with Christopher Morley confirmed that.'

'True. And what happens?' She felt suddenly very tired. 'Dick stages an elaborate gesture.'

'That may be all that is possible at present.'

'But if they did contrive to work out the correct interpretation, I doubt whether they would take any notice.'

'I'm inclined to be more optimistic. I think the City Council will be more cautious in the future. They may be more disposed to acknowledge that they should take public opinion into account. Which could result in the issue's being opened up for debate. If that doesn't happen, though, if we see no direct benefit, I still think Dick's action will have had an effect, however intangible.

'I would never have imagined that he had it in him, but I don't know him very well. A bit of an enigma, would you say?'

'Not now,' and laughed, the tiredness forgotten. At last she could regard him with affection, like a lover whose departure was untainted by bitterness.

'You've been harbouring a magician. Clearing two pubs on a Saturday night and the tosspots having to sit through a play before they can get their hands on a drink!'

'They loved it.'

'Let's hope they'd come again. You know, Nora, I would never have imagined that epilogue could be possible. It indicates a quality in them that I haven't suspected. I need time to reflect. In many ways this project has been a disturbing experience. Don't you agree?'

'Yes.'

'That was tactless. I apologise,' to her mortification demonstrating once more that her preoccupation had been observed. 'I was thinking of myself as well as of the Neatham folk. Perhaps eventually they may dare to claim their portion. But we'll discuss this another time. You will keep in touch? There's something I've undertaken to ask you, though. Have you heard of a Mrs Isabel Driffield?'

'Yes.' Her mind, slower, registered the body's warning, a tension in the muscles, a restriction of breath.

'I met her son in town this morning; I know him slightly. He told me that he'd intended to come to the play but couldn't because his mother died yesterday. He wanted to know whether anything she had recollected had been used. Apparently she was, as he put it, in her eighty-third year so no doubt could remember beyond the First World War. I said I'd find out.'

'No, Peter didn't use any of her reminiscences.' She concentrated on the question, keeping the death at bay. 'He asked me to visit her because at the time he had more material from men than women, their experience was much more hidden. He wanted to redress the balance, but I got little from Isabel, and that was very private and confused.'

'Nora, I'm so sorry! I didn't stop to consider that you might know her.'

'I wouldn't claim that. We weren't friends, but I'd like to believe we were more than acquaintances. I haven't seen her for eight weeks. I should have done. She was clearly deteriorating.'

'She would have resisted interference, wouldn't she?'

'Yes. In fact last time I visited her, she told me not to go any more;

227

and I complied. She seemed in command of her faculties, though frail.'

'You mustn't blame yourself. Her son feels the same but I understand that after her husband's death she preferred to be left alone.'

'She was quite definite on that last occasion. She wanted me out.'

When all's said and done, you have to admit it showed thoughtfulness, going off prompt when asked and not fussing. Anyone else might have put questions, but not her. She knew when to keep quiet, not poking her nose into what wasn't her business and never passing comment about such as the cat and the washer that hadn't seen a drop of water since he had it sent. There wasn't a thing that got by that Nora, Isabel could tell that, but she knew what was her business and what wasn't; she'd been brought up to respect them as kept counsel despite the posh way she talked. No, she wasn't a bad sort of woman, she had known a lot worse. To be truthful, between Isabel and the cat, she was as good as you get nowadays. They don't make them like Maisie any more, or Miss Freiston, or Dot. It occurred to her that she should include Norman since he'd behaved hissen recently, but she'd bother her head with him in due course.

'She was very agitated by a kind of nervousness, impatience or an apprehension that if she didn't pay attention to some thought, it would be lost. Which would be an inestimable regret. That's why I knew I had to leave her.'

'Yes.'

'I shall attend the funeral. How did she die?'

'Well, this week there have been these frosts, Nora.'

When he had told her: 'I see. I would not have imagined that as an ending.'

She was pleased that all the thinking about Nora had got her back to the others, in the same way that Nora had been the one to start thoughts about Dot and what had happened and the scandal they'd made of it Bottom End. As soon as Dot came to her, she'd made sure word got round that if anybody took it upon themselves to play parson, they'd have Isabel Driffield to contend with. Only one came out with it to her face, that painted gabber at number eighteen. 'I haven't seen your Norm recently,' she said, 'but I hear he's learning to bear up.' That made Isabel see red the way it implied that Norman was being put upon and she whipped out with a few choice words describing hypocrites that left her at number eighteen sorry she'd opened her mouth; Isabel could name others that went on the spree while their maisters were away from home. But now, because she didn't seem to have had time for it before, she appreciated Norman being so easy about the arrangement; he hadn't said a word against her taking in Dot and the lad. She felt really upset that she hadn't given him credit at the time and the next occasion she got up and looked in on him, she'd mention the omission. She'd thank him; though it was forty year since, he wouldn't mind. Better late than never was a favourite saying he had.

She didn't want to budge from where she was at the moment, sitting on the sofa with her eyes fixed on the empty grate. She didn't feel particularly cold and she wasn't hungry; her belly didn't start rumbling till it was time to feed the cat so it couldn't be his supper time yet. She couldn't remember when he last showed up. She didn't want to budge because she had to keep her mind on the light; it came from the feeling at the back of her head and it flickered if she didn't keep thinking about Dot; it was something to do with her that had got it going. Started by Nora. And it had to do with the other two that had meant anything to her. Reluctantly she added Norman, not because he figured as a young girl's dream but because she'd seen to him for over sixty years – still was doing, for that matter – and that couldn't be ignored. There were different reasons for feeling how you did about people, and different ways.

Dot.

Well, from the moment she'd first held her, her guts had jumped at the sight, and they did no less as the girl got older; when she was with her, everything was pushed to one side and she was so happy, but frightened, too. Dot always gave her the sensation, it came straight off her skin and out of her laugh, of how precarious, how quickly destroyed, are life's joys. Isabel had ached and wept for Dot long years before she went.

Miss Freiston was another, and the tears for her were as secret but for reasons of need: to have been seen crying would have been like casting a vote against her dad out there in the trenches. Before she died, though, Isabel's eyes had never been wetted by thoughts of Miss Freiston; it wasn't her guts that gave a lurch in her company so much as her brain, which was exactly what the schoolteacher desired. 'Your brain's a collection of cells right there in your skull,' she'd say, 'not some spirit circling above you dressed in a nightie and wings, so you can keep it healthy and exercised and fed. I hope I do give you brain ache as you call it; that shows you've been trying to put it to use. If you've learnt that poem by four o'clock, next time you may pick your own. "Abou Ben Adhem (may his tribe increase!)" It is the last line I want to hear you say, Isabel.' And she had swept to the next desk, her eyes intent, the brooch at her throat sparkling, her feet brisk in buttoned boots, her hair piled into a crest of tawny curls. So, inspired by admiration and respect, Isabel returned to the poem, determined to have learnt it in the eight minutes allowed. Six years later there'd been no Miss Freiston to encourage Maisie. Her place was taken by a man invalided early from the war, sweet, Maisie had reported, and a bit apologetic; and Isabel had wondered whether Mr Repton was uncomfortable about being singled out by the managers for the job in view of the opinion of the teacher he followed. He wasn't as clever as she was, of course, or as vital and fearless, but he could recognise brains when he saw them so when she came to the scholarship exam, Maisie got through.

Isabel had never shed tears for her but there were times when she would've taken the stick to some if she'd had the chance, on behalf of Maisie, the things she learnt about girls at that school. Turning their noses up and not even giving her a greeting when she went into class! It made Isabel's blood boil. No, she didn't feel the same for Maisie as she did for Miss Freiston or Dot. When it came to Maisie, things weren't so straightforward, they were more mixed. She was pleased the way Maisie'd got on, she admired her no end, but she couldn't get past the fact that it should've been her to be first to attend that school, since it'd been her that was first to pass the scholarship, and so she was jealous, she couldn't gainsay that, and Maisie had knew. And the reason why, despite herself, she'd kept part of her open to Maisie was that Maisie didn't cast any blame for it, was that Maisie regarded her as the person to appeal to if she was in a fix, was that Maisie would want to tell her about the lessons and would come round to her to test what she was studying. 'If it'd been a question of one place per family, Bella,' she had once said, 'then you should've had it.' And you can't hate anybody as says that. No, Maisie had cunning; Isabel knew what she was up to, offering compensations, but it was a Christian action and in turn asked for Isabel's charity to accept it without resentment, which she did. In the end, they had a special place for each other, which you'd hope to happen, after a thing like that.

But Maisie had never twisted Isabel's guts like they'd been twisted for Dot.

She didn't know why she kept coming back to Maisie and Miss Freiston alongside of Dot, except that one way or another the three of them had given her pain. Something she didn't want now. And she wasn't expecting it. This light in her head promised better than that. It was exhilarating; she felt like leaping about, doing cartwheels like a young kid, because in the middle of it she was sure that there was something saved up for her, something she had wanted all these years though she wasn't sure even now what that was. She'd know soon, though. And it didn't matter how many times it went dark outside, she could tell the difference between street lamps and daylight; or how many times the milkman knocked to enquire about the milk, she would just go on shouting that she had cancelled the order. It didn't matter if he was growing impatient upstairs, she'd see to him all in good time. She wasn't going to spoil it by pushing it to come too soon.

She wasn't going to spoil it; she had the patience. It didn't matter if it took weeks. For she wasn't going to lose hold of it now. She was certain of that. Because the room too was full of light. It wasn't just there in her head. It dressed the mantel and the chair, soaked into every corner and glinted up at her from the tins lying inside the hearth. It lay like crystals glittering, sparkling everywhere she looked. And it was on the floor, too, startling her feet as she rose from the settee, a streak of it running up her legs from the linoleum and making them tingle. It was like silver dust on the windows when she scratched and she gave her time to it, admired it stuck under her nails tinsel bright, then peering through the circles she had made, she saw that the white shining was there, even out in the yard. She thought: I wonder whether Norman can see it; it'd be nice to share. Which showed she must be going soft in her old age. But recently he'd been more considerate; that encouraged a generosity in return, so: I'll go up, she decided, and I'll take him a clean sheet. There ought to be a pair on the line, but all she could see was a towel hanging by the coalhouse. That'll do, she said to herself; he'll like that; a clean towel is something he hasn't had for a time.

The yard was unfamiliar after so many months and the door knob was cold and pulled at her flesh, but she persevered, stepping a bit dizzily over the flags and hardly noticing when the cracks snagged her stockings. When she lifted it off the nail, the towel stayed in its folds as if it was full of starch and pretty, twinkling like salt. She tried not to spoil the drape of it as she crunched it under an arm. Back in the house she got through the kitchen and gave herself a rest at the bottom of the stairs. It was a long time since she'd climbed them but the dust on the fanlight above the front door couldn't hold back the beam which bore her up to the landing and into his room.

It was less fresh than it should have been, smelling of him, but she could tolerate that, and he stirred, acknowledging her presence, which made her glad she'd come. 'I've brought you a towel,' she told him. 'You can have it when it's aired and I'll give you my news. It won't be long coming.' For a moment his breathing trembled then quietened as, satisfied, he returned to sleep. Then she pulled the chair nearer to the bed and waited in the night's brilliance.

When it came, it came gradually, the light folding back in the way petals do as they open, first one then the next, scattering pollen like golden stars, and there in the centre was the sun.

There had been four of them, and three had done something courageous but she hadn't dared. She hadn't come up to scratch; she had been the only one who hadn't stepped out of line. Miss Freiston had stood against all of them out there in the town, and Maisie had wheedled her dad into letting her go to High School and then seen it through; and Dot, well, Dot, a married woman, had lain with a soldier who was black. And each time she'd felt shown up and despised herself for weakness, though she knew most considered her hard. But the weakness she had was the sort they applauded because it fitted their notion of how to behave. She didn't stand up to her dad when she passed the scholarship and everyone complimented her for bringing in money as soon as she could. She hadn't gone to Miss Freiston's burial and it had been forty years before she'd sought out the grave. She hadn't admitted to Dot that she might not have said no to a soldier though there wasn't the distance of half the world separating her husband from her.

Yet she had done something and it had been so natural, such the obvious thing for her to do, that she'd not noticed at the time, let alone swanked to herself about it. She had given Dot shelter.

She'd taken in Dot and the boy William when the girl's own mother, a poor thing without much backbone, had thrown a fit saying she couldn't stand any more. So Isabel had brought them home, settled them in the spare bed that was by rights her son's when he came on leave, and then she'd turned to face the looks and the comments behind hands and the sneers and contempt that had followed them to this street.

But that wasn't all. Inside this great beam where colours danced as they had in a prism she had held as a child, Isabel could make out something else, tender, protective, equally daring: a journey alone with a small package, a brief ceremony without mourners, but this time she had stood by the grave. Later, Dot had said to her, 'I knew she'd be all right with you, Auntie,' and that was enough.

She was glad she'd found out before she was finished. The years hadn't been so much of a waste as she thought, because ever since she'd lifted up that dead babby, she'd been one of them, those three. She had had dignity. She could hold her head up with them. It was nice knowing before she was finished.

And when she let him into the secret, Norman might be gratified, too. He had offered no objection to her taking in Dot. That must be remembered. She was pleased she'd brought him the towel. He'd accept it as an honour from someone who could hold her head high. She nursed it on her lap ready to give him. It thawed a little, then after a time once again stiffened while she sat, waiting to tell him her news.